Emma Louise.
Babylon forever, darlin'
♡
victoriajames
x x

P.S - I TOLD YOU SO!
P.P.S - You'll win the
lottery next ♡.

1

WITHOUT forever

VICTORIA L.
JAMES
L.J
STOCK

A NOTE TO THE READER:

Without Forever is book five in the Babylon series, all of which are written by both Victoria L. James and L.J. Stock. Book one, Without Consequence, Book two, Without Mercy, and Book Three, Without Truth, and Book Four, Without Shame are all available on Amazon.

For more information on the authors' work together as well as their individual projects, please visit the following pages.

www.facebook.com/Babylonseries
www.facebook.com/VictoriaLJamesAuthor
www.facebook.com/LJStockAuthor

WITHOUT FOREVER ©2019

Victoria L. James & L.J. Stock

This is a work of fiction. The names, characters, places and incidents are products of the authors' imaginations only. Any resemblance to actual persons, living or deceased, events or any other incident is entirely coincidental.

Front Cover Design: L.J. Stock (LJDesigns)
Front Cover Image: ©shutterstock.com

Edited by: Claire Allmendinger, BNW Editing

OTHER BOOKS IN THE SERIES

Without Consequence

Without Mercy

Without Truth

Without Shame

ACKNOWLEDGEMENTS FROM BOTH AUTHORS

With a team of friends around us like we have, it's impossible to express the gratitude we truly feel, but for the final time, we're going to try.

Babylon would not be what it is if it wasn't for the following superstars in our lives.

Claire Allmendinger: Thank you for being your usual selfless self. Thank you for your time, your patience when we miss deadlines and your honesty with each and every story.

Bare Naked Words: AKA Claire Allmendinger (again) and Wendy Shatwell. What started out in 2014 as "just one book we need to get out" has turned into five years of craziness. You two ladies have been there the whole way through, and we cannot thank you enough for your support.

Sue Hollingmode, Mary Green, Charlie M. Matthews, Francesca Marlow, Amy Trevathan, Karyn Lawless Degiorgio, Trish Kitty Taylor, Kristina Hanicar, Valerie DeGeorge, Joanne Bulmer... you guys are just a few names in a sea of loyal friends who have been with Drew and Ayda from the start, and we cannot thank you enough for every single thing you do. From sharing social media posts to beta feedback, you guys are the best, and you'll forever be a part of The Hounds of Babylon MC.

To the Babylon Beta group: Thank you for being there

at the drop of a hat. We appreciate your time and feedback so much.

To The J Team & The Saintly Sinners (our individual reader groups) we owe you guys the world. Thanks for sticking with us when we're quiet and when we're busy. You're the fun part of the book world, and we love you so.

To our families, for always encouraging us when times get hard. For your patience, your support, and your loyalty. Thanks for being the reason we do this.

To each other. Vic loves Lou and Lou loves Vic. Two friends who, just a few years ago, didn't know the other existed but now can't imagine a life apart. Here's to an everlasting, fun, easy, breezy, beautiful friendship, and a whole imagination full of possibilities as to what we can do next. Clear eyes, full hearts, can't lose. We got this.

And finally, as is tradition now... to Drew Tucker and Ayda Hanagan.

Thanks for being our dream couple.

Thanks for coming alive in our minds.

Thanks for being our escape.

Thanks for letting us into a family full of brothers who we believe the whole world will one day fall in love with.

Thanks for the adventures.

The romance.

The angst.

The fantasy life.

Thank you for Babylon.

You'll be our forever no matter what happens.

Vic & Lou

DEDICATED TO

Our die hard Babylon readers. To those who have been with us for the last five years. To those who we've picked up along the way.

This one's for you.

PROLOGUE

ERIC TUCKER
Before the Rescue

"Torch it."

The words passed over my lips as I watched Drew and Ayda get the hell out of the yard that day, the two of them heading out to seal Sinclair's fate with bullets, blades, and revenge.

An odd feeling of vertigo washed over me as I watched my son drive down a path leading to death and destruction. I should have been terrified. Instead, I was proud of the man he had become—a man who took care of business—a lion at the top of the food chain, willing to protect everything around him, even if that meant sealing his fate.

I turned to Slater; his expression blank apart from the obvious desire to call me fucking crazy shining from his eyes.

He was loyal, ready to throw himself under the bus for the greater good if he needed to. I'd always admired Slater for that—appreciated the way he loved Drew and respected the love he held for The Hounds of Babylon MC.

Now I was asking him to step up and do what I knew would hurt him.

"Torch it," I repeated.

Slater's nostrils flared, and his chest expanded as he filled his lungs with courage and fortitude.

"The whole place?" he asked quietly.

I swallowed, the thought of Slater torching The Hut, the yard, and everything around it, making my stomach twist like strings of fiery acid were choking it. The sun always seemed to shine when I had a hard decision to make. It wasn't really my decision to make at all, but there I was with the light in my eyes, squinting at the sky before I took a good look around me and made the decision anyway.

We'd built this world from blood and sweat. My fellow men and I had molded a future from grassroots—a safety net around us made from bricks, wood, and stone. Now I was contemplating setting it alight and destroying it within seconds.

It would free my boy.

It would give Drew a way out—a chance to think about a new life with Ayda and maybe… maybe a fucking child.

I knew what the right thing was. I knew burning it all and setting him free was the way to go.

"Eric." Slater nudged me, interrupting my thoughts. "You want me to torch The Hut?"

Turning back to Slater, I blew out all the air from my lungs.

Another time, maybe.

"No. Training room only."

He deflated at once, still keeping himself upright as his obvious relief bled out of him in puffs of air.

"Burn all the evidence of Owen's blood in there before the cops get here. Make it look like everyone is trying to put the fire out, not start it. You, Jedd, and Deeks… you need to step up now, do whatever it takes to distract attention from

the massacre in there. Don't let them know we know Sinclair was a rat. Don't let them know anything is wrong among our brothers."

Slater nodded slowly, and I looked up at the other men standing around the steps that led up to The Hut. They were gathered around the club's VP, Jedd, waiting for him to guide them. Big men covered in grease and ink who looked like innocent children, some with their head in their hands while others paced back and forth, worried like orphans that knew they'd soon have nowhere to call home.

"Slater?"

"Yeah."

I looked him right in the eye and held his gaze. "You know how to act, right?"

"Act?"

"It's time to put on a show for the ATF. No matter what happens, you don't let them in that training room. You got that?"

"I got it." He looked at Drew's bike then back to me. "What are you going to do?"

"Whatever the hell I need to do to make sure my son gets away with what he's about to do to Sinclair."

"Drew gets sloppy when he's broken, Eric. You need to be ready for the wreckage. We all do."

"I'm ready. I hope he smears Sinclair's blood across all of the asphalt in Babylon. I'm here to clean everything up for him now, no matter what that means for my future. His forever is my only concern."

CHAPTER ONE
DREW

We traveled down the highway with the future suffocating us. Even unable to breathe, I'd never felt more alive with her wrapped around me and the wind whipping over our skin.

Ayda's arms tightened around my waist, her legs squeezing me as she sat on the back of my bike—the one my father had dropped off to us on Sinclair's land before he told us to get the hell out of there.

"What the fuck has happened to Jedd, Slater, and Deeks?" I barked, watching Eric saunter casually toward me outside Sinclair's burning home.

Ayda was standing strong, her hands down by her sides and her legs parted, like some kind of formidable she-warrior who didn't care about the dirt and disease crawling over her skin as a building blazed behind us.

Eric took one look at Owen's home, and that was it. After that, his attention was solely on me.

"They're taking care of business," he answered with no emotion whatsoever.

"By turning themselves into the feds?"

"We had to conjure up some magic, Drew. It's all about distractions."

I searched his eyes, wondering how he remained so calm at every turn. The sound of wailing sirens far off in the distance caught my attention, making me look up at the crows squawking and fleeing overhead.

"You need to get out of here before those sirens head this way. The sky's ablaze," he said calmly, and when I looked back at him, he was smirking. It should have made me angry. Instead, it calmed my soul. A smirk from an arrogant asshole like him only meant one thing: he knew what the fuck he was doing.

"What did you do?" I asked him quietly, my fingers flexing down by my thighs.

Eric glanced at his watch. "Tick tock, Tucker. Time's a wastin'. You need to take your old lady and that precious cargo she may be carrying and get her the hell out of Babylon."

"Out of Babylon? Are you fucking crazy?"

"You're meant to be out on a ride together, unaware of the shit happening on our own porch step. If you rush home now, you'll look guilty, panicked… like you've got something to hide. You're the president of The Hounds of Babylon MC. Do I need to remind you of that? If you march into Sutton's building and tear that ATF woman to pieces, demanding to see your men, you'll look like you've been in on it all along. You need to stay calm, Drew. Like you've switched off your cell to go and enjoy some quiet time with your future wife, and that's why nobody can get hold of you. Not like the whole club is in chaos because they're about to get proven guilty."

"You want me to walk away?"

"We fucking need you to."

I glanced at Ayda whose eyes were bright with adrenaline

and, more importantly, faith. She had faith we would handle this—faith that we could find our way out of this tangled web we had weaved.

Grabbing her hand, I pulled her to my side.

"How long for?" I asked, turning to Eric.

"A few hours at most."

"But they know we chased after Owen when we left Walsh's rally because we wanted to kill him."

"They know you wanted to kill him?" Eric arched a brow. "How?"

I scowled again. "Walsh. He'll have told them."

"You think Walsh would confess to ATF that he knew Sinclair was a rat? You think he'd admit to having intel he hadn't shared with them already?"

Shit. My father was right. Winnie may have seen disruption in our club when we jumped on the bikes and followed Sinclair, but they wouldn't know why we were chasing him. All they could do was assume.

A case couldn't be built on assumptions.

"Are they at least safe?" I asked as the sound of the sirens grew more distant instead of growing closer. "Are my men safe?"

Eric's eyes narrowed. "Do you trust me?"

"Yes," I answered without hesitation.

"Then get the fuck out of here."

"But—"

"Now, son."

And that time, I didn't correct him or tell him he wasn't allowed to call me his son. I followed his instruction without further hesitation. It was time to get my girl out of there.

Smoke seemed to fill the sky around us, and I wasn't sure if that was just in my head or not. No matter which road I tore down with Ayda wrapped around me, sirens sounded close by. No matter which direction I looked up at the sky, it was gray, taunted with ashes.

"Something's not right," I muttered to myself.

My skin prickled, but even though I wanted to turn around and head back to The Hut, I found myself listening to the memory of my father's words.

Do you trust me?

Motherfucker.

I carried on through to the outskirts of Babylon, heading for the one place that was still a sanctuary to me.

Pete's tree.

But demons lurked on those roads that day, and with death still lingering on my fingertips, I began to panic that all my sins were catching up with me.

Fire at the back.

Fire from the sides.

And now what looked like fire up ahead, rising from the tree that held all the memories of my long-lost brother and our time together as young boys.

"No," I breathed in a panic, twisting the throttle to pick up speed. Ayda tensed around me, her arms tightening as she sensed the shift in my mood. Thick plumes of black smoke rose up the branches of the tree, spreading until the once green leaves on it turned chargrilled. Those damn sirens seemed to be following us now, and as I skidded to a halt at the side of the field, all I could do was drop my feet to the ground, stand up over my bike, and stare as my youth and memories turned to ash before my very eyes.

Hell had arrived on Earth—my own personal Hell.

Babylon was burning.

Just as I said it would.

CHAPTER TWO
AYDA

The smell of fresh burning wood made it feel more like a cookout than a funeral pyre. Cloying black clouds rose high above us, but there was nothing we could do to stop the flames now. The fire was in full swing, crawling through the upper branches and into the hazy air above.

I was sickened by the sight of another representation of the club going up in flames, but I couldn't think about myself right now no matter how gutted I was at the sight of Pete's tree ablaze. The man in front of me, the love of my life, was watching one of the most important and significant things in his world turn to charcoal. For Drew, this would be the same as losing Pete all over again.

This was one of the things we'd been fighting for.

Placing my hand on the skull and hounds at his back, I felt his heart pounding even through the leather. I gave him the time he needed to process what he was seeing before we acted on this. I knew this had to have something to do with what we'd done—what we were about to do. Even the tree seemed to whine as it was consumed, creaking under the pressure of the fire.

We stayed there for a few minutes, both of us speechless,

before something other than the blaze cut through the air.

The fire department had arrived.

I could barely hear the sirens over the roar of the fire, but they were there, screaming into the unusually still air. The noise grew louder and louder as we watched something we loved disappear branch by branch, our moment of mourning coming to a sudden end.

Pulling off my helmet, I turned my head and watched as the fire chief's SUV, with full lights flashing and sirens screaming, passed the cattle grate and slid into the empty field. He fishtailed as he neared, dirt and grass shooting out from around the vehicle, bringing it a sliding stop. The driver's door opened with a very purposeful force.

Ronnie Bex, fire chief of the Babylon Fire Department, stepped half out of the vehicle, obviously standing on the side runner as he assessed the fire and frowned in confusion. He waited for a beat, looking around the field to the roads that cut around it before the crash of a branch pulled his attention back to the blaze. Then he turned his bewildered eyes to me.

I knew he registered the mess my face was in, but the small shake of my head when he looked at Drew seemed to appease any negative thought he had there. I hadn't come up with an excuse for that yet, so I needed to deflect any unwanted questions until I figured out something relative and believable. Falling down the stairs and walking into the door were too predictable.

"You call this in yet?" Ronnie barked.

I shook my head and left my hand on Drew's back as I took the lead on the conversation. "We just got here."

"Son of a whore. What the fuck is going on today?" He held up a hand to me and then reached into his vehicle for a radio handset. "Dispatch: we got a Class A out at the junction of Southwest CR thirty-one fifty, and southwest thirty-one sixty."

The radio squawked for a moment before clearing, the voice of the dispatcher coming back.

"Sorry, chief, we have dispatched to two other locations. We're waiting on a third. We don't have a truck for you right now."

"Fuck." He slapped the top of his SUV, squeezed his eyes shut, took a deep breath, and pressed the button again before speaking calmly. "Can you call Randy over in Dawson, see if they have a spare rig they can send us?"

"On it, chief."

I waited for him as he threw the radio back into the passenger seat and watched him swing from his truck before I asked any questions.

"What's going on?"

Ronnie swiped his BVFD cap from his head and wiped his brow with the back of his hand, letting his gaze move to Drew, and then back to me. The town may have accepted Drew and the Hounds to some extent, but that stigma of Drew being a grenade with a loose pin would always be around.

"Christ. You don't know?" he asked in surprise.

"Know what? We've been out on a ride and then came back to this." I flung my free hand at the tree in exasperation, acting as though this was the most significant thing in my world. For now, as far as Ronnie Bex was concerned, it was.

"It's just. Well, The Hut... the Sinclair place, and the remains left at the old factory where..." He didn't bother finishing that sentence, I was pretty sure my expression said it all. "It's... it's all on fire, Ayda. The whole goddamn town is

27

burning."

"What? The Hut? Owen's…" I trailed off with concern, my hand covering my mouth. I hoped to God that Owen's place had burned to the ground before they got to it. I wanted him to be bone when they found him.

"You really haven't heard?" Pulling his hat back on, he stared at the burning tree and shook his head again. "You two should get back to town."

Drew had apparently lost his voice, his ability to move, and his usual sense of leadership. He stared at Ronnie, finally blinking before his entire body tensed—his arms going rigid by his side. Throwing his head back, Drew let out a feral roar of anger I'd never heard from him before. His hands were balled into fists, his body shaking as everything fell to pieces around us—pieces we didn't know were going to fall.

I didn't say or do anything. There are times when you just have to let a moment happen—when the shit that's hit the fan has to fall away so you can assess the damage left behind. I knew Drew wouldn't fall back into the state he'd been in after Harry's death. This wasn't that kind of mourning. This was an exorcism, and it had to happen so we could figure out what the fuck was going on and move forward.

Ronnie's eyes widened at the animal sound coming from Drew, growing wider still when the unexpected sound cut off and an almighty crack broke out from the heart of the tree.

"The tree is splitting, y'all. You need to get out of here."

Drew leaned forward, grabbing the bars of the bike and looking up at the tree in front of him. His breaths were ragged, and he dropped his chin to his chest.

"I can't fucking watch this," he said roughly. "Helmet on, Ayda."

Chancing a glance at Ronnie, he nodded as though saying he had it under control, and I pulled the helmet over my head, muting the crackle of flames. I'd barely wrapped my arms around Drew's waist when he took off, spinning the back wheel out from behind us and heading back to the country road. We had an excuse to head back to The Hut now. None other than the Fire Chief himself had informed us to. No one could question that.

I was in two minds about this. Home sounded like a balm I needed more than anything else. Knowing the rest of the guys were safe was a close second. I just wasn't sure what we were going to find when we got there. Fire. Slater, Deeks, and Jedd in custody. Even the warehouse remnants we'd almost died among were burning again. We would get answers when we got back, but we had to get back there first. As I tightened my arms around Drew's waist, I kept my eyes on the black smoke now rising ahead of us. One was Owen's place—the other had to be The Hut.

The nearer we got to the center of town, the thicker the smoke became. Gray haze wrapped around everything and hung in the air like a thick fog, the curves in the road growing more faded the closer we got to the worst of the fires. Pete's tree had been isolated in comparison to this, and now all three fires were joining forces and blocking the sky.

If Drew hadn't known where he was going with his eyes closed, he would have missed the turns that led us home, but he hit every one of them with precision, barely slowing as we came to the turnoff for The Hut. I heard the dirt and gravel under the tires before the gates came into view. The air was heavy with the smell of burning wood and plastic. It was soul destroying, yet another feeling that seemed to be mirrored by

Drew's body language. Every muscle in his body tensed under my hands as he slowed to a stop next to the fire truck that was running noisily as the men slowly wound back in the hoses and packed up their equipment.

I could see The Hut standing strong where it had always been, safe and secure, still our home. Only there was now a hole in the landscape where the training room once stood. Jagged lines of twisted metal and fallen beams laid in a tired smoldering heap that was slowly beginning to dissipate.

I didn't have time to think much more about that devastation because Drew became my sole focus.

His gaze was on The Hut. For all I knew that the rest of the land and buildings on it meant the world to Drew, The Hut was his home. The place where whiskey was spilled, bonds were made stronger, tears were shed in private, and his brothers' love blossomed. Then his attention turned to the training room... or what was left of it.

And his shoulders relaxed.

All the tension that had kept him wound up tightly by Pete's tree and on the ride back here seemed to bleed from him slowly until I saw the way he inhaled deeply, releasing it all in one big stream.

"Thank fuck," he said, almost to himself.

His reaction to the mess in front of us confused me.

Pushing the helmet from my head, I swung my leg over the bike and stood on solid ground for the first time in what felt like hours. Sickness washed over me. My face and body hurt, and there was a spot on my cheek that felt raw as the helmet brushed against it.

"Drew?"

He locked eyes on mine, searching wildly, as though

hoping I was real and not a figment of his imagination. I usually adored it when he looked at me that way, clinging to me like a dream he was scared to wake up from, but something about it in that very moment, with all the world ablaze around us, made me feel nervous.

"We need to find Kenny," he said huskily.

Right on cue, Kenny came charging down the street, his hand pressed against his chest.

He was heading right for Drew when he glanced at me and slid to a stop. The horror and disgust on his face told me exactly what he saw. He didn't see me though—just what Owen had done to me. I had no doubt they'd been filled in on what happened and told what to expect, but I actually considered putting my helmet back on.

"I'm fine," I told him. I could see him mouthing 'son of a bitch' and shaking his head in disbelief before he continued toward us, his eyes moving between Drew, me, and the firemen still milling about and packing the truck up. "What happened here?" I demanded.

"They moved us across the street. Everyone's there, including Tate," Kenny's response was aimed at Drew, and I knew it was pointless to ask questions.

The king was back in his kingdom, and it was time to reclaim his throne.

CHAPTER THREE
DREW

I parked the bike outside Wheeler's hardware store. Ayda had walked across the street with Kenny and was back by my side within minutes. The three of us pushed through the front door, where Wheeler had cleared a section for all my men to stand in while they watched a part of their world go up in flames.

Kenny made his way to stand by Tate's side, and I didn't miss the look of relief on Tate's face when he saw Ayda, but it only lasted a second before his relief turned to sheer anger at the sight of the swellings on her face. I immediately hated myself for not protecting her, and for not protecting him from seeing her that way.

Moose looked like a giant locked in a rabbit hole, and the rest of them looked too dark and full of dirty history to be standing in something as everyday as a small town hardware store. In the middle of all my men stood one man I didn't expect to see.

Howard Sutton.

Howard's gaze turned my way. No smile came. No acknowledgment. Just a soft puff of air, which I couldn't decipher. Was it relief or agitation?

He glanced at Ayda, flinching slightly when he saw the

state of her face, and I had to close my eyes to stop myself from looking at her, too. I swore she'd never get hurt under my watch again, and of course, I'd let her the fuck down. Now wasn't the time for thinking on regrets. I could do that once everyone was safe and back in the home they belonged in. Now I had to figure out what the fuck was going on.

"Chief," I croaked, clearing my throat and nodding, gripping Ayda's hand tighter in mine.

"Tucker," he blew out, shaking his head. He looked and sounded exhausted. "What in the name of Jesus. Tell me you didn't do this…"

"Do what, exactly?" I scowled, tired eyes narrowing in on him. "Set the whole of Babylon on fire, including my own home?"

"Well, you can't blame me for asking. I mean—"

"I goddamn can blame you for asking. Don't you know me at all?"

Howard looked up, blinking slowly and searching my eyes for any sign of a lie. I hoped to God he saw what I was projecting, because I was angry, pissed off, and just as confused as him.

"You don't know anything about anything. Is that what you're telling me?" Howard asked carefully.

"I never said that."

"Right." He sighed again.

"Who am I talking to right now? Howard Sutton, my friend, or Howard Sutton, the chief of police?"

Sutton glanced back at all the men around him before his eyes landed on Ayda, and then me. "Your friend. I'm your friend."

"Good, then start fucking acting like it and tell me what's

going on with Slater, Jedd, and Deeks. And what the hell happened to our yard, the old warehouse, and Pete's place?"

Kenny stepped forward, reluctantly moving away from Tate to stand beside Sutton. "We've only just heard through Howard's radio about Pete's tree. Is it…?"

"Gone? Yeah. Another memory set alight."

"And you had nothing to do with it?" Sutton dared to ask again.

I took an angry step forward, only stopping in my tracks when I felt the urgent squeezing of my hand from Ayda. *He was just doing his job*, that's what I'm sure she was telling me. *Don't have any regrets. Take a breath. Think, Drew.*

"I swear to God, Sutton," I growled through gritted teeth. "Don't ask me that question again."

He had the decency to hold his hands in the air and retreat. "Okay, I believe you. I just had to make sure. You're sloppy when you're angry, Drew, and I know what your temper is like. It's worse than a toddler's—"

"Chief!" I groaned.

"Sorry." He cleared his throat. "All we know for now is that random fires have been started at the remains of the old warehouse where The Emps' attack took place."

"I'm familiar with it," I said, low and full of judgment.

"Right." Sutton inhaled deep, blowing it all out in one quick stream. "The warehouse fire started not long after you left the yard, but everyone here is claiming they know nothing about it. On that, I'm calling bullshit whether you like it or not, Drew. I can tell you're surprised, but these men behind me didn't dare look me in the eye when I ask them what happened." Sutton thumbed over his shoulder at Moose. "And as for that big dope… if ATF or anyone else from my department questions him, they'll see straight through the fact that he can't lie."

I looked up at Moose who simply shrugged like a useless ape and then scratched the back of his neck. That's when I turned my attention to Kenny.

"What's going on, brows?" I asked him calmly.

"Slater set fire to the training room."

"Motherfucker!" Sutton snapped.

"Sorry, chief. I needed to tell Drew first," Kenny explained.

My eyes widened and my brows rose. "Slater?"

"He was under instruction."

"From...?" I didn't need to hear the name.

"You know who," Kenny confirmed.

I closed my eyes and pinched the bridge of my nose with my free hand.

"But I swear to you, we don't know who is responsible for the rest. Pete's tree, the old warehouse... none of it makes sense."

It made sense, all right, and I knew exactly who was responsible for all of it. It was the wisest move he could have made—if it was him.

Misdirection. Distractions. Magic. It screamed of Eric Tucker.

The tactics of a true leader, but ones that had cost me a lifetime of memories and a place I clung to and used to restore my sanity on my darkest of days.

"And what about Slater, Jedd, and Deeks?"

Right on cue, the doorbell above old Wheeler's hardware store door rang out, and the sounds of heavy boots hitting the floor had all of us turning around. In the doorway, framed by the light of outside, yet somehow looking darker than ever, were my sarge and one of the club's founders.

Deeks and Slater were back, staring at me with fire in their eyes and frowns on their faces.

"What the hell?" Sutton whispered on behalf of all of us.

"Slater?" I croaked, my eyes wide with surprise and confusion. "I thought…"

"We need to talk," was all he said.

"Why? Where the hell is Jedd?"

Slater and Deeks took one look at each other before they crossed their arms over their chests, and Slater stared back at me. "He's not coming back, Drew."

The fire department wasn't willing to let any of us back inside the yard for a few hours until they could confirm we were no longer in danger. Our home was cordoned off, and a bunch of feral Hounds were left to roam the streets of Babylon, knowing we couldn't keep Wheeler's place occupied the way we were doing. It was like trying to cram elephants into a drainpipe.

Ayda had phoned ahead to Rusty's place, and just like that, the guy who barely said two words without waving a spatula had closed the place down to the public, and it was now being used as The Hounds' safe haven.

I was sitting in a booth with Slater and Deeks opposite Ayda and me, while Kenny and the guys lingered close by. Howard had left us, choosing instead to head back to the station so it didn't look like he was a part of this brotherhood.

"We'd barely taken a foot inside the place when Jedd asked to speak to that Winnie chick alone," Deeks told me, his face full of confusion and an aching sadness that made my own heart squeeze tight. "Next thing Slater and I know, we're being ushered into a cell together and told to wait. We didn't even have to wait thirty minutes before the ATF woman was rattling her keys and telling us to be on our way."

I couldn't make sense of it, but one of my greatest fears was that yet another one of my brothers was about to throw themselves in front of a moving freight train in order to save me. Pete and Harry: Take Three. I couldn't let it happen. I wouldn't.

"Explain to me everything that happened the second Ayda and I left the yard to head to Sinclair's place."

Slater's nostrils flared at the mention of Owen, his jaw tensing as he failed to hide his feelings of betrayal and hurt.

"Don't worry. He paid," I assured him.

Slater nodded once and leaned forward, resting his forearms on the surface of the table between us.

"You two were getting Owen in the truck when Eric pulled me aside. One minute you were there, and the next you were riding out, and Eric turned to me and asked me to torch the training room."

"Why?"

"He wanted rid of all the evidence of what we'd just done to Sinclair, but more than that, I think he wanted it to look like Owen had turned against the club, and he'd set fire to it to hurt us, and then he'd run. He was covering his bases. Our bases. I don't know."

"And after that?" I asked, fisting my hands together in front of me. "Once you'd agreed to it?"

Slater shrugged. "I got to work."

"And what did Eric do?"

"He…" Slater stopped and frowned, taking a moment to think. Deeks, too, looked lost in concentration, his eyes searching the surface of the table.

"Last I saw of him, he was talking to Jedd and the kid," Deeks answered.

"The kid?" I sat forward, my heart rate picking up speed. "Rubin?"

Deeks lifted his eyes from the table to me, offering a small, understanding nod for my obvious concern. "Yeah. Rubin."

"Fuck," Slater whispered.

"Did Eric take Rubin anywhere when he left the yard?"

"No," Deeks answered with absolute certainty. "No, Eric left not long after you. He was with Slater before he moved to Jedd and Rubin, and then he threw himself on your bike like it was a Playboy pussy, and he rode the hell out of there."

"Was Rubin around when you set fire to the training room, Slate?"

He reached up to scratch his beard, blowing out a long, tired breath. "Not a clue, Drew. I was lost in wondering how the fuck I was going to do what I had to do without fucking it up. I ran to Deeks to tell him what Eric had asked of me, and the next thing I know, the yard is half empty, everyone's running into The Hut, and Moose, Kenny, and Deeks are heading my way to help me. I think Deeks went into the pawnshop to get some of the documents out of there in case it spread farther than we wanted it to."

"That's right." Deeks nodded slowly.

"And no one saw where Rubin went?"

"I did," Moose called out from behind us. I raised my head to look at him, trying to recollect how many times I'd actually heard him speak before.

"Where did he go, Moose?"

"I don't know, but he had his pushbike with him, and it wasn't long after Jedd went back inside The Hut to grab something that Rubin was pedaling out of the yard as though he was trying to win some kind of race."

I leaned back in my booth, throwing an arm over the back of it and glancing Ayda's way. There wasn't anything I could say to her or ask her, so I simply stared into the beautiful blues that sat hidden behind her marred and swollen skin, still needing that connection, despite seeing her wounds.

"What the fuck is going on, darlin'?" I asked her softly.

Ayda took her time before answering, her glance bouncing around the faces that surrounded us in the booth. The men she'd come to love as her family were mostly all here, but her confusion was still obvious. It looked like she was trying to put two and four together and coming up with one.

"I wish I knew," she finally answered. "Rubin would do anything for any of you, so I know anything Eric asked of him he'd do without hesitation, but that's all I've got."

I turned back to Slater and Deeks. "Did they give you any idea how long they planned on holding Jedd?"

"None." Slater shook his head, but I saw something on his face: a twitch of his nose, a subtle shift in his gaze as he tried to side-eye Deeks before looking back up at me.

"What was that?"

"What?"

I slammed a hand down on the table, making Ayda and the men around me jump before I leaned forward and ground my teeth together. "Slater Portman, don't lie to me."

"Calm down, Drew," Deeks interrupted, shifting a hand to

move on top of mine and trapping it there. "Calm down."

"Then tell me why the hell Slater looked at you that way. What is Jedd doing?"

"What he thinks is best, I imagine."

"Yeah? Like Pete did? Like Harry, too?" I pressed. "Well, fuck that. I'm not losing any more of my men, do you understand me?"

Neither one of them answered, and I yanked my hand out from under Deeks' and looked up at all the men standing in Rusty's diner.

"Do *ALL* of you understand me? Are you fucking listening? Can you hear the words coming out of my mouth? I am your president. I run this show. I make the final decisions whether there's a gavel in my goddamn hand or not, and I am telling each and every one of you here who thinks their life is worth less than mine... it isn't. Cut that shit out, and if I find out any of you are trying to save me by hurting themselves, I'll fucking kill you myself. It's my job to protect you. *Mine.* I've lost too many brothers to bear any more grief, and I cannot, will not—I fucking refuse to have this conversation. If anyone is going to die for this club, it's going to me." I let my raging eyes drift down to Ayda. "I'll fall before this club does. It's what I was born to do. It's who I was born to be."

Ayda didn't say anything. Her hand tightened around my leg, but it was the only indication at all that she'd felt the words and the weight behind them.

She was letting me be who I needed to be.

My brothers had been around from the beginning, through the worst, and they'd be there come rain or shine because they took the honor of their patches seriously. No part of me wanted to consider a future where I'd have to make the call, but it was part of the job.

Turning back to the men, I took in a deep, steady breath and released it with just as much control.

"Now, I'm going to ask this one last time: does anyone in this diner know what the hell my VP is planning while he sits in that shitty little cell all alone?"

CHAPTER FOUR
AYDA

It was late when we finally got clearance to go back to The Hut.

Rusty and Jan were the ever-graceful hosts and fed us two meals as we waited and talked, all coming to the same gloomy conclusion: no one knew a damn thing.

We'd exhausted every avenue we'd had three times over, and there were so many holes in the stories we did have, we only ended up frustrated beyond belief and more tired than I imagined we'd ever felt before. No one more so than Drew. Not having answers made him grumpy.

He'd already lost so much, been through so much, taken on so much, and none of his questions were being answered. He was also now down three men—Jedd, Eric, and Rubin. No one knew where they were, and that only added to the growing pile of questions we all had.

When the call finally came from the fire chief, we all knew we'd be better regrouping where we felt the most comfortable—our own home. Where alcohol would flow, and frustrations could be voiced without scaring Jan and Sam.

The metal of the training room was still glowing hot when we rode back in, but the fire was out, and the smoke had dissipated. The whole landscaping and horizon looked wrong.

Even the stars seemed to stretch out over the midnight blue sky and taunt us.

This had been the longest day of my life.

Longer than the day of my parents' funeral.

Longer than the day Tate and I had lost our home.

It was a close second to the day I thought I was going to lose Drew in that warehouse.

I just needed a minute to clear my head—a second to regain perspective—a moment when I wasn't on display. I finally found it when I had a moment to crawl under the steamy water of the shower in our bathroom. It took everything in me not to look back on the day and focus on the terrible things we'd done. I managed, to a certain extent, but avoidance became impossible when I came to undress and found a few specks of blood above my boot—blood I seemed to understand intrinsically wasn't mine. Drew and I had washed most of Owen's blood from ourselves with Owen's hose, and I had scrubbed Drew's cut while he'd rubbed the worst of the blood off himself waiting for Eric to show up. Not that it had helped much.

Once in the shower, I scrubbed my body until my skin was pink, and ignored the ache in the areas that were most abused by Owen. I didn't want this physical evidence left behind anymore. I didn't want to be the reminder of what had happened, and I felt that's exactly what I would be when they all looked at me. The damage on my flesh was all I saw when I looked in the mirror. Now that I was clean, it stood out even more.

This was why I was wearing Drew's sweats and an oversized hoodie when he found me brushing my hair in our bedroom.

I didn't worry too much about his reaction—he'd already exorcised his demons on Owen's flesh. It was the outlaw's credence. Blood for blood. Blood for betrayal. Blood for treason.

But I could see the tension in Drew's body as he paced the room with a bottle of scotch fisted in his hand. Agitation rolled from him in waves, while all I found myself capable of doing was falling to the bed on my back and staring at the ceiling as I listened to his boots pound their way across the room again and again.

"Sit with me?" I finally asked, raising my head so I could see him. My hair was in damp tendrils because I hadn't had the energy to dry it.

Drew stopped in his tracks, taking a moment to tilt his head and look at me. Of course, there was sadness there as he took in my new bruises and mottled skin, but he wasn't as angry as I once would have predicted from him. It took him a moment, but eventually, he moved, dropping the scotch onto the side before he sank down onto the mattress, resting his ass on the edge and leaning over me. He brushed a hand over my forehead and across my damp hair, his eyes searching mine.

"I mean this in the nicest way possible… but you look exhausted, darlin'."

I offered him a smile. I wasn't sure there was a word that could adequately describe my level of fatigue. I was tired down to the very marrow of my bones.

"Long day."

"Yeah? What you been doing?" he asked with surprise humor lacing his voice.

"Oh, you know, the usual. Mayhem and mystery. Earning my keep."

"You've earned a lifetime of happiness in one day, and then some." He ran a gentle thumb over the creases around my tired eyes. "Do you think you can stay awake until after I've showered?"

"I already told you I'd wait forever for you, pres."

Gathering his shirt in one of my hands, I fisted the material, pressing against his abs, making sure he felt our connection there as I held his gaze. I had so much I wanted and needed to say, and yet none of that seemed like it needed to be said now. I just wanted to be with him, the rest I could deal with later.

I rose up to kiss him, ignoring the bite of pain on my fragile skin as I made the meeting of our lips deeper and more needful.

"Go and wash today off yourself," I spoke against him.

"Yes, ma'am," he answered with his best southern drawl attached to it, and then he reluctantly made his way to the bathroom.

Dropping his cut into a chair, he didn't take much care with the rest of his clothes and shed them on his way to the bathroom. I pushed myself to sit in the middle of the mattress and listened to the shower come on. The sound of water beating down was hypnotic and almost lulled me to sleep several times before it cut off again.

I listened as Drew made his way through his usual routine and soon appeared at the door of the bathroom, one of the fluffy white towels I'd bought for us wrapped low on his hips as droplets of water clung to his skin, unwilling to give up their only moments with him.

"I really wish I had more energy right now. I'd have climbed in that shower with you." I sighed dreamily.

Running a palm up the back of his head, Drew shook more water out of his hair with a rough hand, and he made his way to the bed, climbing onto it from the bottom before he crawled up and over my body, landing carefully beside me so he didn't hurt my already aching body. His skin was still damp, but the coolness of it was drowned out by the heat of Drew being Drew, and him pressing against me like he wanted to hold me tightly.

Propping himself up on one shoulder to give me the space he knew my body needed, he let his gaze drift from head to toe, taking in the many layers of clothes I didn't usually wear for bed. His free hand drifted over them, his nails trailing tenderly over my thigh before he flattened his palm over my waist, across my ribs, and back down to rest on my stomach. Once there, his eyes fixated on it, and a small scowl took over his handsome face.

"I can't remember how it was when I had to do this life alone, without you there at the end of the day to make me believe life was different. That it wasn't always so fucked up."

I swallowed my irrational emotions brought on by fatigue and tried to remember how to breathe. "I'm not sure I existed before you."

"Funny how you feel so alive when surrounded by so much death, isn't it?"

"It's not death that makes me feel alive. It's you. You and the love I have for you." I searched his face for the longest moment. "You do realize I would follow you into Hell, don't you?"

"You already have… so many times. Some days I have to pinch myself to see that you're still here. Thank God you're still here," he blew out in a heavy breath. "But, Ayda, I can't take seeing you this way ever again. I can't. The bruises, the pain you're trying to hide… seeing some guy holding a gun to your head, mistreating you and marking your body." Drew shook his head softly. "I can't do it anymore, darlin'. This is the last time. It has to be. It's killing me. Holding it together right now is killing me. Seeing you this way *kills* me."

I ran my palms over the stubble on his jaw, never breaking the eye contact. "It will all go away. The pain I can handle. The bruises will fade, and everything will go back to the way it was. I'm not made of glass, Drew." I felt him tense beneath my touch, and I continued before he could argue. "But this was also a really unique situation that no one could have predicted. No one will get that close again. You won't allow it, and neither will our family. We've cut the disease out. The rot is gone."

"Everything will go back to the way it was, huh?" His thumb pressed down on my stomach, and his gaze drifted there, eyes thoughtful and his soft sigh somewhat dreamy. "Maybe not everything."

"A few minor changes along the way are inevitable."

I glanced down to my stomach and felt the flutter of emotion rising. I still wasn't sure whether or not there was a baby growing inside of me. Not for sure, but whether right or wrong, I was beginning to realize that I was hoping there was.

"What are your thoughts on all of this?"

"I think I'm scared," he answered without hesitation in the most un-Drew-like fashion while he stared at his hand. "I think I'm excited, too, but mainly scared. It feels like… fuck, I don't know. Like I'm still a child myself, barely keeping my head above water and with not enough arms to keep everyone I love afloat." Drew's head slowly rolled my way, his eyes finding mine. "And I'm scared to love something else the way I love you."

I think I stopped breathing.

Lost in the intricate blue-green of his eyes, I floated somewhere between reality and fantasy as the words slowly seeped below the surface of my brain and settled over me.

He was hoping, too.

Even after all the shit that had gone down, and all the hell that we were about to face together, I felt happy. I felt loved.

I couldn't form the words, though. Not the ones filled with hope and promises of a future that was so uncertain at that moment. Instead, I kissed him, pouring all of the things I couldn't say into the passion that was always present between us. My hands fisted his thick, damp hair, pleading with him via touch to understand what I wanted to say. No one would know as much love as our baby would—not another living soul.

"I feel so much more than love for you," I whispered against his mouth.

"Open your eyes."

I did as he asked, allowing a tear to escape.

Drew lifted his hand and wiped away the tear with his thumb, brushing it away on the towel still wrapped around him before he placed his hand back on my stomach. "I'm going to say something now, Ayda, and I need to say it while I'm feeling this way, and I'm going to need to you to listen to me. I'm going to need you to let the words sink in without telling me I'm being stupid. Is that okay?"

I searched his eyes, but nodded anyway, despite there being no hint of what he was trying to say. .

"Babylon is our home. I belong here, so do you, but this isn't just a place for us to live anymore. It holds a lot of...

history." He exhaled through his flared nostrils, looking away like he was nervous before clearing his throat and scowling, a pain deeper than physical creasing the beautiful features of his face. "If you are pregnant. If by some miracle I've been graced with a boy or a girl, a son or a daughter, twins, triplets, whatever… I need you to make me a promise that you'll see through to your dying day."

More tears fell from the corners of my eyes as the weight of his words hung between us.

I hated it when he asked me to make a promise before he told me what it was.

I would give him anything he wanted, he already knew that, but some promises? Some were impossible to keep, and I hoped this wasn't one of them.

"Tell me," I whispered.

"If anything happens to me, and I don't get to see them grow… get my baby the hell out of Babylon for me. Don't let them live a life like mine."

Biting my lip, I forced the sob back in my throat. This baby—if he or she was in there—meant that I wouldn't be able to follow him anywhere anymore. Not the way I'd always intended to anyway. There would be another life to think about. One more valuable than each of ours.

Closing my eyes for a second, I blew all the breath from my lungs out before opening them again and locking my gaze with his.

"I promise." Even this, I would give him.

His shoulders relaxed, his body somehow moving closer as he scanned mine one more time and nodded softly. His thoughts had drifted, as though he was agreeing with something inside his own mind that only he could hear.

"Thank you," he whispered. "And I'll do my best to make sure I stick around."

"You better." I touched his bottom lip with my thumb and stroked gently. "I don't want to do this without you."

I didn't mean just the baby or the pregnancy. I meant everything. Living. Breathing. Hurting. My life had really only started the day I met him.

A soft smile graced his lips. "You know what's funny? I always thought I'd be okay with dying young. I expected it most of the time. In prison, I longed for it. I had nothing to keep me from sacrificing my life for the sake of the club... not until you. And now I have these crazy visions of us sitting out there on the porch, watching the world go by, our hair gray, our children old, all our mistakes behind us and our good times and memories outweighing the bad. I've never wanted to grow old like I do now," he whispered, leaning closer until his lips were only an inch away from mine. "So, don't you worry, darlin'. I'll cling onto life with dirty, oil-filled fingers for you—you and all the lives we can create together."

I closed the distance between us, my lips attacking his like the kiss was the only thing that would keep me alive. It didn't escape me that I was the only person who would ever hear anything close to words like this coming from this formidable man's mouth, and I cherished every last syllable. If I weren't pregnant, if for some reason my intuition was wrong and I'd lost my mind, I knew that it was what I wanted. I could see this future between us now, and I was craving that. Suddenly, Drew as a father was a huge turn on.

"I wanna grow old and gray with you, too."

"Let's make it happen. You and me."

CHAPTER FIVE
DREW

*H*arry laughed from his rocking chair on the porch. The sun highlighted every weather-worn crease on his skin, and his eyes twinkled with mischief as he let his cigarette dangle from his thin lips.

Pete was sitting on the top step, throwing a ball to some kid I could only hear, not see, and Pete's head came back whenever his laughter shook his entire body.

Deeks, Jedd, Slater, Kenny, and Tate were there, each of them lingering and passing by with mutterings, quips, and sarcastic comments being thrown around in the air like an endless game of word ping pong. The yard smelled of warmth—a ridiculous thing to register, but it did. Whoever had been cooking on the barbeque behind me had created a feast that tinged the oxygen around us, making it feel like we were wrapped in an invisible security blanket.

We were home.

All of us.

"You've not said a word," Harry croaked, coughing lightly on that damn smoke in his mouth. His eyes found mine, and I noticed they were a different color to how I'd remembered them. They were silver now, his skin pinker, too, his smile a lot brighter than ever before.

"Drew doesn't speak much anymore, Harry, remember? He's working on being the brooding silent type," Pete called out over his shoulder.

I looked at him, too, and huffed out a barely-there laugh. He was throwing this ball back and forth, pointing directions at someone I couldn't see… they were too far out of my peripheral vision, and I was trapped, focusing on the two main guys in front of me.

"You gotta work on your catch, kiddo!" Pete called. I wanted to turn to see who the kid was, but I couldn't. I was caught in some kind of tunnel vision that would only let me see so much around me.

Then Ayda stepped out from the front door of The Hut, wearing her tight jeans, a thin white tank, and a sexy little apron around her waist. I looked up to take her in, noticing the way her hair had tinged gray at the roots, and her eyes were cradled by more lines than I remembered her having.

My whole face lit up at the sight of her.

Age had made her even more beautiful.

How was that possible?

"Baby, don't do that!" she called out to the kid Pete was playing with. "You can't give your Uncle Pete the middle finger. What's Mama told you? Have some manners."

"It is kinda funny, though." Pete chuckled, and the sight of him laughing made my chest tighten. The smile on my lips was making my cheeks ache, but I was also filled to the brim with emotion that wanted to pour free.

Almost thirty years of emotion.

My face fell at once, the need to cry like a fucking child threatening to ruin it all.

As if they could sense it, Harry, Pete, and Ayda all turned

their attention my way. I looked from one to the other in a panic, my heart beating faster and the hairs on the back of my neck standing to attention. I wanted to move, to get out of the chair and fucking do something. Shout, scream, release all of this energy, or maybe throw a punch at a swinging bag, but I was trapped, pinned in place by something I couldn't fight.

"Here he goes," Harry muttered under his breath.

"Baby..." Ayda whispered, taking a step closer and bending down to me.

I ran my hands over my thighs to get rid of the sweat collecting there, and I rocked back and forth in my own seat, not knowing where to go or what to do.

Pete rose, the click of his knees making him groan and stumble to the side before he released a laugh and rolled his eyes.

"Don't say it, Pete," Harry warned.

"He needs to hear it," Pete answered, keeping his eyes trained down on me.

I glanced up at him through unshed tears, feeling like a pussy and hating the way it felt impossible to fucking breathe.

I just needed to breathe.

"Oh, boy." Harry sighed, pushing himself to pick up the momentum in his chair. He drew in a long inhale of his smoke, releasing it out into a cloud around him, but I was focused on Pete. My brother who wasn't my brother. The only brother I'd ever needed.

His hand landed on my shoulder, and he leaned down closer.

"Drew..." he said quietly.

"Yeah," I croaked, relieved that I could say anything at all.

A slow smile crept onto his face, his eyes shining with a knowledge I'd never imagine possessing in my lifetime. His fingers squeezed my shoulder tightly, and I only wished he would wrap his fucking arms around me and give me one of those hugs I'd missed for so many damn years.

"Don't worry, kid. It isn't time yet."

"It isn't?" I asked breathlessly.

Pete shook his head. "You're too soon. Get out of here. We'll see you when you're ready."

"When will that be?"

Pete smirked, his mouth parted as his answer began to fall free...

And just like that, my eyes flew open, and I gasped for air.

I was sprawled close to the edge of the bed, my face squished on one side, and one eye closed while the other looked up to see a fucking angel standing above me.

Ayda.

She pulled her bottom lip between her teeth as she watched me. Both hands were behind her back, and her cheeks were flushed under the swelling and darkening bruises. She seemed frozen for a moment before her bright blue eyes sparkled and she sank to her knees beside the bed so our faces were level.

"Did I wake you?"

"Erm…" My voice wasn't working—my mind yet to wake up. "I don't know," I answered honestly, blinking and squinting the one eye that was open as I looked at her. "What time is it?"

Ayda glanced at the clock at the side of the bed and grinned. "Almost one in the afternoon. You looked peaceful when I got up, so I left you where you were and ran some errands with Kenny."

"Fuck, what? Fuck, fuck. I need to… Jedd… I need to find…"

"Nothing's changed. Still slow moving. Howard sent Sloane over to let us know Jedd is fine. Spent the night in a cell, and he's been fed, but that's all he knows." Ayda shuffled on her knees. "Before we take care of that business, I thought we may want some answers, so I had Kenny tail me to town, and I got…" She placed a box between us on the mattress and tapped the top nervously before removing her trembling hand.

I pushed myself up, leaning on one arm as I spun the box around with my other hand.

A pregnancy test.

I looked up at her quickly, my eyes holding hers, seeing the hope shining back at me.

She wanted this.

Ayda had already decided it was real in her mind—now she needed confirmation from her body.

I wasn't sure I could console her if it had all been nothing more than a wild thought, a dream she'd wished to be true. That was a different kind of grief.

"Now?" I asked her quietly.

She looked down at her hands before fidgeting again "It doesn't have to be. I just thought—"

"Do you want it to be now?"

Ayda shuffled closer and folded her arms on the edge of the mattress, resting her chin on the back of her hands as she met my eyes.

"I need to know for sure."

I glanced down at the test sitting between us. It held all

55

the answers we needed to carry on as we were or build new foundations around us to prepare for a life I could never have imagined.

The nerves fluttering away in my stomach were a feeling I'd never experienced before. This was real fear. I'd faced death, murder, prison, grief… everything the world could ever throw at me, and I'd never felt the weight of it like this before.

Pushing the test closer to her, I caught her eye. "What do you need me to do? Where do you need me to be?"

"I have to pee on the stick. But you can do the waiting patiently thing with me. I'm nervous."

I swung my legs from the bed, and shuffled to the edge of the mattress, pulling her to me carefully. I held her face in between my hands and dropped my forehead against hers.

"I've never been so scared in all my fucking life."

"Did you mean what you said last night? Old and gray?"

"You've got me until I'm a wrinkled silver fox, darlin'."

"Then I'll be right back." Tipping her head, she pressed her lips against mine and reached for the box, pulling it against her chest as she slipped from my grip and rose to her feet. She took a moment to run her hands through my hair before padding to the bathroom, doing her best not to rush.

I didn't release a breath until I watched her disappear inside the bathroom, but once she was out of sight, I planted my elbows on my knees and dropped my face into the palms of my hand.

Fuck.

Fuck.

Fuck.

Was I about to be a father?

Was this it?

Could I be what any child of Ayda's would deserve?

Goosebumps trailed up my body from my toes to the back of my neck until they invaded my head and made me feel cold. Yet my heart beat harder and harder, a flood of warmth preparing to flow out to contradict it. There were so many emotions floating around, and I was worried about Ayda feeling disappointed if it turned out to be negative after all. But among the chaos of my thoughts and the mixed reactions of my body, one thing above all else stood out.

And I dragged my hands down my face, resting my fingertips on the edge of my open mouth as I realized what that one thing was.

I wanted this, too.

I wanted this to be real.

I wanted a son or daughter. I wanted a chance to prove I could do it. I wanted something to love from the very beginning, something that was mine, something that was both of us.

I wanted this so badly that I was scared I was about to be crushed with a negative.

I wanted a forever.

For her…

And for me.

CHAPTER SIX
AYDA

Sitting on the closed toilet, I stared at the box resting on the edge of the sink. It was just a plain old box—so unassuming and ordinary—a three-pack of small, plastic test sticks that had the possibility to change our lives forever.

Not just mine and Drew's. This would change the life of every man in The Hut.

The rest of the fallout we could deal with when we had the test results, though. I was already a hundred and ten percent sure I was pregnant, but this would make the whole thing a reality. This test would give us a definitive answer.

Pressing my hand to my stomach, I stayed where I was and mentally tried to ready myself for what was about to come. This proverbial can of worms had been opened now. There was no going back to how we had been before those words had fallen from my lips.

If I wanted the answers, all I had to do was take the damn test.

Something I was suddenly struggling with.

"Man up, Ayda," I mumbled to myself as one foot tapped against the bath mat with nervous energy. It was so easy. There wasn't much to it. Pee on a stick, wait, and the results would be right there. Easy.

Except it wasn't.

Pushing up from the toilet, I stared at my bruised face in the mirror and winced at my battered reflection. I hated it.

These bruises were a horrible reminder of the deepest betrayal we'd felt, and that realization now meant that I also had to consider what my body had been through in the last thirty-six hours. What if the pregnancy test came back positive now, and I went to the doctor only to learn that I was pregnant, but something had happened, and that gift of pregnancy had been taken away? What would that do to me or to Drew—the man who was sitting out there, possibly working through all the same shit I was working out in here? Would it have been kinder to have kept my sudden epiphany to myself when he'd caught me after Owen's attack?

It was too late to think about that now.

This was happening, and there was nothing I could do to change how it had all come about. I still had Drew, no matter what, and the two of us could work through whatever was thrown at us together. We'd been through so much in our relationship already and I wasn't about to let this break either of us, which meant that I had to be strong. It meant I had to hold my shoulders back and be as level headed as he was being right now. Even if that meant I had to be the realist.

The first step of all of this was to take the test, which is exactly what I did next.

Reading the directions twice, I went through the steps and rested the test on the side of the sink while I washed my hands, doing my level best not to look at the damn thing before I was supposed to. I left the other two in the box and finally picked up that little plastic life-changer before I headed back to the bedroom where I'd left Drew.

The moment I stepped through the door, I stopped and took a moment to appreciate him. He was sitting up in bed now, his back against the wall, his bare chest and abs on full display, both riddled with the scars that only ever added to his sex appeal.

He hadn't shaved in a while, either, so the stubble that littered his face made him look more angular and hard. Even with that hard masculinity on full display, all I could think when I studied him was how beautiful he truly was. Handsome, yes. Sexy, absolutely, but Drew was also more. So much more that words failed me.

Easing farther into the room, Drew caught the movement from the corner of his eye and unleashed the intense blue-green of them onto me, temporarily freezing me in my tracks.

He pushed himself up to standing, staring at me like he was waiting for me to remind him how to breathe.

When I finally ventured close enough to feel his body heat, I put my free hand over his heart and felt it smashing against my palm with the same urgency of my own.

"It's going to take a minute or two," I finally said. I bit my lip and tried to think of something more profound to say, but all I could do was look at him.

Drew raised his hands, running them up and down my arms slowly before he let his palms slide up to cup my neck. "Have I ever told you how brave I think you are?"

"Don't say that. I'm absolutely terrified right now."

"You are, but here you stand, with one hand holding our future while your other rests over my heart like you're the one worried about me, when it should be me worrying about you. You're crazy, beautiful, strong, and I'm going to spend my life making sure you know it. Then, whether it's in nine months or nine years, I'm going to make sure our kid knows it, too, and make sure they spend all of their days telling their mama how crazy, beautiful, strong, and fucking loved she is." He smirked and offered me a small wink. "I'll just leave out the cuss words for a while."

The sting of unshed tears was enough to make me blink several times as emotion overwhelmed me. He always knew exactly the right words to say when I needed to hear them. He always knew how to pierce my heart and make it swell twice the size with nothing but love.

"Stop trying to make me cry."

"Not trying to make you cry, darlin'. Just trying to let you know that I've got you, no matter what." He dropped his forehead to mine and whispered, "Because I love you."

"I love you. I hope you know I've got you, too. I've always got you."

I could feel his heartbeat quicken beneath my touch, but he never moved. Drew simply held me with his gaze, trying to create a world where he was my only focus, and all my doubts, worries, fears, and nerves were drowned out by his blue-green eyes.

It worked. It was so easy to let everything fall away and give him my full attention. His eyes were pools I could drown in, and it was exactly what I needed at that moment, even as the small piece of plastic in my other hand seemed to begin to gain weight.

"Is it time?" he asked.

My breath seemed to get stuck in my throat as I broke our gaze and let my eyes fall to my hand hanging limply by my side, clinging to the stick like it was a lifeline.

It was time.

It was time to look at the stick and figure out where the hell we went from here.

It was time to see if Drew and I were going to be parents.

"I don't think I can look. I want this too badly."

Drew swallowed hard. "Then let me do it."

I pressed the test into his hand as I stumbled away. I didn't go far, just turned and dropped my ass to sit on the edge of the bed as I tried to find the air in the room.

Drew gripped it with a white-knuckle force, holding it down by his thigh, never taking his eyes from me the whole time. He dropped to his knees in front of me and positioned himself carefully between my parted legs, resting his free hand on my thigh.

"Ready?" he whispered.

All I was capable of doing is nodding. I just needed to know.

A whispered, "Jesus," fell from his lips before he looked down at the stick, holding it in both of his hands slightly trembling hands. I'd never seen him tremble that way.

"Tell me what I'm meant to be seeing." A small scowl creased his brows.

"Two lines means positive. One is… negative."

He swallowed again, his frown deepening as he nodded in gentle understanding.

I was so focused on the movement on his eyes, I forgot to breathe.

Drew looked up, his face creased, and his eyes glistening with unshed emotion, and my heart dropped into the pit of my stomach.

Biting down on his bottom lip, Drew carefully placed he

test to the floor beside him, and he closed the distance between us, dropping his head to my stomach and burying himself there, a quiet sob I'd never heard him make before pouring free. The rush of his hot breath against my skin made the hairs on the back of my neck stand to attention.

He wrapped his arms around me, claiming me, his fingers curling into my back like he wanted to climb inside me.

"It's positive," he choked.

"What?" I whispered.

"You're pregnant, Ayda.'"

My hands fell to his hair, burying themselves in the strands as I wrapped my body around his head as best I could. Overcome with emotion, I started to cry. The images of the future I wanted and had so desperately denied myself suddenly formed with perfect clarity. Those rocking chairs Drew had talked about, the children, even a puppy all formed in my head and stretched out like a red carpet.

We were going to have a baby. There was a child inside me growing.

Our baby.

"Drew." His name came as a choking sound as I slowly uncurled myself from him and ran my fingers through his hair. He was still clinging to me, his head in my lap, but I needed to see his eyes. I needed to be able to see if this was truly what he wanted. That brief second of recognition had been followed with an emotion I'd never seen on his features before.

When he lifted his head and his red-rimmed eyes locked on mine, he didn't look like my Drew. This man looked lost in his own head, unsure of what to say or do. An unsure Drew wasn't one I knew well. I reached out, cupped his cheek with my hand and watched as his eyes closed and he pressed against my palm.

I took a breath, my mouth opening and closing, trying to form words to say, when the muscles in Drew's cheeks twitched mere seconds before his face broke out into a grin that made him look so young and free, it took my breath away.

All the stress and worry he wore daily was put aside, and all that remained was Drew.

My Drew.

Tears fell freely as I watched him. No words were necessary. All he had to do was open his eyes to see my smile matching his. To see the happiness that I felt all around me. But he didn't open his eyes. He stayed in the moment, so I took advantage and leaned in, pressing my lips over his so he would feel my aching happiness radiating from me. My lips were against his when I finally whispered, "Me, too."

CHAPTER SEVEN
DREW

S he was going to be a mother. I'd finally given her something good and pure. Something untainted by my world that could be raised in any world she deemed fit.

Ayda was going to be a mother.

I was going to be a dad.

The minute her words fell against my lips, I reached up and gripped her hair tightly, holding her mouth to mine and sealing our moment with a kiss so true and heartfelt, it made my skin prickle. Her tears were against my cheeks, and I released her slowly, pulling back to take a look at her beautiful face.

A tear I could no longer hold back fell and rolled over my rough cheek while I stared into her pretty blue eyes.

"We're having a baby," I croaked.

"We're going to be parents." She sounded stunned. Her hands landed on my shoulders, and a radiant smile blossomed over her face. "We made a life."

"I'm ready," I said, without any hesitation or reservations. I was ready. I was ready to have something I could call my own, something I could nurture and protect in a way that didn't require me going to war. Now I would have something that would ground me and remind me that life deserved more than fighting. It deserved peace, and it deserved respect. "I'm ready to do this with you."

"I can't imagine ever doing this with anyone else. I didn't know I wanted this but now..." She gave me another broad grin. "I can't imagine not wanting it."

I released a small huff of laughter and shifted, pushing up until I was standing over her and brushing her hair away from her face. Even beat up and bruised, she was perfect to me, but the wounds of that battle would be the last she'd ever have on her skin.

On my life, they would be the last.

Pulling her to stand with me, I wrapped my arms around her and rested my chin on her shoulder, just needing to hold her tight. She felt tiny in my arms, but the responsibility I felt holding her, and now my child, made my heart want to break free from its chest and shout to the world how fucking happy it was.

I'd never felt anything like this before.

Not with this much power.

"Just promise me one thing," I breathed over her shoulder, emotion closing my throat up tightly.

"Anything," she whispered.

"Promise me this is my baby and not Harry's. I know how close you two were."

Ayda's laugh came as a sputter before her forehead landed on my shoulder, and she unraveled. Her laughter had her shaking in my arms, and took a while to die down, her words coming as a guffaw. "I promise."

I laughed, too, because I had no fucking idea what else to do. The tension was cut right on time, stopping me from choking on my own heart and falling to the floor. I'd never felt such a twisted combination of weak and empowered all at once.

Without another thought, I picked her up, wrapping my arms around her and spinning her around in a circle as carefully as I could. My head fell back, and I looked up at the ceiling, my happiness pouring out of me before I pressed a hard kiss to her head.

"Thank you," I told her sincerely. "Thank you, thank you, thank you."

"You're half responsible for this. I should be the one thanking you."

Planting her back on her feet, I held her and looked down into my favorite blue eyes. "You're welcome. Now tell me that you're okay. Tell me what we do next." I inhaled slowly. "Tell me where we go from here because I don't have a clue, Ayda."

"I'm perfect." Her voice was wistful but honest. She meant it. "As for the rest, I'm as clueless as you are. What I do know is that I need to see a doctor at some point. We probably need to talk about how we deal with this when it comes to our current situation, but aside from that, I was hoping you had all the answers. You normally do." She winked playfully.

I brought my hands around to her flat stomach, resting the heels of my palms together and creating a cradle for my child growing in there. The thought and idea of it was unimaginable. A miracle brought to the hands of a man who had done so much harm and brought so much pain to the world.

Maybe second chances were real after all.

"First thing I'm going to do is get you a doctor," I told her. "Doc can be here in no time, and we'll get you checked over. I need to know everything's okay right now. Once I know you're good, I'm going to figure out a way to get shit out there sorted, get the men out of this mess we're in again, and make sure the life we're bringing this child into is one we're proud to call our own. And *then* do you know what I'm going to do, Ayda?"

"I have no earthly idea."

"I'm going to marry your ass."

"About damn time."

By the time the afternoon rolled around, Doc had been over to The Hut without raising any suspicion among the guys. Ayda had been hurt by Owen Sinclair, and as far as my men knew, I was simply being my usual, overprotective self.

Doc told Ayda he wanted to return during the week, and there was talk of blood tests, scans, appointments she'd have to make, and so much more I didn't understand. All I could do was sit in the corner with my hands clasped together as I leaned forward and watched every move he made on my girl.

She kept asking him over and over if the baby was okay, or was she in danger of losing him or her due to her injuries, but Doc didn't have any clear answers. She was too early into her pregnancy for him to have any, so, for now, it was a waiting game with no assurances to keep our minds from tripping up over all the things that could go wrong.

Once Doc left, I drew Ayda a bath and watched as she sank into the bubbles and tipped her head back against the tub. With a kiss to her temple, I told her I'd give her some time and be back soon.

While the two of us were lost in the clouds of what our future could now hold, my men were out there wondering where the hell I was, and why I wasn't storming down to the station to rescue Jedd.

"Any news?" I asked Kenny as I walked over to the bar.

He was sitting on a stool while Deeks stood behind the bar, leaning against the wall with his head down and his hands sunk into his pockets.

"Nothing." Kenny shook his head.

I dropped my ass onto the stool next to Kenny and leaned against the counter. "Sutton hasn't called?"

"Not since earlier."

"No Eric?"

"No."

"Rubin?"

Kenny sighed, taking a moment's pause. "No."

"Great," I sighed. When I glanced up at Deeks, I saw defeat and concern marring all his features. "You doing okay, brother?"

Deeks looked at me with a small shrug of his shoulders. "How we going to get out of this, Drew? I can't see no way. I can't see the plan no matter where my mind goes."

"We'll find a way, Deeks. We always do," I assured him.

"Not without one of The Hounds taking the fall for it, we don't. You, Pete, Harry, now—" Kenny reminded me, but I cut him off quick.

"No more sacrifices. I promise."

"How can you promise that?"

Staring into Kenny's eyes, I began to see for the very first time how young and vulnerable he could look at times. Sure, he was one of my most trusted men, despite our differences in the past. If there were a fight, Kenny would be standing beside me with his fists tight and his gun ready. He'd die for me—for any of us, and that meant something. It meant everything. But, fuck, he was young and so was I, and was this the life men like us should really be fucking living? Dodging bullets, flexing biceps, growling loud, howling at the moon, too scared to talk about repercussions and sacrifices in case it was our hearts that stopped beating next.

He was looking at me to be the president of the club. I needed to be that now while I was still capable because once that baby of ours came along, shit was going to change.

It had to.

Pressing a hand on Kenny's shoulder, I leaned forward and squeezed him hard. "Because I have a feeling it's our time now, brother. The gods haven't always played in our favor, and we've handled that. Maybe it's time for us to have a little faith. A little hope."

Kenny's forced scowl didn't match the sparkle in his eyes. He wanted to believe in the words I'd spoken, but the bruises of his memory hurt to touch when he thought back over the last few months and years of our lives. It was easier for us to be skeptical than to accept that good shit could happen to us as much as anyone else.

I'm going to be a father, I wanted to tell him… but I didn't because now wasn't the time to share that news. For now, it would stay between Ayda and me. A secret only we knew. A truth in our world we could treasure just a little longer.

"Trust me, Kenny. It's our time."

CHAPTER EIGHT
AYDA

The bath Drew had run for me did me a world of good. The hot water eased the muscles in my body, and the calming scents of the bubbles made me feel more feminine. The room was filled with steam and vanilla, relaxing me.

Even standing in front of the mirror, completely naked, I felt nothing but a strange and out of place, contented happiness.

My body didn't reflect my pregnancy. Not in any noticeable way, anyway. The bruises that were slowly blooming into deeper shades over my skin were a distraction I didn't want, but I tried to look beyond them, unsuccessfully. Frustrated with myself and the barrage of memories, I pulled on a robe to hide the evidence of my confrontation with Owen.

Not that I could hide my face.

I was in the middle of prodding a wicked bruise on my cheekbone when my phone started ringing on the counter. I didn't recognize the number at first glance, so I swiped it from the counter, and answered the call with a cautious, "Hello?"

"Ayda," the voice greeted me in a whisper. There was no mistaking who it belonged to. The little bubble I'd locked myself into popped with a loud burst, and the anxious reality of our situation rose again, growing another head and several sharp teeth.

"Rubin! Where the hell are you?"

"Can't talk," he whispered quickly, his words coming fast as something rustled on his end of the line. He paused, as though waiting, so I held my breath, concern rising with every second. Taking a deep breath, he continued in the same hushed and rushed tone. "I just needed you to know that I'm okay, and to tell you to keep your heads down. I'll call again when I can. Please don't call this number. They don't know I have this phone."

"Are you in trouble? Who are they? Where are you?" I asked in the same quiet tone as I started toward the door to shout for Drew. Unfortunately for all of us, the call had ended before I made it out of the room. "Shit."

I looked at my phone in my hand again and did the only thing I could without raising too much of a ruckus. I sent a quick text asking for Drew to come to our room before I disappeared into our sanctuary to pull on some clothes and finally start the hellish day.

I was fully dressed and pulling on some socks when Drew came into our room, his eyes filled with concern, scanning me for injury or destruction of any kind.

"Rubin called me on a burner," I muttered with little finesse.

"What? Where is he?"

"No idea." I shrugged and repeated everything Rubin had said, word for word. "What do you think it means?"

Drew's eyes had zoned out the way they did whenever he was trying to fit the pieces of a puzzle together. He was glancing up at the ceiling—jaw ticking as his thoughts got carried away with him.

"The kid's in too deep," he finally whispered.

I'd known Rubin most of his life. He was Tate's best friend. Rubin was headstrong, funny, loyal, and bold. I knew everything about the kid, including the fact that he was smart enough to say no when he wasn't willing to take a risk.

"Rubin doesn't do anything he doesn't want to do, Drew. Whatever he's into, he made the decision to do it. He's smart, though, so we need to trust that he has a plan. He'll call us if he needs us." I had to believe that. I did believe that.

"Him being smart isn't my worry. I've seen what he can handle. What he's been asked to do is my main concern." Drew ran his hands over the back of his head roughly, making the longer lengths of his hair stand on end. He began to pace back and forth, his movements controlled as he studied the floor like it held all the answers he was searching for. "Eric walks over to Jedd and Rubin before he leaves the yard," he muttered to himself. "Jedd rushes inside. That's what Moose said." Drew bobbed his head from side to side like his thoughts were making the motion for him. "Slater was asked to torch the training room by Eric. What was Jedd rushing back inside for? Why did Rubin rush out of the yard on his pushbike when he could have asked any of us to get him where he needed to go a hell of a lot faster than his legs could carry him?"

He ran his teeth over his bottom lip, chewing on the inside of his mouth once he released it. Then at once, he stopped, dropped his hands from his head, and looked up at me.

"Eric," he whispered, his face stunned. "Misdirection. The tree. The fucking warehouse." His eyes grew wider as random words fell from his lips. "Do you know something my father always told me as a boy, Ayda?"

I stared at him for a moment. "No."

"If you can't silence a problem, set fire to it, and then bathe in its ashes." His eyes roamed over my body, landing on my stomach for only a second before he let them trail back up to my face. "Metaphorical bullshit back then, but he said those words all the time. If you can't silence a problem, set fire to it then bathe in its ashes." Drew took a step closer to me. "He set fire to the training room. He set fire to Pete's tree. He set fire to the remnants of the warehouse. All places The Hounds of Babylon would never burn to the ground, no matter the circumstances because history and honor come before anything else to us. We'd never torch our own Holy Grails. We'd never burn down our own training room. But do you know who would do those things…?"

"Walsh," I muttered. "Eric created a diversion and misdirection with the fires, making it look like we were the targets while sending a message to Walsh and whoever else he's involved with."

"Because Eric is the original president of The Hounds of Babylon. Because he's the one who needs to save this world he built more than any of us. Because he needs to prove a point, his loyalty, and his allegiance to our brotherhood." Drew dragged in a breath and released it in a rush, a look of unexpected humor flashing across his face. "And because he's a goddamn fucking genius—one I've underestimated. One who is trying to stick to a promise he made me not so long ago."

I wasn't sure what he meant about the 'promise'. After all the time they'd spent together after Harry's death, it could have been anything.

"He's also the only one the ATF aren't focused on." I paused, letting his words catch up to me. As much as I hated to admit it, my curiosity had got the better of me. "What promise did Eric make, Drew?"

"He promised me that if anyone in this club was going to take the fall for anything else, it was going to be him. Even if the blood was on my hands, he was going to make sure he was the one they went after." Drew scowled, his nostrils flaring at the idea of it all. "And now the crazy bastard is actually following through with it, isn't he?"

I blinked at him for a while as the pieces slowly fell into place in my head.

"Except it sounds like he's going to ensure the blood is on his hands, not yours."

Eric was going to try and spare his son. This was probably the most selfless thing he'd ever done for Drew. Yet, I was worried this misguided self-sacrifice would force Drew's hand in other areas, and that scared me. Drew was a loyal man himself; honorable and protective of what he considered his. One wrong move and the whole thing could come crashing down around us.

"We need to find Eric," I said quietly.

"I'm not letting him do this, Ayda."

I held that steely blue-green gaze with my own and felt all the love and pride rise in my chest. This man was mine, and I could see that he was putting all of the pieces together in his head. He knew his father. He knew what Eric was capable of, what he was willing to do, and what he *would* do. No matter how honorable or selfless these plans of Eric's might be, Drew understood that this wasn't the right course of action to take right now—there were too many moving parts on the mayor's

75

machine. Something I wasn't sure Eric had fully considered.

Drew was smarter than Eric in so many ways.

Walsh had laid out a gauntlet for Drew. He'd used a knife of betrayal to wound him, but Drew had just snapped off the blade and was ready to strike back. He'd already started to formulate a plan to cut the legs out from under the monster, and I could see that planning in the occasional glazing of his eyes as he retreated into his thoughts. Drew wanted to play this smart, to ensure the win, and to make sure that when the threat was down, it stayed down.

There was no way in the world Eric could know any of this. He couldn't possibly understand the tactician his son had become. If he had, and he was still doing this his way, he'd underestimated Drew in a big way.

"We most definitely need to find Eric," I repeated.

CHAPTER NINE
DREW

We agreed Ayda would stay behind at The Hut and wait to see if Rubin or Eric contacted her again, because as much as I had loved having her by my side through the stresses of this life I lived in, her main concern and priority from now on had to be the baby.

No more taking risks… whether she batted her little blue eyes and pouted at me or not.

I was standing in the bar, ready to leave, when Slater walked with me to the door and out onto the porch. He, like everyone else, looked exhausted. Despite the sunshine casting warmth on our dirty faces, there was a dark cloud hanging above our world now.

"See that over there?" Slater pointed to a car beyond the yard with two men in the front seats, sitting there idly.

"Shit," I sighed, realizing what it was.

"They're not going to leave us alone now until whatever plan Jedd has formulated comes off."

I stared at the car; eyes narrowed. "Having them around isn't such a bad thing, Slate."

"No?"

"The more people that see us sitting innocently in our home, the better. Let them follow us. Let them watch. We're not running. We've nothing to hide or cover up this time."

"Except the fact that you just brutally murdered one of our own," he muttered from the corner of his mouth.

I huffed sarcastically, folding my arms over my chest. "I've been more brutal than that in my years."

Glancing Slater's way, I saw the subtle twitch of his lips and the way he tried to suppress his smile. "Even though I know it happened, I still can't believe we were betrayed that way."

"It makes you wonder who's going to be next, don't it?"

"You think we have more enemies in our walls?"

I shook my head slowly, focusing back on the two chumps in the car across the street. "No, but I guess we'll never really know. We'll always be suspicious in the back of our minds."

"I fucking hate that," he ground out through gritted teeth. "This is our safe place. Our club is what we live for."

Maybe it's time we tried living for something else, I thought, the ease in which it came surprising me. If anyone loved this club and was willing to die for it, it was me. It had always been me.

"Have faith," I found myself saying quietly. The silence lingered between us for a moment before I exhaled heavily, blowing all the air from my cheeks.

I made my way down the steps of the porch.

"Where you going?" Slater called out.

"Dunno yet."

"You going to take those guys for a ride?"

I glanced back over my shoulder and smirked. "Why not? It'll keep them busy."

"Mind if I come with you?"

"Yeah, actually, I do." I pointed to The Hut behind him.

"You're in charge now Jedd isn't around, and when I'm gone. I need you to look after my woman for me."

"Ayda can look after herself, and we all know it."

But she's carrying my baby now, I wanted to scream from the rooftops, hang banners from every building and place neon signs over our home.

"She's not as tough as she makes out." Throwing my leg over my bike, I curled my hands around the bars, kicked out the kickstand and backed it up, turning to Slate. "I'll be back soon," I promised, knowing I couldn't stay away for long.

I pulled out of the yard slowly, coming to a crawl, and then a stop beside the car that was keeping us under surveillance. Rapping on the window of the driver's side with my knuckle, I leaned down and gestured for them to open it up. My cheesy grin was fixed in place as the driver did. He had black shades in place that made him look like a really bad version of that Reeves guy in The Matrix, and his gray hair was poking through the black at the sides, hanging over his ears. He wore a black shirt with no identification pinned anywhere. For all I knew, he could have been there to kill me on behalf of The Navs, but one look at his partner and I knew they were cops.

Shit cops, too, by the looks of things. The other guy looked like Owen Wilson with his blonde hair, too-bent nose, and his denim shirt hanging open at the collar.

"Hey." I waved sarcastically as soon as the window was down. "You guys need a coffee or a sandwich or…"

The driver glanced at his partner, and even though I couldn't see behind his sunglasses, his eye roll game felt strong.

"No? Shit, okay. Just make sure you have some water.

79

It gets hot around here, and you can't let the A/C run on that engine all day unless you're going to run it on the road. It'll burn out. No good for the mechanics of your motor. If it has wheels, it's meant to roll, if you get my meaning."

The passenger cop tried to hide his amusement and failed, but the driver cop… well, he thought more of himself than to mess with a criminal like me, clearly.

"Where are you going, Mr. Tucker?"

"Out for a ride. Some fucker just burned down half of my yard and I'm feeling pretty pissed about it."

"Lot of those fuckers around Babylon recently."

"You're telling me. Mayor Walsh is a dick." I leaned over the bike and glared at him. "I don't know about you guys, but I've never trusted him. And, I'm not gonna lie to you, if I see that red-headed cocksucker anytime soon, I won't be held responsible for the fist dent I leave in his face."

They glanced at one another, a small scowl here and a twitch of confusion there.

"Probably shouldn't be telling two cops that though, right?" Leaning back, I squared my shoulders, stretched my neck to each side, and let out a small groan of feigned tension. "Anyway. I'm heading out. You can either stay here and watch my place for me—which, by the way, me and the guys really appreciate in case some other fucker comes back and tries to burn down my home again—or you can follow me on the road. If it's me you're actually watching, I mean, and not The Hut."

I stared at the driver and waited, letting him mull the words over in his mind, and then I smiled, winked, and rode away.

Of course, they followed me. I had no doubts they'd

probably called in a second car to go and park itself outside the yard, too. There was no way they could let me ride out of there after everything that had happened in the last forty-eight hours. Not when I was the only infamous convicted murderer around here to have served solid time.

It was too easy to play these fools.

Twisting the throttle, I rode harder. The wind on my face made me want to close my eyes, which would be pretty fucking stupid when riding a motorcycle, sure, but that's the kind of peace it brought me. It hit every nerve ending on my face, whipped through my hair, and made me feel alive.

If I have a son, I'll ride with him one day.
If I have a daughter, I'll ride with her, too.

The baby and its future controlled my every thought as I took the cops on a wild goose chase, taking them on a loop around the outskirts of our town, only to bring them right outside Sutton's police station.

I parked up in my usual bay. When the car pulled into place behind me, I'm pretty sure I saw the driver mouth that I was a son of a bitch while the passenger cop simply shook his head at me, looking like he appreciated it all the same. I saluted both of them and let my laughter pour free as I hopped up the stairs to the station and pushed through the doors.

"Honeys, I'm home!" I called out in the reception area.

A few familiar faces looked up, the women's eyes widening, while a few of the cops at the back rose from their desks and quickly dropped their hands to their gun belts. I rolled my eyes at those idiots and dropped my arms on the counter in front of me, offering the lovely Ellen Moon a smile and sigh of contentment.

"Hey, gorgeous," I cooed at her. Ellen was in her late

fifties, with auburn hair that she still set in curlers most mornings, and a plump face that let everyone knew she was a regular visitor at Lizzy Ford's bakery. "How's my favorite girl today?"

She rolled her eyes, but the faint blush in her cheeks gave away her thoughts about me. Cougar Moon, I called her, knowing full well she'd take me in a heartbeat if I let her.

"What are you doing here today, Drew?" she asked, aiming for indifference as the contradicting red patches crept up her pale neck.

"I need to see my man." My fingers drummed on the workspace between us.

"He's in his cell. No visitors allowed."

"Says who?"

"Says me," came Winnie's voice from behind Ellen. Cougar Moon dipped her head and began shuffling some papers around. The entire station seemed to hold its breath while they listened to the clip-clopping of Winnie's heels on the floor.

Still leaning over the counter, I looked up to see her, and I plastered on a bright, white smile, raising my brows as she drew closer.

"What are you doing here, Mr. Tucker?"

I winced. "FYI: I really hate it when people call me Mr. Tucker. Don't waste your time patronizing me."

Winnie came to a stop behind Ellen, casting her a glance of disapproval before she looked back at me and folded her arms across her chest. "What would you prefer I called you? Mr. Fuc—"

"Don't go there."

"No. Perhaps I shouldn't. I hear the last guy who called

you fucker ended up dead."

"Well, that sounds like a lady of the law is accusing me of a crime I don't know about there, Miss Winnie."

"I really hate it when people call me Miss Winnie. I find it… kinda patronizing," she countered, tilting her head as she studied me.

"I like you." I laughed, leaning over my arms even farther, making sure my biceps popped from beneath my black T-shirt. Her eyes drifted down them before she made her smile tighter, blinked, and forced herself to look up at my face again. The mistake she made then was swallowing and trying to hide it. Body language was my forte, and I loved nothing more than studying someone when I had nothing left to lose. "You could be real pretty if you weren't such a bitch."

Ellen gasped, her eyes rising to mine briefly before she clamped a delicate hand over her mouth and looked down again. Winnie's eyes just narrowed, and her nostrils flared, but she tried to keep that smile in place.

"Sorry," I whispered mischievously, scrunching my nose up for effect.

"What do you want, *Mr. Tucker*?"

"I want my man."

"So do I."

I raised a brow. "He's a good-looking guy. Can't say I blame you."

Heat rose in Winnie's cheeks, and she shuffled on her feet, taking a quick glance around as if she was making sure nobody had heard what I'd said.

Wait a minute…

Did she…?

Fuck, I'd thrown a flippant comment around, and

somehow it had landed on target.

Winnie corrected herself quickly, and I wasn't sure anyone else would have seen her reaction unless they'd been studying her, too, but I'd seen it, and I was sure as shit going to press on that tender spot over and over again until she gave me what I wanted.

"Winnie, you might want to do something about that." I pointed to her face.

"Excuse me?" She scowled.

"The heat in your cheeks. It's screaming desire. I don't know if that's for me, or for my man Jedd, but…" I tsked, leaned in, and whispered. "I'm guessing it's Jedd, and that's really why you're keeping him here."

"You need to leave," she pushed out, straightening her shoulders.

"I will. I'll leave as soon as I've got Jedd."

"He isn't going anywhere tonight. He's here of his own free will, Tucker. He has no desire to leave yet."

If she could read body language, too, then she probably saw the subtle flinch of my eyes at that one. He doesn't want to leave? Fuck that.

"I guess I'll be staying here for the night then."

"*What*?"

"You heard me. You either let me speak to him right this fucking second or be prepared for me to sit over there on those rock-hard chairs all day and night long, just to piss you off."

Winnie stared at me, her eyes on fire as she struggled to keep her hatred under control. She knew I'd been a bad guy. She knew what I was capable of. She probably had proof of shit I'd done and gotten away with over the years, too, but damn, was she having a hard time pinning something on me that would stick in the here and now.

The law was fickle.

Anything could be turned over if the evidence wasn't one hundred percent watertight. Everything she had on me had holes in it, and she was a ship waiting to sink if she let her one lead out of here:

Jedd.

"I know that he's your last lifeline now, Winnie. Jedd's your last chance to bring my brothers and me down. But you should know your value on him means nothing. He's your last hope, but he's my brother, and you'll never win this battle against me."

"Are you threatening me?" She quirked a brow.

"No, ma'am. I'm advising you to choose another game to play."

"And if I don't?"

I exhaled through my nostrils, stared straight into her eyes, and I released a slow, confident smile. "Then you should be prepared to lose."

CHAPTER TEN
AYDA

There was so much going on in my head, it actually felt strange to walk out of the room and into the bar where no one knew what was going on inside of my body. I hadn't realized I'd been in a bubble with Drew about the baby until I looked around and saw every guy in the place meeting my gaze and wincing because of my damn bruises.

For them, the physical abuse was still their main focus when they looked at me, and from the scowls they all wore, the fact that the bruises had been issued by someone they'd considered one of them, stung.

I didn't know what to say to appease the situation. I knew reassurance was pointless. The men of the club looked fit to be tied.

When I spotted Deeks behind the bar restocking the shelves with liquor, I headed straight for him. He seemed like a safe bet, and I was hoping he needed the distraction as much as I did. Sliding into the stool directly behind him, I slapped my palm against the counter.

"What's a girl gotta do to get a drink around here?"

Deeks spun in a jerky motion, his cut slapping his sides as he floundered and almost dropped the bottle of bourbon in his hands. After a quick save, he pushed the bottle onto the counter and shook his head in disbelief.

"Jesus, kid, you trying to kill me?" He paused and reached out a hand, his index finger brushing over the swollen bruises by my eye. He frowned, creating deeper creases in his forehead. "Makes me wanna kill the bastard all over again."

"It's done now," I said, catching Deeks' warm hand and holding it affectionately between the two of mine. "I'm not made of glass, Deeks. They're just bruises."

"They shouldn't be there, and certainly not at the hand of a Hound."

It was my turn to scowl. All that my bruised face was doing was reminding each and every one these guys that one of their own had been working against them for years. It hurt me to know it hurt them to look at me.

"He was never a real Hound. A Hound would never have done any of this. Not to me or any woman attached to the club. A Hound would never have betrayed you guys or done the shit he'd been doing. He wouldn't have stolen your money, given away your secrets... not any of it. The rat bastard was a snake who wore the cut and convinced us all that he fit in. He convinced us that he deserved to be here. But, Deeks, he's just one man, and we can't let that one man be responsible for everything falling apart. Especially not now; not when we need to be united."

Deeks curled his fingers around my hand and squeezed in encouragement, but the hurt he was feeling was still worn right there in his eyes. This wound cut deep and was going to scar the club for good. Owen's betrayal would always be something they looked back on, a shadow cast over that blind trust they'd always had for one another. This realization pissed me off more than anything Owen had physically done or said to me. The asshole had secured himself in this club's history for good. Owen Sinclair would never be forgotten, even when he deserved to been buried in obscurity as though he hadn't existed at all.

"Drew will figure it all out. He always does. Don't you worry about that," Deeks said confidently.

At least that faith in their leader hadn't changed. Belief in Drew was something every man seemed to have in common. I could see Moose nodding at the other end of the bar in agreement. Raising his bottle, Moose mumbled something unintelligible before drowning it out with a mouthful of beer.

Deeks looked concerned for only a moment before turning his attention back to me. "You want a coffee?" he asked.

I would have physically killed for a coffee. My body was craving it with as much enthusiasm as I needed oxygen, but what little I knew about pregnancy, I understood caffeine wasn't a great idea—at least not in the capacity I suddenly needed it. Shaking my head in refusal was far harder than I'd thought it would be, and I watched Deeks' eyebrows rise in surprise. I never said no to coffee.

I guess I did now.

"What? You think Drew didn't feed me caffeine already?" I asked flippantly.

"Smart man. I've seen you without your coffee before. Terrifying." Deeks mocked a shudder.

I stuck out my tongue and grinned at him, releasing his hand when he finally moved to tug it from my grip. His eyes had flickered to the door that was now bleeding bright sunshine into the darkness. I followed his gaze and immediately recognized Howard Sutton strolling in with the same confidence he'd had for the last couple of months. I never got tired of seeing how at home he was in this world now.

Gone was the hand resting on the grip of his gun, and the swagger he'd always used to exert control. The only thing close to that now was his thumbs hanging over the buckle of his belt as he scanned the place.

"Is that coffee I smell, Deeks?"

"Is that a hint, chief?"

Sutton rolled his eyes, but Deeks shot me a wink and headed to the kitchen, leaving Howard and me alone at the bar. Howard settled himself on the stool next to mine and shifted his belt to the side so he was more comfortable before he turned to face me.

"No one gave you steak or peas yet?"

"Jeeze, you asking me out to dinner, Howard?" I asked teasingly, my smile breaking free.

"For your eye, smartass. It helps with the bruising."

"I'm fine. It'll heal."

He nodded but tangled his hands together in front of him on top of the bar. To his credit, he only looked at the door once, but I could see there was something on his mind. If there was anyone suddenly capable of looking uncomfortably comfortable, it was Howard Sutton.

"They're watching The Hut, Ayda."

This wasn't a surprise to me. Slater had noticed them, along with half of the other guys that had come and gone this morning. I'd already received a couple of texts about it. We'd been ignoring them, maintaining the fact that we had nothing to hide, but I could see why that would make Howard uncomfortable. He wasn't supposed to be showing off his connection with us. Not as blatantly as this, anyway.

"You shouldn't technically be here, I'm guessing?" I asked.

"Probably not." He paused and looked around the place, his cheeks ballooning as he released his breath. "You want to take a ride to Rusty's for lunch?"

"Sure. Let me text Drew and let him know."

Howard rose beside me and watched as I pulled out my phone and typed in where I was going, who I was with, and who was watching my back before sliding the phone into my pocket and following Howard to the door. I knew, without a doubt, that Deeks would be following me any second now. He was set on automatic Protect Ayda mode, and that only ever made me smile to myself.

Howard and I were sitting in his car before either of us spoke again. He'd just waved to the two cops watching The Hut, and I couldn't help but smile as they stayed where they were and just narrowed their eyes in our general direction. I wondered whether they would follow Deeks when he pulled out, forcing them to have to put yet another car on The Hut. With all the guys going in their own directions on any given day, I was pretty sure they'd run out of cars long before we'd run out of guys.

"Do they think you're questioning me?"

"Not exactly sure what those a-holes think. They've been at my station moving crap around and making demands of my staff like they own the place."

Howard's frustration was very real. He didn't like that kind of authority hanging around, and from the looks of things, he really didn't like that they were using his station as a base of operations. Especially after they'd all but accused him of betraying his position after the mess at Rusty's.

"You've been working a lot lately," I commented quietly.

Glancing over at me for a second, Sutton quirked an eyebrow before turning his gaze back to the road. "I don't like strangers in my house. They're loud and disrespectful. Why? Has Sloane been complaining?"

"Not that I'm aware of."

Howard gave me a single nod as he turned toward the diner. The man still didn't like to get chatty about his personal life. He never really had. I think that was why he'd always hated when Sloane and Tate had been together. He had to deal with all the pleasantries that came along with that—something Maisey had taken over for him after they'd married. Thinking about Maisey suddenly made me think about the kids they'd had together.

"How are the twins?"

"Growing up too fast," he said after a beat. "They've been asking after their momma a lot. Sloane always manages to field the questions, but she's spending more and more time with Tate and his friends. I've been trying to find them alternative care."

"Bet that's expensive."

"It's insanity, but I can't keep asking Sloane to give up her teen years being a mother she'd never wanted to be." He turned onto the highway and sped up. Rusty's giant sign was barely on the horizon, so I kept talking.

"How's Helen?"

Sutton did a double take on me like I'd lost my damn mind. I supposed it would seem that way after the warning Drew had issued with her release. Me? I was genuinely curious.

"Helen Taylor is terrified, Ayda. Her whole life has been turned upside down. She was being held captive, her husband was murdered, and now her life has been threatened."

"Has she spoken to her girls yet?"

"What is with all the questions?"

"It's called a conversation, Howard. I was just curious. I know Helen was worried about them while she was with us, and I figured the first thing she would have done when she was free was call them."

"She did. Apparently, they're fine and looking forward to seeing their mom."

"That's good."

He looked my way again, disbelief keeping his gaze on me for an uncomfortable moment. It had only been a few days since Helen's release. He surely had to know that we didn't wish her any real harm. We were just protecting ourselves from a very real threat.

"So, you and her have history, then?"

"Nope, not going there. New topic." He was pulling into a spot at Rusty's, and he killed the engine. "Before you ask, I can't tell you anything about Jedd, either, because I still don't know anything. But I appreciate you holding off asking for this long."

"I wasn't—"

"You were thinking about it."

I was guilty to that extent. I had been thinking about it. I just hadn't been planning on asking him. I'd known he wouldn't tell me anything, not before he'd seen Drew, anyway. Those two had an understanding now, and I wasn't going to put myself in the middle of that.

"What is a safe topic of conversation these days?"

"Food."

"Howard. You had me come to Rusty's to sit with you while you eat?"

"Nope. I have a favor to ask." He climbed out of the car and waited for me to do the same, grinning at me over the top of his cruiser when I found my feet again.

"Sounds dubious."

Howard Sutton hadn't ever asked me for a favor before. The last one I'd asked him for had pissed off Drew enough to have him choke the air out of the poor guy, so I figured I owed him. Following him into the diner, I headed to his table with him, only to be distracted by the sight of Libby sitting in her usual booth with another familiar face.

One that stopped Howard in his tracks, too.

Rosie.

Rosie had been a Hound Whore when I'd started working off Tate's debt in The Hut. She'd hated me from the moment she set eyes on me. I remembered her specifically because I'd heard some of the guys talking about her after she left one afternoon and never bothered coming back. Apparently, she'd been seen several times talking to Maisey, Drew's ex, and Howard's now deceased wife. No one knew why Rosie had stayed away, but one of the other girls had happily suggested that it had been my fault. Rosie had set her sights on Drew, apparently. I remember hearing a rumor that she'd been kicked out of Drew's room on a night he'd chosen *her* to mess around with, before changing his mind and rejecting her completely. Another more diplomatic girl had said Rosie was sick of being a whore for every guy but the one she truly wanted.

And now, here she was, talking to Libby. Our Libby, who looked completely engaged and oblivious to our arrival as she held the sobbing woman's hands over the table.

I didn't say anything, not to the two women or to Sutton who looked as though he'd seen a ghost. I guess he had. He wouldn't have seen Rosie since Maisey died, and probably hadn't expected to see her again after she'd disappeared.

"That's Rosie Sullivan," Sutton said as we slid into his booth. I nodded in acknowledgment and put a finger over my lips as I leaned back against the booth in an attempt to listen to their conversation. He nodded in agreement, his hands clasping in front of him as he leaned closer to try and hear for himself.

"–heard about the fires. I was at my mom's when the trucks flew by, and I panicked."

"Awe, honey, I'm so sorry. If we'd known you were back—" Libby started.

"You'd have what?" Rosie laughed, her tone chilly. "Called me? I don't think so, Lib. No one cares about me, or what I do anymore. Not since *she* showed up. Even Gemma told me to stop calling her."

"Gemma told you to stop calling her because you got her kicked out of Slater's bed. Not because Ayda came on the scene."

"Slater? Like Gemma cares about him. Isn't she with that guy with the fucked up eyebrows now? Kenny?"

"No." I started hearing the skepticism in Libby's tone and felt proud of her for keeping her guard up. "He's not with Gemma. Anyway, what does it matter to you? You said you were done with club life."

"I was. I was in a relationship away from all of that, but I still cared, Libby. It's not that I didn't want to be there. I was just in love with someone other than Drew."

"And what? You've just changed your mind and now want in with The Hounds again because you've changed your mood and mind about who to love?" Libby's tone was becoming colder with every word.

"No, asshole. I was dumped."

"By who?"

"You know what? I'm done. I shouldn't have come here."

Silence hung in the air, and I glanced at Howard. There was definitely more to this story than Rosie was giving. There was also another reason Rosie was here, but we weren't going to find out what that was today. Rosie was already slipping out of the booth in a petulant fit of rage and marching to the door without so much as a backward glance.

Apparently, the rendezvous hadn't gone the way she'd planned. Something that was reiterated and underlined several times when Libby finally muttered a simple, "Bitch."

Howard and I didn't dare say anything, and we waited and watched until Libby left, too.

"Damn," Howard muttered in his usual grumble as he threw himself back on his side of the booth. Rubbing his cheek with his palm, he looked part bewildered and part bemused. "I think I owe Drew another apology."

"Why's that?" I asked, suddenly hungrier than I'd ever been in my life and pulling the menu from its place behind the condiments.

"I thought he'd organized her disappearance."

"Whose? Rosie's?"

"For damn sure."

"You really did have him wrong all along, chief."

"All right. Let's not make me admit I was wrong about Tucker all over again. It's becoming too much. Every time I have to say that out loud, a little baby muscle grows in Drew's ego and sprouts up to make him love himself even more than he already does."

My bark of laughter came so hard and fast from sheer surprise, and it turned into a hacking cough that only seemed to spur on Howard's quiet chuckle of genuine humor.

CHAPTER ELEVEN
DREW

I'd been questioned in this particular room a hundred times before. There'd been days in my early adult life where I'd had to sit opposite the town's policemen and women, spending hours convincing them I hadn't done anything wrong—endless hours of them trying to pin down the cocky rebel kid who they saw as nothing more than a nuisance in their otherwise peaceful small town.

I'd stared into each man's eyes with pure hatred pouring out of me.

Now?

Now, I wished it was the town's chief I was looking at instead of the arrogant ATF agent with a bald patch bigger than a baseball diamond on his head, and eyes that wanted to bring me under.

I wished it was Sutton sitting opposite me instead of this fucker.

I stared at the ATF agent as I leaned back in the chair, one arm over the back of it, my other arm resting on the table in front of me. I could stare a guy in the eye for days on end and not feel awkward about it. Especially a guy who was, without intention, declaring himself an enemy.

Time dragged on before I heard the familiar sound of

Jedd's heavy boots stomping down the corridor. When Winnie pushed through the door and held it open for him, Jedd walked in, his eyes cast down before he sat in his chair opposite me.

He rested his hands on the table, leaving me to raise a brow at Winnie and gesture for her to get rid of the asshole in the corner. With a roll of her eyes, she coughed gently and signaled for her colleague to get out of there.

Once he'd left, Winnie shut the door behind her and positioned herself at the end of the table.

"You've got ten minutes," she said, folding her arms over her chest.

"Thanks." I smiled sarcastically, letting my eyes drift over to Jedd.

He didn't look guilty.

He didn't look sorry.

He didn't look angry, scared, or confused.

Jedd, my ever-reliable vice president, looked… peaceful.

A minute must have passed before Winnie blew out a breath in irritation.

She wanted words to be exchanged. She wanted answers; to be on the inside and to see what happened when the president of the MC she was trying to bring down confronted the VP who appeared to have betrayed them.

She'd be waiting a long damn time.

I watched Jedd, neither moving or making a sound other than to lightly drum my fingers on the table between us as I waited for him to look at me.

It happened slowly—a subtle rise of his eyes as he peeked up through his thick, black eyebrows and locked in on me. My nostrils flared, and my lips twitched, but I never blinked or looked away. Jedd held my gaze, and so many emotions ran through me. Fuck, I'd spent so long looking at the club as a whole, as a family, as a group I had to protect… it felt like a lifetime since I'd looked at the men as individuals.

The day I'd found Deeks outside The Hut crying as he looked at the picture of me, him, and Harry was the last time I'd stared deep into the eyes of a brother I loved and really, truly seen him.

It was happening again with Jedd right then.

I fucking loved him, and he loved me. There was a loyalty in his stare that didn't need to be questioned, and I realized at that moment that I'd never needed to speak to him.

I'd only ever needed to see him—to be one hundred percent certain he was still with me.

I raised my chin and released a breath through my nose, but Jedd's face never shifted. His lips never parted, and his eyes never strayed from mine.

My fingers drummed harder, the force finding a rhythm that matched my racing heart and quiet mind.

"Five minutes and not a word exchanged. Don't waste this time, boys. Who knows when you'll get it again," Winnie eventually spoke.

Jedd's smirk pulled at one corner of his mouth, making his long beard twitch.

I huffed out a small laugh and shook my head.

"You're a bastard, Thomas," I told him softly.

"Learned from the best," he muttered, low and quiet.

"We good?"

"You know it."

I nodded once and turned to look at Winnie whose brows were creased, and her eyes narrowed on me like I'd somehow just slipped my brother a fucking chisel to scratch his way out of his cell.

"Thanks for letting me see him. I think I'm done here."

She glanced wildly between the both of us, her chest rising and falling faster and her mind clearly working at a thousand miles an hour as she tried to understand what the fuck had just passed between the two of us. She'd never figure it out. No one beyond the gates of our yard ever could.

This was loyalty.

Blood.

Brotherhood.

Family.

I stood, pushing my chair back and noting the way Winnie flinched as the legs scraped loudly against the flooring. With a single rap of my knuckles on the table, I made my way to the door without looking back at either of them.

"Don't hang around here too long, brother. I think the agent in this room has a thing for you."

Her gasp was loud enough for me to hear. "Wait a minute, I—"

"See you on the other side, VP," I said calmly, and then I walked out of the room, leaving Jedd with my faith, and Winnie with her questions.

Whatever Jedd was doing, he had it under control.

It was time for me to do what I had to do, and hope that we were all going to come back together as a full pack.

"Where are you?" I asked Ayda, my cell pressed to my ear as I pushed my sunglasses into place and stared up at the dying ball of sunlight outside the station.

"Rusty's. Sutton's about to leave and Deeks is about to

take his place. Where are you?"

I spun around to look at the building I'd just left. "Visiting family. Making sure we don't have any more men going rogue on us. Trying to find a way to figure all this shit out without anyone getting hurt. I think that about covers it."

"Is there anything I can do?"

"I just like to hear your voice."

Ayda made a small humming sound that expressed her pleasure. "I'm glad to hear it, but at the risk of ruining the moment, we bumped into an old friend in the diner."

"And by the tone of your voice, I'm assuming by friend, you mean enemy, asshole, or both."

"Rosie Sullivan."

I frowned. "Who?"

"Maisey's best friend. One of the women from The Hut who walked away just after I started warming your bed."

Admittedly, I wasn't good with names, and if someone didn't leave an impression, they were a ghost to me, but the mention of that bitch Maisey—may she rest in Hell—had my brain scrambling like crazy through a sea of female faces. Faces that held no warmth to me, only instant gratification and even that wasn't always instant. Sometimes the effort outweighed the reward.

Rosie…

Rosie…

Rosie…

Then it hit me. The memory of her and Maisey talking to each other on the street corner in Babylon before all hell broke loose in our world. After that, I couldn't remember the last time I'd seen her.

"Fuck," I groaned. "She's back."

"Seems like it. She was meeting with Libby. I didn't hear much of the conversation, and I'm not sure if Rosie saw Howard and me come in, but she was laying it on pretty thick. Libby didn't seem convinced, and Rosie sounded like she was trying to get a toe back in the door. She mentioned the fires."

I closed my eyes and threw my head back. "Please tell me this little bitch isn't involved in all this, or so help me, God..."

"I don't think so. It sounded like she was using it as a topic of conversation—an excuse to call Libby in the first place."

"Has Libby always been close with Rosie?" My head rolled down, and I scuffed my boot across the ground. "Because if she is, and if there's any chance that Tate's lady is playing both sides the way Sinclair was, I've got to be honest with you, Ayda, I will have to fucking end her. Tate's girlfriend or not."

"If that were the case, you know I would back you up all the way. The thing is, it sounded more like Rosie was scraping the bottom of the barrel, grasping at straws and seeing if she could pull the short one. Libby didn't seem to buy it, but it may be worth keeping an eye on her. Just to be sure."

"What's your gut telling you? Can we trust her?"

"I feel like we can. Libby's happy where she is right now, but I can't say for certain what her relationship with Rosie was before you and I got together. But to be sure, it may be worth having Slater ask the HW called Gemma? There was mention of her not taking Rosie's call for getting Gemma kicked out of Slater's bed or something."

I ran my hand down my face in complete and utter exasperation. "Is this what being a father is going to feel like? Constantly dealing with the kids' bullshit?"

Ayda's quiet laugh was full of warmth. "Maybe, just with less life or death shit attached to it… I hope. Hang on, Drew." There was a slap at the other end of the line. "We need to start feeding the guys more."

"Huh?"

"Sorry, Deeks is trying to steal my lunch." She paused, releasing another breath. "Do you want me to follow up with Libby?"

"No, I want you to put Deeks on the phone."

"Okay, but you should know we came to a peaceful resolution about the food."

"Woman, I know you and your peaceful resolutions. Whatever it was, it'll still mean my baby having less bacon or eggs." I meant it playfully, but my voice betrayed me with a hint of seriousness I wasn't expecting. I'd never cared what Ayda did with her body before, what food she put into it or how she chose to look after herself, but suddenly she wasn't just Ayda anymore. She wasn't just one love of my life. She was two, and the weight of that may as well have been an arrow to the chest that struck me hard, forcing me to step back and rest a hand on the seat of my bike.

I was so fucking screwed already.

"The fact that you know I have both bacon and eggs on my plate is scary. Sounds like I need to change some things up and keep my man on his toes."

"Darlin', I'll spend my entire life on tiptoes if that's what makes you happy."

"You realize I'm sitting here with a goofy ass smile on my face right now, don't you?"

"Make sure it stays there. I want to see that when I get home later."

"It will be there all day, but how much later are you thinking?"

Blowing out a breath, I gazed up at the sun again, appreciating its warmth and remembering the cold, lonely days of my prison cell. The sun... I'd never get tired of it.

Maybe that's why I was so determined to marry someone who reminded me of it.

"As soon as I can, darlin'. As soon as I've figured out where the fuck Eric is."

CHAPTER TWELVE
AYDA

Riding back to The Hut on the back of Deeks' bike was just what I'd needed to clear my head. The only thing that could have made it better was Drew being in front of me instead of Deeks. Thankfully, I did love the big teddy bear of a man who navigated us easily into the yard and delivered me safely to the rest of the guys, before taking off to find his ladylove.

I felt a little lost in the middle of the day with nothing to do but wait. I looked around for something to do or someone to bother, but everyone was doing something, and I tried my best to avoid the black hole that showed in everyone's eyes as they worked.

Eventually giving up, I headed to the small mechanic bay where the guys kept tools to work on the repossessed cars and their bikes, knowing Tate would be around that area.

He spent most of his free time in there when he wasn't with Libby.

Wearing a pair of grease-stained coveralls that were tied at the waist, he was sitting on a mechanics stool tinkering with the V-twin engine of his Harley. There was a greasy rag draped over his knee, and a book open at his feet.

"You know what you're doing?" I asked, noting the slight

jerk of his shoulders where I'd surprised him.

"No. I figured I'd fuck it all up and hope for the best," he grunted, the sarcasm in his tone unmistakable.

I stepped around to the other side of the bike from where he was working and bent at the waist, resting my forearms on the seat so I was eye level with my kid brother, Waiting patiently, I held my silence until he finally glanced up at me reluctantly.

"Sorry," he offered.

I waved him off and looked down at the parts he'd spread out in front of him. We'd bought him a brand new bike, but Tate had been purchasing upgrade kits for it at the rest of the club's behest. Everyone had a suggestion on how to personalize it, and the bike was beginning to look better with every alteration. This process of disassembling and reassembling was teaching Tate how to do his own maintenance, which most of the guys had said was priceless.

"So, what are you doing on the bike today?"

"Just taking shit apart and putting it back together again. Eric said this was the best way to learn how the bike and parts *should* look. You know, *before* something goes wrong." Glancing up at me, he offered a small smile. "Eric likes to help out Rubin and me when there's nothing much going on. That one over there is what Rubin works on."

I glanced over to where he'd nodded his head and saw a frankenbike that was almost stripped down to the frame in the corner, looking all depressed and naked.

"That's nice of Eric to do."

"He's not a bad guy," Tate said, glancing up when he realized I'd said nothing in response. "And it kinda meant that I got my bike back, so..."

"I got you." I nodded and shuffled on my elbows. "Still no Rubin?"

"Nope. He hasn't called or been to the extra practices coach set up for the team." Tate picked up the rag and wiped off his hands before picking up something shiny and studying it. His eyes flicked between the part and the book several times before he began reattaching the piece to the bike and picking up a wrench to secure it. I was fascinated, watching him work. "I called his house from school, but his dad picked up, so I hung up. I know Eric sent him off to do something for a reason."

I realized too late that Tate was feeling a little jealous and left out of everything. The Hounds of Babylon had come to mean the world to my kid brother since we'd become part of it all, and just like Rubin, he would have done anything asked of him by any of the men around here. Tate worshipped every one of them in his own surly way. I hated that he felt this way, and I wanted to reassure him that he was just as useful as everyone else, but I couldn't say anything of the sort to him without getting my head chewed off.

"Don't look at me like that, A." Tate worked the wrench competently and picked up another piece without looking up at me. "I'm not mad, confused, or jealous. I'm just keeping busy and staying out of the way until I *can* help."

"You do help."

That got me a head-on glance, but it lasted only a second before he went back to work, attaching the part and sifting through the rest of the pieces with a methodical eye. He really did look like he knew what he was doing, and he was calmer than I'd seen in a while. Something I was happy to see after the craziness of the past couple of weeks.

"Are things finally settling down with you and Libby?"

"We're fine. Everything that happened was just a misunderstanding. Libby got jealous, she's apologized, as you well know, and we've moved on."

"The shower was the apology?"

Tate snorted.

"Do you know any of Libby's friends? Ones outside of The Hut?" I'd said it casually, conversationally, but I'd been thinking about her meeting with Rosie. Had she told Tate about it?

Blowing on a part, Tate looked up at me and shrugged again. "Wasn't aware she had any. Libby spends all her free time here with us. When she's not here, she's visiting her grams in a nursing home down in Corsicana. She doesn't go often, though. Why?"

"Just curious."

Tate rifled through more of his parts and started rebuilding what he'd taken apart. He was quiet while he worked, making sure everything was tightened down before he dropped the ratchet he'd been using and picked up the rag, wiping his hands again. This time he looked up and studied my face a moment before he smiled at me.

"You can ask her."

"What?"

"Libby. Whatever question you have brewing around in that head of yours, whatever you saw, just ask her. It'll bother you until you get an answer."

"I'm not sure if it's that big of a deal."

"Liar." He chuckled when I bared my teeth at him. "How long have you been bossing me around?"

"Since birth."

"Exactly. I know something's on your mind and it's going to nag away at you until you have answers. I can't give you those. I ain't tied to Lib's side all day, so you're going to have to ask her directly yourself."

I slapped the saddle of the bike and rose to my full height. It was pointless trying to get anything more from him now that he'd called me out. He was also right; I needed to ask Libby if I was suspicious, but I wasn't sure that was something Drew would want me to do. For now, I'd hold off.

"Don't forget to eat, jackass."

I ruffled his hair as I passed, and he barely dodged me, he was so invested in what he was doing.

"Yes, Mom."

I left the bay, laughing, my hands in my pockets and face to the sun. I needed to find something to occupy my time or I was going to stare at the clock and count the hours until Drew got home. If he was looking for Eric, there was no telling how long that would take. Eric knew this town well, even if he hadn't been here for a while. If that man didn't want to be found, he wouldn't be found.

Tate stayed in the bay working while I wandered aimlessly, looking for something to occupy my time. The air still had the smell of overheated metal on the breeze, as well as mutilated plastic. It wasn't something that would just go away, even when the rest of the guys seemed to refuse to so much as acknowledge it. Part of me wanted to gather some of the guys together and start gutting the place just to rid us of the constant reminder.

When inspiration for a distraction finally hit, I locked

myself away in Drew's office, sat at his laptop, and started researching. There were some terms I remembered from the paperwork I'd found in Harry's room, as well as Owen's home. Going incognito, I typed in some of the terms and read through the findings. There wasn't much to glean without specifics, so I moved my search to the land and the sale. There were no public records on file for the land, and in order to get a more detailed report, I wasn't willing to give them my credit card or payment information. Not without discussing it with Drew first, anyway. Having my name on that paperwork wouldn't be a good thing.

When I finally threw myself back in the desk chair, almost two hours had passed, and I still wasn't any more informed than I had been when I'd begun. I sighed and started searching pregnancy and babies instead, quickly losing myself down a rabbit hole of self-diagnosis, which was a horrible idea. Having everything that could go wrong plastered over a screen was doing nothing to stop my concerns, and not having a clue how far along I was in the pregnancy only fed into a whole set of other fears I wasn't prepared to face alone.

An hour later, and I was a mess.

"Ayda?"

Glancing up, I found Autumn standing in the door, her beautiful face clouded in angry shadows as she caught the bruises that I continued to forget about. Her frown didn't last long, though. Her gaze had already drifted to the screen sitting open on the desk. In a blink, she was beaming at me.

"You can't say anything, yet." My words were fast and jumbled as I rushed to shut the pages I'd been working on. "Don't freak out. Please."

I held my hands up, a half smile on my lips, my fingers

trembling. I hadn't intended anyone to find out by accident. Even though Autumn and Janette were probably the first two people I would choose to tell after direct family, anyway.

"You're…"

I nodded.

"How long?"

"No idea."

"Have you seen a doctor?"

"I saw *the* doctor, but not a specialist. Is there a specialist?" I asked, covering my face with my hands, the words falling from me so quickly they began blending together. "I'm so underprepared for this. I have no idea what the hell I'm doing. All I can see is a tiny baby with Drew's sparkling eyes, and I melt. Everything practical goes out of the window. Then I get this image of Drew with a tiny baby in his arms and it's like an orgasm that smashes me off my feet. After that, the questions and concerns just flutter away. No one knows yet, either. Just Drew and me. Well, and now you, and we don't want—"

"Jesus, Ayda, breathe," Autumn sang, throwing her hands up in the air as she stepped closer. "This ain't gonna happen tomorrow, sugar. I know you feel blindsided, but you've got months and months to get ready for this."

"Months," I agreed. My cheeks flamed as I looked at her again and grinned. "I'm sorry, I started searching online and freaked myself out all over again. And that stuff I said about Drew—"

"Daddy Drew does it for you. No shame in that." Autumn wrapped her arms around me, and I rested my head on her shoulder as I attempted to find my breath again. "How did he take the news?"

"Surprisingly well. I think we're both scared. With things as they are right now, it's hard to think too far into the future, but... Autumn, he's going to be amazing." I glanced up at her and smiled tearfully. "It's the only thing in all of this that doesn't terrify me."

"A baby," she said quietly, squeezing me tightly.

"It doesn't feel real. I was on that porch, a gun to my head, figuring I was going to be saying goodbye to Drew, trying to make my peace with leaving Tate and y'all. Suddenly, the baby was just a thought in my head, like, *oh, I guess that could turn out badly. I need to rethink this*. I just... I knew, Autumn."

"Intuition."

"It's not like I sat there counting down to my last period. How could I possibly have known?"

Autumn rested a hand over my heart, and I looked down at it. "I know I'm an old hippie with unconventional thoughts, but whatever it was, head, heart, or sixth sense, I'm glad it helped you to fight for survival when you were ready to say goodbye."

"Oh, I wasn't ready." I huffed out on a forced laugh. "I was ready to fight and knew that it might not turn out well, but I wasn't about to just roll over and die."

"That's my girl."

I thought back to that night, and how fast it had all gone down. Every punch, slap, and piece of manhandling Owen had served only adding minutes of pain to his life. I'd felt the fight rise in me. I'd been so tired and full of pain and exhaustion, but when I'd caught Drew's eyes, I'd known. I would not accept death, and neither would he.

When he'd pulled me out of Owen's reach, and our eyes

had met, it had been a light bulb going on over my head.

I shuddered almost violently as the memories of that night flooded me again. It felt like a hundred years had passed since then.

"You still with me?" Autumn asked gently.

"Yeah, sorry. Just thinking about it all."

"Would you like a distraction?" Pulling back, she flashed me a bright smile and raised her eyebrows in a challenge. She pulled her braid over her shoulder and stroked it like a wicked genius.

"What do you have in mind?"

"Movies," she said proudly, dropping her hair with a game show hostess flourish. "Great movies with junk food and tissues."

I couldn't remember the last time I'd sat down and watched a movie from beginning to end without any explosions or auto chases involved. When you were outnumbered ten to one by men, you didn't really have much say in the matter.

"What kind of movies?"

"Baby Boom?"

I groaned. I'd walked straight into that one.

"*She's Having a Baby*?"

I started laughing while Autumn continued to name movies from the '80s that involved pregnancies and babies. Finally, I agreed and gave her final choice while I went to pop some popcorn.

At least it would kill some time until Drew got back.

CHAPTER THIRTEEN
DREW

I rode for hours, waiting for inspiration to hit. A sixth sense inside told me Eric wasn't far away. I could almost feel his history on these roads, haunting my every move, steering me in ways I'd never realized he steered me before. I was my father's son, whether I liked to admit it or not, and the two of us had an instinct that flowed through our blood—one which we could neither explain or describe. But it was there, and the power of it told me to keep riding until something stuck like gum to my wind-chapped face.

At the border of The Navarro Rifles' turf, I skidded to a stop and stared down the road, unable to ignore the tingling of my spine.

Dad had set things in place to take the spotlight off our club—to keep The Hounds of Babylon clean in the eyes of the ATF and the law. The fires, if I'd guessed correctly, were his doing, and now he was in hiding, trying to plant evidence we'd collected, and to make sure our enemies would have motive to destroy us.

Since the demise of the Emps and Chester Cortez's charter, The Navarro Rifles were our biggest rivals. Travis 'Trigger' Gatlin had placed a target on my back since his half brother Jacob Hove had strode back into Babylon. Trigger was in deep with Walsh and Jon Taylor, that much we were certain of, but the rest…

The rest we were guessing.

At least I was. Did Eric know more? Had he always known more?

My chest rose as I dragged in a hot breath and held it there for just a moment before I blew it back out.

Go to The Navs, Drew. Find out for yourself. Stick a gun in someone's face, risk your life, cause mayhem, and worry about the consequences later. Win the war for your brothers.

That's what the old me was screaming in my head. But his voice was now muffled behind a gag. It was a muted plea from someone I used to know. The new me had a voice much louder, clearer, and more understanding, and the way he was talking surprised every me I'd ever known.

Ride away. The battle isn't here today. You can't do this anymore without consequence. You cannot go to them without mercy and patience. You cannot fight this war without truth and knowledge. You cannot do this to Ayda without shame and regret. Drew, you can't fucking do this alone without forever being different to her after its all over. Be careful which road you take. Everything has changed now.

I swallowed hard, turned, and rode away, circling in loops every direction I could go. When Mayor Walsh's house came into view on the open road, I slowed to a crawl and looked up at the windows on the first floor, hoping to see some sign of Rubin and get a single look into his eyes the way I'd done with Jedd. All that stared back at me were reflections and disappointment. Walsh's car wasn't anywhere to be seen. The house looked deserted.

The bike remained strong beneath me, forever my faithful

steed when my mind wasn't sure where to guide us. Before I knew it, I was crawling down the main road of Babylon, glancing at the all too familiar stores and buildings. That instinct of mine kept trying to tug at loose threads of my memory, taunting me with weak theories or possibilities I just couldn't seem to cling to or turn into something solid.

Eric hadn't been at Pete or Harry's grave. There'd been no clues left behind.

He hadn't been with Jedd. He wasn't hiding in plain sight—or sight that I could actually fucking see. But the one thing I knew about Eric was that he was like me, and if I were him, I knew I'd be in the faces of the very people who expected me to hide.

My bike weaved in and out of the traffic. The sound of my engine and the cut on my back attracted the usual stares. My heart went wild one minute only to level out the next.

Where would I go?

Where would I go?

Where would I...

And then it hit me.

The very people he was hiding from weren't our enemies.

He was hiding from The Hounds. From us. And if he wanted to hide in plain sight...

"You bastard," I ground out, tensing my jaw and working the muscles there as I gripped my hands tighter around the throttle and made a sharp right out of Babylon.

"Seriously?" I stared at Eric on the top step of the wrap around porch.

He smirked confidently. There he sat at the safe house,

wearing the same outfit he'd been wearing when I last saw him outside Owen's burning home. His face looked dirty, and his hands were black, the same smears covering the gray flecks of his facial hair and actual hair.

Eric's legs were parted, and his hands hung limply over the edges of his knees as he stared at me smugly.

"Took you fucking long enough," he finally said in that low, calm, confident voice of his. "I thought this place would be the first place you thought to come looking."

"I didn't think you were that obvious."

"No need to over complicate simple decisions, Drew."

"You're an arrogant motherfucker."

He huffed with amusement, his body barely moving. "Yeah," he sighed. "I know."

Dropping my hands into the pockets of my jeans, I took a few steps closer and stared down at the ground, hearing the stones crunching beneath the heavy weight of my boots.

"So, Ayda's definitely pregnant, huh?" he asked casually.

My head snapped up at once, and I held his gaze—mine serious, his breezy. I searched his eyes, looking for something. A warmth, maybe? A connection. Something that made me think he'd felt the same way I felt when he found out Mom was pregnant with me.

Eric wasn't like that, though. At least not the Eric I knew. He had complete control. None of us ever truly knew what he was thinking.

"Yeah," I eventually answered.

He nodded slowly, processing his own thoughts.

"She's pregnant, Eric."

"You ready for it?"

"Honestly? I'm both dying inside with excitement and

dying inside with fear." I curled my shoulders in and shook my head. "Now is, quite possibly, the worst fucking time in the history of our club for us to be bringing another life into the fold. I'm only just beginning to figure out who I am. There are so many demons circling above me—I wake up some days not knowing which one is going to drop down to grab me first."

"Son?" I didn't flinch when he called me that then. His slow smile grew, the light of the porch making something I'd never seen before shine in his eyes. "It's all going to be okay," he said quietly.

I swallowed the lump in my throat, unable to look away. "You think so, Dad?"

He nodded once. "On my life."

Reaching up, I scratched the back of my neck awkwardly and looked back down at the ground.

Dad. Son.

We'd used those two words quickly tonight, and neither of them had made my skin crawl. I wanted to go to him, sit beside him on the porch with a beer in our hands, stare out into the night and clear a lot of old history away. There were still so many questions to ask, but only a few mattered that night. The rest could be answered when he was older, grayer, less... Eric.

With a sigh, I dropped my hand back into my jeans pocket and walked over to stand in front of him. No words passed between us before I allowed myself to drop into place on the porch steps beside him. Okay, so we didn't have the beer or the perfect timing, but we were there, and I had my questions as we both looked out into the inky night.

"Where've you been?" I asked, resting my hands over my knees—a mirror image of him. Harry would be choking on his smokey laughter looking down on the two of us and our awkward relationship.

"Ready for this, too?" Eric side-eyed me.

"Probably not, but let's hear it anyway."

He spread his hands out, revealing the dirt and grease upon them as he turned the palms up to the sky and stared at them in front of him.

"The stuff Ayda collected from Harry's room and from Owen's place was good, Drew. She's got an eye for what's important. After you guys rode off from Owen's place, I gathered it all up and got the hell out of there. Dumped it all in the repo vehicle, rode someplace remote, not too far, to the outskirts of Owen's land. There was water there. Did you know that? Water I could drive the front end into, flood the engine, make it so no one could move the thing without a tow truck."

"To make it look like whoever burned Owen's place and him to the ground also stole the car and wanted to get rid of it quickly?"

"Maybe."

"What did you do with the evidence? There was a lot of it."

"Left some of it in the car. I had a little time to flick through some of the paperwork. I didn't leave much. Just enough to tie Owen, Jon Taylor, and Mayor Walsh in together. After you guys rode out of Babylon chasing Owen that day, you had a lot of witnesses to say he'd gone rogue. You also had a lot of witnesses see the look on Walsh's face, by the sounds of it."

"How do you know that?" I scowled, turning to study his aging yet familiar face.

He stared forward, his amusement lighting his eyes. "I have my sources."

"Have you had those sources the whole time you've been gone from Babylon?"

Eric turned to face me, his movements slow and controlled. "I'm your father. I needed to know. Sometimes I hated seeing your life through other people's eyes. Most days, I convinced myself a day like this would never come—a day where you sat next to me on a porch step, trusted me, and listened to me."

"I don't trust you," I lied, the croak of my voice giving me away.

"Okay." His lips twitched on one corner.

I looked out into the trees again, imagining a million pairs of wolf eyes staring back at me, or a hundred guns, pointed and ready.

"What did you do with the rest of the evidence?" I asked quietly.

"Gave it to Rubin."

"Rubin?" I called in surprise, looking at him once again. "The kid has our club's future in his hands?"

"I hope not. Not anymore, anyway."

My scowl was deep as I shook my head, telling him I didn't understand.

"Trust me, Drew. Trust him. The kid is smart."

"And how the hell would you know that?"

Eric tilted his head to the side and released a slow, long breath of air from his lungs. "Gut instinct."

"And Jedd? What have you got him involved with? Why the fuck is he in a cell and looking proud of the fact?"

"You've seen him?" Eric raised a brow, clearly surprised.

"You're damn right I have. He's my VP. You think I'm just gonna let him rot—let any of you just fuck off like a trio of vigilantes trying to bring down the bad guys, while me and my future wife raise a pretty little girl with pigtails for the rest of my life. I don't think s—"

"You think it's a girl?"

I paused, my heart feeling like it stopped for a second, and my eyes unblinking as I stared at him.

"I…" I hadn't even thought about it. Not until now.

"A girl?" he asked with reverence lilting his voice.

My mouth opened and closed four times before my shoulders relaxed, and I shook my head. "I don't know, Eric. I just can't allow myself to believe it could be another boy for us to bring into this mess and fuck up with ego, bravado, and bullshit the kid doesn't deserve."

Eric's face fell, and all the regrets I'd longed to hear him speak of were written across his face as he stared at me.

"I haven't made many promises to you in your life, Drew. Never felt the need to. Never wanted to make one and break it or let you down. I've lived a life where the truth has been both my addiction and my tonic. I figured truth could be yours, too. I was wrong to do that. Truths are often twisted and ugly and sharp. They don't always make things better. Sometimes truths make things so unbearable, you feel like you can't breathe. A long life of mistakes has taught me that. The truth isn't always a good thing. I drowned you in it for years, and then I hid behind lies I thought would protect you. I'm one big fucking mess of a father, and I can assure you, no one knows that more than me."

I ran my hand across my forehead, not knowing what to say.

"But I'm going to make you a promise today."

Looking up, I held his gaze and saw that never before seen emotion there again.

"Before your child is born, there won't be a mess for you to bring them into. The mess will be gone. No matter who has to pay the price for it, the next generation of Tuckers are going to be born into a world of peace. The kind of peace you and I have never known."

CHAPTER FOURTEEN
AYDA

S pending time with Autumn for most of the afternoon had helped my weird flash of anxiety. By the time Deeks came to get her, we were sprawled out on the huge bed laughing our asses off at nothing in particular. She always had good stories to tell me. Being on the fringes of the club all these years, she'd experienced everything with them, and had watched a fair few of them grow up. Drew was one of those. Happier memories were always welcome to me, and I relished in them when she decided to regale me, but it sometimes felt as though Deeks had a second nature and knew when she was telling a story about one of his indiscretions as a younger, less inhibited biker. The one she been telling me, she'd promised to finish later, and I planned on holding her to that.

Drew hadn't made it back to The Hut yet, so I'd found myself reverting to old habits to keep myself busy and distracted. I had worked my way through a couple of loads of laundry and had made a chili that could be reheated for anyone looking for sustenance later. I also managed to direct Moose in the direction of a room where he could sleep off the crate of beer he'd inhaled since we'd been allowed back inside.

I wandered around the building looking for a distraction

after that, soon finding myself at the door of the club's heart.

The War Room.

Nothing in the room matched, the chairs were all different shapes and sizes, and the reaper and hounds were etched into the surface of the table. If you inhaled hard enough, there was still that lingering smell of Harry's cigarette smoke in the air. I didn't dare enter their sacred space, so I leaned my head against the frame and stared, mentally filling the chairs around it. My brain seemed to stutter over the seat that had always been occupied by Owen. I wanted to wheel the damn thing into the yard and burn it, but we'd already had more fires than we could explain. I couldn't imagine we'd be able to make excuses for my rash decision, especially if we were trying to sell ourselves as being in mourning.

It made my skin itch to see Owen's seat there. It also triggered another memory.

"Hey, Kenny?" I glanced over my shoulder at him and waited for a response.

"Huh?" Kenny was already behind the bar, but he was watching me.

"Did you ever mess around with one of the club's women called Gemma?"

Sliding his beer onto the surface of the counter, he considered my question. One thing I loved about these guys was they didn't get prudish talking about their conquests with me. I'd become another one of the guys to them.

"Oh, yeah, that little blonde with the tight ass? Once, I think, but that was before Drew got out of Huntsville. Her and Slater used to fuck frequently, I think."

"You seen her around lately?" I asked, my body turning so I was facing him. Kenny shrugged a shoulder and swiped his beer from the bar, downing half of it and belching before replying.

"Haven't looked for her. Why?"

"Someone mentioned her name the other day, and I couldn't remember seeing her around."

"I heard she's studying beauty shit at Navarro College."

"Beauty shit? That an official course title?"

Kenny flashed me his middle finger and a grin. I wrinkled my nose and playfully bore my teeth at him, making him shake his head in humor. Figuring I'd taken the questions about Gemma as far as I could without raising questions and suspicions, I changed lanes.

"Have you seen Libby today?"

"Last free question. I'm gonna start charging after this one."

I made another face at him. "You do that, and I'll start charging you for beers."

Kenny glanced down at his hand and back up at me before he rolled his eyes and smirked at me.

"Libby's with the kid. She came in looking for him earlier, then headed out to the bay to see him."

"Thank you."

Sliding his bottle along the bar until it dropped off into the trashcan, Kenny waved me off with a grunt and turned to grab another. Things around The Hut still weren't back to normal, and it was like an elephant sat in the corner of the room for all of us. As much as I hated the impact Owen had on us, I knew that in time, once the distrust had passed, we would find a new normal, and we would make it work.

I still wasn't sure whether or not Drew wanted me to talk to Libby yet, either. I knew where she was. I knew what *I* wanted to ask her, but waiting for a game plan while everything trembled around us felt like torture.

I had no idea what Drew was planning on doing with half the information he'd obtained, both from me about Libby and Rosie, and with all the information and evidence we'd gathered against our enemies. But *I* needed to know if Libby would try and hide the meeting she'd had with Rosie Sullivan or not. Part of me couldn't imagine that she would. Libby had met Rosie at Rusty's, which was my territory as well as The Hounds favorite spot these days. I couldn't imagine her thinking that it would stay a secret. There were so many other places the two of them could have met had they been in cahoots with each other.

I wasn't sure what I planned on asking her as I headed out the door and onto the porch, but it all became a moot point the moment I heard the bike pull off the main road and into the yard. My attention was immediately diverted to the president of The Hounds rolling to a stop in his usual spot, and pulling off his sunglasses with a sexy flip of his wrist.

Hopping down the porch steps, I pushed my hands into the pockets of my jeans as I approached him.

"Any luck?" I asked after he'd killed the engine and glanced up at me.

Drew's small yet confident smile was his answer as he swung his leg off the bike and slowly closed the distance between us. When we met in the middle, with only a few inches between us, Drew glanced over my head at The Hut before he focused back on me.

"I need to keep that father of mine on a leash."

I grabbed the front edges of his cut and pushed to my toes, pressing a kiss to his chin. "Wouldn't that be like keeping an alligator on a leash?"

Drew's hands slid around the lower part of my back. "He's too controlled to be an alligator. Despite it hurting to admit this again, he's a quiet genius, and I've been stupid to underestimate him since he came back to Babylon."

"I think it's safe to say that we *all* underestimated him."

Metaphorically speaking, Eric was the lone wolf. Being pack animals at heart, they all understood that they had to look after one another, but having imposed himself to isolation after being ingrained with that pack mentality for most of his life, it had forced Eric to become smarter. This wasn't something you thought much about in terms of humans and their interactions, but Autumn had alluded to that little fact when she'd talked about Deeks and Eric in the past, and it made sense now.

"People tend to do that when your last name is Tucker. You sure you want to marry into that?"

I couldn't help the grin that flashed at the thought of marrying this man. It had been one of the first thoughts every morning since he'd put the ring on my finger. "It can't happen soon enough."

"Let's get you inside. It's getting late. I need a shower, and we need to talk."

Rocking back onto my heels, I nodded in agreement. The thought of seeing Drew in the shower never hurt. Sweeping his hand up in mine, I backtracked toward the porch and through the bar, where Kenny was no longer alone.

"You want me to grab a bottle and meet you in the room?" I asked, already knowing the answer.

"Sure thing, darlin'."

I watched him saunter away for a moment before heading to the bar where Kenny already had a bottle and two glasses waiting. The crazy eyebrows of his were high on his forehead as he smirked at me.

"You want me to tell Libby you were looking for her?"

"Nah, I'll find her later."

"She won't be difficult to find."

I sent Kenny a glare. His tone had filled in the blanks. I hadn't needed the mental image of my brother and his girlfriend, but Kenny lived to torture me.

"Kind of like Sloane and you then?"

"Ouch. Was that supposed to hurt?" He chuckled and shook his head.

"You know I could be much meaner, but it's not in my nature."

There was a cough at the other end of the bar that I ignored as I picked up the bottle and glasses. With a dramatic roll of my eyes, I headed back to my room and followed the sound of running water to the bathroom, where Drew was already under the steaming flow of water.

I admired him for a moment.

It was hard not to.

Drew had one of those bodies that demanded your attention. His skin was scarred, inked, and stretched over muscles that always rippled under the surface as he ran his hands through his hair. I never got used to seeing him like this, and I didn't think I would ever lose appreciation for my good fortune. I knew what that body felt like under the palms of my hands, knew the heat that bled from his flesh when he wrapped himself around me. I had memorized that iron grip of his and the feeling of safety it always afforded me. When he turned to grab the soap, and I got a glance at his ass, my decision to join him was made.

Sliding the bottle of whiskey onto the vanity, I stripped out of the clothes I was wearing and into the shower behind him, my hand covering his as he worked the soap over his chest, the other rested against his shoulder, absorbing his body heat.

"You talk, I'll scrub," I whispered, brushing my lips over his back.

Drew filled me in on everything Eric had alluded to, his eyes closing as temporary peace drifted over him under my care. The bitter edge to his voice when he spoke about Eric had disappeared, and in its place was a slight air of admiration and surprise.

Eric had orchestrated the fires. All of them, including Pete's tree and the warehouse. Misdirection, as Drew had suspected. Who he'd got to start those fires was still a mystery—one Drew didn't like being in the dark about, but one Eric assured him he didn't need to know about. Not yet, anyway.

Jedd was a part of the plan, occupying the ATF with promises of treachery so their time was wasted on him rather than Drew, Eric, and most importantly, Rubin.

Rubin.

Just a friend of my younger brother's, now playing a vital part in the MC's future. How was this possible? How had all of this come full circle to Rubin, the mayor's very own son, being the one to save us all?

When Drew turned around in my arms, letting me run my soapy hands over his chest, he opened his eyes and let the water rain down his handsome face.

"Do you want to know a secret, Ayda?" he whispered.
"I do."

"I'm losing control of the club."

I blinked in surprise and rocked back far enough to catch his eyes with mine. I'd needed to see if he was serious, and he was. I could see it in the lines of his face, the clarity of his eyes, and the set of his mouth as he studied me right back.

"What the hell are you talking about?"

"Can't you see it?" His expression was blank, accepting, and I had to imagine Drew saying those words without fury tainting his tongue when I first met him. His club had always been his everything. It was the blood running through his veins. The ink on his chest. It was the beating of his heart and the light in his eyes, but now…

Drew sighed softly and then drew in a breath. "I'm good at reacting. I'm good at being at the front of the pack when they need someone bold enough to bark and howl from the rooftops. They know I'm loyal. I was born to be who I am—the president of the mighty Hounds of Babylon MC. And all that's been a part of my life I've had to accept, even on the days when I've felt more alone than a man standing at the top of a mountain. But things are different now. People don't come to me to ask my advice like they once did. They don't need my approval to respond to a situation. They don't mind keeping me in the dark when they think it's for the greater good. That's something Slater, Jedd, Kenny… fuck, all my men… it's something they wouldn't have done before I went to prison. When I came out, they wanted a leader to return, and I guess for a bit, I did. I was angry enough to do it. I was vengeful enough to want it, but now…"

"Now…?" I echoed.

"Now there's only gratitude. Revenge is more motivating than gratitude. It gives you a greater drive. I think I've lost that drive now. All I want is… peace."

I rinsed my hands quickly before framing his face in my palms, and I pulled in a long breath.

"I think you're wrong. I think that this club has grown and evolved since you've been out of prison, but I don't think that means you're losing control, Drew. These guys trust you. They idolize you, but you've also let them know that you trust and respect them, which means they have the freedom to make these choices for the good of the club. For you. That doesn't tell me you're a bad leader or that you're not angry and vengeful enough to lead them. It means that you're thinking, and you have them doing the same. Every single one of us loves this club, but the club isn't what it is without all of you. Or without you in particular. You're the heart and soul of this place and every last one of those men knows that. They feel that."

"I never said I was a bad leader, Ayda," he said softly. "But I am an honest one, and I have to be honest with myself about what's in my heart. And right now…" He trailed off, glancing down at my bare stomach, a small scowl creasing his brows together. "Now there's more to life than death for me. More than motor oil, patches, and enemies. I'm losing control, whether you like to think it or not." His gaze rose slowly, taking in every inch of my naked skin before his eyes locked on mine again. "And the truth of my heart tells me I'm okay with that," he whispered.

I released a long breath. Inside, I already knew what I felt. It had always been there. It was a mantra that played every time I looked at him. I'd always thought that it meant something different. I'd thought it had meant destruction, but now I realized that the possibilities were as endless as the love

I felt for him.

"I will follow you anywhere, Drew Tucker."

He smiled softly, the force of it barely moving his lips, but I saw the real happiness in the crease of his eyes. "All I want is a life filled with you."

"You couldn't get rid of me if you wanted to." I felt tears stinging my eyes. I was happy. Happier than I felt I had any right to be in this moment while the world around us was on fire, but it was there, right in the center of my chest: an overwhelming love that would always eclipse everything else in my universe. "I can't wait to marry you. I don't want to wait."

Drew wrapped me in his arms, curling my body against his as he held me tight and rested his cheek against the top of my head. "Call Autumn in the morning. No more waiting. Life's too short. Arrange the wedding of your dreams. The fires can wait until we're ready to put them out. There's nothing I want more than to marry you and marry you now."

I threw myself at him, catching us both off guard as his back hit the tile and our mouths crashed together. There just weren't enough words to express my feelings. There were also no clothes to keep us apart.

Drew took control easily. I may have made the first move, but his hands were slow and gentle, running from my shoulders and down under my arms. No matter how hard and fast I wanted him, he was setting the pace tonight, and from the looks that he aimed at me, he was in the mood to appreciate the time we had together and worship every inch of skin he could reach in his own time.

I wasn't going to complain. He could have me any way he wanted me.

Drew's thumbs brushed the edges of my breasts in a slow, teasing slide, slipping under the weight of them with a hum of appreciation. He twisted us, my back now pressed against the wall so I was fully at his mercy. He spread his palms over my ribs and lowered himself just enough to press his mouth over my right nipple, his teeth grazing the taut skin as the water beat down around us.

My breath rushed out in a mass evacuation from my lungs, and my head fell back and hit the wall as a moan of pure appreciation left my mouth at his sudden attention. Drew knew my body. He knew every dip and valley of my flesh. He understood where to touch, where to lick, and even where to brush, so gently that I would beg for it to be harder. If my body had been a puzzle, he'd know where every piece connected, and he proved it every time.

He moved slow and languorously between teasing with his tongue and teeth, working my body into a heated frenzy that I wasn't sure I would be able to control for long. I wanted it all and more. I wanted his fast and hard—his slow and attentive. I wanted to see his eyes and watch the green flare into dominance as he pushed into me. I wanted it all because I knew he could give it to me. I knew that every contradicting thought and need would be met and that only seemed to make the ache between my thighs grow.

My fingers fisted in his hair when he switched his attention to my neglected nipple by dragging his hot mouth and tongue over my chest, exploring the skin there. I moved quickly in sudden desperation, one leg riding up his thigh and hooking over his hip in an invitation as I fought, and failed, to draw in a breath and regain some control over that physical connection between us.

Drew didn't take the invitation. He reached past me, turning off the water as our eyes met, and I knew tonight was going to last a while. The intensity that burned in his eyes promised it and was followed when he swept me up against his body, my legs wrapping around his waist as he carried me out of the shower and into our room.

He didn't so much as acknowledge how wet we both still were as he laid me on the bed and then stepped back to look at me. His gaze roamed over my body, taking it all in. I knew when his focus landed on the marks I'd tried to hide from him. The blue and green of his eyes lit like fire, stoking the flames of anger before he let them give way to arousal again.

I couldn't say I wasn't taking my chance to look at him also. Drew Tucker was a sight to behold naked, but glistening in the dim light with droplets of water gathering in the ridges of his muscles was something I was having trouble finding words for.

Climbing on the bed, he took his time making his way up to me, his lips brushing up one of my legs while his hand trailed up the other. He stopped on the creases of my hips, licking the water from them one at a time before brushing his lips to my belly and closing his eyes. I'd never in my life known that being touched like this, so gently and reverently, could make my body ache with a need for satisfaction. I watched him crawling up my body, my hips rolling as he tended to every mark and bruise that had been left on my skin, his mouth brushing over each one as his eyes met mine and made those silent promises over and over again.

When he finally reached my lips and settled his hips between my thighs, I was ravenous—my skin a raw nerve that trembled under every brush of his breath as he hovered over me. He must have known what he was doing, and when my eyes met his, I knew for certain. That beautiful smirk that said everything he refused to say had curled those beautiful lips and made my tentative control snap completely.

Pushing up on my elbows, I crashed into his body, our lips colliding so violently that teeth clicked and nipped the skin of the other. My palms found his damp skin, sliding over the muscles and bone as I tried desperately to pull him closer, needing to feel him inside of me.

"Drew."

It was all I needed to say—that one word—full of pleading and desperation. I sometimes forgot that he'd set the world alight if I asked him to.

Holding my gaze, Drew pushed himself into me with such urgency—such need, it felt like the world shifted below us. He paused for only a moment, his eyes holding mine, reading everything that sat there like an open book for him to devour. When he looked at me this way, I knew he saw love, happiness, safety, trust, and our forever staring back at him.

Drew sucked in a breath, one corner of his mouth twitching in satisfaction before his patience waned and he snapped, giving us both exactly what we wanted and needed.

With him inside me, I knew there was no way on earth I would ever get used to the way Drew Tucker fucked me.

CHAPTER FIFTEEN
DREW

S eeing Eric and Jedd had given my soul a sense of peace, even though I still had a thousand questions and a million reasons to stay awake. The only thing I'd needed after the day I'd had was her. The need to make her come and have her whisper my name in my ear was stronger than ever. No better feeling existed.

With Ayda's head resting on my chest and her breaths falling against my skin, nothing else seemed to matter. I was tired. So tired. Not just from recent events, but from my life. All of it. The expectation, the damnation, the purpose, the leadership…

I was fucking exhausted.

I'd listened to Ayda's quiet, heavy breathing for a while. The ceiling held my attention for only a few minutes before dreams of a peaceful life, a wife, and a healthy baby filled my world.

A world I was beginning to wish I could drag into reality.

It felt like I'd only been asleep for a minute when I felt the gentle tugging of my hand that was hanging off the edge of the bed. With a groan of protest, I rolled my head on the pillow, facing the direction of the tugging.

"Tucker," came a rough voice.

It took one thunderous heartbeat for my eyes to fly open and my body to tense.

Jedd was hanging over me, his silhouette the only thing I could really make out as the light from the adjoining bathroom poured through the crack in the door. He had a finger pressed to his lips, and his dark eyes narrowed as he used his other hand to point to Ayda.

I glanced down at her blissfully asleep against me. She was holding on tight, clinging to me in a way that made me want to curl into her even more and spend a week there. But Jedd was back, in the middle of the fucking night, telling me to be quiet, and the peace Ayda had shrouded me in was slipping away by the second.

With a sigh, I peeled Ayda off my body, making sure not to wake her as I lifted my groggy head from the bed and began to slide out from beneath her. Jedd was backing away toward the door, his silent instruction clear.

I walked out into the corridor, blinking against the muted lights that lit the way. I'd dressed in some loose fitting, gray sweats, and was pulling my white T-shirt down over my body when I froze in place.

It wasn't just Jedd waiting for me.

Eric was there, too.

I'd barely had time to blink when a groggy-looking Slater Portman was shuffling into place beside me, rubbing the tiredness out of his eye as he struggled to stifle his yawn.

I looked between all three of them before I began to walk forward, Slater dragging his bare feet behind me. Eric was standing behind the bar, as stoic as ever, and Jedd was standing by his stool with a suppressed grin on his face.

"What fucking time is it?" Slater croaked.

"About one in the morning," Jedd answered.

I blew all the air out of my cheeks and glanced between him and my father.

"What's going on?" I asked roughly.

Jedd gestured for me to take a seat on the stool as he slid into place on his. Dad uncapped the bourbon, lined up four glasses, and poured heavy measures into each one.

"They let you out in the middle of the night?" I questioned, scowling at Jedd just as Eric slid a tumbler into my hand. The gulp I took sent a burning fire into my chest— one that woke me up without fail before I dropped the glass back to the counter.

"They offered to let me go two days ago."

"That's a joke, right?"

Jedd glanced at Eric, as though waiting for his instruction rather than mine. When he eventually looked back at me, his eyes were light, the darkness I'd come to know him wear so well... gone.

"I was free to walk any time I liked."

"But you stayed..."

He nodded slowly. "All part of the plan."

"To create trust with that Winnie chick?"

"That, and..." He trailed off and glanced down at his finger running circles around the rim of his glass. "The thing is, Drew, everyone in this club loves you. You know that, right?"

I scowled harder, not needing to answer him when his eyes looked up to meet mine. I knew. That didn't mean I had to say it aloud.

"We love Ayda, too," Jedd said quietly. "It's weird. In the grand scheme of the club, she hasn't been around long. You two haven't been together for years. I don't even think you've celebrated a birthday together yet, right?"

That was right. April 10th was approaching, marking the celebration of the birth of the greatest woman I'd ever known, and my birthday was June 3rd—a summer child with a winter heart. It was hard to imagine Ayda never being in my life. In such a small amount of time, we'd endured, felt, and survived so much, my heart often tried to convince me that she'd always been around.

That I'd always loved her.

"Right," I found myself breathing to Jedd.

"So, when Eric began speaking to me on the sly just a week or so ago, and he said that he wanted to set backup plans in place that would save both you and Ayda, you know I had to hear him out, too, yes?"

My jaw tensed, the muscles twitching as I glanced at Slater and Eric. "Right." I swallowed hard.

"It wasn't just about saving you, Drew. It was about saving Ayda. It was about saving you as individuals, and as the couple we've come to love having around here."

"Tell me everything, Jedd," I begged him quietly.

He did. Jedd told me how Eric had approached him, warning Jedd of something big on the horizon. Something he didn't know the finer details of yet, but something that had his gut warning him that they needed insurances in place in case The Hut came under attack from anyone. Things that would keep the club, as well as Ayda and me, safe. Since the ATF arrived in town, the plan had always been for Jedd and Eric to slip away and cause a distraction when the time came.

False promises of intel.

False teases of turning rat in order to get out of it all.

More misdirection.

Eric had asked Jedd because he knew Slater was too loyal to keep secrets from me—even ones that would protect my future in the long run. He'd been right in that assessment, too. Slater was loyaler than loyal. The guy struggled to look me in the eye when a lie was resting on his tongue. I'd have figured him out straight away. But Jedd...

Jedd was a natural born VP.

There wasn't anything he couldn't do if it served the greater good.

He had all the makings of being president.

He was controlled, a tactician, a military soldier dressed in leather and ink.

I, more than anyone, knew Jedd would lay his life and reputation on the line to defend his president and his club.

"Harry had hinted to me before that the club had a rat, but in typical Harry fashion, he called it a mole—just a man or a whore with a big mouth and loose lips. He never said anything about it being Owen Sinclair who would betray us."

"And that made you wary of everyone around here," I added, purposely making it a statement rather than a question. "And that's why you've been asking more questions lately, brooding more, looking disappointed at all of us and having me think that, for all this time, you've been disappointed in me."

It was Jedd's turn to frown. "How could I ever be disappointed in you?"

With a shrug, I answered honestly. "Because I went and fell in love with a girl who took up more space in my heart than this club ever could."

The silence was tense between all of us when my eyes

met Jedd's again.

"That's what you think?" he eventually asked, his voice hoarse.

"The thought had crossed my mind once or twice. You blamed me for disappearing after Harry died and—"

"I blamed you for closing the fucking doors on us all, Drew, not for disappearing or falling in love with Ayda. Fuck me, do you know how many people in this club wish they had what you have? Do you know how many of us lay on our beds, letting random whores suck our dicks while we look up at the ceiling and dream of a love like you've managed to find?"

I leaned back and straightened my shoulders, unable to hide my surprise at his admissions.

"You don't get to make assumptions, Tucker," Jedd told me. "Not you. That's not who you are. You've always been upfront, straight to the point. Next time you think I've got a problem with you being happy, either ask me outright or fucking man up and realize that I could never have an issue with you finally wearing a fucking smile on that grim-ass face of yours. This isn't just about you anymore. Get that into your thick skull once and for all. You don't get to be the only guy around here making sacrifices that send you off to jail for five years. Harry did it, and if I want to do it, too, then screw you, I'll fucking do it whichever way I see fit."

Eric's huff of laughter had me looking his way, watching as he dipped his chin to his chest to hide his smile and ran a hand over his forehead.

I turned back to Jedd, resting my elbow on the bar. "You quite finished with your dramatic speeches, you big pussy?"

"For now."

"Right. Bravo. Glad you got that shit off your chest." I smirked, unable to hide how good it felt to know a man like Jedd cared so much about Ayda and me, he was willing to do whatever it took to keep us safe. "Now tell Slate and me everything we need to know. What does Winnie have on us?"

"If she wanted us all to go down, she has enough evidence to put a few of us away for life."

My face fell, and all the nightmares of returning to prison swirled above my head like a dark, cold cloud of doom.

But Jedd's flat smile slowly rose into a contradicting shit-eating grin.

"What do you mean, *if* she wanted us?"

"We're not enough for her now. She's got bigger men to chase—ones that could earn her the promotion she's always dreamed of. While I was inside, Eric was putting things in place to tie our very own Sinclair, Jon Taylor, and Mayor Walsh together."

"How?" I asked, looking at Eric who was now leaning back against the bar wall with his hands folded over his chest.

He shook his head like the information he was about to part with didn't matter. "I took a trip to Dallas to visit Clint's family. They send their love, by the way." He paused, taking in my reaction and seeming somewhat pleased with himself. "They gave me Clint's old letters. I even got the ones mentioning Harry in them. I took them to Jon Taylor's house. Jon's widow was very accommodating in getting me the key to their place via Howard Sutton."

"Sutton's been in on this?" I scowled.

"Not really," Eric answered. "But the guy loves you, too, and he was happy to help. So I got the key, planted the letters in Jon Taylor's house, along with some of the evidence Ayda pulled from Owen's place and Harry's files. Evidence that made it look like Taylor was confiscating the letters from the prisoners before they were sent, and keeping them in safe hiding for Mayor Walsh and Sinclair."

I blinked hard, trying to keep track of it all, but Eric's voice was soon taking over the room again.

"Mix that with the evidence I left in the back of the repo truck I dumped in the water just off his land, there was enough to suggest some shady shit has been going down between those three men. Shit that was done in an attempt to pin murders, corruption, drug deals, and money laundering on The Hounds of Babylon."

"Fuck," I whispered, looking back at Jedd. "How did all this get back to ATF?"

"When Sutton was on shift, he came to visit me in the cell. He told me whenever Eric had a message, and he passed those messages on."

"Messages telling you the evidence was in place, and you could give the ATF your suspicions?"

"Something like that." He beamed, clearly proud of himself.

"And she bought it? Winnie trusted you?"

It was Jedd's turn to swallow, a look of bashfulness creeping over him for a split second before he smoothed down his long, black beard and cleared his throat. "Let's just say that a bond was forged in there. One I think Winnie actually believes exists mutually."

I raised my brow in question.

"It never hurts to have people in high places wanting to fuck you."

"You fucking snake," I forced out through a proud smile.

I had no idea if there was more going on with Jedd and Winnie than he was letting on, but right now, I couldn't think about that. "Okay, so what about Walsh? Where does Rubin tie in with all this? I know you said he's working for us on the inside, but how?"

"He's getting ready to set his father up as we speak."

"Just like that." I shrugged sarcastically. "No remorse, no guilt, no questions?"

"Apparently not."

"And how does he plan on doing that? How does he plan on going against someone with Walsh's obvious experience of being a two-faced triple threat?"

"You need to have more faith."

"I need to have more facts."

"Fine. Rubin has the laptop Ayda grabbed from Owen's place..." Eric interrupted, dragging my attention to him. "Once I got it unlocked by some guys I used to know down in Corsicana... I guess that's when I really knew we were going to be okay."

I found myself leaning closer, desperate to put myself nearer a definite happy ending that was being dangled in front of me like a fucking carrot.

"Cut the shit, Eric. Give it to me straight. Tell me what we've got on him."

"Yeah, man, spit it out. I'm fucking dying over here," Slater grumbled behind me.

"It turns out Owen really did have a lot of insurances in place of his own: taped meetings between him, Jon Taylor, and Mayor Walsh. Photographs of warehouses filled with guns, drugs, and a basement or two that showed pictures of safes being stuffed with money by guys dressed in black. Owen knew he was running a dangerous gauntlet, and that fucker wanted crash mats all around him if anyone from the other side ever decided to turn."

My blood boiled at the thought of one of our own deceiving us that way, but then my mind went to something else. "Which meant he had all those insurances on us, too."

"He had a fucking *lot* of shit on us, Drew."

"What kind of shit?" I asked, my heart picking up speed.

He tilted his head to one side, his sympathy pouring out of him in the form of a sigh. "Owen had cameras all over The Hut. In cars out in the yard, on bikes."

"*My* fucking bike?" I asked in a rush. "How the fuck wouldn't I have seen those?"

"They make them the size of a needlepoint now. You'd have to be looking, and since we didn't expect a rat..."

"We didn't see shit." I slammed my fist down angrily, pushing my fists into my forehead as the rage built up inside of me. "Tell me what he had," I ground out, too furious to look up. Memories of random kills in the nights with Eric taunted me, where grief provided too much of a blinker on any consequences, and rage was the fuel that kept us hurting people. Flashes of Hernandez and The Emps. Nights where Ayda and I had ridden out and...

My head shot up at once. "Did he have pictures of Ayda?" I growled. "Did that sick fuck have pictures of my girl?"

"Drew, you—"

"Tell me, Eric, or so help me..."

He blinked twice before he answered. "He had pictures of everyone. Videos, too."

I found myself jumping from my stool, needing to burn off the energy by pacing back and forth.

"Jesus *Christ*," I hissed.

"Brother," Jedd said as he tried to reach for my arm, but I shrugged him off. Sinclair had seen my girl naked, hadn't he? He'd seen us… both of us… doing… what? Everything. Every fucking thing. What had he seen? What had he heard? What had he passed on to Walsh and Taylor?

Placing my hands on my hips, I came to a stop, closed my eyes and let my head hang.

"If he wasn't already dead, I'd rip that man to pieces all over again. I'd tear his tongue from his mouth and feed it to the sewer rats. I'd spoon his fucking eyeballs out and then shove them down his raw, bleeding throat."

"What's done is done, Drew," Eric told me firmly, no emotion in his voice. I looked up slowly and met his gaze, sadness coating my eyes. "And everything he ever had on us is gone," he added. "Tomorrow, we'll get Kenny and Slater to sweep every building we own. They can make sure there are no more cameras in place."

"Did you see it?" I asked sharply, not caring about tomorrow, just needing to know. "Did you see the shit Owen had on my girl?"

"I'm not that sick to watch."

"And where is it all now?"

"It's like it never existed," Eric confirmed, his confidence shining through with the slight lift of his chin.

"How do we know he hasn't, you know…" I waved a hand around flippantly. "Whatever Tate and Rubin always say they're doing with their cells. Backed stuff up or whatever?"

"The guys in Corsicana helped me delete all the accounts it could be connected to. If any of it is in cyberspace, it's a million light years away."

"And you can trust those tech guys?"

Eric narrowed his eyes. "Never work with anyone you don't have a hold over. I've got my own shit on them. Don't you worry. They're too afraid to look me in the eye, never mind cross me."

"You're a real shady motherfucker, ain't you?" I asked in absolute seriousness.

"When it comes to those I love, there isn't anything I wouldn't do to protect them."

And despite all his years of absence, I was beginning to struggle to find any hint of a lie in his statements.

Running my hands through my hair, I blew out a breath and held them at the back of my neck. "Okay, so now what do we do?"

Eric glanced at Jedd, and Jedd turned to me, holding my gaze. The baton had been handed back to my VP.

"Now, we wait for Winnie and her crew to raid Walsh's house. Once they've got him, all of this is over, Drew."

"Nothing is ever that easy for The Hounds of Babylon, Jedd."

"Well, there is one more thing we need to take care of before all this is set into motion. Something that we can't overlook now I'm out of custody."

I frowned harder. "Why do I have a feeling I'm not going to like what you have to say?

Jedd's smile could have outshone the sun, and his eyes twinkled with delight. "One of our men just died, pres. It's time for us to dig out the black outfits and turn on the crocodile tears. We've got an entire town to convince, not just the law. If we don't mourn that son of a bitch, we're back under the spotlight of suspicion. Whether we like it or not, we have a funeral to arrange."

CHAPTER SIXTEEN
AYDA

Organizing a memorial in three days was so much easier when you hated the son of a bitch who was being mourned. The fact that every man riding behind the hearse would have rather set the coffin inside on fire than put it in the ground was neither here nor there. We'd had several ATF SUV's following us through Babylon, and we'd had to make our mourning convincing. Owen was supposed to be one of us, so we'd sold it as best we could.

Drew had taken the whole thing in his stride, and I'd ridden behind him, my arm's tight around his waist. He stroked my hand with one of his and steered with the other as we rode. Calm, but stoic because that's what had been expected of him. When we'd pulled into the cemetery we'd found as far away from Babylon as we could without being suspicious, Drew removed his helmet and gloves, and he led me in without a word.

How the boys didn't just throw the casket in the hole was beyond me. If anyone noticed that Owen's box was missing the adornments that Harry's had, they didn't say anything. Inside and out there was no reference at all that he'd ever been part of The Hounds, and there never would be. This was one more thing that the ATF and people of Babylon didn't need to know. It wasn't like any of them had been there to compare the two.

Autumn and I hadn't even bothered to have the ceremony overseen by a religious figure. Though Autumn had suggested finding a Satanist to ensure his worthless soul was sent to the right part of Hell where he would suffer for the rest of eternity. I felt it was a waste of money, and Drew had agreed with my assessment. In fact, his response had been that I should spend less time on that fucker's hole in the ground and more time on our wedding.

We'd talked about our wedding a lot since we'd decided to move ahead with the ceremony. In those moments when it was just he and I, Drew seemed to have an odd sense of peace surrounding him. He was composed, levelheaded, but never complacent. He seemed to understand that this was the calm before the storm but was confident that all the moving parts were doing what needed to be done. Jedd and Eric were back in their roles, but Rubin was nowhere to be seen. Something else Drew didn't seem too concerned about, as it had been a part of the plan set in motion the night of the fires.

I wasn't used to seeing this side of Drew. He'd always been relentless and in control of every piece of the machine that was his club. Since he'd come to the conclusion that he was losing control, he was more open to discussing what was happening next and spending extra time in the war room with Eric, Jedd, and Slater to discuss how they needed to proceed. That left Autumn and me free to use his office to plan the wedding.

Which was how I ended up standing in the middle of a bridal shop in Waco.

There was so much white and tulle in one place, it

made me anxious. Autumn insisted that we make a day of it, and Deeks was currently in a bar across the street killing time so he didn't have to be a part of this *women shit,* as he so gracefully put it. Drew and he had decided that Deeks would take up his role as unofficial bodyguard again until the shitstorm had been dealt with. I was about five seconds away from following Deeks to get a shot when the over-helpful attendant pushed a tall glass of champagne into my hand.

"Oh, thanks, but I can't..." I didn't bother finishing. The glass was swept from my hand by Autumn and traded for a simple but stunning white gown. It was an off-the-shoulder dress in what was called a mermaid cut. There were beads, sparkles, and a train that looked like a deathtrap. "What's this?"

"Cocaine."

The assistant looked almost shocked by the response and took one step back, attempting to appear busy by organizing some of the dresses Autumn had stacked on a rolling rack for me to try. No two were the same either. She had corsets with full skirts, empire waists, princess, ball gowns, and some with so much tulle it looked it had been made from a cloud.

"You know what I mean." I snorted.

"None of these are your style."

"Right."

"It wasn't a question," Autumn said, grinning at me. "I already know what dress I think you should get that will knock Drew off his feet."

"But…"

"I'm asking you to indulge me. You have a figure that I never had and never will have. You're getting married, which I never will do or want to do. *And* you're the only daughter I will ever come close to having. You see where I'm going with this?"

"You're seriously going to make me do this?" I whined playfully, holding up the dress and studying it. Autumn already knew I would do anything for her, but when she held her silence, I was forced to glance back at her.

"Not make, sugar. I would never *make* you do anything, but beg? Blackmail? Guilt into? Abso-freaking-lutely."

I studied her and let my shoulders sag. There was a part of me that said this could be fun, but that part was tiny and insignificant—the same part that had said goading Owen into bitch slapping me was a fantastic idea. That part of my brain was the den of bad decisions. I eventually conceded anyway.

"Fine. Pick five of your favorites, and then I want to see your serious pick."

Autumn did a victory spin on the back of her cowboy boots and waved me toward the changing rooms with the champagne glass, while she headed to the cart with a dozen dresses already hanging from it.

I moved to the changing room with the gorgeous but *not me* mermaid style dress. I stripped out of my jeans and tank with hesitance, looking down at my black lace bra with a rebellious grin. Staring back up at the dress, though, and that sense of victory quickly died. This was going to be a long afternoon.

Five dresses and two hours later, Autumn seemed nowhere near ready to give up on her escapades. I, however, was exhausted. Wedding dresses were not light. You had to be a contortionist to get into some of them, lacing, buttoning, or hooking your way into the confines of them was nothing less than a full on pain in the ass. The corseted princess dress, with thousands of blinking beads and a fuller-than-full skirt, was my last indulgent dress. Though I admittedly felt pretty and looked the part of a bride, I was ready for the torture to be over.

"Wait. Tiara and heels to finish the look. Get up on the little stage with the mirrors." I hesitated and glared pitifully at Autumn. "What? We have to do pictures of this one, too."

She'd thrown veils, heels and every other bridal accessory imaginable with every dress before sending me to a small raised dais in the middle of a full three-hundred-and-sixty-degree mirrored room. Then, she'd taken pictures.

Seeing that much of myself was not good for the ego.

"My God. Are you doing this to bribe me later in life?" I asked petulantly.

"Hell, no. This is to throw those boys off the trail. They have bets on."

I groaned and rolled my eyes, dropping my hands to the cinched waist of the dress and attempting to pull in a deep breath.

"Don't they always?"

Raising her camera as I dropped the veiled tiara on my head, I struck a pose and blinked as the flash bounced off every mirror and blinded me a dozen times over.

"You sure you don't like this one, doll? You look gorgeous."

I growled at her.

"Okay. Okay. You want my choice, or do you wanna look?"

"I've looked, I don't see anything that…" I trailed off and stumbled down the platform on the teetering heels as Autumn held out a dress with a broad, knowing grin.

The dress now holding my attention was backless with spaghetti straps, a plunging neckline, and it was made of crocheted lace that fell into a gathered waist with modest, pooling train. The dress was lightweight, simple, and beyond perfect.

"You've had that all along?"

"I saw it the moment we walked in," she said proudly, holding out an arm for me to steady myself on as I stepped from the heels and ran my hand over the gorgeous material. "You wanna try it on?"

I nodded, unable to speak as I took the dress from her hands and headed to the changing room slowly. Autumn trailed behind me, unbuttoning the seventy buttons on the back of the dress's corset. By the time I stepped into the changing room, I was able to just bounce out of the one I was wearing.

I held up the new dress and admired every detail on the bodice before I pulled it over my head and smiled at the gentle slide of fabric. I knew this was the dress the moment I slipped it on. It fit perfectly. No clips were needed, and no straps needed to be loosened. The bohemian style felt like me, and my reflection made me grin back at it.

"Autumn." I could hear the smile in my voice as I spoke but ignored the need to giggle as I waited.

The moment Autumn stepped into the changing room, she started to cry. She gave me a once over, covered her mouth with her hands, and shook her head.

"Happy tears," she mumbled, waving me away with a watery chuckle when I tried to comfort her. "Do you like it?"

I twirled. "I love it. This is the one."

"You don't want to look somewhere else?"

I shook my head and glanced at the mirror, bouncing on

my toes and ignoring the fading bruises that were beginning to look like I had jaundice. "This is it."

Autumn nodded and watched as I checked every angle. Eventually, she helped me out of it and took the dress with her to wait for me, while I dressed and tried to hang the other dresses I'd tried on as neatly as I could. When I'd redressed in the clothes I'd arrived in, I walked out and found Autumn standing with Deeks, the two of them looking proud of themselves while the sales assistant bagged the dress.

"What did you do?" I asked, looking between them.

"It's our gift to you," Autumn squealed wringing her hands. She flung a hand out at the dress, sending her hair swinging over her shoulder. All the air left my lungs for a moment before I remembered how to breathe in again. I gaped at the two of them with an open mouth—the credit card Drew had given me suddenly weighing a hundred pounds in my back pocket.

"Guys…"

"Don't gush," Deeks begged with a wink.

"You really didn't have to do this."

"We wanted to." Autumn took the dress from the sales assistant and draped it over her arm. "I'll keep this at my place so the guys can't take a peek. I've sent Deeks the pictures of the other dresses to throw the boys off. So, the only thing left to do today is the flower market."

"I'm going back to the bar," Deeks grumbled, only half joking. He looked so out of place amongst all the whites and off whites, I wasn't surprised when he eased the dress from Autumn's grasp and mumbled something about taking it to the van and meeting us at the market.

It felt good to stretch my legs and body as we headed

toward the flower market that was only a couple of blocks over. The area we were in was full of small boutique shops, small bakeries, and coffee shops, too. The smell of coffee beans filled the air as we passed the door of one of the smaller coffee shops, and when I glanced in, ready to bemoan my self-induced coffee ban, I froze in place.

Tucked in the back of the small shop were several intimate loveseats and armchairs. The one in the corner held my interest the most. In that loveseat sat Rosie Sullivan, wearing a slutty little low-cut dress as she leaned over to reach her coffee, flashing major cleavage. In the chair opposite her was a guy with lank, dark, shoulder-length hair, broad shoulders, and he was wearing a leather cut.

I thought I was seeing things when he eased forward and slid his index playfully into the neckline of her dress, tugging it down a little farther for him to get an eye full.

This was a casual move that any couple could have exchanged, and it wasn't what had transpired that had thrown me off, but more the comfort in how it had been executed, as well as the couple that had shared it.

"Autumn?"

"Yes, sugar?"

"Look in there, in the back, on the right. What do you see?"

Her gasp was all I needed to hear. The Nav's patch on the back of the man's cut was as clear as Rosie's face.

"We need to get back home," I said, steering her toward the van. I hated to cut our little shopping trip short, but this mess suddenly took precedence. "Flowers next week?"

Autumn nodded in agreement before glancing back into the coffee shop one last time.

"Jesus Christ," she muttered under her breath, taking over to guide me back to Deeks.

She could say that again.

CHAPTER SEVENTEEN
DREW

I pulled down the peak of my black baseball cap, scrunching my eyes shut before I pushed the cap back up again. This headache of mine had been lingering for days as the responsibilities of life began to mount.

Weddings. Babies. Enemies. Brotherhoods.

I was twenty-nine years old—feeling like a hundred.

With my free hand, I spun the bottle of beer around on top of the table, staring at it as I waited for the other men to arrive. Life had gotten so hectic for us all around here, I couldn't remember the last time we'd sat at the table this way like we were still a full functioning club—one that I was the head of, with the gavel resting next to me, waiting to be brought down once a decision had been made.

I'd made the choice to purposely leave Deeks out of this meeting, sending him on errands with Ayda while she got things in place for the wedding. The sooner she became my wife, the better.

The door creaked open, and Kenny walked through wearing a sad smile of acknowledgment, soon followed by Slater, Jedd, Moose, and a few other guys who each had their smokes hanging from the corners of their mouths. I squinted against the cloud of gray air they brought in with them, instantly thinking of Harry.

Get it together, son.

Right, Harry.

Clearing my throat, I messed with the peak of my cap again and readjusted the cut on my shoulders. Jedd and Slater flanked me on either side and once all the men were in place, I looked up at them individually and scowled.

"Someone's missing," I told them.

"Deeks is out with Ayda," Kenny reminded me, but I shook my head slowly and glanced back at the closed door that led to the bar.

"I'm not talking about Deeks. We need Eric in here."

Whoever coughed roughly failed to hide their surprise, but I didn't flinch. I just waited for someone to get out of their fucking chair and go to get him.

Slater moved quickly, the screech of his chair against the hard floor sounding like a sharp knife against my already aching head.

"Bold move," Jedd muttered beside me.

All I could do was offer him a weak half smile and a raise of my brows.

"Makes quite the statement," he added.

"What do you want me to do? Leave him out of this shit when he's the one leading the way?"

"Not even a little bit." Jedd leaned back in his chair with satisfaction, his eyes trained on the door he was waiting for Slater and Eric to walk back through.

When they did, Slater led the way, and Eric followed closely behind him. His hand rested on the edge of the open door, and his eyes found mine immediately. There were no looks, no subtle gestures, or any words spoken. I gave him to the count of ten to see the certainty in my face and sit the fuck down, and luckily he did just that, taking the empty seat that was once Harry's.

The significance of it didn't go unnoticed.

Nobody had sat in that chair since Harry's cancer-riddled ass had ruled us all with a quiet manipulation we hadn't seen at the time. Now there was another scheming bastard keeping that seat warm, and I had no doubts in my mind that Eric had the same good intentions for the club that Harry had had while alive.

Looking around the table, all eyes were on me, and for the first time in a very long time, nerves attacked me. The pressure tingled my spine. Being president didn't feel as natural as it once had, and I had no idea why that was or what that meant for my future.

"First things first: this is long overdue, but I feel I owe each and every one of you here an apology," I announced.

Slater's scowl was firm, and his shoulders became set, while Jedd had to press his lips together to stop himself from scolding me—that much was clear.

"Since being released from Huntsville, a lot has changed in my life," I admitted, looking down at my clamped hands, my fingers twisting together. "When I left you all to deal with the club, and the aftermath of Pete's death, I was a selfish bastard who couldn't see the light even in the daytime. All I saw was darkness. Everything here was blurred," I waved a weak hand over my forehead, frowning as I did, "drowned out by the screaming rage and venom in my head. I never thought about any of you. I never thought about this club that had raised me from a child and taught me things I could never dream of being taught. I only saw the bad in everything. I saw the loss of my brother as a personal attack, and I was the only one injured from it. I didn't care who in here was hurting. I didn't care about your pain. The only thing I had on my mind was survival, and the thoughts about the desperate need I felt to escape and punish myself for believing we were indestructible. It was self-flagellation because Pete was my religion, and I'd obviously done so many fucked up things in my life that his death was my penance—something I brought on myself without realizing it. It had to be. The pain I felt, it was my fault."

Glancing up, I met each of their gazes as I looked around the table.

"As if that wasn't selfish enough, I then had the nerve to waltz out of prison and fall in love with a girl."

A few of the men laughed and cheered like it was a celebration rather than my apology. Waving them down, I rolled my eyes and rubbed my palms together again.

"She took over everything, and because of that, I let things slip. The club became an excuse for me to be violent when things went wrong with her, or she got hurt, or someone dared to burst this bubble we were in—the bubble I could never dream of being in."

"Drew, you—"

"Shut up, Slater," I warned quietly, cutting him off. His shoulders sank, as did his chin to his chest, and I could see by his tense body language that he wasn't a fan of my apologizing for my happiness—or anything, actually. In Slater's eyes, there wasn't much I could do wrong, and if I were ever to slip, he would be the one to pull me back up to safety. He saw it as his duty. "I need to say this… just once, Slate. Please."

He nodded slowly and leaned back in his chair, releasing a sigh.

"Nobody blames you for loving Ayda, Drew," a brother named Stones said from the far end of the table. Stones was a man I'd never gotten too close to, but one whose loyalty was as apparent as his biting sarcasm toward his MC.

"We've all fallen for her," Moose interjected.

"And the kid's all right, too," Ben, who barely ever fucking spoke, piped up. I wasn't even aware he registered half the shit going on unless he was being told to fix up a motor, help on a repo, or work on a bike.

"The Hanagans brought something to the club that was always missing, Drew," Moose said in his deep, slow, almost-haunting voice. "Before them, we only had Autumn and the women out in that bar for female company. Autumn rarely came here, and those women… well, we ain't exactly treated them with the respect they deserved, have we? Ayda coming here with a young brother in tow taught us how to respect women again. She reminded us how important it is to have someone like her around to keep us in line. She brought heart to the place."

"She also reminded us which sex is really in-fucking-charge," Jedd laughed.

"Amen, amen," a few of the guys joined in, their rough laughter making me wish Harry was here to see it.

My smile rose as I studied each of them. "I was going to apologize for making her my only focus, and letting you guys fall behind again, just like I did when I decided to go inside for five years. But, I can tell from the way you're all looking at me like goofy little pricks that you've all made her your focus, too."

"We just don't get the added extras you do." Jedd chuckled, and he dodged quickly as I lashed out an arm in an attempt to hit him.

The whole table came to life, and I pointed a finger at each and every one of them. "And none of you ever will. Is that crystal fucking clear, ass wipes?"

A few jokes passed through the room, and I almost allowed myself to get lost in the comfort of it. Suddenly, my nerves were gone, and being at the head of the table seemed like the most natural thing on earth. The only one not to speak yet had been my father.

I turned to him when the noise faded away again.

"We have many things to discuss today. One thing I need to talk to you all about openly is the return of my father."

Eric's eyes shot up to mine, a look of worry etched on his face.

"When he first came back, I didn't trust him," I told them with honesty.

Slater shifted uncomfortable, the clearing of his throat his giveaway. Kenny scratched his etched-up eyebrow, and Jedd's jaw tensed when I glanced around at them all.

"Every single one of you here already knows I didn't trust him. You also know that the last thing I ever like admitting to is being wrong. So, get your cameras out, boys, and record this shit if you need to because here it comes." I tilted my head and narrowed my eyes on my father. "Eric, I was wrong. I was wrong to think you wanted to hurt the club rather than save us. I was wrong to be angry with you for running away when I did the same thing after Pete. I've been wrong for a lot of things when it comes to you, and even though I still think you've got a million skeletons in your closet that will someday come back to haunt us both... as far as I'm concerned, you're a part of this MC and this table now."

"Hell, yeah." Kenny nodded.

Eric blinked twice and swallowed hard, his eyes never leaving mine until I broke contact and glanced around the room again.

"Any objections?" I asked my fellow brothers.

And though some still looked uncertain, no verbal objections came, and I brought the gavel down on the table for the first time in a long time, enjoying the vibrations of power it sent up my arm.

"Next on the list... Road Captain."

I put it to the guys that, if he was willing to accept it, Deeks was the man I wanted to take over the role of Harry Rogers. He was the man I trusted to lead the club out on the road, and the only man that could ever try to wear the same boots Harry once had.

The vote was unanimous, and the hollering and cheering that came forth, along with the hands being banged on against the table, made my smile grow too big as I lost myself in a moment of temporary happiness with my brothers.

Tell them about the baby.

Tell them about the baby.

Tell them about...

But somehow, I held it back.

We discussed Sinclair openly for the first time, each of us staring deep into the other's eyes as we spoke honestly about the betrayal we'd felt knowing one of our own had been against us. We discussed the possibility of it happening again, and the consequences that would bring about. We discussed putting each other first more, communicating, loyalties, and the way we saw the future of the club going should we manage to drag it into a perfect world. We spoke of the training room and how we could rebuild it, with old ghosts buried and bad memories burned to the ground. We assigned new roles for the pawnshop since Harry had left a gaping hole in that business, too. Kenny and Slater were taking over security, stepping it up by doing regular sweeps of all our buildings, fitting more cameras to the entrances of the yard and the land surrounding it.

And finally, we discussed the code.

The code of what would happen if, in the not so unlikely event, one of us got taken in for more questioning by the ATF. After all, the body count surrounding our world over the last few months was higher than it had ever been.

The Emps, including Cortez, Hernandez, and Ramirez.

Maisey fucking Sutton.

Jacob Hove.

Jon Taylor.

Clint.

Owen Sinclair.

And Harry.

Despite the recent plans laid in place by Eric and Jedd, nothing in this life was certain—especially not the happy ever after we now dreamed of. The only thing we could guarantee was trouble. It was up to us how we handled that, and for us to decide who we wanted to be once this hell was over.

If it ever would be.

Tell them about the baby.

Tell them about the baby.

Tell them…

My lips had parted to speak when the door to the room

was flung open in a hurry, and there stood Ayda with nothing but uncertainty in her eyes and her hand resting over her stomach as she tried to draw in a breath.

CHAPTER EIGHTEEN
AYDA

Deeks had grumbled under his breath all the way back to The Hut. Autumn sat up front with him—a calming presence when he was agitated like this. I knew that a lot of his heightened emotions came from the memories of what had happened the last time Autumn and I had been that close to a Nav, and I couldn't blame him for reacting that way. They weren't my idea of fun either.

I wasn't sure what this meant for Libby after seeing her with Rosie. All I'd managed to obtain had been that Rosie had been snuggled up to a Nav, and she'd looked more than comfortable.

Talk about a shitstorm.

We'd been halfway between Waco and Babylon when I'd noticed the flash of chrome behind us. From the flicker of Deeks' eyes in the rearview, he'd noticed it, too. I'd felt the subtle shift in our speed, the growing tension in his shoulders and his glances at both Autumn and I as he assessed how much he could do to save us if the shit hit the fan.

We were being followed.

Whoever Rosie had been with, he hadn't been there alone. I guess the thought should have occurred to me the moment we'd seen them together in the cafe, but I'd been too shocked by what was going on in front of me to really think about anything but the implications that her association with the Navs had. I'd also been stupid enough to not take in my surroundings outside of Deeks, Autumn, and the van. From the appearance of the bike tailing us about three cars back, I had to assume that this guy *had* been paying attention and, he'd not only noticed us but recognized us, too.

I wasn't scared like I probably should have been. I knew Deeks would never let him get close to the van, and as we passed into the Babylon border, I could have kissed him for it.

The moment we pulled into the yard of The Hut, I was on my feet and yanking the door of the van open, forcing a bark of surprise from Deeks as the vehicle came to a stop, and I slipped out at a dead run, hefting the door closed in my momentum.

The Hut was pretty much empty when I entered, blinking away the dots caused by the bright light from the sunny day. There were a few of the girls lounging around sleepily, and Tate was behind the bar, a beer halfway to his mouth and his wide eyes on me. I glanced around, noting the door to the war room was closed. I barreled toward it, not even bothering to announce myself as I pushed into the sanctity of the room.

The moment the door was out of the way, all eyes were on me. This wasn't normally my style of entry to any room, and the moment I met Drew's eyes, the words formed without a cohesive thought about the reaction they would get.

"Navs were in Waco. One of them followed us back," I breathed out, hand on my stomach as I tried to suck in air.

Drew's eyes landed on my stomach, the small V of worry forming between his brows before he finally looked up at my face. He was out of his chair in a second, the sharp scrape of the heavy wood against the floor making me wince. "Fuck, are you okay?" he ground out as he came closer, his hands finding the tops of my arms.

"Winded." I took a breath and spared a glance at the other guys who were in varying states of shock—some half out of their seats as they waited for more intel. "We were heading to another store when I glanced in a coffee shop and saw one of them—a Nav—in there cozying up with Rosie Sullivan. Remember… that Hound Whore I told you about? But I didn't think to look closer and see if the Nav had backup. We just headed straight back to tell you. That's when we caught him on our tail."

Drew glanced up at the men, each of them focused on him—awaiting his instruction. I didn't know what passed between them all, but between one blink and the next, Drew's jaw had tensed and he'd given a curt nod that made Slater, Kenny, and Moose move while the others stayed in place.

The three men marched past me, making their way through the bar to the yard.

"Ayda?" Drew said my name softly, drawing my attention back to him. "I'm gonna need you to take a deep breath for me, okay, darlin'?"

The sound of his voice helped my brain catch up with the rest of me. I'd been so determined to get in here and tell them what was going on that everything else had been pushed to the side, including basic bodily functions. I drew in a long breath through my nose, held it for a second and released again, calming my panting breaths enough to find a normal pattern. Hiding my grimace, I met Drew's eyes and nodded with more confidence.

"I'm good."

"Good. That's good. Now, can you tell me where Deeks is?" he asked, and I knew he was trying to control his anger at me for being there alone.

"He was still trying to park when I jumped out of the van," I said sheepishly. "He's probably on his way in now."

I didn't want him to be upset with Deeks who had been pretty amazing, considering the white knuckle ride we'd just made back here in record time without being pulled over by a State Trooper or Nav.

Drew stepped back, his eyes widening. "You did what out of the what now? Because I know I didn't just hear you say you jumped out of a moving van."

"Moving was an extreme exaggeration. It was more of a smooth rolling stop really." I put my hand on his chest and ignored the other half dozen sets of eyes trained on me. "I landed on both feet just fine," I whispered.

I watched as he stepped back from me, dropping one hand to his hip while he pushed his other fist to his mouth and tried to keep whatever he had to say inside him. His eyes were sure to set fire to me he was glaring that intensely until he finally let his eyelids drop for just a moment before he looked back up at Jedd who was still standing over his seat at the table.

"So help me God, this woman will be the death of me," he mumbled behind his fist.

I didn't want to antagonize the situation more than I'd already done, but I also didn't appreciate the kid gloves returning. I wasn't made of glass.

"I'm fine. I knew what I was doing, and I wasn't at risk. I saw a risk in Waco and I made my way back here. I did everything you asked of me."

His gaze drifted down to my stomach, nostrils flaring before he let out a sigh and refused to make eye contact.

"Fine." Drew looked back at Jedd and was just about to open his mouth to say something when Kenny's voice rang out through The Hut.

"Pres! Get out here!" he called.

"Shit," Jedd groaned.

In the blink of an eye, the rest of them were moving through The Hut with urgency.

I stayed where I was, waiting for Drew to make the first move. I didn't want to hide this time. I didn't want to stand behind Drew and peek out to see the threat like I had done during his first confrontation with Chester Cortez, but I also wasn't going to put him in a situation that could make matter worse.

"Give me a gun, just don't make me stay in here," I whispered.

He stared at me, his jaw ticking and anger rising. Kenny's voice called out to him again, and Drew shook his head before he began to move in the same direction as the men.

"I'd never ask you to stay if you didn't want to, but you can find a gun yourself, Ayda. If that's what you want to do out there, fine, but don't ask me to put one in your hand and plant you and my baby into the middle of a fight now. It isn't just about you and me anymore. It's about that child. The last thing I want is our baby standing in the midst of this, but it's your body and your mind. Do whatever your gut is telling you to do. I'd never ask anything else of you. How can I now? This is so far beyond my realm of expertise, I haven't got a fucking clue anymore."

"No gun then," I said as agreeably as I could, my hands

palm up as I sensed his disapproval. I'd thought it was a fair compromise. Something that would set his mind at ease, not agitate him further. With the tension already rising, it was a stupid inclination. "I don't want to be in any kind of fight. Not with this baby inside of me. I promise you. I will leave long before any of that even becomes a concern. If something should happen—if that asshole out there tries to start something, all I ask is that you look after yourself, okay? I will be long gone protecting the two of us."

I put my hand on my stomach so he would understand.

"I haven't died yet, have I?" He managed to smirk, despite his irritation.

"Keep up the good work. We need you." I let my eyes flicker to the yard and back again.

"Pres!" Kenny called, just as Deeks came stumbling toward the war room.

"I gotta go," Drew said quietly.

I nodded my head in the direction of the door and gave him a small smile, reassuring him. We had no idea what was waiting for us out there, but I'd meant every word of my promise. The first sign of real trouble and I would flee.

Drew gave me one last lingering look before tugging his cut down and heading to the door.

I followed him, stopping just as the light ate him up and chased the last of the darkness from my vision. I was outside, but only just, my back against the wall next to the door, ready to make an escape should it be necessary.

CHAPTER NINETEEN
DREW

My boots hit the loose stones at the bottom of the porch, kicking up dust after I'd jumped down the steps in one. When I looked up, my men were standing by the gate of the yard, their circle formed, and the confusion on their faces clear.

Ayda lingered somewhere behind me. I was aware of that. Right now, I had to be the president of the MC. Family life had to be put on hold when the enemy was currently riding up and down the street your home was built upon, revving his engine for the whole of Babylon to hear.

Slater and Jedd flanked either side of the opened gate, their guns aimed high and their bodies following the direction of the single bike that seemed to be taking great pleasure in riding back and forth for the joy of taunting us.

Shrugging my shoulders in my cut, my footsteps fell heavier the closer I got, and soon Kenny was beside me, his words rushing out.

"He just keeps riding up and down the street this way, Drew. He's taunting us, playing some kind of game. Moose can't see anything or anyone else on all the surveillance cameras, and Slater wants us all to stay behind the gates until we know if anyone else is out there. He thinks it could be a trap to lure us out there into open space."

I chucked my chin to acknowledge him, my strides determined until I was among my men. They parted for me, letting me through to the front. When I walked past Slater and Jedd, I heard their cries and ignored them anyway.

"Tucker!" Jedd called out.

"Get the fuck back here, Drew," Slater cried.

The men grumbled behind them, but I never looked back as I stepped out into the middle of the road, watching as the bike holding the Nav in question spun around to face me. When he saw me standing there, he twisted the throttle over and over, making noise and waiting for me to cower. My response was simple: he was in my town. These were my streets. I wasn't going anywhere.

Standing with my legs apart, I carefully folded my hands over my chest and waited.

Slater and the guys were muttering among themselves, while I stared at the Nav in front of me.

He set forward at once, the slow build of his engine gathering power, making the town around us vibrate with his attempt at intimidation. He was aiming straight for me, no other direction in mind, his speed growing while my feet remained planted on the asphalt.

The Nav was getting closer, closer, his path set to go straight through me if he had to.

I held my position, not moving an inch.

If I could have seen his eyes behind his glasses or hear the words falling free from his moving lips, I'm sure I would have known for sure that he thought I was a crazy bastard.

The guy had no idea how crazy I could be.

"Drew!" Jedd called again. "Get out of the fucking—"

He rode closer, and just when I wasn't sure if he was going to swerve, the Nav twisted his bike to the right, gliding around me in a flurry of activity, his body nothing more than a black mass of leather and grease as I slowly spun on my heel and turned to face the direction he'd ridden off in.

Had the guy had any sense, he'd have carried on and hit the roads out of Babylon, but he wasn't here by chance, and I, more than anyone, knew this little performance was both planned and for my benefit.

When he stopped and spun the bike around again, his hand twisting the throttle as he revved the engine, I tilted my head to one side and offered him a sarcastic smile, my slow blink controlled.

Ayda is going to kill you, I thought to myself.

The Nav set off again, repeating the same process, testing my nerve and seeing defiance glaring back at him before he swerved around me on the right, riding back to his original position.

"I don't like this, Drew!" Slater called out to me.

"Stay where you are, Sarge," I warned him calmly, never taking my eyes off the target in front of me—the enemy on my turf.

"He's not going to go around you a third time."

"I'd be pissed if he did," I muttered to myself, holding my position.

The Nav's bike roared to life again, charging straight at me.

I waited.

And waited.

And waited.

And at just the right moment, when he was far too

175

invested to ride away from his commitment, and I was so close I could see the rise of his cheekbones, I moved fast, my body shifting as I reached into the band of my jeans, tore out my gun and fired it straight at the front headlight before I fired off a second shot at the front fender.

The bike swerved wildly, the rider's body going rigid and his mouth falling open the second he realized he'd lost control.

It took less than two seconds for the sound of his bike hitting the metal gates of the yard to occupy the air. The Nav bailed before impact, throwing himself to the side and letting his modified Harley V-Rod take the full force of the crash. It buckled against the metal, the back end rising before it all came to shit and fell to the ground.

Squinting against the smoke from the tires, I let out a sigh of frustration and walked over to The Nav. He was a crumpled heap beneath my feet, curling up into himself and clutching at his ankle. His weathered face was creased with pain—his eyes scrunched together as he whispered something I thought was Spanish.

I crouched down and rested the hand holding the gun over my knee. "Name?"

"Fuck you," he spat.

"Your mother must have hated you."

The Nav looked up, his hatred for me palpable before he raised his chin in defiance and muttered something else I didn't understand. Whatever he said, it was far from a compliment, the venom in his words producing spit on the harsh rise of his voice.

I rolled my eyes and sighed again, not looking at him before I twisted around and pressed a hard hand on his injured ankle. He gritted his teeth instantly, his hiss of pain making my body sing.

"You sound in pain, brother. Pity."

"I'm not your fucking brother, *hijo de puta*," he spat. His phlegm landed on my cut, and I looked down at with a raised brow.

I reached up to wipe away the flecks of moisture slowly before I looked up at him through hooded eyes and tensed my jaw. My teeth ground together and nostrils flared as I stared at him. The Nav swallowed hard. "Don't ever do that again," I warned him, my hand twisting around his ankle with a grip so fierce, it made my fingers throb.

He cried out, the agony making his body twist to the side and his back to arch.

When I released him, I stood, dropping only to fist the hoodie beneath his cut before I dragged him up to me like he was nothing more than a stray dog. I pushed him toward the gate his bike had created a massive dent in, and then I threw him against it before dropping back down to crouch in front of his crumpled body.

His face twisted, and sweat dripped down his cheeks. I leaned closer to smell his fear.

"You stink like shit, brother," I told him quietly. "Like trash. I like to keep the streets of my town clean, which means you aren't welcome here."

"Tu club se está muriendo. Tus calles ya no importan."

"If you have to insult me in another language, you're no threat here."

The Nav curled his lip in disgust. "Your club is dying," he whispered.

"We're all dying, brother. Some sooner than others."

His eyes searched mine wildly, and a quiet hum of tension

took over. I heard some of my men move around behind me, right before the bike was backed away from its collision spot by them, the creaking of metal and the sound of glass hitting the ground taking over.

The Nav's eyes drifted to the left, and I reached up to squeeze his chin, forcing his attention back to me.

"Count yourself very lucky I didn't aim four inches higher and a little to my right. Your heart was in my line of sight, *hermano*, and I let you live. But let me make one thing crystal clear. If you ever follow and intimidate my girl again, I won't just shoot you in the chest. I'll tear you down and stick my gun up your ass before I fire upwards to make sure your heart stops beating. Do you understand me?"

I squeezed his chin harder, forcing his mouth to pop open.

"Do you understand me?" I growled quietly.

It pained him physically and emotionally, but he nodded anyway, his acceptance of defeat a blow to his ego and probably his reputation with The Navs, too.

"Did Trigger send you?" I asked him.

"Fuck you," he whispered.

I blew out a heavy breath and shook my head. "You people never learn."

"It's The Hounds who never learn. You're in so deep, and you can't see your end is in sight," he croaked.

"It seems you know more about my own club than I do. Enlighten me, bleeder." Releasing my tight hold on his chin, I reached up and wiped away a strand of blood that had broken through the grazed skin on his left cheek. "Tell me why Trigger sent you. Deliver your threat. Make me tremble with fear." Then I wiped the blood from my thumb down his other cheek, never taking my eyes from his.

"Keep your father off of Navarro Rifles' land, Tucker," The Nav said coolly.

"My father?" I asked, looking up to find Eric through the gates. Standing next to him was Ayda, her eyes fixed on mine intently.

"His threats against us can't save you. If the ATF has something on you, keep it on you. No more deflecting to us. Trigger is watching—always watching. You don't even know. We all are."

"Trigger is watching us?" I smirked, turning back to him and leaning in closer. "*Us*?"

The Nav nodded once, swallowing his ball of fear again, no matter how small he tried to keep it.

"Then he should know that I'm about to bring him and all his crooked army down. Taylor's already dead. Walsh may be next. After that, who knows where I'll lash out? I'm not playing anymore. You tell him that from me."

That set him off, his rambling in Spanish sounding like a yapping puppy I wanted to roll over with the front end of my bike. Looking up at Eric and Ayda again, the blood rose in my cheeks along with my need to hurt something or someone. As the shit bag next to me spoke, and the more he went on with his rambling, the angrier I grew.

Not at Eric.

Not at Ayda.

Not at any of them.

I was angry that someone had the nerve to threaten me and my family again. I was angry I'd let them all think I'd become *that* soft, and it was around the point of The Nav's ramblings turning to Spanish again that I finally had enough, and my fist lashed out to connect with his jaw.

"That's one way to shut a man up," Slater sighed above me when the enemy crumpled to the ground in a heap.

My response hung on the edge of my tongue, cut off as a slow-rolling vehicle turned onto our street, the familiarity of it not lost on me. I rose at once, stretching out my legs as I turned toward the mid-afternoon sun.

"ATF," I whispered. "Great."

"Want me to do anything?" Slater asked.

Glancing down at the unconscious Nav at my feet, I closed my eyes and gave myself ten seconds to come up with a plan. When I opened them again, I found myself spinning back around to the cop car and waving my arms in the air for them to stop.

"What the hell are you doing?" Slater mumbled, and the rest of my brothers grunted behind me.

I stepped out into the street, flagging the car down, and when it stopped, I made an effort to jog to the passenger window, tapping on it for them to roll it down.

The two cops I'd given snark to before looked at one another, their confusion clear before the one nearest to me reached for the gun on his belt.

Time to act, Tucker.

"Boy, am I glad to see you guys," I huffed out, faking breathlessness. The Owen Wilson lookalike glared at me, his scowl deep like he was waiting for this to be a setup.

"What's happened here?" he asked, gesturing to The Nav and his bust-up bike.

I looked behind me and pointed at Slater. "My man was just about to call 911. This guy here was riding past our yard, firing off shots in the air blindly. I've got women in there, man. Women. We came out, opened up the gates to try and wave this guy down, and the next thing we know, he's hit something on the road, his front end has gone, and he's smacked straight into the gates, twisting himself up. He looks pretty beat up from the fall."

He glanced at his partner before looking back at me. "And let me guess? This guy who happened to run into your property just so happens to be a member of a rival MC. An enemy?"

"We have enemies?" I frowned hard, pulling my chin back and tugging down the peak of my cap.

"Cut the shit, Tucker."

"I thought all our enemies were dead when they tried to blow us, the innocent ones in all of this, up. Remember? The warehouse job gone wrong..." I pressed my hands to the window frame of his door, leaning forward and holding eye contact as the guy quizzed me with expressions alone.

"Funny how you always claim to be innocent."

I grinned as I panted for breaths and shrugged a shoulder. "Sometimes the truth just happens to be funny, sir."

"Sir?"

"I can call you buddy if you like."

"Your sarcasm isn't welcome here, Tucker."

"Neither are these delays. We need to get this guy a medic of some sort. Get the cops down here. Let them review this shit. Sutton will help. If The Navs are coming after us at The Hut, we're going to need you guys to keep an eye on things." I glanced back at the yard, seeing Ayda's beautiful face staring back at me. "I have my girl in there, officer. I can't let anything happen to her, no matter what."

The cop sighed as he brought his radio to his mouth, pressed the button and called for assistance.

When I turned back to face my men and my girl, it felt like every damn one of them had their mouths hanging open as they stared at me.

Everyone except her.

CHAPTER TWENTY
AYDA

I'd changed in the past couple of months. I'd been through so much shit, seen so much crap, and lived through nightmares that the person I had once been no longer existed.

And I didn't miss her at all.

Standing at those gates, watching Drew with those agents... it became so clear to me.

I wasn't condemning him for his lies. I wasn't doubting his tactics, and I wasn't standing there wondering if he'd lost his mind because I knew he hadn't.

I was standing at those gates thinking: *This man is a goddamn genius*.

There was no way of following through with this lie of the bike crashing, especially considering there were bullets in the bike, but that didn't matter. This was a point that needed to be made, and he'd made it. The bike was now on our property—the very property owned by Drew, Eric and The Hounds of Babylon. Conveniently, Texas had what was called the castle law. You were well within your rights to protect your property if you were threatened, and I had no doubt in my mind that The Nav was packing heat.

Drew was also using this opportunity to send a message

to anyone willing to take him on now. It was a declaration. He wasn't fucking around. This wasn't a game he was playing. All of his pieces were slowly coming together and he was willing to act—to do what he had to do in order to protect what was his.

This was a warning to Trigger and anyone else who thought we were fair game because the ATF happened to be on our doorstep.

We weren't going to back down now.

Not in the twenty-fifth hour.

Not when it counted the most.

Not when we had this much to lose.

The tactician in Drew was smart, collected, and deadly in ways most people couldn't conceive. This was beautiful to watch in action, and, though it was probably just my opinion, it was hot, too. Standing with the rest of the club, watching him bullshit his way through an interaction with the cops was just the tip of the iceberg. When I met his eyes, all I could do was offer a small smile of encouragement, and wait for the cavalry to arrive.

It didn't take long for the agents to realize they would have to be the ones to arrest the guy. Continuing the concerned citizen act, Drew even offered to load the bike and drop it off at Sutton's office. Once the ATF had driven away with the Nav face first in the back seat, the yard cleared of Hounds quickly. After his quick assessment of the bike, I'd followed Drew back into The Hut.

"You want me to grab the keys to the truck?" I asked, needing something to do before the crash from the short adrenaline rush hit.

Drew turned to look at me, those blue-green eyes of his narrowing ever so slightly as a look of concern took over. He opened his mouth to say something, clearly thinking better of it before he swallowed whatever words had been there and offered me a gentle nod. "Sure thing. You want to ride out with me?"

"Hell, yeah." I started to back away from him, turning on my heel and disappearing into the office before he could respond. I grabbed the keys to the flatbed and met up with him again in the bar, where a few of the guys now lingered, as though waiting for something more to happen. The Nav on our doorstep had managed to put everyone on edge, and for good reason. I'd hated that we'd been the catalyst to his faux pas— that we'd given him an opportunity to stroll up to our door and deliver a bullshit message that hadn't really needed to be said. We were in the middle of a damn war, and none of us needed reminding of that. Glancing around The Hut, the evidence of its effectiveness was clear. Thankfully, the only person with even a modicum of calm now was Autumn who was chatting with some of the girls while playing cards in the corner.

God bless that woman for being as steady as a rock, I thought as I caught up with Drew. I followed him out of the door and turned to where we normally kept the trucks, aiming the key fob at them to unlock the flatbed we needed. That's when I found myself blinking stupidly at the empty parking spot, then down again at the keys in my hand.

"Uh, Drew…?"

His gaze followed mine, a slow look of acknowledgment flashing in his eyes before he looked back to where The Nav's twisted bike should have been. Slater hopped off the porch steps, his boots kicking up dust as Drew turned to him and pointed to where the bike had disappeared from.

"Slate? Where the fuck is the bike?"

Slater frowned. "Eric said he was bringing it into the yard. Didn't you hear him?"

"Eric?" Drew growled, his face dropping and jaw tensing.

"Yeah. But…" He looked between Drew and me. "Ah, shit."

Drew turned to look at me, his anger evident. "Eric's taken the damn bike, hasn't he?"

"He must have taken the spare key to the flatbed and got the bike on." I looked at the gate again and shook my head. "But why? Where would he have taken it?"

"If I know Eric—" Slater began.

"He's gone to deliver it back to The Navs himself," Drew whispered, cutting Slater off. His eyes glazed over as he looked over my head, his thoughts and theories making him distant. "The bastard has a death wish."

I wasn't sure that was the case.

As much as Eric and I had our differences in the past, I was beginning to see that all of this secretive shit he was pulling was his attempt to help. He obviously had a plan of his own, and I wanted to believe that it was to protect Drew. I just wasn't sure if Eric understood that Drew had already set a plan in motion before he tore off and did shit like this without consulting anyone else first.

"What do we do? Do we go after him?" I asked, looking between Slater and Drew.

"We?" Drew asked calmly. "Wherever Eric is right now is not a place for any 'we', Ayda."

"It was a *royal we*," I corrected him quietly, grabbing

for my phone that was suddenly vibrating against my ass. Glancing down at the screen, I saw Sutton's name printed across it. *What now*? suddenly became the loudest thought in my mind as I glanced back up at Drew and Slater. "It's Sutton."

Swiping the green circle on the screen, Sutton's voice filtered out from the cell long before I could get the thing to my ear. It was unusual for Howard to be anything other than composed, but I could hear the worry in his voice long before I could make out what he was saying.

"… and Drew okay—" he said hurriedly.

"Howard?" I interrupted before he could continue with his panicked diatribe.

"Drew! Is he with you, Ayda?" I glanced up to meet Drew's eyes.

"I'm looking right at him. Why? What's going on?"

A long-suffering sigh filtered down the line. "We have a Nav being booked in at almost the same minute that the insufferable Winnie woman and her boys here start talking about a warrant."

"A warrant for who?" My heart was in my throat, making me feel like I was choking as Slater stepped closer to us and Drew tipped his head in question. I put the phone on speaker and held it out between us all. "Howard, you're on speaker. Who was the warrant for?"

"It's for Walsh. They had a search warrant and an arrest warrant. One of her guys said the judge just signed off on it."

I looked at Drew again, my rush of fear and worry beating its way through my veins for an entirely different reason now. Drew seemed to come to the same conclusion as our eyes met.

Rubin.

CHAPTER TWENTY-ONE
DREW

"S later, round up Jedd and Kenny," I demanded, walking past him to get to my bike. "You guys get on the road as fast as you can."

"Where are we going?" he asked, right behind me.

I spun to face him, bringing us both to a halt. "You three need to stall ATF from getting to Walsh's while Ayda and I get Rubin out of there."

"You think the kid is in danger?"

"I think his kid is too close to his father when this shit is about to go down, and if Walsh catches wind of anything Rubin's done, he's going to try and take him down with him."

"The sick son of a bitch."

"It's up to us to make sure that doesn't happen."

No more had to be said before Slater was charging back into The Hut to rally the men, leaving Ayda and me to jump on my bike and tear out of the yard as quickly as possible.

There was no doubt in my mind I needed her for this. Rubin was a teenage boy with too much testosterone and even more enthusiasm. In front of me, he'd try to play big, and no doubt get himself hurt in the process. Ayda being there would ground him.

At least that's what I hoped.

Sirens and engines roared to life in all of Babylon, our somewhat peaceful town suddenly tense and alive with activity it didn't want or need. Every time I took a sharp bend and felt Ayda's arms tighten around me, I was reminded who I had to protect and how much being safe instead of reckless mattered now.

We had to come out of all this unscathed.

Walsh's mansion came into view from the far end of the road, and I slowed the bike to a crawl before parking it in place in the driveway of an abandoned home farther down the road, behind several thick bushes.

"No cop cars. Slate and the others must have stalled them," I said aloud. Ayda's body wrapped around my back as the two of us stared at the building across the way.

"Does it feel too quiet to you?" she asked, reaching for the strap of her helmet.

It felt like the calm before the storm, but I wasn't going to repeat that thought to her. I'd been in enough tight corners and situations in my life to ignore it when my gut twisted the way it was doing then.

So, instead, I helped her off the bike and began to walk farther up the driveway we'd trespassed, holding her hand in mine the whole time while I kept my eyes on Walsh's home.

"Quiet isn't always a bad thing," I told her. "It isn't always a good thing, either, but we're no good way back here." I turned to look at her, holding her gentle gaze. "You sure you're okay with doing this?" I asked, aware that I was becoming neurotic already.

Her hand squeezed mine. It was strong, her way of reminding me she wasn't made of glass. "I will help you any way I can, but if I need to protect the baby, I'll make it my priority. I promise you that."

"That's all I ask."

Ayda scanned the house and turned her gaze back to me with a resolute nod. "Things I know: Rubin always said he didn't need a key to go home at any time of the night. Their back door was always unlocked. They have a covered porch back there, it's right under his bedroom apparently, so he uses it to sneak out. Things I don't know: is that bastard expecting us? And has he hired security?"

"I guess there's only one way for us to find out…" I said, looking back at the house myself. "Rubin isn't contactable. We're the only ones here before Winnie and her crew storm the place, and we're running out of time and ways to save him. The kid needs saving. He needs getting out of there. Even though he might think he hates his father, seeing that father being dragged away in handcuffs will scar Rubin for life... if it gets that far. Though that isn't my main concern. I need to get the kid out of there because I don't doubt for one minute that if Walsh can find a way to pin this on someone else in that house, knowing Rubin's association with us, he'll pin it on him. Turns out I like the boy too damn much to let him take any more heat because of our MC."

"Don't underestimate how much Rubin hates his old man. I think he'd be happy to see him dragged off in cuffs, but you're right that we can't let him take the fall." She tensed, her hand gripping mine tighter. "Let me go first. I can go around the back, climb the porch and knock on his window. Get Rubin out that way. If his mom catches me, I can just tell her I was concerned about him. Tate hasn't seen him in school… he's been associated with the club. If Walsh catches me, I'm the best case scenario for Rubin."

I stared at her, seeing the confidence in her eyes. It was hard to place my trust in her abilities when my heart was screaming at me to keep her safe, but I, more than anyone, knew how capable Ayda was, and how much faith she'd lose in me if I didn't show some faith in her in return.

"I'm an idiot for agreeing to this," I muttered reluctantly. "Okay, baby. Lead the way. Be careful, though… please."

Ayda smiled cautiously and pressed her lips to mine before giving me a quick nod of agreement. Dragging in one deep breath of preparation, she took off at a slow run toward the Walsh house. She slowed when she got to the street, making sure to keep it casual like she was always supposed to be there. Slowing at the end of the Walsh's drive, she headed toward the house. She glanced through the windows as she moved past them, careful not to linger long enough to be caught.

The backyard was fenced off, the edge of the porch barely visible from where I was standing, and Ayda slowed as she neared it. She pressed against the wooden gate gently, peering inside the yard. She didn't move for a long time, then, with one glance over her shoulder in my direction, she slipped into the small gap and disappeared from my sight.

I never wanted to lose sight of her, so I followed, moving where she moved, keeping myself as hidden as possible, considering I was six-feet tall.

I didn't have to wait long to catch sight of her again. Ayda slipped out of the gap she'd made for herself in the gate, her face pale and eyes wide as she searched for me where I'd been standing when she'd headed to the house. The moment she found me closer to her than she'd expected, she rushed forward, panic pressing her lips together.

"Rubin has a gun on Walsh." Her voice was shaking almost as violently as her hands.

My body froze, eyes popping wide as I stared at her and let the words sink in. "Rubin has a gun on *Walsh*?"

"I saw them through a window. I think it's Walsh's office. It looked like he was in the middle of something–" She cut herself off and shook her head. "They're arguing."

"Fuck." I moved quickly, swerving around her and placing the two most important things in my life behind me as I began to march forward. I knew she'd follow, no matter what I told her to do. "Remember your promise, Ayda," I called quietly over my shoulder.

"I know, Drew." She followed me to the gate and pointed at a large bay window located farthest from where we were.

I looked up at the high points of the building, checking for cameras or any type of security. There wasn't anything in my sight. Even though I knew that didn't mean it wasn't there, I pushed on, desperate to get to Rubin and stop him from doing something that could see a bright young kid like him spending years in prison. Anyone could pull a trigger. Not everyone could handle the consequences that went with that.

I reached the window, pressing myself against the brickwork of their home, back and hands flat to it as I peered around the edge of the window. Just as she'd told me, Rubin was standing in front of his father, his hands raised high, legs shoulders width apart as he held the gun out like that of an experienced shooter.

Maybe I was underestimating him.

Maybe he had this under control.

'Maybe' wasn't enough of a guarantee for me.

Glancing back at Ayda, I signaled for her to remain quiet, and if necessary, for her to stay out here until I could guarantee Walsh didn't have a weapon, too. She gave a nod of understanding, and I saw the flash of love she had for me shining back. I held onto that for a few seconds longer before I slid my gun from the waistband of my jeans, knocked off the safety, closed my eyes, and counted down from ten.

Then I moved, swinging a foot out to turn me around before I shot at three edges of the window, the noise piercing the air around us as a distraction. Glass shattered, and I raised a heavy boot to the edges, kicking it out as fast as I could, ignoring the rain of it falling around. As soon as I had enough clearance, and with my gun aimed high, I jumped over the low ledge, and stepped into the mayor's home, looking up in time to see Walsh's face turn pale, and Rubin's eyes light up with relief.

"Don't you fucking move," I warned the mayor, aiming my gun directly at him.

"Get the hell out of my home," he fired back, his tone authoritative and full of arrogance.

"Go fuck yourself, Walsh. This is my town."

"Nothing around here belongs to you."

Shifting some stray glass from under the soles of my boots, I kicked them to the side and eyed Rubin.

"Wanna tell me what's going on here, kid?"

Rubin's face was pale, despite his obvious relief at me being there. His arms had begun to shake, and I wondered how long he'd been holding his father in place with his threat of bullets and pain. Rubin looked at his dad, and he licked his dry lips to get his mouth to work properly.

"You're in so far over your head," Walsh said sharply.

"You shut your mouth," Rubin croaked.

I looked between the two of them, taking in the body language and the obvious hatred for one another. Hatred was a strong emotion, and knowing the love I already had for my unborn child, I struggled like hell to understand how a father could look at their son that way.

"The Hounds have got inside your head, boy. You don't know what they're really like."

"I know they're better than you. I know they appreciate loyalty and family. I know their lies are always meant to protect those they love, rather than to make them rich and feed their greed like you."

"You have no idea what I've done for you, you ungrateful piece of sh—"

I shot at the mayor's feet at once, purposely missing by an inch, close enough to scare the son of a bitch into watching his mouth. His shoulders jumped, and he raised his hands in the air, a sharp, hard swallow making his Adam's apple sink and rise with obvious pain.

"Your boy may have doubts about shooting you, Mayor, but I can assure you... I don't," I told him.

The crunch of glass behind me told me that Ayda had approached, but she didn't enter.

I stretched my neck to one side, making sure to focus on the problem in front of me.

The mayor's sadistic eyes were locked on me, and even with his fear evident, he still managed to look cocky as fuck.

"Do you realize what I can do to you, Mr. Tucker?" he said slowly.

"Nothing you haven't already done, I imagine."

It was his turn to raise a brow now, his surprise clear.

"Dodgy judges, rotten cops, prison officers in your pocket... I was on the receiving end of them all, Walsh, and I paid for my sins via your games and need for power."

"Yet, you're still here, meddling in my business, turning my family against me, pointing guns at me without a care for your future, or those in it." His eyes drifted to Ayda behind me, a slow smile creeping on his face.

I took three steps closer, my face twisting with anger, and my jaw ticking as I raised my gun higher.

"You look at her again, and I'll put a bullet in your dick before I plant one in the center of your skull."

Walsh's attention slid back to me. I could practically smell his fear.

"This is where you and I differ," I began, taking another step closer. "This is where I'm the man and you're the boy because I don't need to operate in dark, seedy corners. I don't need other men, more capable than me, to do my dirty work. There's no fun in that, Mayor. No fun at all. I like to see the fear in my enemy's eyes before I pull the trigger. I like to dig their graves with my own bare hands. I like to pack that soil and dirt in real tight, stamp on it with my heavy boots and let Hell know I've sent another bastard its way. If I want to kill someone, I do it myself. So, if you think I've got any fear of following through with my threat to end your life, and if you so much as acknowledge my girl behind me, you might want to think again, because I will put your fucking light out faster than you can blink."

Silence filled the air as we stared at one another, his eyes searching mine for any sign of a lie, while I remained still apart from the subtle flex of my finger over the trigger.

"Noted," Walsh eventually whispered.

"Good." My nostrils flared, and my finger pressed down gently on the trigger, skin meeting metal, desperate to extinguish another enemy while it was in my line of sight. Reality soon kicked in, and I released it, exhaling through my nose and side-eyeing Rubin. "Kid, I'm going to need you to lower your gun and go to Ayda."

He shook his head violently. "Can't do that, Drew."

"Yes, you can. You're safe. We're here. Nothing's going to happen to you now. I promise."

Rubin's arms were really shaking now, his emotion taking over. His sad eyes filled with moisture as he stared at his pathetic excuse for a father.

"Rubin," I urged. "Go to Ayda."

"He threatened to kill me," Rubin eventually said on a shaky breath. "He said he knows what I've done, Drew. He said the judge who signed off the warrant had tipped him off—told him that they suspected something in this house that would send Dad down for a long time. He knows it's me. He knows what I've done."

"And none of that matters because the ATF are on their way, Rubin. We need to get you out of here as quickly as possible and let them come take care of this asshole you have to call a father."

"If I can get away in time, so can he. I'd rather stay here and hold him in place. I need him to pay."

Walsh sighed heavily, the slight roll of his eyes making me want to fly over there and punch the guy in the fucking throat.

"Pay for what?" Walsh groaned. "For keeping this town safe? For trying to rid it of the only problem it has ever had?"

"The Hounds are my family," Rubin hit back angrily, his

arms shaking wildly.

"Rubin," I called out, my tone firmer. His head snapped my way, eyes wild and his body out of control. I could see the pain he was wearing and the torment running through his mind, and I wasn't about to let him fall down a hole I'd fallen down one too many times myself. "Listen. Focus," I mouthed to him. "Go. To. Ayda."

As though something clicked, he began to lower his gun, both hands gripping it tightly as he pointed it to the floor.

"Go to her," I whispered. "Get out of here. I'll hold Walsh in place. I'll stay here until the cops get here if I have to."

"You're not getting in any more trouble for him, Drew," Rubin said quietly, shaking his head. "That's what Dad wants."

"Then I'll get out before they see me here. Trust me."

Rubin looked at me for guarantees, and all I could give him were promises with my eyes. Promises I intended to keep.

Slowly, Rubin began to move, never breaking eye contact the entire time as he made his way to the window ledge where Ayda was waiting, no doubt with open arms.

"Rubin?" Walsh called out to him.

Rubin turned, just as he approached me, looking back at the man who was meant to be his father.

"You'll pay for this," Walsh warned him. "You'll die for this."

I blinked hard and turned to look at him. I'd seen some fucked up shit in my time, heard even worse, but watching the mayor of our town tell his only son that he'd kill him had to be one of the most messed up pieces of shit I'd ever heard fall from a man's tongue.

"Fuck you," Rubin spat before he turned to walk to Ayda.

Caught off guard, I found my attention drifting to Rubin, both proud of his response and concerned for how this would affect him later in life. What I hadn't realized as I looked at him, however, was that I'd lowered my gun.

In a moment of weakness and concern, I'd taken my eye off the target, and while Rubin climbed over the ledge of the window, Walsh took his opportunity to strike, charging at me with so much force and at such a speed, I didn't have time to respond.

My body hit the floor hard, the shards of glass forcing my back to arch and my eyes to scrunch tight. Walsh was on me, a fist flying across my face before I could find the energy to strike back.

I took two hits to the face, sending my chin one way only for him to send it flying back in the other direction before I was able to lift a knee up between us and hammer it into his groin. A groan of pain erupted above me, but Walsh didn't falter or move, and as I tried to raise my gun to his head and shoot, he hit the weapon out of my grip, sending it sailing across the floor.

I was about to fight back when I heard the unmistakable sound of the cocking of a gun.

A second later, a bullet soared through the air.

It hit Walsh and sent him crashing the floor beside me, a limp body crying out in pain, leaving me to whip my head back in the opposite direction.

There, by the window, stood Rubin. His eyes narrowed, jaw set tight, and his arms out with the gun aimed directly at his father.

"And fuck you once more," he pushed out through gritted teeth.

CHAPTER TWENTY-TWO
AYDA

My ears rang violently. The shot was in close quarters, and Rubin was standing just in front of me, within reaching distance. To his credit, he'd squeezed off his shot without hesitation. Rubin heard and saw the fight between Drew and Walsh, turned and raised the gun, pulling the trigger all in the space of a single heartbeat. He was still standing, legs shoulder width apart, both hands on the gun, and his grip completely steady. The only difference now was that his trigger finger was lying against the guard and no longer on the trigger itself.

My hands were trembling, and my legs felt weak. My heart was also having a real hard time finding it's normal rhythm again.

Drew seemed as equally shocked as me, his eyes on the kid and filled with a disbelief I was clearly identifying with.

None of us moved, even with the sound of sirens growing louder and louder, and the mayor writhing in pain, only a foot away from Drew. I gave him a cursory glance, but it was all I was willing to give him after the hateful shit he'd thrown at his son. He was lucky he wasn't dead.

He deserved to be.

The sound of the sirens continued to get louder, even as

we stayed frozen, and it was only when Rubin lowered the gun that Drew and I seemed to find our motor functions again. If his father's words or the venom in his tone hurt Rubin, it didn't reflect in his eyes. They were still trained on Walsh, his normally smiling mouth now a flat line, and his jaw set even harder.

"We're running out of time," I whispered, the sound distorted by the fading ringing inside my ears. "We have to get out of here. Now."

Drew moved quickly, scrambling to his feet as carefully as he could. Stunned wasn't an emotion he showed often. I could count on one hand the number of times I'd seen the look he was wearing as he glanced at Rubin and back down at Walsh, repeating the action over and over again.

He took a moment to think, scanning the possible exits before his eyes settled on the window ledge. "Ayda, take Rubin to the bike. I'll grab Walsh. He has to come with us now."

I nodded my agreement, letting my eyes move between the two men before tapping Rubin on the elbow to get him moving.

"He keeps the keys to his BMW on the hook in the kitchen. Mom has the Land Rover with her in Dallas," Rubin said as he pushed the gun into the back waist of his jeans. He glanced at me with a small nod as stepped out of the shattered window, the glass tinkling and crunching before he hopped over the edge with ease and landed beside me. He left without a backward glance at his father, and I only stayed long enough to meet Drew's eyes before rushing to catch up.

"You okay?" I asked, unable to help myself as we slipped through the gate at a slow loping run. I pointed to the house three doors down and let him take the lead.

"I'm fine."

He wasn't, but that was something we could deal with later. Right now, I needed him away from this scene before the cops showed up. If we managed to get away with the cops not seeing Drew's bike, all the better. We moved quickly over the yard, avoiding the main street, and slipped back to where we'd left Drew's bike. It was something comforting and familiar for me, but anxiety bled from Rubin as he thought about riding it.

"You know any back roads?" I asked, attaching Drew's helmet to the back and offering Rubin mine. Rubin took it from me and pulled the standard helmet over his dark hair, still avoiding eye contact as he worked.

"I ride my bike everywhere. I know every back road." He paused and rested his hand on the bike's tank, swinging his leg over it and looking more natural than I thought he would. Glancing up, he stared at me. "I'll try and avoid damaging the bike, but I'll make sure it's not seen."

I nodded, not really needing the assurance. "We trust you. Just be safe."

"What should I tell the others?"

I glanced down the drive we were standing on and watched as a sleek black car pulled up to the end and idled quietly.

"Tell them Drew will call them if something changes."

Rubin nodded and kicked the bike below him to life, with a nervous glance at the BMW now crawling to the end of Mayor Walsh's drive. I didn't know where this was leading any more than he did, but I fought the sudden instinct to hug him. Rubin wouldn't have wanted that to happen in front of Walsh, I was certain of that.

"Go. Be safe."

With a twist of his wrist, he took off slowly down the drive, and I followed, noting the subtle nod he gave to Drew as he made a small turn between two houses and disappeared.

Slipping into the car Drew was now driving, I finally found enough air to breathe and glanced over at him.

"He's taking the backroads so he won't be seen."

Walsh groaned behind us, followed by him hissing through his teeth. Drew turned to look at him in the back seat, taking the opportunity to glance out of the rear window while he was there.

"We can't head back to The Hut. Not with him in the back," he said, staring at Walsh but clearly talking to me. "The note I just made this fucker write pleading his guilt should stall ATF for a while, but it won't be long before they scour every inch of Babylon for him. The first place they'll look is our property. It's where they know Rubin's been lately. We need to take a ride out of Babylon and dump this fucker, once and for all."

"What are you gonna do?" Walsh croaked. "Kill me?"

"Tempting." Drew narrowed his eyes. "Very fucking tempting. I should kill you for disrespecting your son alone, but we'll discuss the particulars of your fate later."

Drew spun back to face the steering wheel, his hand curling around it with force. "You okay?" he whispered, reaching out to take my hand.

"That little bastard ain't no son of mine," Walsh spat before I could respond. He coughed out a bitter laugh and shifted in the back seat.

If he was stalling for time, it was a pointless gesture. Drew was already gunning the engine, his free hand squeezing mine as I tried to ignore the barb on Rubin's behalf. The moment we saw the flashing lights of official vehicles heading closer, Drew pulled into a drive of a home and killed the engine, waiting as line after line of official vehicles sped past, not so much as glancing at the BMW on their way.

My heart was beating so loudly in my chest, it was a wonder the two men couldn't hear it. All it would take would be one of those cops to glance up the drive and see the plate, and they would know who the car belonged to. They probably knew everything about him as they were heading to his home to arrest him. As much as that was on Walsh, the fact that he had a fresh hole in him, and he was currently being forced to ride in the back of his expensive car was problematic.

Whether it was divine intervention or pure luck, the last of the cars sped past without so much as a pause, and I pulled in as much air as I could, bracing myself as Drew checked all the mirrors and backed from the drive like it was completely normal. We hit the road again and pulled from the subdivision like the Devil himself was on our heels, thankful to see that not one cop was sitting, waiting for an attempted escape.

"Where are we going?" I asked, wriggling to sit up in the soft leather.

"I don't know," he muttered, his eyes flying in all directions. "I was thinking we could—"

His phone rang in his jeans pocket, cutting him off from whatever he was going to say.

Drew glanced at me and raised his ass, gesturing for me to retrieve it for him as he navigated the roads at high speed. When I pulled it out, Eric's name lit up the screen.

"Thank fuck. Put it on speaker," Drew told me, his relief obvious.

I kept my eyes locked on him as he stared down at the screen, and I accepted the call, lifting it between us both.

"Eric! Where the fuck are you? I need you!" Drew barked.

Silence lingered, the tension created in a second before a familiar, sadistic voice filtered through the speaker. "Well, well, well. The big, bad Drew Tucker needs his daddy."

My eyes lifted from the small handset in my grip where Eric's name was steady on the screen, and I met them with Drew's. My blood felt like it had been filtered through ice. The voice made my thumb twitch. I'd never wanted to end a call so much in my life. I was scared but Drew held my gaze before flickering a glance to the road and back to the phone.

"Trigger?" he said in question, his voice low and rough.

"The one and only," Travis 'Trigger' Gatlin answered smugly.

Drew's hand tensed around the wheel, his eyes glazing over with fire and anger. "Where the fuck is my father?"

"He's... hanging around."

Drew glanced at me, his frown deep and filled with worry. "What the hell does that mean?"

"Now, now, Drew. You sound like you're getting frustrated. Pull the car over. Take a breath. Think things through. I wouldn't want you crashing that beautiful car you're in when you have cargo in there that belongs to me."

I wanted to spin around and look behind us. I wanted to see if Walsh was in the back seat with a phone, or if there were bikes that would have the Nav's Reaper and Rifles painted onto the tank. Not that it mattered. Trigger knew where we were and what vehicle we were in, and that wasn't a coincidence. We were in trouble.

Unexpected trouble.

My eyes flicked to meet Drew's, pretty sure I knew what I would see there. He was going to regret having me in this car and regret that he'd taken me with him to begin with. Regrets and more regrets. I just had to make sure that I didn't show him how scared I was and give more power to those thoughts. We were in this, here and now, and we were in it together. Nothing could be done to help that.

Drew gritted his teeth, his control slipping as his foot seemed to gain weight on the accelerator. "Where's my father, Gatlin?"

"About ten feet away from me."

"You bastard," Drew ground out, knuckles turning white on the wheel as he threw his body back into the leather seat and tore down the road. He suddenly had a direction, and he was heading there without thought, taking a tight right turn at once toward The Nav's border. "If you've touched him, hurt him, so much as whispered too close to his face, I'll—"

Trigger laughed, the tone dripping with sarcasm. "What? What are you going to do, Tucker? Fuck things up like usual? Lead with the fists and escape death by the skin of your teeth like usual? Kill that stupid motherfucking mayor who's bleeding all over those beautiful, cream leather seats, and then deal with the wreckage later… as usual? Get one of your other innocent brothers to take the fall because you're too loved up to suffer the consequences of your actions like fucking usual?" He blew out a breath, chuckling on the end of it. "God, it must be real damn tiring having you as their king."

Drew's jaw worked back and forth, the red mist taking over. "Keep talking, Trigger. Keep talking."

"How about we talk face to face? Deal with this like real

men?"

I was staring at the screen, but the moment Trigger said it, I looked up and stared at Drew's murderous face, already knowing the answer.

CHAPTER TWENTY-THREE
DREW

"W here?"

"FM fifty-five. My men are waiting for you."

Casting a side-eye at Ayda, I knew I was caught between a rock and a hard place. There was no way we could head back to The Hut, not now everything in Babylon was finally coming to a head. If I dropped Ayda off at the side of the road and told her to make her own way back, anyone could grab her. If The Navs had gotten hold of Eric, they'd be able to throw Ayda in the back of a van without worry. I couldn't even drop her at a motel. For all I knew, Trigger had Walsh's BMW rigged up with a camera the same way Owen Sinclair had set up our yard, bikes, and home.

She had to stay with me, no matter what. At least this way I had a chance of keeping her safe rather than setting her free to fend for herself.

I smacked a hard palm against the steering wheel, my growl of anger shameless.

Trigger laughed down the line. "You always make this too easy."

"I will fuck you up, Trigger. I will fucking end you."

'I can't *wait*. See you soon, Tucker. Don't kill my cargo before you get here. I'd hate to have to do the same to your old man." The sound of something hitting something else rang out, like a swift kick to a body, and it was soon followed by a deep, painful groan, one I instantly recognized as Eric's.

That sound made my stomach twist with nausea.

Nobody else.

I couldn't lose anybody else.

Snatching the phone from Ayda, I ended the call and threw the cell in the footwell by her feet, crying out in rage, "Mother*fucker*!"

"You think this car is rigged?" she asked quietly, glancing back at Walsh. "I don't want to make it worse by saying something more if they can hear us."

I caught Walsh's eye in the rearview, watching his slow, smug smirk creep into place, and his brows rise.

"Let's find out, shall we?" I spun the car to the side of the road, coming to a sharp stop. There was no time to waste as I turned in my seat, leaned into the back and grabbed Walsh by the throat, squeezing it tight with one hand while my other came up to press a thumb on his gunshot wound.

His cry was high-pitched and wild, his face scrunching tight as the pain took over.

"Seeing stars yet, fucker?" I pushed out through gritted teeth, my eyes practically bleeding with venom.

"*Argh*!" he hissed, his pain a noise I wanted to drown in. "Stop, Tucker. Fuck."

Walsh tried to push me off him, but my fingers were pulsing and my rage wanted to snap his neck in one move. I wanted his blood on my hands and to feel nothing but pride that I was the one who caused him so much agony.

"What the *fuck* has Trigger got on you?"

"I…" Walsh groaned again. "I can't… talk…."

Releasing my hold on his neck, I let him drag a sharp breath in, my hand hovering there. "You have twenty seconds."

He coughed hard, his head rolling back. I may have let him breathe, but the pain he'd be feeling in that gunshot wound alone should have been enough to knock him out as I pressed on it.

"He'll want me dead," Walsh croaked. "But he'll want me dead by his own hands, not yours."

"Why?"

"Because he hates *you*. He hates you more than he wants me dead."

My nostrils flared like a bull ready to charge—my body surging with adrenaline as I pressed hard on Walsh's throat again. "Give me one good reason why I shouldn't kill you right now just to piss him off."

"Do it." Walsh hit back, his eyes widening. "If you kill me, Trigger will kill Eric, and then my death will be worth it. It'll all have been worth it."

My frown was hard as I studied his face, struggling to connect the dots as to why Mayor Walsh would want my father dead… and want it so much that he was willing to put his own life to an end to see it through.

"What don't I know?" I pressed. "Tell me. Give me something. Give me anything that gives me a reason to save you as well as Eric."

Walsh scowled that time, his eyes crossing over as he no doubt saw stars in front of him before he managed to refocus on my face. "Save me? Why would you want to save me?"

"I don't. I want you buried under my front porch so I can stand on your fucking skull every damn morning and every damn night. But I know a kid who says he hates you and probably, somewhere deep down in that confused, young brain of his, actually loves you. I know what it's like to think you hate the man who brought you into this world. I know the way it twists your gut up every day you're breathing, and even though I despise you, I kinda like him, so consider yourself fucking blessed." I pressed my thumb down hard on his wound. "In agony, but blessed."

Walsh looked up at the corners of the car, his eyes drifting all around before he opened his mouth to speak. "You need to be careful."

"And you need to speak. We're running out of—"

The phone by Ayda's feet rang again, and I closed my eyes slowly, knowing what was coming and who that was.

Ayda looked at me for only a second before she reached down and picked it up, flashing the screen my way, where Eric's name was in lights, demanding our attention. With a slide of her thumb, a dull thud and quiet groan filled the small interior of the car, drowning out Walsh's pained breaths.

"Put my toy down, Tucker, or I'll put yours down for good."

I growled and released Walsh slowly, making sure to push him back as hard as I could before I spun back around and slid into place behind the steering wheel.

I took the phone from Ayda as carefully as I could, bringing the speaker close to my mouth.

"Let me take my girl somewhere safe first," I demanded, my voice no longer sounding like my own as it struggled to hold back a million threats. "I'll bring Walsh, but you—"

Trigger's laughter was manic, and I had a vision of his throwing his head back as his amusement poured out of him. I sighed heavily, the weight of my worries falling from it as I turned and locked eyes on Ayda, offering her more silent apologies.

"This isn't a negotiation, Tucker."

"She doesn't need to be a part of this."

"I have a device placed in Walsh's car that can blow you three up with a push of a button. She's a part of this because I say she is. Now start the engine. Put that delicate little foot of yours on the gas. Push it down, and get... the fuck... here. Now."

Ayda's eyes slid closed, and her hands twitched in her lap, but she only needed a moment before the stubborn tilt of her chin set in and her shoulders squared. She wasn't happy, but she was okay. She turned and gave a resigned nod of agreement.

There was nothing more I could do other than hang up the phone and slide it back into her hand.

"I promise you, I'll die before I let anyone lay a single finger on you, Ayda."

"Don't." Ayda let her eyes flick to the mirror where I assumed she could see Walsh with his hand pressed against his shoulder, his face creased in pain. They dropped to her lap and unlocked the phone, her delicate fingers navigating through screens quickly. She barely looked down, her chin still high with that stubborn tilt. "We're not doing the goodbyes this time. We're not giving up before we've gone in there. You understand me?"

Ayda angled the screen my way. There was a small marker in the middle of the highway just about where we were with a speech bubble that said SOS above it. With a swipe of her finger, the screen was on a menu and in her lap again.

"Now, let's go deal with this sadistic fucker. And then, let's go home."

CHAPTER TWENTY-FOUR
AYDA

S ending the SOS out through the phone-finding app was a risky one. Slater had walked me through it a dozen times. After the last couple of confrontations with our enemies, and after having been isolated, it had been a good call. Now, I hoped this worked as quickly as Slater had said it would because I knew they were up to their eyeballs in shit, too—a whole other kind than we were experiencing.

I stayed quiet as Drew drove, hating that we couldn't talk, that everything we said and did was being scrutinized.

My eyes moved between Drew and the mirror that reflected Walsh's face. The mayor had his hand pressed against his bullet wound, his face creased in pain, but it was hard to avoid the smug smile that curved the corner of his mouth when he dropped his head back on the leather and stared up at the roof of his car. I was sure he knew what was about to go down.

My heart was flip-flopping between fear and impotent rage. I felt so helpless.

Like Chester Cortez, Travis Gatlin had a mean streak as wide as Texas. Unlike Chester, Trigger was, in all actuality, batshit insane in the most clinical sense of the word. The memory of him shooting his half-brother Jacob, without so much as a blink of an eye made my stomach roll. Travis was volatile, feral, and hungry for something he couldn't see. He was searching for that high that would sustain him. He had nothing to lose, no conscience to speak of, and was a vindictive son of a bitch to boot.

We turned onto FM fifty-five and saw four Nav bikes and riders sitting on either side of the road, on the shoulders, like sentries, just as Travis had promised.

Four.

"*If I remember rightly, you guys never travel anywhere in big numbers because you prefer to slip into the background and shoot people in the back of the head rather than fight them up front.*" Those were Drew's words spoken to Travis on that fateful night at Rusty's, and I remembered them then. Four, we could probably handle.

I glanced at Drew, noted the rigid line of his jaw, and hoped to God he had a plan.

"Our escort," Walsh started and broke off to drag in an exaggerated panting breath that ended in a sardonic laugh.

Drew's face was still, his eyes drifting to each rider and their bikes. Ever the tactician, he was fascinating to watch. I just had to wonder how many more times we were going to have to see each other this way, on the frontline, about to go to war.

"This is too rehearsed," Drew muttered in a barely-there whisper, his attention jumping from Nav to Nav. "It's been planned for a while. All of it."

"You should have been dead a long time ago," Walsh croaked through his pain.

"Tell me something I don't know." Drew sighed.

Once the Navs spotted us, the lead rider, who was sitting

atop of a Chopper, turned his bike around, and the others stayed in place until Drew had driven through the middle of them. They formed a diamond formation around the vehicle we were in: one up front, two at the side of us, and one at the back.

Drew never stopped eyeing every rider around him, his forearms tensing as he twisted his hands around the steering wheel over and over again.

He was right about it being planned. You didn't have to know the rules these guys set in place to see that, and when they eased us from the road to a dirt turnoff, the building that sat at the end of it brought another round of ice to my blood

A warehouse that was almost identical to the one in Babylon we'd blown up.

They weren't unusual in this part of Texas. They popped up on the horizon no matter what direction you went in. This one, however, was too familiar, and it held a foreboding that sent chills down my spine, aches through the long-healed scars, and my hand to squeeze Drew's thigh before I could think about what I was doing.

"Drew," I whispered.

He turned the wheel in the same direction the bikes led him, coming to a stop outside a huge entrance that was only partially lifted from the ground. Drew wasted no time in reaching out for my hand and squeezing it tightly, leaning in closer as he looked all around.

"Whatever happens, Ayda, do what I say." His eyes found mine, his face stony and serious, the look he gave me warm—contradicting the rigid form of his shoulders and jaw. "Do you understand me? No heroics. Not this time. No trying to save anybody but yourself and…" He drifted off, swallowing hard.

I nodded, the action followed by a mumbled verbal acceptance of his request. Fear should have been the most prevalent reaction, but that had begun to fade as we'd neared the building. I'd somehow managed to file that away and replace it with trepidation and a small bubble of anger that simmered under the surface. Staring up at the red brick and mortar, holding Drew's hand, a small mantra started playing in the back of my head like a whisper. One I was determined to ignore for now.

"What now?" I asked quietly.

He raised my hand to kiss the back of it, looking up at me through heavy eyes. "Wait here. It's me they'll want to speak to first." Then he turned back to look at Walsh. "You lay a finger on her, and the next bullet hole in your body will be straight through your head."

Drew left me no time for anyone to respond. He opened the driver's door and climbed out, his hand on the roof to pull himself up before he slammed the door shut and walked around to one of the Navs who had now jumped off his bike. For a short time, it was just one and one, and Drew was walking closer, looking more confident than I knew he felt. He hitched up his jeans, expanded his chest, and walked to the hood of the car, glaring at the Nav closest to him. He looked like he was about to say something when the other three drew closer, each one drawing out their guns, aiming them at Drew's head, forcing him to stop in his tracks and raise his hands above his head.

My whole body leaned forward at the scene. I scanned the men around him, swallowing the groan when Walsh let out a coughed snort of laughter from the back seat.

"You brought this on yourself, Ayda. Messing with trash

like Tucker."

"Shut the fuck up," I muttered, watching as one of the guys checked Drew for guns and pulled out a couple of Glocks he always carried on him.

"Was it worth it? They're going to kill you both. They'll make him watch as they torture you first."

I was beginning to understand how Rubin was able to shoot the man with such detached precision. If I'd had a gun on me, I would have done the same. For someone with a hole in his shoulder, he talked a lot of shit, seemingly ignorant to the fact that Travis would shoot him with just as much ease as he would shot any one of us.

"You know—"

The mayor didn't get a chance to finish the sentence before there was a butt of a gun knocking against the glass of his door. The guy at the other end of the gun shook his head. With the brief reprieve from the narrative from the back, I turned my head to find Drew again.

His eyes were wide, staring right at me until one of the Navs pulled his arms behind him, held them together, and pushed Drew forward with a hard shove at his back. A second later, my door was opened by a rough looking man who had to be in his late forties, at least. His beard was wiry and wild, all the different shades of it covered in dirt like he hadn't washed for months.

"Time to join the party, blondie," he said roughly. "Get up. Make it quick."

I dropped my cell phone between the seat and the center console, hoping to God that if they took Drew's phone and shut it down, The Hounds could at least follow mine. I slipped from the car, my eyes scanning the building again as the guy gripped the top of my arm roughly.

He started leading me forward, and I played the scared woman part as best as I could, stumbling over my own feet as he forced me up the couple of steps to the front of the building. With a quick glance at the car over my shoulder, the mantra in my head started playing again and again, only louder this time. Loud enough that I couldn't ignore it now.

This can't be the end.

CHAPTER TWENTY-FIVE
DREW

*D*on't fuck this up.
        Stay calm.
        What the fuck ever.

No mantra was going to help him or me if that son of a bitch pushed me in the back one more time. No words of my own wisdom were going to save any of us if they didn't get their hands off Ayda.

We made it to the rolling door, where one of the Navs pressed a button to send it creaking all the way up. He turned to me and smiled, half his teeth missing and eyes creased with fucking dirt. He was a giant among men, placing himself as Goliath and leaving me to be David, but I'd faced bigger men than him before and lived to tell the tale.

Just.

I rolled my head to the side and checked over Ayda, making sure she hadn't been harmed already. Her chin was standing proud and her eyes, even though scared, were determined.

I couldn't believe we were here again. After so many promises to keep her safe, we were back in another enemy's grip, being thrown around like chew toys. I was tired of it all. Sick, tired, and motherfucking angry. Looking down at my feet, I took a moment to try and control my breathing as it picked up speed.

Kill them all.

If any mantra was going to stick, it was, without a doubt, that one, but I even shook that one away when a smartass Nav smaller than Rubin came to stand in front of me like he could take me if he wanted to. He was young, dumb, full of come, and messing with guns he sure as shit better know how to handle if he was going to aim one at me. The guy was in his early twenties, with flopping black hair that fell past his ears, and a face thinner and longer than a fucking horse's. His eyes were narrowed, and he ran a thumb under his nose, parting his lips to say something.

I probably should have given him time to speak, but he was there, and I was angry, and when he took a step closer to me—so close that I could feel his whiskey-coated breath on my face—he left me with no choice. I drew my head back only to snap it forward, smashing my skull into his with a force that knocked that little fucker straight to the ground while I stood there watching over him, barely flinching.

"You fucking—" the kid spat out as he rolled around at my feet, but the rest of what he had to say was drowned out when the Nav to my left threw a precise right hook straight across my jaw, making me stumble to the side until I could hear nothing but a wild ringing noise in my ears for a few seconds.

I then blinked hard and shook my head, unable to help the playful smile that tugged on the corner of my mouth.

"Sorry. My head slipped," I croaked out, only to be pulled back by my bicep by the giant, my hands yanked behind my back hard before he twisted them up, making me rise on my toes and grit my teeth against the painful stretch of my limbs.

"Next time you lash out, we'll hurt the girl," he growled in my ear. "We might fuck her, too."

If I got hold of a gun during any of this, I made a vow to kill that motherfucker first.

There was a grunt from Ayda behind me, but it wasn't the kind that told me she was in pain. More than she was unstable on her feet and struggling on purpose. Reminding me that she was there and witnessing everything—yet again.

When the rolling door reached its full height in front of me, I found myself staring at nothing other than rose petals on the floor in an open, empty space, their path in a neat little line that led around a dark corner I couldn't see.

Whatever was about to happen, Trigger intended to put on a show.

I swallowed down the sharp stabbing in my gut that warned me this was going to be bad, and I found myself moving when Goliath pushed me into the path of the petals.

The inside of the warehouse was much like the one we'd burned to the ground with The Emps inside of it. Muted light filtered through from dirty windows up high, out of reach. The floors were covered in debris with a few boxes stacked up here and there. The four Navs led Ayda and me around the corner, and when we turned it, I froze in place, unable to move.

The path of rose petals led to a white altar with a flowered arch over it. Two rows of chairs were set about ten feet in front of it, the whole scene surrounded by pillars and ropes that made it seem like a wedding ceremony had been set up inside a ground-level boxing ring.

Beyond all the details, the white decorations hanging from the high ceilings, and the ribbons that hung off the back of the chairs, there were two things that turned my stomach into angry knots of nausea.

One was Travis Gatlin, standing beside the erected altar, wearing a crisp white shirt and a black tie under his leather cut. A smug smile dominated his face as he stood there watching me, his hands clasped together in front of him.

The second thing to turn me sick was my father.

Unconscious.

Strung up the exact same way the Emps had strung me up in that warehouse of nightmares. Eric's arms were spread out like he was Jesus, with long, thick, steel chains keeping him in place. The tips of his toes barely touched the raised platform of the altar, and his chin hung down to his chest, the blood dripping from his mouth in slow droplets.

"The guests of honor have arrived," Trigger called out. "Come!" He raised a hand and beckoned us forward.

I wasn't going anywhere.

My eyes were locked on my father.

Flashbacks of that night in the warehouse tore through my mind.

The knife cuts through my skin.

The sound of Ayda's screams.

The agonizing ache in my limbs.

The mental torture.

The fact I almost lost *her*. I could have fucking lost her.

"Move," the giant behind me growled, pushing me harder—so hard I couldn't help but shuffle forward, my feet moving on auto. Everything else had stopped working, and my head was still ringing from the punch to the jaw only moments before.

If we got closer, though, this wouldn't end the same way

as our last performance with The Emps had. We weren't going to be gifted with a second miracle.

Digging my heels in, I came to an abrupt stop, holding steady when the Nav behind me smacked into my back and openly cursed me before trying to push me forward again.

"No," I growled, my teeth grinding together as I stared at Gatlin. "I'm not doing this. I'm not playing this fucking game, Trigger. You want me? Come and get me. You want to mess with my head? It's yours. You want to fuck me up and leave a mark. Let's do it, but we do it without your henchmen around. We do it one on one. And we do it without Ayda."

Trigger's smirk grew, and he tilted his head to the side to study me.

"You're such an angry little thing, aren't you, Drew? Let's not be angry today. This isn't The Emps you're dealing with. I am not Chester Cortez. I don't need to shout and scream and roar to have fun. I don't need to see fear in your eyes to know it's there. Do as I tell you, and maybe, just maybe, some of you will get out of this in one piece."

"What do you want from me?"

"Your cooperation."

"I'm here, aren't I?"

"Now, you simply need to listen." He grinned.

I searched his face, realizing just how fucked up Travis Gatlin was. I'd come across so many evil fuckers in my life that I'd almost thought I'd become desensitized to them. But there I was, staring at the greatest psychopath I'd ever encountered, knowing my blood wouldn't be enough for him.

He wanted something more.

Something I couldn't see.

Something I wouldn't be able to live without.

"The less you resist, the easier this will be," he assured me, and for just a moment, there was a sense of calm. "Or, we can do this." He lashed out his right arm, striking it across Eric's chest and cutting through his already open shirt. Eric was out cold, the only reaction he made being the swing of his body in the chains, but when Trigger peeled back the edges of my father's shirt, he showed me the damage he'd just inflicted. There was a small knife with a sharp blade curled in the center of Trigger's palm, and he'd sliced straight through Eric's skin like butter, causing more blood to pour out.

My jaw set, my breaths getting heavier and heavier. All I could do was move forward, taking tentative steps closer.

"Much better." Trigger smiled like he was fucking proud of me.

When Ayda and I arrived at the end of the rose petal pathway, Trigger held up a hand, bringing us to a halt in front of him. My arms were set free, as were Ayda's, and I immediately reached out to grab one of hers, holding it down between the two of us and moving closer to her, my eyes never leaving Trigger's.

He moved closer. The guy had always had confidence. Now, however, he seemed on another level. His arrogance was indestructible. He was the dictator, about to execute those who didn't fit neatly into his regime. The smug bastard stared into Ayda's eyes for an uncomfortably long amount of time, trying to intimidate her before he turned his attention to me. With a contented sigh, he held his hands up and turned them over, palms facing the ceiling.

"Dearly beloved. We are gathered here today to witness the union of two lovers. We have a bride. We have a groom. We have a father figure to give his blessing." Trigger flashed his teeth, his amusement glowing. "The only thing we need now are witnesses. Some guests."

And right on cue, the sound of several Harleys drawing into the yard outside made the ground beneath our feet shake—the noise I'd once lived for now sending cold shivers of dread down my spine.

"Ask the Lord, and you shall receive," Trigger whispered.

I closed my eyes, squeezing Ayda's hand tight, and I did that thing I'd refused to do a lot of in my life.

I fucking prayed.

CHAPTER TWENTY-SIX
AYDA

I'd always thought the sound of the cavalry showing up so quickly would make me feel better; that the familiar sound of those Harley's pulling in behind us on any battlefield would be a comfort. They'd managed to get here so quickly. So much faster than the last time we'd found ourselves in a precarious situation such as this one. Only this time, I didn't feel like I was about to be rescued. I didn't feel like we were out of trouble.

It didn't take much to understand that Travis had not only expected this call for backup, but he'd planned for it, too. From the look on his face and the cackle of laughter, he'd actually fucking hoped for this to happen.

The crazed glint in the president of the Navarro Rifles eyes made him look scarily maniacal. Travis wasn't looking at me right now, though. His eyes were on Drew. All of this was for an audience of one with the sole purpose of torturing Drew any way he could.

Slater and Jedd were the first to enter the warehouse. Both of them had their guns raised, and their steps were cautious as they rounded the corner, waiting for the situation to present itself. The moment the two of them saw the odd altar with Drew, Travis, Eric and me staged in front of it, they froze in place. Neither one of them seemed sure what to do next, but it was too late, anyway. Another four Navs stepped out from the shadows with their guns aimed true at our men's heads.

So much for small numbers.

"I'm impressed," Trigger spread out his hands like he was a leather-clad messiah and smirked. "Why don't you take a seat and join us, boys? The party's just getting started."

With a glance at Drew, both Jedd and Slater stepped forward, remaining flanked by the armed Navs.

Deeks, Kenny, and Moose came next, already disarmed as they were followed by another four Navs who had assault rifles pointed at their backs. I was pretty sure that there would be no more rescuers. I figured they'd have left some of the guys back at The Hut to keep it safe. But, before Travis could go on, another disturbance came through the back of the building, and two more Navs pushed Ben through with such force he lost his footing and hit his head against one of the rusted old machines at the back.

Ben hit the ground hard, a loud crack breaking the odd silence that I hadn't realized had descended over us.

I tried to move to help him without thinking, but I was pulled back by the grip on my hand, my body brushing against Drew's, while my eyes watched a slow, steady stream of blood pool around Ben's head. He groaned and rolled over onto his back, his eyes opening as he raised a weak hand to his temple. Ben wasn't dead, but he was no use to Drew now.

My movement seemed to attract Trigger's attention, his upturned palms balling before releasing again. He still didn't think much of women from what I could remember of our last meeting. His dark eyes assessed me coldly, disgust passing behind the soulless pits as his lip curled to reflect his distaste.

To Trigger Gatlin, I was merely a means to an end, a tool to be used against Drew. The chill in his eyes made my stomach roll violently because it was at that moment that I truly understood what my part was in this little performance he was putting on.

Drew cared about a lot of things in his life, and he loved a lot of people, too. Over the course of our relationship, however, he'd made it more than clear to his friends and enemies that I was important to him, and Trigger knew that to truly hurt Drew, to really get under his skin and wound him, he had to hurt me first.

I was expendable. His plan would be to torture me and kill me, then he would move on to Drew's brothers, completely obliterating what was left of the club before killing him, too. He wanted to hollow Drew out and send him into Hell with nothing but the dark, desperate memories that would stay with him in his damnation.

I couldn't let that happen.

I *wouldn't* let that happen.

Glancing up at the man next to me, the man I loved, I ignored the growl of Trigger Gatlin. That silent communication we used so often and came so naturally made it easy for me to let him know I was ready for this fight, that I wasn't going to cower, and I wasn't going to risk our child either. I was going to fight for our family, every last one of us, and I would fight for survival, even if I had to kill for it.

"Looks like we have the last of our witnesses," Trigger mused with smug satisfaction, drawing my eyes to him. "Now, where was I?"

"How long have you had this planned, Trigger?" Drew asked. There was a steely coolness in Drew's expression, his voice calm yet powerful.

Trigger turned to Eric, pointing up at him before he glanced over his shoulders to look at every Hound, including Drew. "Does this look at all familiar to you?" He frowned. "A recreation of anything, perhaps? Like you're experiencing deja vu? I can't quite put my finger on where I've seen this before." Trigger ran his hand over his chin, his expression turning pensive. This great act of his now in full flow before he brightened and dropped his hand to click his fingers together. "Oh, that's right." He nodded slowly, moving closer to Drew until he was standing toe-to-toe with him. "This reminds me of the live footage Chester Cortez streamed to me of you hanging in chains, blood oozing out of your fresh knife wounds. It reminds me of the way you swung helplessly in those chains, the rattling metal sending delicious shivers down my spine when I realized that you, the once great, formidable Drew Tucker, was about to die at the hands of the weaker enemy: those stupid, gun-happy, over-inflated egos we used to laugh at. The Emps."

A few chuckles of rough laughter came from behind us, The Navarro Rifles men clearly enjoying their position of power.

"Tell me, Drew," Trigger began, "how did it feel to know you were bested by those fools?"

"I'm still breathing, aren't I?" Drew said through gritted teeth. "I'm flesh and bone. They're nothing more than ash."

"Hmm." Trigger smiled. "So you are."

I probably should have been shocked that Trigger had such an insight to our own personal nightmare, but the whole situation with Owen, and learning about how deep his betrayal ran, I wasn't—not even close.

Drew shifted, leaning closer. "You want my flesh,

Trigger? Come and fucking get it," he ground out. "But quit the dramatics. I've played enough games with enough pricks to last me a damn lifetime. For once, I wish an enemy would have the balls to cut to the chase and get to the point. This flair for wanting attention y'all are breeding is really starting to piss… me… off."

Trigger's face fell instantly, his eyes turning icy as he stared right into Drew's.

"What. The fuck. Do you want?" Drew whispered coolly.

"Nothing you can provide me with can get you out of here, Drew," Trigger answered, his voice as low and steely as Drew's. "You involved us when you buried that Emp on our turf. You disrespected our club when you acted out ghastly deeds wearing a fake tattoo of our patch on your skin. You put the target on your own back when your actions resulted in the death of one of my own—"

"Hove?" Drew laughed, making Travis and me flinch in surprise. "Jacob Hove is why I'm here? I don't recall being the guy who put that bullet between his eyes. That was you."

"Opinions vary." Trigger smirked. "Few people know that. What would our families think?" He sighed softly.

"They'd probably wish it was you who took the fall, not him. I'm sure their lives would be richer without—"

Travis struck out, the gut punch he planted in Drew's stomach so fast, it had almost been impossible to see. Drew's groan was deep as he bent forward, curling himself into the left where Travis had landed a hit on him.

The satisfied look on Trigger's face was despicable and made my anger rise. It felt like my insides were too hot to contain.

"Does the truth hurt, Travis? Do you forget how well I

know your mom?" I smiled cruelly. "You know, she hated the way Jacob was always seeking your approval. She said it would only get him into trouble one day. I don't think that it would surprise her to learn that you shot him in the face point blank to prove a point."

Travis didn't try and hit me as I'd expected him to. Instead, his hand grabbed my chin roughly, angling my face, so the spit from his forced words laced my cheek. "My mom thought you were a fucking cunt. I say it takes one to know one, right?"

I smiled at him. "Mommy issues?" I asked, trying not to make a sound to alert Drew that Travis was squeezing harder.

A familiar roar of anger was set free, and before Travis could offer any retort, Drew had moved, grabbing hold of Trigger's neck with every ounce of strength he had. His face was twisted with rage, veins popping in his head as he growled and tore Trigger from me, throwing himself on top of him, sending Travis to the ground with such force, his head was the first point of contact, connecting with the edge of the raised platform that Eric was swinging upon.

"Don't you *fucking* touch her," Drew spat, using all his power and might to pull himself back just enough to swing his arm up and back down onto Trigger's jaw.

Drew had been quick—his reaction had been faster than any of Trigger's men had been expecting, so it took a moment for them to catch up. All of their guns moved from The Hounds to Drew, and the Nav closest to us pushed the barrel of his 9mm to the back of Drew's skull and made him freeze.

"Now that's the Drew Tucker we all know and hate," Trigger grumbled, spitting blood from his mouth and smirking. He glanced up at me and back at Drew with a smirk that was too calm. "Every time you throw your fists around, I will give your bitch a new scar to take to Hell with her."

Drew closed his eyes, his breaths ragged as his whole body sagged.

Trigger rose, his body stumbling to the side, which only made his sadistic laughter grow as he wiped the corner of his mouth with the back of his hand.

"Hell of a good fighter, though. That could work in your favor today." Trigger tugged on his cut to straighten it down, his chest rising as he pulled in a breath of air and surveyed everyone within the warehouse with a terrifying amount of control.

It was only then that I allowed myself to listen to everything else going on around us. I could hear the grumblings of every man I'd ever shared The Hut with—their growls and fights quieter than Drew's had been. When I turned to look back at them, each one was being held by two or three men, their arms pinned behind them as their fight became weaker.

"Contrary to popular belief, I'm not a total bastard," Trigger said smoothly, pulling my attention back to his smug face. His eyes were zoned in on mine, focused. "I do believe some people are entitled to a happy ever after, don't you, Ayda? Good people. They deserve the chance to fight for their fairytale ending."

There was no answer I could give him that would satisfy his sick need to gain the upper hand and use us as puppets in this little production he'd organized. His smug smile only grew as I glared at him.

"Come on, it's a simple question." He reached out to touch me, and the growls that spread around the place just made his humor more evident, even as I swatted his hand away. He leaned closer, dropping his voice to a whisper. "Shall I let Drew fight for yours, Ayda? Shall I let them all fight for your happiness? Let some of them die so you get to live your dream?"

"No." If he thought for a second that I was willing to sacrifice even one of these men for my life… he was wrong. So very wrong.

CHAPTER TWENTY-SEVEN
DREW

"Too bad you think you get a say in any of this, little lady," Trigger told her, his smile making my stomach twist up like a thousand knives were stabbing the lining of it.

If Ayda got hurt, I'd lay my body at their feet, look up into their cold, angry eyes, and I'd tell them to take out my beating heart and put it in a fucking trophy cabinet for them to fawn over for the rest of their lives.

A victory! Look who took down the president of The Hounds of Babylon, once and for all.

Like any of that shit even mattered.

The 9mm pressing into my skull wasn't enough of a deterrent for me.

I glanced up at my father, watching his face, studying it for just a heartbeat more than I should when I thought I saw the gentle fluttering of his lashes as his body swung in subtle waves. He was alive. I could feel it in my soul.

The Nav behind me pressed down harder, making sure I could feel every bit of the cold metal against my head. On my knees, they thought I was helpless, but I'd been on my knees a thousand times before and survived. I could take that gun out of that pussy's hand without breaking a sweat, and suddenly it seemed worth the risk. There was just something I needed to do first.

"Trigger?"

He spun around slowly, the movement smooth and controlled. His eyes were wide as he looked down at me, the master of the universe, while I looked up at him, temporarily helpless in his eyes, my club at his mercy.

"I'll fight," I told him, ignoring Ayda and her wishes. "If that's what you want me to do, I'll fight for her happiness. I'll fight for all of them. If that's what gets you off, and if that's what all this is about…" I glanced around at the altar, the flowers, the ropes around the edges of the setup, and at the chairs he'd lined up for some private viewing. "I just ask one thing first, before any of this happens."

Travis turned his intrigued smile upside down, and he tilted his head to one side.

I held eye contact with him for an uncomfortable amount of time, not blinking, watching his every twitch, his every fluttering of confusion he struggled to hide behind a fake smile, and I watched the way, as time went on, his shoulders relaxed, as though he didn't have to be on high alert with me on my knees in front of him.

Then I moved quickly, dodging to the side so fast that the guy putting all his weight down on the gun against my head stumbled forward, losing his footing enough for me to bring the edge of my palm down over the gun he was holding and watch as it fell to my feet. There was no scrambling, no plea for survival, or any poor timing on my part. I had that gun in my hand the second it bounced, and then I jumped up on my feet, ignoring the weapons that were moving closer around me, and I pressed that fucking gun against The Nav's head, holding myself upright as I glared right at Trigger.

"Do not fucking underestimate me throughout any of this," I told him, my jaw tense, and my eyes murderous. "You might know what you're doing, but I can assure you, I do, too."

"Always so dramatic," Travis smirked. "You never disappoint, Tucker."

"I never miss a shot, either, so bear that in mind when you're fucking with me, Travis." I raised my brow—jaw tight.

"Noted." Trigger tipped his head in acknowledgment before he took a step closer to me. "But my men never miss either, and you're currently outnumbered three to one. Unless you want me to give the signal for one of mine to put a bullet in one of yours..." He held out his hand for the gun in my grip, waiting patiently.

I glanced up, looking at my brothers.

Slater was furious, his face set to thunder. Jedd looked more patient, a calm having washed over him that only Jedd could ever carry in such circumstances. Kenny was weighing up how to help—I could tell by the way he was looking in every visible corner of the warehouse, checking the high windows, scoping out the place. Moose was, even under the circumstances, waiting for my instruction, and Deeks...

Deeks looked fucking sad as he stared at me, the oldest of us all, tired and worn out with this side of life as much as I was.

I thought of Harry.

I thought of Pete, too.

And then my eyes found Ayda's as I slowly let my shoulders sag and held the gun out for Travis to take from my grip. He knew what I could do. I'd had my way for a minute.

Now it was time to play his games.

Once the gun was in Travis's hand, the Nav I'd taken out groaned and got to his feet, stumbling to the side before Travis jerked his head, effectively dismissing his own brother. The guy left, having failed his club, and I saw the anger in the way his fists curled in and out beside his thighs as he begrudgingly walked away.

"Brothers," Trigger called to his men. "Bring them closer."

Jedd, Slater, and the rest of them were pushed forward, and hisses of cuss words thrown back at The Navs came from each and every one of my guys, as the Navs tugged them back sharply, making them freeze in place behind the row of white chairs that had been lined up in front of the altar.

Trigger turned to Ayda.

"Unfortunately, this isn't going to be pretty for you."

Ayda scowled at him, turning up her lip in disgust. "*Fuck* you."

Travis huffed in response, and he signaled to one of his men. Ayda was grabbed from behind, her upper arm used to drag her to the altar where my father was hanging, blood still dripping in slow falling, lengthy droplets from the corner of his mouth.

There was a desperate need for me to cry out and tell Travis to leave her alone; she was *pregnant*. But I knew men like Travis, and I knew they would use that as even more leverage.

Travis came closer, so there was barely any room between us. "I have a proposal of my own to make to you."

My scowl was immediate—silence my only response.

"You've done a lot to piss me off, Tucker. You and your

237

merry band of fools don't need to look for trouble, that much is clear. It finds you. You're incapable of living a quiet life, of keeping your head under the radar, of being a true tactician and a worthy outlaw. You let your emotions sit on the surface, which lands you and those you love in trouble at every turn. If you keep that up, you'll be dead before you get a chance to walk your pretty little lady down the aisle. Or she'll be dead because of you."

I swallowed hard, unable to look away from him, my heart beating wildly and fists curling down by my sides.

"But I also see you have potential to be something greater than what you are now."

"What the fuck are you talking about?"

Trigger's smirk grew slowly. "I'm a big believer in survival of the fittest. Natural selection, shall we say. I think those who die from their mistakes deserve to die. Those who are weak have no place on this earth. Those who fall too easy don't deserve to get back up. I want to hate you, Tucker. A huge part of me does. I've had many dreams of bathing in your blood and being the one to tie you up in chains like Cortez managed to do, and I've thought about standing over your grave with a smile on my face. But then I thought about why I wanted that. Why did I want you dead, beside the heat you tried to put on my club? Besides the way you seemed to think it was okay to mock my brothers? Besides the fact that you messed with my drug trade in Babylon, and how you put us under the microscope of the likes of the ATF? And once I'd put all those things aside, that's when I came to the honest conclusion that I hated you because a part of me feared you. You may wear your heart on your sleeve, and that may make you weak, but it makes you reckless, too. Reckless can be deadly." He grinned like the evil motherfucker he was. "I like deadly. I want deadly on my team."

"Over my dead body."

"That may be an option." He turned to Ayda. "Or hers." When he spun back around to me, he pressed his lips together and raised his brows. "We could make this a marriage of both clubs, Tucker. If you prove yourself to me, if you do exactly as I say, we could eventually work together to create something Texas has never seen before. I'd protect you."

"At what cost?"

"All the evidence you've planted against us concerning Owen Sinclair and Mayor Walsh." He paused for dramatic effect. "And a little show of strength from you, dear president."

I glanced at my father and Ayda, side by side. I saw every flicker of pain Ayda was feeling and the way her eyes were pleading with me not to agree to any of this.

Closing my eyes to find some strength, I turned back to Trigger and opened them slowly. "What do you want me to do?"

"Fight," he said simply. "You and your club. Show me you're worthy of our allegiance. Your men against mine. We have the ring set up. We have spectators. This is everything you need, right? You did used to fight in the underground if I remember correctly. You're used to these kinds of do-or-die battles, no?" His smile broke free again, and I knew exactly where the fucker was going with this.

Pete. The fucker was referring to Pete's death.

"Did Cortez show you Pete dying, too?" I asked through gritted teeth.

"Who do you think pulled Cortez's strings?" he

countered, raising a brow. "Everything he did was because I manipulated him into thinking he could do it successfully. My mistake. I made an error in choosing The Emps. I never put them to the test. I never found out if they were truly worthy of being associated with us. I won't make that mistake twice. I won't choose a weak club again."

My body shook as his words sunk in. My limbs trembled, and my jaw was about to break because my teeth were grinding together so hard as I stared into his creepy fucking stare.

He'd been responsible for Cortez's actions?

Which meant he'd been responsible for so much more than I'd ever imagined. And now he wanted my club to fight against his so that we could prove we were worthy of his supposed loyalty.

The game had been flipped on its head, and now the rage rolling through my body needed an outlet.

Rolling my shoulders, I shrugged slowly out of my cut, never taking my eyes from Travis as I pulled it in front of me, folded it carefully, and then laid it out on a chair just a few steps away. I began to lift my T-shirt over my head, sliding it off my arms as carefully as I could before I tossed it to the side, ignoring the grunts and quiet protests of my brothers around me.

I was focused on one man and one man alone for now, and that man had never looked more satisfied with himself than he did right now.

"Each fight goes to the end," I told him calmly. "Until the other man can't get off his knees and he has to be dragged away."

Travis nodded. "And which Hound would you like to

offer up as your first sacrifice?"

I shook my head and flexed my fingers out before I curled them into fists. "There won't be any more sacrifices in my club."

The audible groans and gasps from my men had to be blocked out. I was too focused on the narrowing of Trigger's eyes.

"Are you suggesting...?"

"That I fight every man you've got? Yeah. I am. If someone else is going to die for my MC, it's going to be me. No more sacrifices. Come and test my strength. Come and find my weakness." I raised my chin and glared at him, waiting for my chance of revenge on everyone I'd ever loved and lost. For every man behind me with a hound on their chest, and for the man bleeding out in front of me who'd brought me into this world. Mainly, I wanted revenge for my girl, and for the misery that this motherfucker had brought into our lives when all we ever should have been doing was loving one another and living life.

"I can't decide whether you're brave or stupid," Trigger whispered back at me.

"Both." I sucked in a breath and rolled my neck to the side. "Let's go."

CHAPTER TWENTY-EIGHT
AYDA

No matter how many times I'd been there in the training room for one of Drew's bouts with the other Hounds, or how desensitized I thought I was about watching him warm up for a fight, there was nothing in the world that could have ever prepared me for what was about to go down in this warehouse.

The air around us crackled the moment Drew conceded, a cacophony of noise exploding as Hounds and Navs alike shouted and talked over one another, desperate to encourage or issue threats. I wouldn't have listened if I could have avoided it, but as it was, I was frozen to the spot, my heart in my throat, pounding so hard it drowned out most of the noise, while an odd sense of my future thrummed in my gut, reminding me what was growing there.

We couldn't escape this now, and the part of me that was beginning to think like Drew understood why. Wars were made up of battles, and Drew and his Hounds had fought so many of them defensively over the years that this final round, where it mattered the most, meant he had to scale an offensive, even when our enemy had the upper hand. Drew wasn't thinking about me, the baby, or his men as he rolled his shoulders and bounced on the balls of his feet. He was thinking about the future. About freedom, security, and more importantly, peace, even if that meant we had to live it without him.

Tonight was his final stand. The night where he showed his enemies every last one of his strengths.

The rolling bloodlust that was slowly traveling around the room and transforming every man inside of it was now seeping inside of me. Tendrils of it worked through my flesh, setting my nerves alight until my whole body thrummed with it. I needed something to sate this new thirst because that volatile drive was the only thing stopping my emotions from overwhelming me.

With a desperate and angry swipe of my hand, I knocked away the arm of the Nav still holding me, and I pushed closer to the love of my life.

"Drew!" I called out, my body coming to a stop as arms folded around my waist to stop me from reaching him. I pushed them away again but stayed where I was as I waited for him to acknowledge me.

He flinched, his face twisting at the sound of my voice. He couldn't look at me, but I saw the way he swallowed down his regret as he ran a palm over the knuckles on his right hand before he gave in and glanced up through hooded eyes.

His apology was there. I could see it.

But I also saw that he had to do this.

There was no other way out.

"Win," I said loud and clearly. "You win."

Drew held my gaze for a second, allowing himself a moment to take me in, but that moment flew by too quickly, and then Drew was bouncing on the balls of his feet, his neck stretched and his chin raised high as he stared back at Trigger like he was capable of killing him with nothing more than a look.

"I take a guy out—you let one of mine go. We got a deal?" he asked Travis one last time.

"We have a deal."

"You try back out of that deal, find a loophole, throw any surprises, and I'll kill you first."

Travis raised both brows, and after careful consideration gave Drew a nod of approval.

Drew exhaled heavily in response, never taking his eyes from Trigger as he continued to bounce on his feet and point at Eric.

"I win this round, and Eric gets cut loose."

Trigger hissed, dragging air in through his teeth. "Let's save the most important ones for the later rounds. I'm not about to make this easy for you and give you a reason to stop fighting after two rounds, Tucker. Ayda and Eric go last."

I expected Drew to argue at that, but he merely closed his eyes to compose himself, drawing in another breath that seemed to set his adrenaline on fire before he released it quickly and opened his eyes again, this time pointing at his brothers across the room.

"Moose."

"Moose it is," Trigger agreed, and then he summoned a man of his own.

The giant who'd pushed Drew into the warehouse was the first to take him on. The towering body of steel creaked when he walked into the space between Trigger and Drew. Trigger wanted to tire Drew out fast, and he clearly thought this was the best way to go about it.

The guy was huge. His face twisted in concentration as he

sized up Drew and obviously underestimated him. That was something I wasn't willing to do, but it didn't stop that icy finger of fear from tearing down my spine.

This wasn't like boxing I'd seen on television. There was no announcer telling me when the fight would start. There wasn't a bell, a whistle, or a referee. It wasn't even close to the contests I'd seen in the training room. It started the moment the giant stepped forward and took a swing, his long limb lashing out and curling around faster than I'd expected him to be able to move.

Drew dodged it, leaning away and pulling his chin back before he danced backward, his hands up high as he bounced from side to side. The giant Nav threw another punch, his steps heavy and hard as he marched forward, and Drew moved like he knew where his opponent was going to go before the move was made. His eyes had changed, shifting from being concerned, to being alive with adrenaline. No one else was in the room with him but his enemy as he waited patiently to strike.

The Nav charged, his pace picking up until they were both at the ropes, and a large growl came from the Nav as his anger took over and he made another swing at Drew, only to miss as Drew ducked under his arm, bounced around and danced behind him on the balls of his feet. His back was to me, all flexing muscle and damp, bare skin as he continued to send the Nav in circles—the dirty giant who now looked like he wanted to eat Drew alive.

"Son of a…" The Nav growled, lunging forward to Drew, expecting him to move, but this time Drew stayed firmly in place, unmoving as the Nav walked straight into the hard, well-placed uppercut Drew planted under his jaw, sending the

Nav's teeth rattling and his eyes rolling into the back of his head.

Drew wasted no time in throwing a sharp right hook across the guy's jaw, the sound of flesh breaking bone enough to make everyone around me wince and cry out in anger and excitement.

The giant stumbled and Drew attacked. Three hits to the guy's chest barely making him breathe heavy before Drew ducked under a weak attempt at retaliation, only to land a hard hook directly into the Nav's groin.

He was history. He fell, and Drew didn't stop. He wanted blood, and he was getting it as The Nav rolled around on the ground, unable to dodge anything Drew rained down on him. Within seconds, The Nav was on his back, and Drew was smashing his fists into his face for fun, blood flying back up and spraying his face.

Just when I thought it was over, and Drew stood upright over him, Drew did the unthinkable, and stomped his boot hard onto The Nav's face, not even looking down on the man whose bones he'd just crushed beneath his sole before he stepped off of him and walked over to Trigger, his breaths ragged.

"Deeks goes next," he rasped.

My eyes flashed up to where Moose was standing. The Nav that had been standing as close as his shadow had backed off, but Moose stayed where he was, his eyes moving to Deeks as mine did. Loyal as ever, his men were staying where they were. They were never going to leave Drew behind. My heart swelled, even though I knew it hurt every one of them to know that Drew was going to keep doing this in their stead.

Travis nodded his agreement, and the rowdy crowd

stirred.

Another Nav entered the weird, makeshift ring we were all a part of—this man much smaller, but somewhat faster on his feet. Drew assessed him as he approached, taking in everything about him before the fight began. The younger Nav was cocky and clearly pissed off that the man before him had done such a shit job. He was handy with his legs, too, more like a specialist of martial arts than a boxer. His leg was the first thing to swing out, lashing out high to reach Drew's jaw in a surprise move, but Drew seemed somewhat ready for it, and his hand flew out, stopping the foot in its tracks with a hard thud before he grabbed the guy's ankle with his free hand, turned to the side and flipped him over onto the ground. The fight lasted all of thirty seconds before the guy's face hit the hard, concrete floor with a bloody crack, and he passed out, his foot still in Drew's grip.

Drew simply looked at Trigger and raised a brow, holding eye contact before he eventually let the guy's leg fall, and he pointed to The Hounds.

"My brother Kenny goes next."

This whole thing was like nothing I could have ever prepared myself for. The smell of sweat and the tangy coppery scent of the blood already spilled was almost surreal. My fear and anger were two separate beasts that battled inside of me for dominance. I felt helpless. There was nothing I could to stop this from happening.

One guy was dragged away, another replaced for Drew to face.

He'd yet to look over and see that the men he'd already fought for were refusing to leave.

Drew fought on. A fighter around the same size and

weight as him entered the ring, eager and ready to charge.

Drew dodged the first punch, swinging under it only to mistime the way the guy swung back, his opponent shocking him with a Southpaw surprise, sending Drew's jaw the other way with a mighty crack.

The whole room hissed and held their breath. It was the first shot to land on Drew's body, and the fighter he was facing made it count. When Drew regained his footing, he ran a bare-knuckle over the corner of his mouth, a slight curl to his lip making it look like was smiling when he looked back up at the man he was facing.

That blood was a reminder for him to not get complacent and Drew charged forward, his biceps tense and bursting at the seams. He threw a sharp left himself—telling the world he was ready to fight to the death.

This round was much more even, a couple more shots hitting Drew hard in the stomach, turning his tanned skin raw and red, but no matter how much of a good fighter that Nav turned out to be, he wasn't a true match for Drew—the man who'd been taught how to survive using his fists by Pete.

The Nav crashed to his knees suddenly, his nose bloody and his body weak, and Drew brought his own knee up under the guy's chin, sending him backward at once. His descent to the concrete floor seemed to happen in slow motion before all eyes turned back to Drew.

For the first time, he was bloody, and now the game had changed.

He spat a mouthful of blood to the side, refusing to look at me when he pointed to his brothers and croaked roughly, "Ben."

And off he went again. Another man. Another fight.

Another round of pure, agonizing torture for him and for the rest of us.

No matter how strong he was, he was only human, too. Fatigue was setting in, and I could tell by the groans and the growls of frustration he was letting slip free that he was finding it harder as time went on. This Nav came out with brass knuckles on his right hand, and Drew's eyes widened as he took it in.

"Come on, fucker," his opponent taunted sadistically, and Drew froze, his brows rising high.

"What did you just call me?" he whispered.

The man sneered, smug and arrogant, waving his clenched fist back and forth as a promise of destruction. "Fucker."

The corner of Drew's mouth twitched in amusement. He lunged forward, not throwing a punch, instead stepping into The Nav's personal space, grabbing his wrist, and bending that wrist back with a hard snap until all that could be heard around the warehouse was the high-pitched screams of what sounded like a dying cat.

"My fucking wrist! It's broken!" the Nav wailed, dropping to his knees as his face turned purple.

Drew didn't even look at him. He paced in a circle, his chin to his chest and his eyes cast down, that jaw of his that I'd kissed so many times now unapproachable as it clenched and twitched to keep him under control.

"Slater!" he cried.

"The man's a fucking machine," I heard a man in a Nav cut mutter beside me.

He wasn't wrong. As Drew paced like a caged animal, the back of his hand running under his nose, the man I knew no longer existed inside of him. It wasn't forever, and it didn't scare me as much as it should have. He'd buried that part of himself in order to do what he needed to do.

Eric groaned somewhere behind me as my guard stepped to the side. With one glance over my shoulder, my eyes met Eric's. I couldn't read Eric like I could Drew. There was no open communication between us, but a shadow of his own regret haunted those eyes that were so familiar to Drew's.

The tone of the crowd shifted, bringing my eyes back to the circle that had now formed around Drew. His new opponent—a guy with a wide chest and a bald head—parted the crowd and stepped into the circle of bodies with a smirk of arrogance in place. His face and head were covered in ink, the words and images bleeding together, making him look deranged. He curled his body for attack. His large hands gripping the thighs of his jeans and tugging to make more room for movement.

He didn't mess around like the others.

The punch he landed on Drew's face split his left eye open, the blood spurting out in a rush—the force of the shot so hard, it sounded like he'd snapped a bone.

Drew had barely said two words during all of this… until now. There were mutterings of pain being grumbled under his breath in the few seconds he took to himself before he righted his body, brought his shoulders back, and stumbled to the left, his vision clearly off.

"Ya like the taste of that fist, tough guy?" the fighter teased.

"Now, we have a fight," Trigger mused.

Drew blinked wildly, his eyes as wide as he could get them before he blinked again and shook his head to try rid himself of whatever was causing him a problem.

There was so much blood.

So damn much.

"Again!" Trigger called, and the Nav moved, his arm pulled in tight before he landed a left fist in Drew's ribs, bringing his body in on itself as he took the pain with a grunt of acceptance.

It was the first sign of weakness I'd seen in Drew, that any of us had seen, and the way Trigger leaned forward with a sick, satisfied grin on his face only made the rage inside of me flare into a full-blown wildfire.

The whole room was focused on the two men in the middle now. Even the man supposed to be guarding me was too invested in the possibility of his asshole friend besting Drew. The noise that rose from the opposing sides was thunderous. The Hounds hollered out encouragement, advice, and told Drew to focus—to get his head in the game.

The noise made my head swim, and the words made my world vibrate painfully.

Kill him, being the loudest of them all.

Drew managed to avoid the next swing, but the guy recovered. It was barely enough time for me to step out of the line of men, but it was enough for me to deliver my message as Drew glanced my way through wounded eyes.

"End him!" I cried.

CHAPTER TWENTY-NINE
DREW

My bones sang—their song a haunting melody of pain that made the world tremor beneath my feet. The only thing I could see with any clarity was the bright balls of light flashing in the blind spot of my left eye.

The blood, although warm, felt cold against my skin.

Pain sliced through my ribs.

And then she said those two words.

End him.

It was that easy. That's all I had to do.

My opponent swung again, and I swayed, a bout of good fortune landing in my lap, which forced the dude in front of me to miss and his body to rock forward. I saw Ayda again, her concerned face mouthing something else at me as her arms flailed around in front of her in a hurry.

I wanted to go to her—make love to her one last time.

I wanted to kiss her and taste her breath, feel her warm hands on my bruised skin and beg her to whisper something sweet in my ear before everything turned to black. A smile tried to tug at my mouth as I looked at her, but she was telling me to look elsewhere, and it was a good job she did. When I turned to look on my blind side, a fist was swinging my way, and I ducked under the flying arm in time to spin on my feet, see my enemy, and throw a punch in the guy's kidney.

He groaned in surprise, and I launched, feeling the fight return.

One.

Two.

Three.

Bam, bam, bam. I made those punches count, my knuckles throbbing; split wide open, and my wrists aching from the force of the blows with no gloves on.

He was out on the ground soon after, but I didn't have the drive to stamp on his head and crush his teeth into the concrete. All my energy needed to be saved now.

Tilting my head up to the ceiling, I felt my eyes roll back, and a rush of blood flow down my throat as I sniffed up. The need for air was desperate, and I gasped, pulling it in before I shook out the shock of my hits and let my head roll back down.

When I saw Trigger's face, he looked like a lion that had just devoured an all-you-can-eat Zebra buffet.

"Jedd," I croaked roughly, never taking my eyes from his.

"Now it's getting interesting, Drew." Trigger paced in front of me, but my balance was off. It felt like an ear had exploded, as well as my eye, and all I could feel, taste, hear, and see was blood.

I stumbled again, my footing making my body lean to the right before I corrected myself. "I said Jedd."

"You're one hell of a fighter, I'll give you that," he said quietly, thoughtfully, like the tactician he was.

"Save your compliments for someone who gives a shit, Trig, and get me my next fighter."

"Drew!" someone called out to my right.

I recognized that voice, and my body turned on instinct, looking up to see my VP staring at me with pleading eyes. Everything else around him was fuzzy, and I struggled to take him in as more blood poured out from the cut above my eye, forcing me to swipe the back of my hand across it to clear it away.

"You don't owe anyone anything," Jedd said calmly.

I stared at him as best I could, wishing I could tell him all the love I had for him and his unrelenting loyalty. I owed him everything. I owed them all everything.

"We can do this another way," Jedd told me.

Raising a weak hand, I offered a shit smile and pointed right at him. "Do your job, VP. Get every fucker out of here before these bastards ruin us."

"Drew…"

"You heard what I said."

I turned away, scrunching my eyes tight before opening them with a flash and staring at Trigger.

"The next guy I want setting free is Jedd. You fucking deaf?"

"Suicide Tucker. That's what I'm going to call you from now on."

"Whatever gets you hard. I'm sick of your show. Give me my next victim."

Trigger smirked that smirk I wanted to smash right off his face, and he called in a man who was standing to his right.

"A VP for a VP," he said calmly, and I let my eyes drift down to the cut on the next fighter's chest.

Vice President of The Navarro Rifles.

That just happened to be a fancy badge on an idiot's

chest in the end. He had that fire in his eyes and the loyalty marked by the ink on his skin, but everything else was weak. He wasn't big, he wasn't strong, and he sure as shit wasn't a fighter... although he tried. Gerrard Gates gave me a rest, even when I was prancing around like a ballet dancer. I managed to catch my own breath and wipe away more shit by the time he'd gotten close, and even when he made his fist connect my cheek, it was pathetic. In the end, he became mush beneath my legs as I knelt on his chest and pounded my fists into his face like he didn't matter.

He didn't matter.

None of them did.

I was at war, and I was going to fucking survive this.

When I jumped off him, sated, yet thirsty for more, I raised my chin and opened my one good eye to look at my woman properly for the first time. There was more blood on my skin than running through my veins as our eyes connected, and I let my lips fall apart to drag in more air, taking a moment to just... look at her.

See she was alive.

God, I loved her.

Tears were swimming in Ayda's eyes, but her chin was up and shoulders back as she held my gaze. Her lips trembled as she said something, but she had to stop and start again, her words clearer the second time around.

"Come home to me."

I lifted a bloody fist and pressed it over my heart, my breathing ragged as I pushed it into my chest before I released it and pointed right at her, a silent, "You" falling from my lips.

She closed her eyes, then opened them a defiant glint in her eye. "I love you. Live for us."

When you love someone as much as I loved Ayda, it was easy to get caught up in whatever spell they cast. My body was breaking, heart aching, limbs shaking, and yet all I could focus on were those six words she'd just delivered to me. It made me a sick fuck to smile with blood in my teeth and crimson stains on my face, but I smiled anyway, wishing I could have appreciated every moment I'd ever had with her a thousand times more than I had done.

Then Trigger's voice brought me back to the present.

"Bring him in!" he called out, and it made me blink quickly, scowling soon after as I spun to see him from my good eye.

He was facing someone I couldn't see, and the crowd around us began to mumble and mutter to themselves, their whispers growing louder until I picked out a name I instantly recognized.

Walsh.

Walsh was soon shoved in front of me, his body limp. His shirt was undone and his tie loose, but even with one fucked up eye, the only clear thing I could see, and smell, was Walsh's fear as he looked up at me through worried eyes.

His body was bent over; the bullet wound causing him more pain than he could handle in his ripped up, pretentious navy suit.

I glanced up at Trigger who was hovering above him, and I shook my head. "Is this a joke?" I ground out.

Trigger folded his hands behind his back and paced slowly around the Mayor of Babylon, staring down at him like he was nothing more than a sewer rat. "Do you know, Drew, how many times this man right here has stood in front of me, whether he's been in my drug lab asking for cheap rates, or he's been handing over intel on money launderers, arms dealers, crooked prison officers…" He paused, glancing over his shoulder to raise a brow at me. "…fellow MC men like myself." Trigger sighed and turned back to his task. "And all he's begged me to help him do is bring down The Hounds of goddamn Babylon." Trigger raised his hands, palms up and facing the ceiling like he was talking to himself. "Every single time we'd meet to discuss some new venture together, it would always, always come back to The Hounds."

I glanced at Walsh and his scared eyes and messed-up red hair, my face tight and angry.

"This man wanted every one of you dead. Every single last one of you. Men, women, girls, boys, innocents, guilty criminals, he didn't care. If you were associated with The Hounds, you're damned in his eyes. It was like he was obsessed. I never quite understood it. He sold his hatred of you to me by saying you were ruining his town, but then I looked into it. I got Chester Cortez and The Emps to look into it, to rile you up and rustle your feathers a bit. I got Sinclair to set up the whole teenage copycat club to lure you in. I got each and every man working for me to go out there and make you *snap!*" Trigger spun on his heels, the twist of his body smooth and controlled as he eyes shot to mine. "But I never got them to catch you *starting* the trouble. I never got them to catch you being fools for the sake of being fools. You were fools because your hands were tied. You were forced to be those men. Which only made me dig deeper. And do you know what I found?"

I remained silent, apart from my ragged breaths.

Trigger bent down over Walsh, his lips resting by the mayor's ear as he looked up at me and spoke. "I found a bitter man, jealous of your MC, who was making men like me deal with his enemies because he was too scared to handle them himself." He looked down at Walsh. "Isn't that right, Mayor?"

The mayor simply shook, a big man full of shit staring back at me with wide eyes and fear hanging over his shoulders like a cheap, shitty suit.

"He just doesn't fucking like you, Drew," Trigger told me. "He's asked me to kill you and your family so many times. He'd ask me to kill you now if he thought I would."

"Why don't you?"

"Because I don't do shit for anyone unless I want to. Unless it benefits me. I work for no one. Do you understand that? Everything I ever do is because *I* want to do it. Because I'm in control. I rule this town. I rule all the towns. Texas is mine."

"And you want me to kill him now?" I asked carefully.

"I want to see how you fight for survival against those closer to you than we are."

Shifting my feet, I stood with my legs wider apart, my fists flexing down by my thighs. "Get up," I told Walsh, not caring for Trigger's need for his ego stroking, only caring to extinguish one more threat. "Get up!" I said louder, losing patience.

"I... I can't fight you," Walsh stuttered. "I can't..."

"Either get up, or I'll drag you the fuck up."

"He sounds serious, Mayor," Trigger teased, and for a moment, I thought he was on my side—if he had been the kind of man to take sides at all, but then I saw him dip his hand into the inside of his cut and ever so slowly, ever so carefully, pull out a knife, slipping it into the hand of Walsh as he looked up at me. "Consider this an advantage from me to you, Mayor. I think you'll need it."

Walsh stared at the weapon, turning it over in his hand before he looked up at me carefully.

"If you think you need it, use it," I told him.

"Suicide Tucker," Travis said through a sleazy, bright smile.

I ran a hand under my nose and sniffed, blinking away the trickle of blood that was swimming in my eye. "Cut my father down," I told him, pointing Eric's way before I pointed at Walsh and bounced on my toes. "Cut him down, and I'll fight this fucker: knife or no knife."

"No!" Walsh snapped, turning back to Travis, the panic in his eyes. "No. You promised me that Eric would die. You told me he would hang."

Travis seemed to study Walsh, his expression unmoving as he took him in.

"You told me your word was your bond," Walsh rasped.

Travis's smirk broke free, and he leaned closer to Walsh. "I lied."

The words *I lied* fell easily from the mouth of the man who once claimed that lies were punishable by death.

With a click of his fingers, Travis had given the instruction to bring Eric down. The chains rattled around him, and his red, raw, bleeding body swayed as two Navs began to lower and release him. Eric's knees weren't about to hold him up, though, and I opened my mouth to shout for someone to catch him when I saw Ayda moving quickly from the corner of my good eye, her agile body slipping past the men in leather until she was by Eric's side in a flash. Her arms flew around his stomach a second before the chains released him, and his body fell against her. She took the brunt of it, stumbling back only a few steps before she lowered both of them to the platform as carefully as she could.

"You son of a bitch," Walsh hissed.

"You said you wanted to end Tucker's life, Mayor," Travis whispered. "You begged me to let you be the one to sink a knife into his chest if my memory serves me correctly. You just never made it clear which Tucker you were referring to."

"You know I meant Eric," Walsh ground out. "You've set me up. You lying, crooked bastard."

"Careful. I can always take that knife away from you and let young Tucker kill you with his bare hands. There's hunger in those bust up eyes of his, and he looks ready to hunt."

Walsh turned back at me. His weak, shot-up arm limp as he pushed himself off the ground and began to stand on shaky feet. He looked all around him, at every man and woman within in his sight, the fear of what was about to happen taking over.

There were no tricks he could pull here.

No deals to negotiate.

No bodyguards standing in front of him.

No way for him to slip away unharmed.

He was terrified, and I fed off it, raising my chin proudly as I stared back at him.

"You're all going to die for this," Walsh whispered, more to himself than anyone around him. "And if you don't die, you'll rot in prison for the rest of your lives."

Travis stood, too, and with a sigh of impatience, he pushed Walsh in the back, sending him stumbling forward and into the makeshift ring.

Walsh took one last look around, sensing his fate, and then he leaped forward, his footing off as he lunged the knife right at me like a damn musketeer. Hopping to the left, I dodged his feeble attempt and reacted quickly, my fist landing on the edge of his jaw, sending his head back and his teeth practically rattling in his mouth.

He groaned and found his feet, shaking off the punch and blinking wildly to try and refocus on me. He moved again, this time aiming for the other side where I couldn't see so well. The tip of the knife grazed across my left bicep, right at the same time as I landed another uppercut under his chin, sending him crashing back until he was sprawled out on the concrete.

I straddled his chest, reached over for the knife in his hand and spun it around in mine, wiping at my face with my forearm to clear more blood away. It was trickling down faster now, spots of red landing on the mayor beneath me, making me dizzy.

Walsh's eyes were wide. But the mayor was a coward, and cowards were only able to win a fight when someone else was doing the dirty work for them. Now he had to use his own fists, the fear of what would happen if he did had taken over, and every ounce of arrogance Mayor Walsh had ever owned was officially as dead as he was about to be.

Leaning forward, I gripped his throat tight in my hand, and I held the knife horizontal above my fingers, pressing the edge of the blade against his throat as I looked down at him.

"Give me one good reason why I shouldn't kill you," I whispered.

"Drew, I beg of you." His panic sent a shiver of icy coolness up my spine. I'd seen many a man cower before me this way, and I'd never felt the way I felt holding Walsh's life in my hands, knowing I could be the one to make him take his last breath.

"Would you have mercy if this fight had gone the other

way?"

"Kill him… Drew," my father croaked, his cough rough and dirty, making me glance his way. The relief I felt from hearing those three words had my hand loosening around Walsh's throat. I was too lost in the visual in front of me. Eric and Ayda, both of them alive.

Walsh buckled under me, bringing my attention back to him. I pinned him back in place, lifting him and smacking his head down onto the hard concrete beneath us with a sharp crack. His body sagged, and he released a groan.

"Don't," he cried weakly. "Don't kill me. T-think of Rubin. Think of him. Think of how he'll hate you. I'm his father, Drew. I'm his dad. His only dad. You end my life, and he'll never forgive you. Rubin deserves so much mor—"

"Fuck you," Eric spat, venom tainting his every word.

"Drew," Walsh croaked up at me, his eyes getting wider. I could feel the panic in the pulse around his neck, and I watched as the veins in his head became more prominent, and his skin turned a deeper shade of red. "If you care for Rubin at all, you won't kill me. You won't kill his father."

"You're *not his fucking father!*" Eric roared, his raspy voice, painful and distressed. When I glanced back at him, he was on all fours, coughing up more blood, staring up at Walsh and me through narrowed, desperate, pleading eyes. "You're not Rubin's father and you know it. We both know it," he breathed.

I frowned hard, staring at Eric. When he looked up at me, I saw a million apologies and a single request staring back at me.

"What?" I frowned, my whisper strangled.

Eric sucked in a breath, and on his exhale, my whole

world shifted. "I'm Rubin's father, Drew. He's *my* son—the reason I had to leave Babylon. The Navs, Walsh… they forced me out. Walsh didn't want me around Rubin. I had to get away from him and Walsh's wife, Carolyn. I had to do it to save you. If I didn't, they were going to kill you and every Hound we knew." Eric coughed again, his body swaying into Ayda who was wide-eyed and trying to hold him up. Blood fell from Eric's mouth and he fell, but his pleading eyes never strayed from mine. "Do what I should have done ten years ago. End that son of a bitch. End Walsh. Do it for me. Do it for you. Do it for *Rubin*."

CHAPTER THIRTY
AYDA

Everything seemed to just stop. Even the pounding beat of my heart slowed to a crawl as I held Eric, now panting with pain, upright as we knelt together under the altar he'd been strung up on

Eric Tucker was Rubin's father?

He'd slept with Carolyn Walsh?

Drew's eyes were on Eric, even while his grip around Walsh's neck stayed unrelenting. It took me a moment to realize that Travis didn't seem as surprised as the rest of us were, and if he was in any way shocked, he hid the emotion well. Trigger crouched close to the mayor and Drew, his forearms resting on his knees as he studied the two men with a triumphant smirk on his twisted mouth.

I hated Travis Gatlin even more at that moment because I realized a few important things about him. The man had no honor to speak of. He certainly had no morals. And more importantly, I knew he wouldn't ever stop this war of his.

Travis cared about nothing but satisfying his sick need to break everything in his path. Whether that obstacle was a man in high standing like Mayor Walsh, a rival president like Drew or Eric, or one of his own men. Trigger's only objective was to win by any means necessary, and he wasn't a go around the mountain kind of guy. He would always choose to go through, to take down everything in his path until there was nothing left and the whole world was leveled under his boots.

The worst part was that he seemed to enjoy it.

"The way I see it, this is all the more reason to kill this worthless motherfucker, Tucker."

Trigger pointed at Walsh casually with one finger, but his eyes were on Drew, waiting for a reaction, knowing that this revelation would only complicate things further.

Drew stared at Travis, his mouth tight before he looked back at Eric in disbelief. "Rubin? He's my brother?" he asked, his voice one I barely recognized. It was so soft and almost innocent-like. A harsh contrast to the broken, bleeding man who looked capable of being nothing but murderous toward the person in his grip.

My heart ached for him. The hits were coming one after the other lately, and as much as I wanted to go to Drew, to help in some way, I knew that we were in the middle of a fight for our lives and that wouldn't be welcomed. Instead, I helped Eric straighten as much as he was capable, encouraging him to respond while my eyes moved to Trigger.

Eric sucked in a breath and nodded once at Drew.

"So many secrets. So many lies," Trigger whispered, enjoying every minute.

Drew's attention snapped back to him. "You shut the fuck up, Travis before you find yourself trading places with Walsh."

Trigger laughed roughly and held up his hands, mocking Drew as he pretended to concede.

Drew looked down at Walsh, the muscles in Drew's arms popping as he used all his strength to pin the mayor down. It seemed like his whole body was shaking as he stared down into his eyes. "Is this true?" he ground out.

"Y-yes," Walsh croaked, struggling to grab a full breath as Drew pressed down.

"Fuck!" Drew snapped, removing his hand from Walsh's neck at once. Walsh reached up to touch his throat, his red face on the verge of turning purple, and he managed to pull in a rough breath, the sound of it harsh, forcing him to wheeze and cough.

Drew knelt over him, the heels of his bloody hands pressing into his own forehead.

His head had been in the fight, his guard up and walls in place, but now his thoughts were elsewhere, on a boy who was probably sitting in The Hut, wondering if the man he thought was his father was still alive.

"Finish what you started, Tucker."

Dropping his fists to his thighs, Drew opened his closed eyes and glanced at Trigger. He rolled his chin back and forth, studying the Nav in front of him. Then he glanced at me, at Eric, finally settling on Mayor Walsh beneath him.

"I should…" he began quietly, flexing his fingers out before curling them back into tight, bloody fists. "I should finish what I started. I want to. I want to end this son of a bitch's life for everything he's put my father through. For everything he's put my club through… me through. He's responsible for every bad thing that happened to me inside Huntsville, which means a lot of my demons belong to him."

"Son…" Eric tried to interrupt but Drew ignored him, his focus on Walsh as he talked about him like he wasn't even there.

"I should want to draw his last breath from him for Rubin… because no kid hates the man they think is their father the way he hates you, Walsh. Not unless you've done some fucked up, shitty things to him." Drew leaned closer, and Walsh's eyes were wide, his body too weak and his heart too cowardly to react. "But you don't deserve to die. You deserve to live—to look over your back every second of every fucking day, wondering where the bullet to end your life will come from. I won't be the guy to give you the easy way out. You're not worth being another life on my conscience. You're not worth shit." He spat, making sure it hit Walsh's chest before he slowly began to climb off him, coming to a stand by his side.

Drew looked up at me, and he held my gaze. "I believe I only have one person left to fight for. Let's get this final round over with. I want to go home."

With a flick of Trigger's wrist, Walsh was pulled to the edge of the fight circle and dumped between two of the Nav's who were nursing their wounds.

"Walsh won't let this go," Eric grunted, panting through the pain as more of his weight came against me. "He won't stop until I'm dead, the club is destroyed, and Rubin is broken, Drew."

Drew paced like a caged tiger, all strength and focus as he scanned the crowd waiting for the next man to step up. He was tired, but his spirit was still there. He was determined to get us out of this.

"I doubt Trigger will let him walk out of here alive," I said under my breath, all of my focus on Drew as he rolled his shoulders.

"Ayda, don't be naive," Eric hissed in my ear before coughing in pain. "Trigger's not going to let *any of us* walk out of here alive."

The freezing fingers of realization worked their way down

267

my spine as Eric's words sank further than just the surface of my skin and began to take root there.

He was right.

When my gaze found Trigger shrugging his cut from his shoulders, I started to see all of this through the eyes of Eric, a sight that didn't have the light of hope tainting the edge of it.

Jesus Christ, I was stupid.

It was all so clear to me now.

Travis was planning on taking on Drew in this last round, and he wasn't intending on following any of the usual fighting rules Drew was adhering to on this battlefield he'd built. Trigger wasn't going to allow Drew to walk away from this warehouse tonight no matter what happened, and he was going to make damn sure the boys and I would be another set of nails in that coffin for him.

"You heard the words from his mouth yourself. He lies," Eric whispered as Trigger's shirt came off and his scarred and tattooed chest appeared. A reaper with a scythe and assault rifle spread from the middle of his chest to his lower waist like a death omen.

Beating his chest with his fist, Travis released a sadistic laugh that made my chest ache in trepidation. I watched him wind himself up, pace along with Drew, his strides wider and stronger because he was fresh and full of energy. Then he pointed his fist at Drew—his eyes bright and full of murder.

"My turn, motherfucker."

Drew's eyes narrowed, and I wished I could know what he was thinking as he stared at Trigger through one eye, the other too swollen for him to see anything clearly.

"Cat got the Hound's tongue?" Trigger asked with glee, his bounces energetic, his muscles sharp and flexing, ready for the fight.

Drew followed him, his gaze unwavering, going wherever Trigger went as he danced around, stretching his neck from side to side.

"This wasn't part of the rules," Drew pushed out.

"There are no fucking rules, pup. Not today. Not after you recently accused me of being a coward and avoiding a fight. What was it you said? That I slip into the background and shoot people in the back of the head because I'm too afraid to fight them man to man? Well, here I am."

"You don't want to do this," Drew warned him.

"Damn, I do. I've waited a long time to sink a fist into your flesh." Trigger smirked, and he lunged forward at once, his arm jabbing out sharply to hit Drew on the left shoulder, sending his body in a twist until he corrected his footing.

The Hounds stepped forward, stopped by the men flanking them all on either side, their rifles pointed high. They'd chosen not to leave, and they were going to see this through to the end. Jedd was looking around him, the VP trying to save his president by any means necessary, before he leaned into his cut, his mouth moving as he whispered something to himself. If he was choosing now to pray, I wasn't going to argue with it.

"Kill him, Drew," Deeks shouted, sounding less like Deeks than ever before.

"Yeah." Trigger grinned, bright and sadistic. "Come kill me, Drew." He beckoned him closer with his hands, but Drew was no fool.

He waited patiently, flicking his head to remove the blood that was dripping into his eye whenever he could. Frustration poured from him, but so did his ability to fight. Trigger looked like he could take any man in here. Drew looked like he'd already done it and won a thousand times already.

"One more round," Drew said quietly.

CHAPTER THIRTY-ONE
DREW

*O*ne more round.

My arms had turned to lead—the pain in my knuckles and fists like acid on the skin, yet it was my mind that hurt the most.

I'd got out of so many situations by the skin of my teeth, and now I had it all to win, the sense of loss hung over me, ready to bring me to my knees. I'd met some sick motherfuckers in my time, but Travis Gatlin was up there with the worst, and whether I won this fight or not, he wasn't about to let me get out of this alive. I just had to make sure Ayda and the baby got out. That was the one goal that kept my body driving forward with a need to kill.

It didn't matter if I died, as long as they got to live.

My thighs throbbed, my chest fucking ached, and my feet were getting sloppy as the disruption to my vision made everything off balance.

"Come on, Tucker," Slater hissed at me.

"You've got this, Drew," Kenny shouted to me. "Get off, motherfucker," he snapped at someone else. I didn't have time to look or listen to any of them.

Trigger's smile had slipped as he concentrated on the thrill of the kill and pulling in enough breaths to keep him moving. His first serious shot came in triplicate, my jaw taking the first hard jab, and my chest tensing against the second before he rounded it off with a hit that made my teeth rattle.

Grunting and shaking it off, I blinked away to move the blood, and I tried to see through the red spots that were blurring the world around me.

Trigger's teeth were bared through his smile, his amusement clear.

"Too easy," he panted, two-stepping closer to me to throw another, but I managed the dodge this time, and Travis went past me, quickly finding his feet and bringing himself back around.

"If it were that easy, you wouldn't feel the need to stay on your toes and bounce a-fucking-round like that."

Trigger planted his feet in place, his legs wide apart, his shoulders sagging as he looked at me. "This better for you?"

I moved quickly, my left fist aiming for the fucker's eye. If I could only see out of one, he sure as shit was going to have the same impairment.

Trigger's head snapped back from the impact of my fist to his face, his laughter sadistic, and I took the chance to hit him in the chest over and over while I had him. Speed was no longer my friend, and I was going to make the most of every opportunity I got.

When I bounced back on my toes and took a chance to drag in a feral breath, I watched Trigger lift a hand to the eye I'd hit, his fascination clear when he pulled it away to find a stream of blood on his fingers.

"Damn, that felt good," he whispered, looking back up at me. "I'm going to enjoy this."

He was soon moving again, circling me effortlessly, and

taunting me at every chance he got. Trigger was too quick, and before I could maneuver my body to launch an attack on him, he was on me, pouring every punch he could muster onto my already bruised and beaten body, making sure he got my face, my arms, my stomach, and even throwing in a punch to the side of my head. I drew my arms up, blocking him as best I could, but I couldn't see for shit. It was raining red in front of me, and I was a blind man having to feed off sounds and energy, knowing I needed to make an escape before this turned into the very thing I was trying to avoid.

"Fuck!" Trigger laughed, his panting breaths as loud as his cries of victory when he stepped away from me. "Come the fuck on, Tucker." He punched me again, my chin taking the brunt of it, sending me stumbling back until I had to press my hands to my knees and pull in some fucking air.

"Kick his fucking ass, Drew. You've got this." Ayda's voice should have been lost in the sea of people, but it was the only feminine sound in the room, and it stood out from the rest.

I blinked hard, opening my eyes as wide as I could get them as I looked up through fucked-up eyes to see Trigger staring at me, waiting to kill.

This wasn't a fight for me. I was fighting for her.

The grunt I released drove me forward, and I swung at him harder than I'd ever swung at anyone, the roar of survival tearing at my throat. My fist hit him like thunder, the smack to the left side of his head making his eyes roll to the side, his mouth to fly open, and his body twist and turn to the side. I caught his impending fall with a returning left punch to the right side of his face, my features twisted in anger and the blood rushing to my brain, my rage uncontrollable.

Trigger was gone, his head and body shook as he stumbled back, right into the arms of his waiting Navarro Rifle's brother, who caught him in his arms. When Trigger's eyes opened, his lips parted, and he stared up at me, dazed and somewhat confused.

I stood there, fists hanging down by my sides, and I stared right back at him, my teeth grinding together and my nostrils flared as I struggled to breathe.

"Get up," I demanded quietly.

He stared. His silence his only response.

"I said... get up."

Trigger swallowed, letting a slow smile grace his bust-up face as the Nav behind him guided him back to his feet. His body swayed as the aftershocks of my attack rattled through him.

That's right, motherfucker. Feel me in your bones. There's more where that came from.

He leaned into his brother and whispered something, following it with a wink before Travis turned back to me and tapped his fists together.

"Okay, Tucker. You've shown me your strength. Can feel it in my damn balls, brother." He laughed roughly. "No more performances. Now it's time to fight how real men fight."

I had no idea what the fuck he meant. I could hardly see anything, and my head felt like it was about to roll off my body, the lightness of it making the room spin around me. My feet seemed to move of their own accord, and I stumbled to the side, forcing my shoulders back and my chest out in a bid to stay upright.

Every Hound around me grew louder, their voices one big sound of noise I could no longer decipher, and when Trigger stood toe-to-toe with me, I saw my short future playing out ahead of me.

But only one voice stood out.

One voice I hadn't heard in a very long time.

Pete:

"A true leader looks their enemy in the eyes and he says, 'I'm never gonna back down, no matter what you throw at me and no matter how beaten to the ground I am. If you want to win this fight, you're going to have to kill me.' Do you get that? There's no in between. No middle ground. No negotiations. This is do or die. A leader—a true leader— they'll do whatever it takes to make things go their way."

The memory of him was so real that I had to blink hard to refocus on the world in front of me.

My body swayed as I widened my eyes to stare back at Trigger.

"You with me, Drew?" he asked in a whisper, taking a controlled step forward.

Widening my nostrils, I inhaled and exhaled slowly, watching as his eyes taunted mine.

"I'm not a man of honor, and I'm not ashamed to admit that. What I am is the real deal. I'm a real man, and real men do whatever they have to do to win," he whispered at me, taking a final step closer until there was nowhere else to go.

He stared into my eyes, holding them hostage.

And then I felt the nick of something sharp slice through my skin, just under my ribs.

Wincing, I pulled in on myself, scowling up at Travis, who simply stared at me with no emotion.

I'd been cut, deeply, my head spinning from the pain.

The noise of my brothers grew around me, but I was

locked in on my enemy. The rest of the world was fading to nothing.

"Fuck you," I spat as bile rose in my throat.

"See you on the flip side, brother," Trigger breathed, and in a strike so powerful, he rained his punches down on me, one after the other, after the other, after the other.

I brought my hands up to fend him off, my body not giving in just yet, and I fought back, ducking and weaving, despite everything being on fire while the icy fingers of death trailed its finger down my spine at the same time.

Scars were being reopened.

Skin was being torn from my chest.

Sweat mingled with the blood.

Stars appeared in front of me, mixing with red and black until I wasn't sure where I was or who I was with anymore.

With one last swing, I lunged forward, hoping to connect with something that felt like flesh and bone. Instead, I missed, and my legs gave out from under me.

I fell, my body straight and uncooperative, sailing to the cold, rough ground with a thud, my cheek hitting the deck and bouncing back up before hitting the concrete once more.

The sound went off, the silence piercing and painful in my ears.

The taste of warm metal collected in my mouth.

And when I tried to open an eye, my whole world tilted, with Ayda's blurry face scrunched up in the distance.

I love you, darlin'. I failed you.

Then the pain stopped, and I closed my eyes, letting myself sink into the black.

CHAPTER THIRTY-TWO
AYDA

The moment Drew's body hit the concrete I was on my feet. Across the room, The Hounds were in various states of attack, trying to break free from their guards so they could reach, and save their president. Jedd was doubled over, one of the two Navs surrounding him coming in for another swing while he was down. Slater was in a knockdown, drag-em-out fistfight with two more enemies, his hair a mess. A bloody streak tore down his chest as he moved from one Nav to the other, only allowing himself to be distracted by Drew's body when he was between the two attacking him. Kenny was face down on the concrete, held down by a couple more as he bucked and struggled, his cheek being pressed into the dusty rubble beneath him, and Deeks was holding his own with two men over by one of the machines he'd tried to circle around. Moose was with an injured Ben, the two of them working their way through the swarm of Navs that stood between them and Drew, neither one of them caring for their own lives anymore... only the club's president.

It was pure bedlam, but all I could think about was Drew and the dark pool of blood that was slowly growing around him. I tried to run, to get to close enough to help him, but

I found myself just as restrained as the rest of them. Only none other than Eric Tucker himself was holding me back. He was still weak. I could feel that in his shaking limbs, and his desperate grip on me was using every last vestige of his strength.

"So help me, God, if you don't let go of me!" I screamed in a blind rage, my hands swinging at his arms to dislodge him. "Eric, let me go!"

"Ayda, think, goddammit."

Think? He wanted me to *think* while Drew was laying face down on concrete, very likely bleeding to death.

"Do you want to end all of this once and for all?" he growled, his hand tightening around my upper arm as he pulled himself to his feet, using me as leverage. I was so close to hyperventilating, my body trembling like a tuning fork. All I could think about was getting to Drew, and my pathetically weak body was being restrained by a man who'd been half beaten to death.

"W-what do you think?" I finally stuttered, trying to shake him off. Panic was rising, clawing its way from the deepest depths of me.

"Trigger is going to kill Drew, and he'll kill *you* if you get in his way. Drew won't fight to live if you take yourself away from him on some suicide mission. Don't you get it, Ayda? Drew's got too much to lose, so you have to keep yourself safe, and give him something to damn well live for."

Those words made me stop and stare at Eric. His eyes were so similar to Drew's that looking into them made my heart ache. A quiet keening of pain rose in my throat, my gaze flickering to Drew.

"This motherfucker said no rules, right? Which means

his assholes can't contest anything we do to help Drew win that fight now. That asshole is showboating for his men. He's egging his boys on to take out The Hounds, knowing they will fight to the death to save Drew. You and me are all that's left. You gotta get out there and get me a gun. I swore to Drew that... I can't..." He sounded as frustrated and worried as I felt.

We both glanced to where Trigger was circling Drew, the knife catching the light as he moved, both of us growling as he kicked Drew's side and sent a ripple of anger through The Hounds that were already fighting. Eric was right—Trigger was trying to stir up every guy in our MC, and taunt them to continue the fight.

He wanted every one of us to die, and for it to look like it was our idea.

It was up to Eric and me to stop this.

I turned back to Eric. "Where the fuck am I going to find a gun?"

Releasing a painful lungful of breath and wrapping his arm around his ribs, Eric nodded to one of the guys guarding Travis. His back was to us, his broad shoulders filling out the cut with the Navs' patch across the back.

"He has one in the back of his pants. If you can get us close enough, grab the gun and get it to me. I'll do the rest." He gave me a stern look—a look that Drew had once given me himself. He reminded me so much of his son. "After that, you get yourself to safety."

"But—"

"Trust me." He groaned in pain. "For once in your goddamn life just *trust me*, Ayda."

I stepped into him, my shoulder easing under his armpit to support most of his weight. I moved us as quickly as I could manage, dragging him away from the altar and into the fight that raged around the open space of the warehouse. It felt like I was standing in the middle of a football game. Men were throwing themselves at other men, the coppery smell of blood and sweat mingling and tainting the air, making it thick and heavy. The grunts of pain and growls of rage were followed by thunderous steps as they charged at one another like raging bulls. Eric and I were walking straight through the center of it all.

Eric grew heavier with every step we took. More of his weight seemed to come down on me as exhaustion and fatigue set in, his breaths hard and labored while blood oozed from the cuts Trigger had left on his chest. If Drew's life hadn't been on the line, I probably would have slowed down and helped him more, but my driving force was now in my line of sight. Although every step felt like I was carrying three men on my back, I took it, and forced myself to go to the next and then the next until I was panting with as much effort as Eric was.

"Leave me here and go now," Eric groaned when we were only ten feet from our target. He was holding his side with his other hand and fighting to stay on his feet when he uncurled his arm from my shoulders and stumbled forward. "We're running out of time."

He wasn't wrong.

Trigger was already growing bored with the fighting around him, and Drew was beginning to stir at his feet—two things that didn't leave us with much time to get the job done.

"Be careful," Eric said, barely blinking as I stepped away from him.

I nodded, focusing on the one thing that could force me forward.

Drew.

I broke through the fight that Kenny was in the middle of. Kenny had been surprised at my presence and had worked around me, his instinct to get me the fuck out of there overruled when another Nav stepped in on his other side and took a pot shot. I'd seen that defiance in Kenny's eyes and pushed onward, finding myself barely three feet from the Nav that Eric had pointed out to me.

I could see the gun sticking out from the waist of his jeans, and I hoped to God that the weapon would be in my hand long before he realized what I was doing. But before I could take so much as a step forward, one of the Navs smacked into my body, sending me surging into the guy who I'd been sneaking up on.

The moment I collided with his broad back, he was spinning with a roar of rage. On instinct, his hand wrapped around my throat, and he held me close, reaching around to his back to grab his gun, but it was too late for him.

The moment our bodies had made contact, I'd moved without thinking and pulled the thing free.

"Bitch!" He said it with so much rage and hatred, spit splattered across my cheek, and I saw Trigger's attention move to me from the corner of my eyes.

I mentally pleaded with him to keep his attention on me instead of Drew. Watch me die! But Trigger didn't care about me in the grand scheme of things. He cared about winning, and I now happened to be in the perfect place to watch him murder Drew mercilessly.

In a pure moment of desperation, my heel slammed into the Nav's instep before I bounced my foot from the concrete and swung my knee up, sending his balls traveling to his throat, the pain forcing him to release his grip on me.

As I stumbled away, my first instinct was to check on Drew. Trigger was already bearing down on him with his knife raised, ready to end it all while Drew was out cold.

It just couldn't end this way.

It couldn't.

Fear made a scream form on my lips, but fear also made me swallow it whole.

Drew's life was now in my hands, and I only had a second to make the call.

I knew that I wasn't a good enough shot to hit a moving target, and the only person I knew for sure who could, was more than ten feet away on the other side of a fight. There was no way to make a run to Eric, and I turned to find him in desperation and found him frozen, his eyes on Drew and Trigger with horror painted over his features.

"Eric." The sound came out strangled, yet he heard it, and he looked right at me.

One glance.

Eric gave me that one glance, and I risked everything by tossing the gun through the air with all the strength and determination I had.

It was a one in a million shot.

A risk I shouldn't have taken, and when Eric snatched the gun from the air and closed his hand around the grip easily, it made me blink in shock. One twist of his wrist and he had the barrel aimed at me in a heartbeat.

"Down."

I fell to my knees and heard the shot just as the shocking and painful impact of my knees on concrete rocked through my body. I scrambled on hands and knees, spinning just in time to catch the look of amused shock on Trigger's face as a drop of blood trickled slowly from a small hole in his temple.

His eyes remained open, a look of shock forever etched on his face, and the knife tipped over the edges of his fingers, falling from his hand as his muscles seized.

The moment Trigger's body fell, so did the silence of the warehouse, making the impact of him hitting the concrete ring out all around us.

The fighting had stopped as suddenly as it had begun.

Yet, my thoughts were on one thing and one thing only.

Drew!

The scream of his name in my mind was so clear. I was moving, scrambling on hands and knees toward him before I'd made a conscious thought to do so. I reached out with force, my fingers finding the chilled skin of his, the screaming truth of our reality now brutal in my mind as I crawled closer.

No, no, no, no, no.

Drew still wasn't moving.

He was cold.

I raised my head to scream at anyone to get help, but the sound was muted as a blast came from the front of the building. An army in black stormed the room like a flood in the desert. The white ATF badge emblazoned across their chests as they held their guns raised on the men bleeding and bruised, all staring at Drew and me with the same horror I felt inside.

Pressing my head against Drew's in resignation, I wrapped an arm over his motionless body in an attempt to protect him.

The way he'd given his everything to try and protect me.

CHAPTER THIRTY-THREE

HOWARD SUTTON
CHIEF OF POLICE
BABYLON, TEXAS

"**N**obody move!" Winnie shouted, her voice sharp.

"On your knees!" an ATF officer yelled.

"Hands behind your head!" another cried.

There were noises everywhere. Grunts, cuss words, angry faces, and bloodstained skin all around.

With my gun aimed in the air, I scanned the crowds, seeking out The Hounds' patch on leather and only seeing Navarro Rifles tattoos and colors at every turn.

"I said nobody move!" Before I could turn to see who Winnie was yelling at, a shot rang out, followed by a heavy, guttural moan that sounded like three-hundred pounds of man flesh falling to the ground.

Then I saw Jedd.

Followed by Slater.

Kenny, too.

Relief flooded me when Moose's long hair was pushed from his face, his hands rising slowly in surrender.

My eyes, slowly adjusting to the diluted light, looked up

toward the faux altar that had been placed inside the ropes of a ground-level boxing ring, and then they fell to the blood-splattered floor.

I saw the body of Travis Gatlin first, and I swallowed in relief, unable to scream with joy because of the law enforcement around me.

A small whimper came from somewhere nearby, and my eyes followed the sound, finding Ayda on the floor with her head pressed against another as she ran her hand over a lifeless body.

The body I soon realized belonged to Drew Tucker.

"Jesus Christ, no," I breathed out, unable to stop the cold shiver of dread that spread down my spine, turning my toes cold as I slowly lowered my gun. "No."

CHAPTER THIRTY-FOUR

KENNY PALOMO
Patched Hound

I couldn't look away from Drew.

He hadn't moved in so long.

Why wasn't he fucking moving, man?

The ATF were shouting out orders left, right, and center, their men and women armed and moving through us like we were all strapped up and set to detonate. They were taking no sides. Every living creature inside this warehouse was guilty in their eyes. The way their bodies were crouched as they moved through us, smooth but cautious, ready to fire at any moment… it said it all.

I should have been scared.

A life behind bars was calling. *I should have been scared.*

But the only fear I felt was for our president—the one who hadn't moved or even flinched since an army of people came charging in to handcuff us all.

"Why the hell isn't he moving, Slater?" I whispered, my mouth slack before I managed to swallow the ball of fear residing in my throat. "He isn't getting up. Drew always gets up."

CHAPTER THIRTY-FIVE

SLATER PORTMAN
SERGEANT AT ARMS

"Get the fuck off me," I hissed, shrugging an ATF fucker away when he came around the back and pressed the butt of a gun to my skull.

"Hands at the back of your head... *now!*" he yelled like he thought I even gave a shit.

Raising my hands slowly, I entwined them and did as he asked, pushing up on my knees so I was at his mercy.

None of this mattered.

The ATF didn't fucking matter.

The only person who mattered was unconscious, face down against the ground, blood pouring out of his limp body. Ayda lay next to him with tears streaming down her face as his name fell from her lips over and over. She couldn't even hear the ATF around us. She couldn't see Sutton charging toward her like a father desperate to protect his child.

She couldn't see the way we were all holding our breath, waiting for our president to move.

But he wouldn't move.

He. Just. Wouldn't. Fucking. Move.

Tears filled my unblinking eyes as I stared at my brother. My best friend. The man who'd done more for me and this club than I could ever put into words. The man I'd never seen stay down for so long—not even with a bullet in his arm or a knife wound across his chest.

Ayda's wails of desperation tore free, the sorrow and grief in her screams echoing around the warehouse, sending goosebumps across every part of my body.

"Come on, you son of a bitch," I whispered through gritted teeth. "Get up, brother. Please. Do it for me."

Drew always gets up. He always gets up.

CHAPTER THIRTY-SIX

RICHARD 'DEEKS' TWEEKS
ORIGINAL
Patched Hound

I'd lived long enough to sense real fear in a room.

Half the men were staring at their dead leader, wondering what the hell to do next.

The other half were staring at their leader, wondering if he was dead, too.

I glanced around the men, tearing my eyes away from the desperate way Ayda was clawing at the love of her life: angry, desperate, and so lost it made my chest ache, wishing my Autumn was here to help her.

Kenny's face was pale.

Slater's eyes were filled with unshed tears.

Moose had his head bowed, in respect as well as fear of the unknown.

And Jedd… he had his eyes closed, his hands behind his head, and his chin tilted up to the ceiling.

This was real fear.

All the battles we'd fought. All the times we'd gotten lucky. The men we'd lost. There was no amount of fist-swinging that could save us now. A change was coming. I could feel its return like a long, lost ghost, feeding its way through the cloying air around us.

The memories and dread were crashing into every Hound

around me, leaving each man breathless and weary, too scared to accept what they were seeing.

When I turned back to Drew, he still hadn't moved, and Ayda's body hung over his, her head pressed to his temple as her tears fell in rivers of distress. Her cries of agony made even the strongest of ATF men lower their guns as they stood over her, unable to help, yet unable to stop themselves from the onslaught of sympathy they clearly felt.

They were lovers torn apart, and Ayda was the one left wailing at the skies as her heart cracked wide open for everyone to see.

Howard Sutton was screaming something into his receiver, his arms flailing everywhere, and his mouth moving quickly, but all the words he was shouting were being drowned out by the constant ringing in my ears.

The sense of dread that made me old heart freeze.

And the way my eyes had focused in on Drew's unusually pale skin—paler than I'd ever seen it.

Blood.

Sweet Jesus, there was so much blood.

"Please, Lord," I whispered to myself. "Take me instead. Take me. Let him live. Let Drew live for Ayda. For all of them."

CHAPTER THIRTY-SEVEN

JEDD THOMAS
VICE PRESIDENT OF THE HOUNDS OF BABYLON
Loyal to my brothers.
Undercover for the ATF without
any of my men knowing.
Currently wearing a wire.

I couldn't get enough air into my lungs.

Just breathe, I repeated over and over again.

Those two words were silenced by a more dominant thought:

They should have been here sooner. Winnie promised they'd be here fucking sooner.

I couldn't look at Drew, and I couldn't look at Winnie.

I'd let them down.

She'd let me down.

All her guarantees of our safety—her promises to keep every man free from harm and safe from death now sounded like fucking shallow lies to get me to where I currently was—in a warehouse, surrounded by blood, unable to look at my president who was truly unresponsive for the first time in his life.

Winnie's voice called out to Sutton, her words sharp like a knife in my chest. "Medics on route. Everyone else stay the fuck down."

She should have been here sooner.

"Is he breathing?" Winnie asked someone I couldn't see.

"He'd better be fucking breathing," Deeks muttered to himself.

"Drew, for fuck's sake, man!" Slater's voice was cracked and desperate, his pitch breaking on every word.

Dropping my chin to my chest, I slowly peeled my eyes open and stared straight ahead, the scene in front of me shattering my heart into pieces.

Time froze to imprint that scene to the forefront of my mind for the rest of my life, and when I caught sight of someone moving closer to me, I glanced up through narrowed eyes and watched as Winnie came to a stop and stared down at me with her lips pinched together.

Her regret shone like a dark star.

Her unspoken apology hung in the air.

Her need to hear me say it was okay was obvious.

"Go fuck yourself," I whispered roughly, making sure she heard every ounce of venom I had within me for the traitorous bitch. She held my gaze, unblinking, before I turned away and focused on my president.

I waited for him to move because that's what Drew did.

He always moved in the end.

He always got the fuck up again.

CHAPTER THIRTY-EIGHT

ERIC TUCKER
FORMER PRESIDENT OF
THE HOUNDS OF BABYLON

D rew was on the floor, chest down, the blood we shared now spilling out around him from an open wound in his side.

Everything I'd tried to control had come to a head, bringing us to this very moment.

A moment when I suddenly became useless as I stared at the one person I loved more than anything else in this life.

My son.

While Ayda cried and the air became thick with tension, I closed my eyes and pictured a face I hadn't seen in so very long. A face I missed. A face I needed to come to our rescue.

My sweet Shelby. I'm so sorry for all the mistakes I've made since you left us. I thought I could do this alone. I thought I could be the father he deserved. I've failed you both. I can't do this anymore. I need your help. He needs your help. Save our boy, darling. Please. He needs his momma now.

CHAPTER THIRTY-NINE
AYDA

I t felt like hours I'd spent trying to warm Drew's cold body, waiting for anyone that looked like a paramedic to show up. I wouldn't let anyone touch him as I pressed my hands against the gaping wound in his side, trying to staunch the bleeding. I was so afraid that one wrong touch and the shallow rise and fall of his chest would cease, forcing me to lose the only thing that was reminding me to breathe myself.

Drew was still alive, but glancing at him, I wasn't sure for how long.

Everything seemed to move around us both. The thunderous beat of panic hammered through my chest and deafened me as my heart pumped blood through my body. I couldn't have told you whose hands touched me or who spoke because none of that mattered.

Nothing but Drew mattered.

He had saved me so many times. He'd put his life on the line too much for me, and I wasn't going to let him down now. I couldn't. I kneeled by his side, tears blinding me.

I was so lost in my pleas and cries for him to wake up that I barely noticed when the paramedics finally rushed to our sides. In the blindness of my panic, I tried to fight them off, protectively covering Drew's body with my own to shelter him from the onslaught of new people rushing closer. I didn't see their uniforms until I blinked away a fresh round of tears, and only then did I relinquish control. This forced me to watch impotently as they did their best to save Drew's life, while I batted away any arms of comfort that tried to close in around me.

I would not be moved from his side. Not now. Not ever again.

I tried to keep my composure as they worked on him, throwing around words like internal bleeding, collapsed lung, concussion, but the shivering that worked its way through my limbs made me feel like I was a walking vibration. My teeth clattered together too loud in my own head, and my hands, covered in Drew's blood, trembled wildly. I was a mess, and I knew it, but my wide eyes always stayed on Drew's chest.

The two men working on Drew asked me question after question after question about how he'd got in this state. They asked what he'd been stabbed with, so I pointed to the knife at Trigger's feet.

They asked me how many fights Drew had had. The answer of *too many* stayed in my mind, but I heard another voice from around me—one I recognized as Slater's—offer a number when I couldn't.

"Were there blows to Drew's head?" they asked me. *Only when the other bastards cheated*, I thought. Again, Jedd answered with the number I didn't have as I mumbled under my breath for Drew to wake up.

"Was he hit with anything heavy? Where did he take the worst of the abuse?"

I answered as best I could; reliving every painful memory

as we'd all watched Drew fight for his life.

Slater and Jedd were standing behind me now, and the rest of The Hounds were no longer being detained by ATF agents, each one of them looking stunned as they watched the guys wearing the Nav patches being cuffed and lined up on their knees along the wall farthest away from us. I wasn't entirely sure what had gone down, or why only The Navs were being arrested and taken away. In that moment, I didn't really care what was going on outside of Drew.

I was unwillingly eased away from my place next to Drew enough for them to get him on a gurney, but they couldn't keep me away for long. I stepped right back by his side, my hand on his wrist, running alongside them as they wheeled him out of that fucking hellhole where the midnight blue sky held a spattering of stars. I breathed in my first breath of untainted air only seconds before Drew was loaded into the back of the waiting ambulance.

No one could keep me from climbing into the back of the rig next to Drew. Not the cops, the ATF, nor the paramedics, but they tried. I elbowed one of the agents in the ribs when he tried to hold me back forcefully, an action that was followed by a whole MC growling in defiance. No one else seemed inclined to come close to me after that, so the paramedics made room for me, and I took my seat next to Drew, watching as the paramedic affixed more wires and tubes to various parts of his body.

Terrified, I hadn't said much since they'd asked their questions, but my tears fell uselessly, and my heart pounded painfully as I watched them moving around him.

There was eventually a beep from a machine that had wires connected to pads over his heart. It sounded too slow to be his heartbeat, even in that weird juxtaposition with the sirens screaming all around us as the rig began to move. I didn't know what any of it meant, so I continued to watch that rise and fall of his chest, my breaths moving with his to assure myself he was still alive. Still breathing.

In and out.

In and out.

In and out.

Then... nothing.

Drew had stopped breathing.

So I did, too because breathing without him felt too hard.

I froze in place next to Drew, my breath a heavy weight stuck in my chest as pain pierced my soul, the words: *no, no, no, no, no,* stuck on repeat bouncing around my brain while my lips parted in a silent scream.

I watched as the paramedic sitting on the other side of Drew pulled out a defibrillator while screaming the words, "*He's coded,*" over and over again at the driver who grabbed for a radio and gunned the ambulance. The urgency forced a roar of sound to rise from the engine and tangle with the already long drone of the flat line of the heart monitor and scream of the siren.

My hands were thrown from Drew, leaving me to only blink wildly as the technician pressed the paddles to Drew's bare chest. I flinched when he shouted at me to stay back, and I watched helplessly as he shocked Drew with so much power, his body bounced and arched from the gurney.

I was dying inside, filled with layers of pain and darkness, thoughts and emotions aflame and burning me alive from the inside. I was now a silent ball of torture. I wanted to scream along with that deafening siren that was unrelenting overhead, but I had nothing left in me to give to the outside world. I had no breath in my lungs to release. All I had were tears, rivers of them falling in a constant line that burned my skin as they trailed down my cheeks and dropped from my chin.

I couldn't do any of this without Drew.

I couldn't live without Drew.

I couldn't love without Drew.

I couldn't breathe without Drew.

How was I supposed to survive this without Drew?

I watched silently as the paramedic continued to work over him, placing a mask over Drew's face, the heel of his hand rubbing over Drew's chest doing God knew what. My muscles were now frozen as the paramedic rocked back, placed the paddles against Drew's chest and shocked him again, pausing to watch for a reaction.

Any reaction.

The machine's screen maintained that straight line.

The whining of the machine played that consistent torturous sound, taunting me with its lack of life.

Unwilling to give up, the tech replaced the paddles and dropped one hand to Drew's wrist, watching his screen. I stared at Drew's chest, at the patches of ink… at my name tattooed on his heart, and I waited for those breaths to come back as words of silent prayer fell from me.

"Breathe. Please, Drew, breathe."

I leaned in, my forearms on the edge of the gurney as my lips moved closer to his ear.

"We need you, Drew. We *all* need you. Breathe. Please. Just. Breathe. I love you. Please."

"Just. Breathe."

"Just. Breathe."

"You promised me, you son-of-a-bitch." My voice cracked. "Breathe, goddammit."

The last words tore out of me in rage, but the sound in my throat died with another wail of the siren. I stared at the man I loved with all I had, and I silently pleaded one last time.

Please.

At once, emotion caught in my throat, and I saw Drew pull in a breath only a second before the monitor beeped in that slow stuttered rhythm again.

Alive?

He was *alive*.

For now.

But it was a start, and my Drew never quit on me. Not after he'd made me a promise.

I watched vigilantly, breathing with him.

In and out.

In and out.

Silently begging him to stay with me while my hand held his and my tears fell.

When the ambulance finally came to a violent stop, the doors were yanked open from the back of the ambulance, and a whole team of people greeted us in a cacophony of sound and motion.

Voices, loud and controlled, shouted over one another, making me gasp with surprise and blink against the shock of my reality.

Medical terms were thrown about, and hands tried to grab at me, pulling me away from Drew.

I pushed and shoved them away again, fighting to get close to him, utterly undeterred by the call for security as we ran with the gurney into the bright white lights of the hospital.

I winced against the sudden light into submission, until I clearly saw the rise and fall under the too pale skin of Drew's chest. He struggled to stay with us. His fight was weak. He looked too ghostly under these bright lights, his lips a blue tint under the mask they'd placed there, and his face whiter than the pure driven snow. The sight of it was terrifying, but I swallowed my endless sobs and ran alongside him, ignoring their continued encouragement for me to step aside.

They slowed at a set of doors.

"You can't go any further."

"He's in the best place."

"We just want to help."

"You have to let us do our jobs."

"Let us save him."

And that was the one that finally stuck.

"*Let us save him.*"

I shuddered violently to a stop as they continued, and I watched as Drew disappeared through a set of swinging doors with a team of doctors. Arms barred me, pushing me back as the doors swung closed and locked me out, away from my only lifeline.

"Let us save him."

"Let us save him."

"Let us save him."

"Save him," I quietly demanded of no one in particular while standing feebly on weakened legs, my arms wrapped around my stomach, trying to hold everything together as my world crumbled and shattered into painful shards around me.

I wasn't sure how long I was standing alone there—

waiting.

People and staff came and went through those doors over and over again, walking around me as I stared at the seam of the doors waiting for someone who would tell me what was going on.

Eventually, a kindly woman in scrubs stepped out from them, and with a small sympathetic sigh wrapped an arm around my shoulders and led me into a small area with chairs and vending machines.

I sat, and she took the seat next to mine, her voice a murmur as she asked questions and offered reassurances that went unanswered. I trembled so violently, my teeth made an awful clicking sound, and the tears continued to fall. I knew it was helping nothing, achieving nothing, but the fear of losing Drew, the very thought of not seeing him scowling at me when I did something stupid or seeing that smile he gave me when no one else was looking, or the touch of his strong hands when I needed him the most… it all crushed me.

I had shared so many firsts with Drew in our short time together. I'd discovered so much about who I was when I was loved by the right person. But I hadn't learned every one of his emotions yet. I hadn't taught myself what every line on his handsome face meant. I hadn't explored every scar and muscle on his body. I hadn't had enough time to worship him the way he deserved to be worshipped.

I wasn't ready for everything that we'd shared to be the last of anything.

Our last kiss.

Our last I love you.

Our last smile.

I hadn't had him long enough.

He was my forever, and the thought of saying goodbye crushed me under the weight of it.

I was barely aware that the nurse stayed with me until some familiar faces began crowding the room around me. I wasn't even sure who the faces belonged to.

I was numb and cold, unable to see anything but the door that Drew had disappeared through, my heart barely held together by the last string of hope that I would see him again as people moved around me.

I think The Hounds came in first. The faces I saw were bruised and covered in blood, each one heartbroken and cautious as they studied me like I was a bomb that was about to go off.

The Babylon Police Department showed up in force looking pained, unsure how to approach me or what to do as they set themselves up as a barrier between The Hounds and the ATF.

The ATF agents who had showed up behind them were standing around the information desk, looking concerned and bored at the same time.

The Babylonians who showed up wanted news.

Family, friends, and neighbors alike were all worried about Drew, but I couldn't tell any of them apart because my eyes were still on those fucking swinging doors.

Waiting.

My eyes were still crowded with tears.

Waiting.

My heart still full of hopelessness.

Waiting.

All I could do was wait.

I was waiting for anything.

News.

Information.

Pain.

Torture.

The end of the world as I knew it.

I wouldn't let anyone touch me.

I couldn't.

I couldn't have comfort because I knew it would only allow me to fall apart, and I wasn't sure I would ever be able to put myself back together if I let go of that tentative hold I had right now.

The only beacon of hope I had was focusing on those doors, and any news about Drew that would eventually come through them. I'd almost lost myself to the pain when Tate and Rubin finally sat on either side of me, each picking up a hand and holding the same silent vigil I was holding.

I breathed through the pulsing, painful emotions enough to find my breath encouraged by the strength they loaned me, but almost lost my shit all over again when Autumn took the seat behind me and stroked my hair in that loving maternal way of hers that promised comfort I didn't deserve. There were so many people offering me love and support, and I only wanted the arms of one person.

Drew.

My Drew.

The man who always got up.

The man who had all the answers.

The only man I had ever really loved in my life.

The man that every single person in this room with me loved as fervently as I did. Did he even know how much love existed in this world *for* him?

As if I knew what was about to happen, I looked up a second before the doctor stepped through the doors that Drew had disappeared through. The whole waiting room shifted in that direction, the clatter of chairs and a rolling murmur moved through every last one of the people occupying the space. It had to have been hours since we'd arrived, and not a soul outside of those of us waiting for news on Drew was in that room. The mood was too volatile.

"Mrs. Tucker?" the doctor asked, stopping about four feet away, trying his best not to stare at the crowd that had gathered behind me.

I rose to my feet and felt Tate's hand steady me as I rocked on my heels and tried my best to find the strength in my legs. I nodded, not even attempting to correct him.

"I'm Doctor Atwood," he said, pausing again and glancing behind me. He motioned me forward, and I stepped to him. Lowering his voice, he continued quietly. "We had to take Drew into emergency surgery to stop the bleeding. He's still in critical condition, and he may need more surgeries before the night is over, but his father, who was also admitted, suggested that your husband would do better with you in the recovery room with him."

Doctor Atwood swung a hand out to the doors in an invitation for me to walk with him, and selfishly, I didn't so much as glance back at the men behind me as I started walking.

My only need at that moment was to get to Drew.

He was alive.

I took my first real breath in hours and caught up with him.

I listened to the doctor talk as we walked through the

hospital with quick steps, his words not really sinking in as he threw around medical terms I couldn't understand. I caught a few important things. Drew had swelling around his brain, which could be a concussion. The knife that had gone through his side would have punctured his lung had it not been for his rib, which now had a fracture from the blade. He had four broken ribs, an orbital fracture, in which they had immediately realigned at the sphenozygomatic suture line, and they were watching his blood work to make sure there was no internal bleeding. Aside from that mouthful of medical terms, I did pick up some extra key points that I'd needed to hear.

Drew was in critical condition.

He'd won a single battle for now but was still amidst the war of recovery.

Lastly, I needed to be prepared for what I was about to be faced with.

I was very glad about that last warning.

Walking into the hospital room and seeing all of the wires and tubes connected to Drew's body almost broke me. He looked frail, lost amidst a sea of gray and white plastic, while small lights flashed on monitors and machines beeped, not allowing for silence. I stumbled inside with my hand on my mouth—my tears filling my eyes again as I sank down into the chair next to his bed and just stared at him.

"I'll send in a nurse with some scrubs for you to change into, and something to eat. Your father-in-law also said you were pregnant."

I nodded. Not really paying that much attention to what he was saying now. Being this close to Drew, seeing his breath forcing his chest to rise and fall helped, I could finally see with my own two eyes he really was alive.

"Doctor?" I asked suddenly, my voice hoarse and broken.

"Yes, Mrs. Tucker?"

"Can I…" I stopped and took a deep breath as my voice cracked. "Can I touch him?"

Doctor Atwood paused at the door, a kind but sad smile passing over his lips. "You can eventually, but first I'll send in a nurse with a change of clothes for you, and some toiletries. You're still covered in his blood, and your husband is in a delicate state. He can't afford an infection."

I looked down at my hands and studied the long-dried dark blood that coated my fingertips and forearms. I nodded in agreement. When I looked up again, the doctor was gone, and I was finally alone with Drew and a room full of machines that were keeping him alive.

A shower was a good idea before I touched him, I decided.

Leaning in closer, I whispered to him, hoping to God that he could hear me.

"You better come back to me, Drew Tucker."

CHAPTER FORTY
AYDA

After that first shower, I only left Drew's side to use the restroom and wash my hands. Nurses came and went, and tests were performed. Some of the guys came to the door to check on us both, and eventually, Drew was wheeled from recovery to intensive care, but I stayed by his side every step of the way.

My body and mind were mostly numb to the goings on around us both. When I slept, it was with my hand under his, my head on the edge of his bed waiting for him to move, to squeeze my fingers and wake me up.

He didn't so much as twitch a finger.

All too soon, that first hellish day rolled into another, and then another. The windows slowly grew dark, casting us in shadows and then, as the machines continued to beep and tick it soon became light again, but still, Drew didn't so much as stir.

The nurses in the intensive care unit encouraged me to speak to Drew almost as much as they insisted on me eating... for the baby's sake. His baby was growing inside of me, and the promises I'd made to Drew helped me keep it all together. A bean and a promise were duct tape on a gaping wound in my soul that wouldn't ever heal until Drew flashed those blue-green eyes at me again.

But a promise was still a promise, and I ate what they put in front of me. I drank the water they set on the surface next to his bed, too—the only space not taken up with machines, wires, and charts.

I paced his small room when my muscles ceased, curled up in the uncomfortable chair like a contortionist while they changed his dressings and checked his stitches, and I also insisted on being the one to help clean him with warm towels.

Drew's face was swollen, black and blue from the fights, and no matter how much the urge to stroke the brow I longed to see frown at me, or run my finger along the lips I loved to see curl into that sexy smile that was mine, I somehow resisted, keeping the slow strokes of my fingers along his arms, where the bruises weren't so intense.

It was a never-ending nightmare that I couldn't escape from. A night terror that I was too scared to step away from in case something changed when I wasn't there. When things were quiet, and I had all the time in the world to think, desperation and fear became my constant companion. That's when the what ifs hounded me relentlessly.

It was in one of those moments that I suddenly found myself not alone anymore for the first time in hours.

"Ayda?"

I looked up to see one of the nurses standing at the door, her smile still holding that sympathy I didn't think I would ever get used to as she studied me.

"Hey, Katie."

"Drew's father is asking if he can come visit with y'all. Is that okay?"

"He's here?" I asked. The last I'd heard, Eric was in

a room of his own being looked after under duress by the nursing staff.

Katie gave me a knowing smile and stepped aside as Eric Tucker shuffled into the room wearing a flannel shirt and jeans, his face almost as bruised and battered as his son's.

"He discharged himself," Katie said with a click of her tongue, her eyes meeting mine to make sure it really was okay before offering a quick nod and stepping out to leave us alone.

I studied Eric for a moment as he limped toward the bed and stared down at his son. He was hunched, one arm plastered to his side, telling me that his ribs were also worse for wear. The pained look in his eye wasn't for his own suffering. That look was for his son. He hated seeing Drew like this almost as much as I did.

"How bad are you?" I asked quietly, moving across the room to grab him the only spare seat in the room. It was hard and plastic, but he seemed grateful for the gesture.

"Fine," he answered robotically, his eyes trained on Drew. It was obvious to me that he wasn't fine, but you couldn't argue with Tucker men. That was one thing I'd learned along the way. "And you?" Eric asked, looking at me reluctantly. "The baby?"

"We're..." I paused, not wanting to use the same word he'd used. "The baby is doing well."

I made my way to the other side of the bed and slipped into my chair, pulling my legs up against my chest as I met Eric's familiar hazel eyes with a pang of sharp pain in my chest at seeing them so vibrant on a face that wasn't Drew's. It was a cruel thought, but I blinked it away as I reached out and slipped my hand under Drew's again, needing that physical connection between us.

"Have you talked to any of the guys?" I asked. As much as I loved the guys, I hadn't put much thought into how they were handling things. It was selfish, but I would deal with the fallout of my guilt for that later.

"Yeah," Eric croaked, leaning forward to rest his arms on his knees as he clasped his hands together and studied Drew again. "They're worried. We all are. I can't seem to hear what they're saying too much when they speak, though… just that they refuse to leave the hospital. Slater's going crazy."

There was a small pang of regret in my chest as I thought about what the rest of them must be going through, especially Slater and Jedd. I knew the two of them held themselves impossibly responsible for this whole thing. When Slater had managed to get past security briefly, I'd pretended to be asleep, unable to face him because I had nothing new to tell him.

"How did it all get so fucked up, Eric?" I asked suddenly, glancing up at him. I wasn't holding him accountable for what had gone wrong by any means, but part of me needed to know how they'd gotten a hold of him to use as bait for Drew.

"You want the long or short answer to that?"

"I just want an answer."

"Short answer: I thought I could take care of things and spare Drew any more shit from men like Taylor, Cortez, Walsh, and specifically Travis Gatlin, so I went to deal with it myself. I tried and failed. Long answer: Travis Gatlin was ready for me, and when I went to drop that Nav's bike back at their club, he decided to make his move. One minute I was outside their yard, staring at Travis and a few Navs I'd seen a thousand times before. The next, he was taunting me, asking me how my son was, how you were, how the whole damn club was. He couldn't get a rise out of me no matter how hard he tried and that pissed him off. Before I knew what was happening, a van pulled up behind me, Navs popping out from behind every wall, gate, tree, and car. You name it, they sprung from it, and I was thrown into the back of the van." Eric's face creased, as though the memory caused him more pain while he stared at Drew. "They did some fucked up things," he whispered. "They had fun with that shit."

I was glad he didn't elaborate. I was pretty sure I'd seen the tame end of Travis's sadistic games twice now, and I wasn't looking for an in-depth insight into the inner workings of his mind. Especially not when it came to someone Drew loved.

"He'd set it all up, already knowing how it would play out," I said, blowing all the air from my lungs. "He knew the guy was following me. He knew Drew wouldn't stand for him being in Babylon, and he somehow knew that one of you would make sure that Nav, or his bike, would make it back to him at one of your hands. Did he know they had a warrant for Walsh?"

"I think Travis Gatlin knew more than any of us could ever have imagined," he offered quietly, a soft sigh of defeat falling free. "I hope he burns in the darkest depths of Hell."

"He said he was the one pulling Cortez's strings," I said, looking down and rubbing my thumb over the back of Drew's hand. "Even Walsh didn't argue that he had some control over him too. How far back does this go?"

Eric turned to me, his eyes searching mine carefully. "Far enough," he eventually answered. "And most of it probably began because of me. Because of what happened with Rubin's mom. Because of the mistakes I made. Nothing breeds corruption like a need for revenge. Everything bad begins because one man's ego became bruised."

I understood that to some extent. Walsh had been a proud man for as long as I'd known him. He looked down his nose at almost everyone in Babylon, but the only times it had ever really bothered me was when he'd taken it out on Rubin. That kid had done everything in his power to be what his father had wanted him to be. He'd made himself sick trying to make the man proud and all the time and effort had been pointless. Walsh was never going to be proud of a boy that wasn't his, but his ego wouldn't let him admit that his wife had cheated on him because appearances were worth more than anything else to him.

"What happened with you and Carolyn Walsh?" I dared myself to ask.

Eric sighed softly, the regret obvious. "We crossed a line we shouldn't have crossed. My Shelby had died. Carolyn was lonely, stuck in a marriage she hated. She's always been a beautiful woman and… things happened that weren't meant to happen."

I could tell he wasn't willing to expand on that, so I had to respect it… at least to some level.

"How long have you known Rubin was your son?" I asked, my thumb gentle over Drew's swollen knuckles.

"From the moment he was born."

I felt a stirring of anger in my belly for the first time in days but swallowed it.

"Did you know Walsh treated him like shit?"

He looked away from me. His movements slow as he stared at Drew and mulled over his response. Eric's shredded hands twisted together, his pose thoughtful and calm, forever in control, even when it seemed that his emotions were sitting closer to the surface than ever before. "I knew he treated Carolyn like shit, and that should have been enough," he answered quietly. "But a moral code isn't something we always get to stick to in this life, Ayda. Everything I did, right or wrong, I did with the intention of it serving the greater good. For the most part, I can admit I got that wrong."

"I understand." I did, I honestly did. I saw some of the decisions Drew had struggled through since I'd known him. "Are you going to tell Rubin you're his father?"

"I can't think about that yet. I can't think of anything that could happen beyond me being in this room with my broken son."

I let a humorless laugh fall from my lips as my eyes clouded with my emotion again. "I know that feeling." I leaned forward, brushing my lips over the dry skin on Drew's knuckles, and I breathed him in. "For the record, I don't think he'll be upset about you being his father. Just maybe that you waited so long to tell him."

"Upset, I can handle. I've had a lot of practice handling that with Drew."

"That doesn't surprise me," I said, my lips curling into a small smile. "You know they say your kids are worse than you just to punish you. What do I have to look forward to? How bad was Drew?"

"Oh," he said through a laugh, straightening his shoulders as a twinkle returned to his eyes. "Drew was an asshole from the moment he could talk. A real pain in my Shelby's side. He was born to be trouble. Anything else, and he'd have been disappointed with himself."

I let off a watery chuckle and gently squeezed Drew's

hand. "Do you hear this, Drew? Are you going to let your old man talk about you like this?"

"Did you know Drew's first word was fuck? Came out as 'uck while Shelby was collecting bread from the bakery. She'd forgotten her purse, and she thought she'd cussed to herself under her breath, but Drew was listening like a hawk, always paying attention. He shouted that word so loud, Shelby didn't dare show her face in town for three weeks. Back in those days, your boy could get a reputation for that kind of language at six months old."

This time I fully laughed, my free hand covering my mouth as the sound cracked from me. Laughing wasn't something I'd done in what must have been days. It sounded foreign to my ears, but hearing about Drew as a child, imagining him at six months old… it made me think more about our baby, about who he or she would look like. How much of Drew would they have in them? How much of my favorite parts of him would translate into his mini-me? It was the first time since we'd arrived in this hospital that I'd thought of anything outside of his health and these four walls, and even now, with him broken in the bed in front of me, I could still see Drew in that future.

He had to be there to share these memories with me. There was no alternative.

"I can't lose him, Eric," I whispered feeling weak and hating myself for saying the words aloud. "I'm not sure I can survive it."

"When has Drew ever quit on us all?"

"Never," I barely said the word aloud as I stared first at Eric, and then the hand covering mine. Drew had never once quit on me since he'd figured out I was what he'd wanted.

"Not once."

"Then we have to believe he isn't about to start quitting now. He's just being a little dramatic."

A stray tear loosened itself and slid down over my cheek as I shook my head with humor. "I'm sure he'd have something to say about that if he was awake. Like it's a trait he gets from you." I sniffed, wiping the back of my hand under my eyes and swiping at the tears. "But I'm kinda hoping he'll be over the drama soon."

"Drew?" Eric smirked. "Never."

CHAPTER FORTY-ONE
AYDA

I shifted on the examination table and cringed at the crinkle of the paper that was there for sanitation reasons. I'd been away from Drew for less than an hour, but that was an hour too long. The nurses and doctors who'd talked me into this had promised me it wouldn't take longer than thirty minutes, and yet here I was wearing a hospital gown on the forty-fifth minute as they examined me.

It was the last time I was going to be doing a 'favor' for anyone.

Damn Eric to hell for suggesting to the nurse that I could be spared.

It was the first time I'd left Drew for more than a toilet break since they'd taken me to him. All I could think was that if anything were to happen while I was gone...

"Okay, as far as we can tell you and your baby are in good health, but with some of the trauma you've faced, just take it easy and get on those vitamins," the hospital gynecologist said with a pat to my leg before she removed the glove from her hand with a snap. "We can give you a scan to make absolutely—"

"No. Not without Drew there," I said over her as I pushed myself to a sitting position. "I can't see the baby without the father being there."

The doctor, whose name escaped me, gave me another sad smile and glanced down at the chart she was holding. It felt very much like she was avoiding meeting my glance, but I turned away before she looked up again, my eyes lingering on an image of a weird cross-section starring a child in mom's uterus.

"You can get dressed now, Ayda. I'm going to ask you to make an appointment with your gynecologist when you can, or come back and see me so we can do a scan. All precautionary."

I slipped behind a room divider and pulled on my own jeans and a hoodie that had been brought to me by Autumn via one of the guys. I was glad of the comfort of it, and I shivered once I was buried in the hoodie again. It was always so damn cold in this place.

"I will," I said, stepping out from the divider so I could push my feet into my boots. "Is there anything I should be eating? Drinking? Other than the vitamins?"

"Stay away from too much caffeine. There are some leaflets available at the front desk, which give you some good guidelines on foods to avoid, etc."

I nodded and headed for the door, with another quick thanks as I rushed through the halls to get back to Drew in his room.

Hospitals weren't always a good place for hope to blossom.

From what I could estimate, it had been five days since Drew had been admitted here, and with every hour that passed, my mind seemed to fall into a deeper pit of despair. He hadn't deteriorated any, but he hadn't improved much, either. Drew

317

was in a stasis that left every single one of us who loved him in a holding pattern, waiting for some kind of hope we could cling to with both hands.

I was so lost in the world of wires and tubes and schedules that I had no idea what was going on outside the room. None of the agents had been to talk to me. Not even Howard had tried to bring up what had happened in the warehouse when he'd looked in on Drew late one night. Up until my talk with Eric, I hadn't been in any shape to talk to any of the guys as they'd drifted through.

My only concern had been Drew. Even now, his name was in every step I took on my way to his room, thinking constantly about what needed to be done before the nurses came in and took more blood. One of the physical therapists had shown me how to help with some movements to keep his muscles active while he was in the bed, and this little side trip had postponed that.

I was so lost in my thoughts that I found myself skipping to a halt the moment I was in Drew's room, surprised by the reaper and hounds staring at me from the backs of Jedd and Slater as they stood shoulder to shoulder looking down on Drew.

"Hey, guys," I squeaked, then coughed and tried again. "Hey."

They turned to take me in; their faces unchanging as they studied me until Slater let out a low whistle and shook his head.

"Shit, Ayda. When was the last time you slept?"

I pushed my loose hair back from my face and walked casually to the other side of the bed to check on Drew. He was still there, still unmoving, still with wires pouring from his body like strings.

"I sleep in the chair," I said, tipping my head in its direction. "You two doing okay?"

Slater glanced down at Drew. "Never been worse."

Jedd shifted, moving around to drop down into the chair Eric had taken while there. His leather creaked as he rested his elbows on his knees and planted his chin on his joined hands. Jedd's face was filled with responsibility and regret, the weight of all this clearly heavy on his shoulders.

Slater reached out to grab Drew's hand, his rough fingers touching Drew's skin only for him to quickly pull back as he shook his head. "I thought him going to prison was bad. Seeing him like this is so much fucking worse."

I'd never had to live through him being in prison, but I understood. At least behind those bars, Drew was up and breathing on his own, that mind of his always working on something. Like this, he was an echo of the warrior we knew and adored. Here, but not here, which was heartbreaking to see.

I reached out to lay my hand on Slater's big forearm in comfort. I didn't know what to say to him, or Jedd, who was watching the scene from under his dark lashes.

"We can't give up on him now. It's bad, but..." I trailed off and looked down at Drew's face, losing the words I'd been saying. "Gotta think positive."

"Yeah," Slater said, his word holding no conviction.

Jedd shuffled his feet, dropping his head into his hands to cover his face. It was a move so un-Jedd-like, it had Slater and me looking at each briefly before turning back to Jedd.

"Slate. Can you give me a minute alone with Ayda?" Jedd asked, dragging his hands down his face, resting his fingers on the edge of his mouth. His eyes were on Drew as he spoke. "Please."

"Now?" Slater asked, surprised.

"Now." Jedd nodded.

Glancing between the two of them with uncertainty, I met Slater's gaze, accepting the wink of encouragement he shot me before turning and leaving the room after one last look down at Drew.

Jedd was watching me, and I saw the bob of his Adam's apple under his beard as I slowly lowered myself to perch on the edge of the chair I now considered mine.

"What's on your mind?" I asked, my voice trembling.

"There are some things I need to tell you. I need to tell Drew, too, but he ain't waking up any time soon like I hoped he would, and the weight of all this is killing me." Jedd closed his eyes, taking a moment for himself before he opened them again and directed his attention to me. "When everything was going down in that warehouse, I was wearing a wire for the ATF."

I blinked at him. Unsure that I'd heard him right.

"What do you mean?"

"When I spent those nights in the cell at Sutton's station, I made a deal with Winnie, the ATF chick, that, I hoped, would get The Hounds off the hook. They had a lot of shit on us Ayda. Nothing solid, but enough to ask a lot of questions. I had to do something, and Eric and I had…" He paused to sigh and run a hand over his forehead. "We'd talked about things. About how we weren't willing to let Drew take the fall again. How we could stop the club from burning to ash and half of us spending a lifetime behind bars. We'd talked about strategies and different roads we could take if we needed to. Drew has a reason to be more than just the president now. He has you, and Eric and I wanted to protect that for him. When you and Drew drove off with Owen that day, I decided that it was my turn as VP to step up and become the buffer between the law and Drew. So, I volunteered my time, and I drip fed Winnie selective information to get her on side. I needed her to see we were the good guys, constantly thrown in shit situations. It started out with her being... well... she was a real bitch. Cutting me off every time I answered a question, applying the pressure when she thought she could press on a weakness. I hated her, Ayda. But something happened during my time in that cell, and I slowly began to break her down. I talked about my brothers, the life, and how we always seemed to be in the wrong place at the wrong time. I planted seeds about Walsh, Taylor, The Navs, the whole lot, and I let her add things up in her own head. The minute she saw the chance to take down someone as prolific as Mayor Walsh, she got promotion stars in her eyes and became a hell of a lot nicer. She agreed to back off the club if I..." He raised his brows, waiting for me to fill in the gap he'd left open.

"If you wore a wire," I finished, pushing to my feet and wrapping my arms around myself.

I stepped to the blinds over the windows and stared out between them at the landscape. The sun was shining too brightly for what I was feeling inside. It was so dark and twisted right now. The one thing I loved about these men was their inherent need to protect Drew and the club. I knew it was always born from a good place. Brotherhood. Camaraderie. Loyalty. I couldn't fault Jedd for that, and if it worked...

"Did she get what she needed?" I asked, holding back the inevitable question that was sitting on the tip of my tongue;

one I knew Jedd was waiting for also.

"Eventually," he muttered roughly. "When Slater told us we had to get to you guys after your SOS, I made the call. I told Winnie we were heading out to get her the proof she would need. Kenny hooked me up with the kit she'd given me—the fool believing me when I told him it was our own kit that I was using to try and entrap the Navs with. Kenny's loyal and obeys rules. They all do. So when I told each and every one of them before we left that they were only to move when I moved, they listened. That's why they watched him fight… because of me." Jedd rubbed his lips together in thought, his brows creasing together. "I had to stand by and watch Drew take punch after punch, unable to go to him and fuck with The Navs because I knew who was listening in. Winnie promised she'd be there sooner. I kept waiting for them to charge through those doors and put an end to the fucking carnage, but one fight turned to two, two to three. I honestly didn't think it would go as far as it went. And now Drew is like this, and we're on the brink of losing someone else who held us all together." His voice cracked on the last word—a big man reduced to sounding like a small, broken boy as his emotion and guilt took over. "And all of it's because of me."

"This isn't your fault, Jedd. She had everything she needed when Trigger put Walsh in that ring with Drew," I snapped harsher than I intended. It wasn't aimed at him. At that moment, I almost wished it were that bitch standing in front of me. Days of anger and fear were coming together inside of me like a ball of rage I couldn't control. "Why the fuck did she wait as long as she did?"

"I've not been calm enough to stand in front of her and ask that question yet." His jaw ticked as he turned his attention back to Drew, his eyes glazing over. "Sutton told me the minute he got there that he was the one to press the button and force them to make the move inside the warehouse. Apparently, he's doing everything he can to make sure Winnie gets her ass out of Babylon and leaves us alone for good, but… I don't know. I don't know if that's for the best since we had her on our side. I don't know if we can trust her or not. I don't know anything other than I should have fought instead of waiting. I should have put myself in front of every man who challenged Drew, and I didn't. I didn't do for him what he would have done for any of us."

"He wouldn't have let you," I said, releasing all the breath from my lungs. "He put himself in that position. He wasn't going to let anyone else go down for him." Another slow and painful truth started to rise with the statement. "He wouldn't have put my survival on anyone else's shoulders."

"I shouldn't have given him a choice."

"You honestly think Trigger would have given a shit about that? He was more than happy to give Drew what he wanted. There were no rules, but it was still his game to play. We were the mice—he was the cat. He wanted every one of us dead."

Jedd covered his eyes with a rough hand. "I keep going over and over in my head when it all got so fucked up, and why it constantly happens to us. We can't lose any more men, Ayda. Especially not him. The club may as well fold if he… *fuck,*" he hissed, unable to say it out loud.

"Drew's not going anywhere," I replied stubbornly. "He can't. He has too much to live for." I studied his face for a moment and glanced back at Drew, stepping toward the bed so I could run my hand down his arm. "He promised he was going to marry my stubborn ass, and Drew never breaks a promise."

CHAPTER FORTY-TWO
AYDA

I was rambling as I worked Drew's legs in a slow stretch to warm his muscles up. It had been a week since we'd arrived in the hospital, and we were finally in a room rather than intensive care, which meant we were dealing with more and more visitors. I had a nifty chair that now unfolded into a bed, so I could lay out and wasn't waking up stiff. That didn't mean the nurses weren't tripping over me during their night checks. Every night, Deeks helped me drag that heavy thing next to Drew's bed before he left to sit in the waiting room all night. My hand would be in Drew's while I slept, just in case he decided that was the moment he wanted to wake up.

The longer we were confined within these walls, the longer Drew stayed motionless in that bed. With that, more hope began to bleed from me. I managed to keep those emotions contained inside. I covered that wound inside my soul with duct tape again and again as they widened into a canyon that began to consume my soul. Those moments we had alone together, I would talk about the future I saw for us. I warned him of my grand plans for building a home for us because we couldn't raise a baby in The Hut. Not really.

Day after day.

Hour after hour.

Minute after minute.

Drew stayed still, stuck in his repose.

Stretching out his leg to its full length, once again, I released an exaggerated put-upon sigh that would have had him rolling his eyes at any other time.

"You realize that I miss admiring your butt, right? Most mornings, when we're at home together, I fake being asleep just so I can watch you walking naked to the bathroom." I rubbed my palms up and down his leg with a quiet chuckle. "My favorite mornings were the ones when you caught me out. It was probably one of *those* mornings that you knocked me up."

I bent his leg again, pushing his limb gently toward his chest before pulling it straight and easing it to the bed, where I trailed the sheet over it. I headed back to the top of the bed where it was angled up, the wires still hanging from him. Glancing down at his face, I sucked in another long breath and released it slowly, leaning in so my lips were only inches from his. The whistle from the air tube under his nostrils was louder when this close to him, but it didn't deter me. I moved slowly around him, my hand sliding to its normal place under his palm as I studied his face.

"I miss you."

Something moved over my hand, and I shot back, thinking there was someone else in the room. After glancing around, I realized we were still alone. The door remained closed, the usual hospital murmur relegated to the other side of it. My eyes drifted down to his hand and studied every inch of his flesh, but it was as it had been every day for the past week; sitting steadily, palm down at his side.

"Drew?"

Looking back up at him, I stared at his face for so damn long I thought I imagined the twitch in his jaw, but after a second of holding my breath, I saw it again, an elated cry falling from my lips, making his foot twitch in reaction.

I wasn't imagining it.

Was I?

Raising my trembling hands, I placed one against his cheek and leaned in again, my lips brushing over his and watching as his eyes moved under the thin membrane of skin too quickly to be just a twitch.

My heart pounded in my chest so loudly I was surprised it hadn't alerted those walking past.

Drew was moving.

He was moving, and it was becoming more and more apparent with every twitch he made.

"Hold on, baby. Just hold on."

I raced to the door, throwing it out of my way and barely flinching when it slammed against the wall. I checked on Drew, and then I stuck my head out into the hall. There was no way in hell I was going to leave him now, and I didn't care who the fuck I woke up in the process.

"Nurse!" I screamed, my eyes flashing back to Drew and noticing his fingers twitching. *"Nurse!"*

I saw the bustle at the station, all of them heading in my direction, so I let the door swing shut and rushed back to the bed, my breathing erratic and heaving as my hand found his. I'd barely squeezed it when his eyes flashed open and those beautiful colors I'd missed so damn much searched the room frantically before finally settling on my face.

"There you are," I whispered.

CHAPTER FORTY-THREE
DREW

Eyes I'd craved to see again stared down at me. Shades of blue I remembered well—the memory distant and groggy in my mind, but there nonetheless.

Shades of blue that reminded me of home: safety, warmth, passion, and strength.

She was smiling as tears fell down her rosy cheeks.

Her face was a dream.

A beeping noise grew faster somewhere to my left, but all I could focus on was Ayda as my body throbbed to life.

My eyes felt sticky, glued together by sleep—sleep that made no sense to me. I'd been away from her for too long.

I opened my mouth to speak, the word I wanted to say getting stuck in the back of my dry throat as I studied her beautiful face. It was a face an angel could only dream of possessing, and one I wanted to spend forever waking up to.

"A-Ayda?"

She released a chirp of sound before she leaned down, her lips now closer to mine.

"Oh, Drew. You scared me."

I bathed in the sound of her voice. So real. So alive.

"S-sorry," I croaked, not really understanding what I was

apologizing for, but hating the pain that creased her face.

The beeping seemed to grow louder, the noise gathering momentum at the same speed of my aching heart.

"You came back to me," she whispered as a loud commotion stirred behind her. "You did it, Drew." She pressed her palm to my cheek carefully.

The contact made me suck in a breath.

More memories attacked.

Waking up to her against white sheets. The sunlight shining across her golden skin, prickling from the way I trailed a finger up and down her arm.

Ayda showering while I watched, taunting myself with a craving I was waiting to sate.

Her among my brothers, laughing and joking, her smiles like a galaxy of stars among an oily ocean of leather and darkness.

"You came back," she repeated softly.

A soft smile tugged at my cracked lips as I looked into her bright blue eyes and whispered roughly, "You're the only place… I wanna be."

CHAPTER FORTY-FOUR
DREW

Since waking, the men had been drip fed into my room over a period of days. I was broken and receiving sympathy that didn't sit well with me. Sympathy should be saved for those who hadn't walked into the lion's den the way I had so willingly. My protests went ignored. They were giving their sympathies to me whether I approved of them or not.

Ayda barely left my side—her smile forever fixed in place every time she looked over and saw my eyes open. Every now and again, she would stand by my bed and press her fingertips to my heart, and her eyes would mist over with gratitude.

My body had been in pain for days, but Ayda's heart had suffered just as much.

After some emotional reunions with Slater, Jedd, Deeks, Kenny, Tate, and the others, it was finally time for me to see my father and the kid brother I never knew I had.

Brother.

The thought of what we could have been to one another, had we known, haunted me every time I thought about it, but I shut those thoughts down most of the time with a reminder to myself that, while Rubin hadn't had it easy with Mayor Walsh, he'd also never had to put himself too close to the blade to survive the way I had.

There was a small grain of gratitude toward my father and Carolyn Walsh for that.

Ayda had been making small talk to keep my foggy mind busy while we waited for them both to arrive, and I was grateful for her efforts, though they still didn't stop my heart beating faster when Eric gently tapped his knuckles on my hospital room door before he opened it up slowly, his eyes instantly connecting with mine.

There isn't a son in the world who doesn't long to see pride shining from their father's eyes, but even I had to admit that the sight of it took me by surprise when he walked in with a tired-looking Rubin following behind.

Ayda's hand slipped into mine and squeezed gently. "Hey, guys."

Dad tipped his head at Ayda, with Rubin offering a feeble wave and a soft, "Hi," before he took me in for the first time, and his face fell.

"Shit," he whispered.

"I know I look bad, kid, but is it really *that* bad?"

Rubin stood there, his expression blank.

"We need to work on his game face," Eric said roughly.

"No kidding." I smirked, leaning back on my pillow and releasing a tired sigh. "It's nice to see you, too, Rubin."

"Sorry, Drew. I just couldn't imagine it being true, that's all."

"What?" I arched a brow, eyeing him as he shuffled and tugged the sleeves of his hoodie down over his bunched up hands.

"That you could ever get beaten that way."

I felt Ayda's hand tense in mine for only a second before it relaxed again.

"This is what happens when a sadistic fuck is given too much power," she said quietly.

"She doesn't mean me," I whispered back at Rubin, tipping my head her way while offering him a paralyzed wink.

A quiet snort fell from Ayda. "They know that. I have better names for you."

"I can imagine," I mumbled to myself, looking up at Dad who was standing at the end of my bed, his good hand now tucked deep inside the pocket of his jeans. He was wearing his signature flannel shirt, the sleeves rolled up to the elbows, open at the chest with a dark gray T-shirt underneath. The man wore his clothing like a uniform—a signature look he somehow managed to carry off like he invented it.

"Missed me, Eric?" I asked playfully, my throat scratchy and sore still.

"Yeah, actually."

"No sarcastic comeback. Wow." I glanced at Rubin. "Don't tell me y'all have gotten boring since I got knocked out."

Rubin looked up at Eric, his eyes wide before he let them drop back to me, and I wondered if he saw it the way I could see it so clearly now—the way I should have seen it all those days and weeks before. He didn't look the same as Eric and me, but Rubin held the same respect for those he saw as above him, and he carried himself in a similar manner. Honesty shone from his face, whether he meant to hide it or not, and he always found a way to read the room he was standing in.

"What's wrong, Rubin?" I asked quietly, knowing he had lots of things to say and many questions to ask.

"Nothing."

"You're a really bad liar."

Rubin looked at Eric yet again, as though seeking permission for something I clearly wasn't aware of.

When Eric side-eyed him, he gave a subtle nod of approval, and I watched as Rubin's shoulders fell with relief. He moved across the room carefully, coming to stand on the opposite side of the bed from Ayda. There was a look in Rubin's eyes I'd never seen before—a peace, almost, and a young boy who was transitioning into the man he'd always wanted to become.

"I spoke to my dad the other day," Rubin began.

"Yeah?" I croaked, clearing my throat and looking at Eric who was giving nothing away before I looked back up at Rubin.

"Yeah." Rubin nodded. "I got to sit down opposite him for the first time properly. We were like two adults having this conversation I couldn't keep up with at first. He was throwing all these words at me I didn't understand, saying he was sorry, asking for my forgiveness and begging me to give him a chance."

"How did that make you feel?"

"Weird." Rubin sighed. "He said he's made a lot of mistakes in his life, done things he shouldn't have done. Said things he shouldn't have said. Hurt people he shouldn't have hurt. He told me he always managed to sleep okay at night because, deep down, he thought his intentions were good."

Good? I wanted to cry out. Walsh didn't have a good intention in his bone marrow, and he wasn't the kind of man to beg for forgiveness. All my nerves were tingling, waking up from their slumber, telling me to say something that would wake Rubin up from this dangerous path he was about to go down, but then he spoke again, and everything I wanted to say got swept away with the words he breathed in front of me.

"Do you believe him, Drew? Do you believe *our* dad? Do you think his intentions have always been good?"

He knew.

The kid fucking knew.

My lips parted in shock, and I turned back to Eric, eyes wide and heart beating in that hectic rhythm it had gotten so used to recently.

I stared at Eric Tucker like it was the first time I was seeing him, and there he stood, proud and unashamed, an innocence shining through as a small smile tugged at the corner of his mouth.

"Well, Drew?" Eric asked, bunching his shoulders together. "Answer your brother. Do you think your father's intentions have always been good?"

"I can't believe you found the balls to tell him," I whispered back, my lips barely moving.

"Where do you think you got your balls from, son?"

"You could have given me a head's up."

"I asked him not to," Rubin said, bringing my attention back to him. He was now smiling too. A glint of excitement shining from his eyes. "Brother…" he added.

"Holy shit, the kid's got balls, too."

"Not really. I'm not brave like you—more relieved to know that the man I shot isn't my real dad. Relieved to be away from him. Relieved that I don't need to feel guilty about not feeling guilty that he's going to spend a long time in prison... some of his sentence thanks to me."

"That's a lot of relief." I sighed.

"Maybe you can teach me to be brave one day."

"As long as he teaches you to be brave and not stupid," Eric interrupted. I didn't need to look at him to flip him the bird, my own weak smile trying to break free when I heard his responding laughter.

"How do you feel about it, kid?" I dared myself to ask.

"Honestly? I don't really know yet. I guess it makes sense why The Hut always felt like home, and why defending The Hounds always came so easily to me. It was like some kind of…"

"… connection," I finished for him.

"Yeah. An indescribable bond that didn't make sense to me when written on paper, but made sense to the way it made me happy to be around Tate and you guys."

"You've always been a part of my family, Rubix cube," Ayda teased. "But once Drew makes an honest woman of me, it'll be official."

"And once Ayda stops calling you Rubix Cube. That's way too cute for a Hound."

"Still better than some of the names I have for you."

I squeezed her hand back as firmly as I could, which, given my current state of being weaker than piss, wasn't very firm at all. "Ah, my sweet, loving future wife." I smiled up at Rubin. "Don't you just love her and her smart mouth?"

CHAPTER FORTY-FIVE
DREW

After my time in hospital, Ayda nursed me back to health the way the doctors told her she should, only adding a flair of Hanagan aftercare that proved to be more powerful than any drug I could ever have been prescribed.

The progress was slow at first. That tired, beat-up body of mine had had enough of life, enough of me putting it in the path of danger every chance I got, and enough of my shit. Any thoughts I had about being stronger than any enemy were blown to pieces the first time Ayda had to help my limping body make it to the bathroom to take a piss.

The need to exert my masculinity over her was replaced by my admiration for the raw power of her femininity and the way it exuded a strength too powerful to be contained in something as simple as muscles.

She took charge of me, my recovery, and the club.

She ran the businesses as best she could with a lot of help from the guys, offering them advice and stepping up to help with the plans to rebuild the training room into something fresh and new. Watching her blossoming into a role she seemed born to be in was a thing of beauty. The men around me didn't just love her, they respected her too. The Hound

Whores had found a place in their hearts to take her in, every woman who once stared at her with narrowed eyes now finding a way to smile shyly, offer her a wave, and ask her if she needed any help with anything.

I may have been the president of the club, but Ayda was the fresh glue securing us all together.

Weeks seemed to roll on by with news coming in about Mayor Walsh and The Navs along the way. It seemed Winnie did, in fact, have her sights set on a major takedown that would lead to her getting a promotion within the ATF, and a move to where she wanted: to live and work in Washington, D.C.

After Jedd's deal with her, and him having worn a wire inside the warehouse, they'd secured enough evidence to send Walsh down for a series of charges, including conspiracy to commit murder, blackmail, embezzlement, racketeering, false testimony… the list went on and on and on. Carolyn Walsh was still living in their home in Babylon, and even though I'd yet to go and meet with her and tell her this for myself, being Rubin's mom had earned her a lifetime of protection from The Hounds if she needed it. I could only hope that Walsh hadn't turned her against us along the way with his false accusations, need for revenge, and desire to see us buried six-feet underground.

It turned out Travis 'Trigger' Gatlin had been involved in so much more than any of us could have ever predicted. Harry's and Clint's letters had given us clues into corruption, but the depths of that corruption were unfathomable. Money laundering, drug trafficking, talks of human trafficking, too… you name the crime, and Winnie and her men had found links that traced back to The Navs. How much Walsh was truly involved with was anyone's guess, but his face had appeared on every news channel within the state of Texas—his name living on while his life would forever be spent behind bars.

Justice, it seemed, had been served.

Sutton's station was back under his command—the ATF sated with their need for something big to secure their superiors for a while. I didn't need to say the words to him directly, but seeing him riding around in his cruiser, his cowboy habits back in place, made me happier than I could ever have imagined it would. Babylon may have been ours to protect around the borders, but the heart of it belonged to Sutton. I guess it always had, and the two of us had a bond thicker than blood—one the Drew Tucker of twelve months ago would have found nauseating to even think about. He was my brother in arms, and even though I wasn't in a rush to, I'd lay my life down for him and his girls as much as I would for the men with the hounds and reaper on their backs.

Sometimes enemies are only enemies because we're too afraid to admit we see something in them that we admire way more than the stuff we see in ourselves. Humans are fucked up creatures, made from blood and complications, living their lives with fear they refuse to acknowledge in their hearts. That fear keeps us away from some of the best things we could be blessed with.

I was happy to be blessed with Sutton now.

Rubin had taken to spending his days at The Hut and had worked alongside Ayda to give me a headache most days with the need to ask me if I was okay every two damn minutes. He was taking his new role as my younger brother seriously. But as the weeks passed by and turned to months, and my movement increased, along with my desire to spend quality time with those who mattered, I found myself *wanting* to take my new role as his older brother seriously, too.

We'd often be in the yard, looking over the repo cars and the bikes, and I'd look up to find Eric standing on the porch of The Hut with his arms folded over his chest and his attention on the two of us. He didn't have to say it, but my old man was proud to have his sons together, I could tell—even more than he was relieved to have the secret off his shoulders. The weight of that had held him down and kept him away for years, and as stupid as that seemed to me now, I, more than anyone, knew how easy it was to make a snap decision that changed the course of everyone's lives for the worse.

That fragile life of mine had flashed before my eyes one too many times. Any grudges I felt against my father had fallen away with the ghost of who I used to be before Ayda came into my life and dragged my body into the light.

She was four months pregnant now, her stomach barely showing to those around us. They'd taken the news of her pregnancy and latched onto it like it was the miracle they'd all needed at the time.

We'd spent so long waiting for people to leave us. Now it was time to wait patiently for this new beating heart to join our family and consume our every waking thought.

Deeks had cried—Slater, too. Jedd hugged the shit out of me in a manner unlike the Jedd of old. The rest of the men, including Tate and Rubin, had vowed with their every breath to protect the baby with all that they had.

And before we knew it, we'd made it through one of the hardest winters of our lives, pushed through spring, celebrated Ayda's 26th birthday, my 30th, breathed new life into the club, and we were embracing the sweltering heat of our Texan summer.

The summer.

The heat

I spent every morning sitting on the porch, awake before everyone else, letting the sun and warmth of being alive wash over my face like an old man contemplating his remaining days, rather than a thirty-year-old with his whole life ahead of him.

Reflection had become a new form of meditation for this rugged, tattooed biker. A reformed bad boy who wanted to watch the sun rise and set every day—to feel the gift of air entering his lungs and enjoy the way his heart beat to a different tune depending who was around him.

It was 6:10 a.m. one Thursday morning in the height of Summer, and I was out there on the porch again, soaking up the ridiculous heat of the early hours. You could see the warmth bouncing off the yard in waves already, and I glanced to the edge of the patch of land to the left of The Hut, excited about my plans to build a pool around the back there for the kid to enjoy summer days in when it was old enough. Images of a baby boy running around with Ayda warning him to be careful floated through my mind. Images of a baby girl crying out for her daddy to throw her in the pool made my smile grow as I let my imagination run wild.

We had so much to look forward to.

So much.

My daydreams were cut short when an orange Ford Gran Torino with a black stripe down the hood came crawling in front of the gates. It was a thing of beauty, and I pushed myself up in my seat, watching as it came to a stop outside our yard.

The motor enthusiast in me wanted to go to it, take a closer look and appreciate the mechanics of it all, but the sunlight was shining against the windows, and I couldn't see who was driving. Another tourist appreciating the fact they were stumbling upon a motorcycle club like we were the damn Sons of Anarchy? Another local out making sure we were behaving, keeping ourselves in line?

The window rolled down slowly, an arm and elbow appearing to rest on the ledge before I saw the familiar face staring back at me.

Winnie.

My stomach rolled with nausea, but I found myself moving anyway, making my way across the yard at a leisurely pace before I stood behind the gate and peered at her through the metal bars.

She looked different now. The hard edge to her features had gone, as had her bright red lipstick, replaced instead with a fresh-faced look that made her seem… human. Her eyes trailed up and down my body before landing back on my face, the bruises she'd last seen now gone, and only a few extra scars on my skin left as signs of the fights I'd been in my whole life.

"Nice car," I said, nodding toward the hood of it as I folded my arms over my chest somewhat defensively. "I didn't have you down as a Torino kinda woman."

"What did you have me down as?"

"Something more… beige."

"I see someone has healed just fine." She raised a brow in return, her lips twitching.

"Getting there."

"Was that a limp I saw when you walked over?"

I cleared my throat, hating the slow nature of my healing. "Nothing more than rusty morning joints still waking up."

"Ah." She nodded, not buying it. "The formidable Drew Tucker. He's still as strong as ever."

"Stronger."

"That's the message you're wanting to put out there, right?"

I shook my head. "No, I'm quite happy to live under the radar from now on."

"I bet." She smirked, her eyebrows bouncing before she looked past me and to The Hut.

"Care to tell me what you're doing here at this time of day?" I asked her, bringing her attention back to me. "I sure as shit hope it isn't to stir up more trouble."

"Trouble? The Hounds of Babylon? Never," she mocked, her laughter somewhat light and carefree. "Don't worry, Mr. Tucker—"

"Uch," I groaned, cutting her off.

"Sorry. Don't worry, *Drew*. You're safe."

"Yeah? For how long?"

Winnie smiled, her eyes narrowing as though she was contemplating her answer. "For as long as you behave."

"Behaving ain't exactly our style."

"Not your old style. Something tells me that it will be from now on. You're not a bad club, Drew. You're a good club who always managed to find a way into bad situations. That's a skill—one you might want to get rid of, but a skill none the less."

"Gee, thanks, Miss Winnie."

She chuckled again, her eyes drifting behind me. For a moment, I thought someone else may have been there, but when I glanced over my shoulder, the yard remained quiet and empty, the others in bed, unprepared to start their day so soon. When I turned back to Winnie, she was staring up at me as though I was a friend. It made the hairs on the back of my neck stand to attention, and my gut tingle with anticipation. With people like her, you never knew what was coming next, and I'd grown tired of surprises.

"I'm actually here to ask a favor," she admitted quietly.

"What kind of favor?"

"I'm heading to Washington today."

"D.C? Fancy. The Walsh takedown really did help with the promotion, I see."

"And I couldn't have got him without Jedd."

Jedd. So, this was about my brother, and the look in her eyes suddenly made sense.

"No. You couldn't. But we couldn't have gotten out of that warehouse without you, so the gratitude needs to work both ways, even if you were late to the party."

"Right." She swallowed lightly and glanced down at her arm resting on the window ledge before looking back up at me. "But I don't think Jedd sees it that way."

"What do you care how he sees it? You got what you wanted in the end, didn't you?"

Her eyes narrowed again, the words she wanted to say seeming to get stuck on the tip of her tongue.

"Mostly," she eventually whispered. "I don't make a habit of visiting those I've had under investigation before, Drew."

"We're flattered."

"You should be. He should be. Just…" Winnie sucked in a breath, releasing it like it hurt to do so. "Tell him I'm sorry, okay? Tell him thank you, and I'm sorry."

I stared at her for far too long, the memories of the awkwardness between Ayda and me at the beginning of our relationship coming back to the forefront of my mind. I couldn't be a hundred percent certain of what I was seeing, but if it was what I thought it was, I felt sorry for the poor woman. There wasn't a chance in hell of Jedd ever returning any kind of admiration or mutual feelings for Winnie. If anyone so much as whispered her name in The Hut, he would growl and storm off, unable to listen to the six letters that made up her moniker.

"Sure. I'll tell him."

"Thank you."

Winnie turned to stare out of the front windshield, looking at the road ahead of her with apprehension.

"It's a long way to D.C," I said quietly.

"There's a whole world waiting for us outside of Babylon, Drew," she said, turning back to me and dropping her arm from the ledge to hold onto the wheel with both hands. "Maybe you should think about exploring it one day."

"I've got my whole world inside these gates. No need to go searching for things I've already found."

"Congrats on the baby," she offered with a soft smile.

"Congrats on the new life."

"Congrats on getting away with murder over and over again."

"Congrats on reminding me why I really don't like you." I huffed out a laugh, and Winnie nodded once in acknowledgment before she started up the engine of the Torino, offered me one last glance, and drove down a road that would lead her out of Babylon.

When I turned back to look over the yard, I saw Jedd

walking out onto the porch like a lump of dark hair and tattooed muscle. His arms were stretched up to the sky, his body reaching up before he dropped a hand to his eye and rubbed at it wildly.

I couldn't help but smile at the sight of him.

My brother. My VP. The man who saved the club in ways I'd never have considered doing.

Walking over to him, I laughed to myself when he shook his head and pretended to check an imaginary watch on his wrist.

"Don't you ever fucking sleep anymore?" he asked roughly, his voice still not awake yet.

"Nah. It's a waste of life," I said, hitting the bottom step of The Hut and coming to a stop.

"Who was that?" he asked, nodding to where Winnie had disappeared.

"The Torino?"

"Yeah."

I shrugged, tucking my hands into the pockets of my gray sweats. "Nobody important." I sighed.

Jedd blew out all the air in his chest and looked out over the yard. "Another day closer."

"Sure is."

"You ready for it?" he asked, turning back to me.

"I think I've been ready for this my whole life, I just didn't know it for a very long time."

Jedd's grin grew slowly. "What was life like before she came into this family? I can't remember."

"Who knows? All I remember is being angry with everyone all the time. Thinking hurting others would take away the pain in my own chest. Life was foggy before Ayda came along. Now it's…"

"Filled with sunshine." He smirked.

"Soft bastard." I joked, and Jedd's rough laughter joined mine, filling my life with more love and appreciation than I could ever have imagined existed.

"You guys are gonna have a good life, brother," he told me. "And that starts tomorrow."

"It's going to be the best fucking day of my life."

"Until your kid is born."

"Fuck," I pushed out through a heavy breath. "A husband and a father in the same year. Who the fuck am I?"

"There's not a man on this earth who deserves it more." Jedd made his way down to the same step I was on, his hand landing on my shoulder as he looked beyond me to the rest of the yard around us. His fingers pressed into my skin, the emotion I saw in his eyes making my smile fade, and my chest swell with pride. "Sometimes, the best lives start in the murkiest of waters. Yours hasn't always been easy, but the good times are waiting. Enjoy every second of them… be selfish, no matter what that means for the rest of the club. It's about Ayda and the baby now. You, Ayda, and the baby. It's what Pete and Harry would want. The club has to come second after tomorrow, Drew, and you have to be okay with living this new life."

"This feels like some kind of goodbye, brother."

"You wish." He laughed, walking away and leaving me standing there, staring at the door to my home—to our Hut.

"No more goodbyes," I whispered to myself. "Only good mornings."

CHAPTER FORTY-SIX
AYDA

I hoped I would never get used to the feeling of waking up to Drew Tucker. Every morning felt like the best kind of gift, the more relaxed version of the man I loved had made me fall deeper and deeper in love with him.

And it always started with this moment—the one where I opened my eyes and saw him sliding a mug of coffee on to the nightstand, those fully reformed muscles rippling under his inked skin before he unleashed that stare of his on me.

I knew how lucky we were. We had one another, we had the club, and we'd come out of the other side of it all with a few scars, but we were still alive. We'd settled into a nice kind of calm that felt natural—months with no drama—outside of the teenagers that still insisted on acting like toddlers occasionally, anyway.

As Drew sat on the edge of the bed, the sun shone over the scar just under his ribs and, like I did most mornings, I ran my fingers over it, flashing him a smile when his eyes lit up.

"Morning."

"Morning," he whispered adoringly.

"How long have you been up?" I asked, stretching out like a cat and rubbing my hand over the small rise of my belly where our baby was growing.

"A couple of hours. Not too long this morning." His gaze drifted down to my stomach where he placed his hand over mine. "Everything okay with my two favorite people this morning?" he asked, leaning down and brushing his lips against mine.

"All the better now you're here. We've decided that it's gonna suck not waking up next to you tomorrow, but the tradeoff is totally worth it." I twisted my hand under his and linked our fingers together. "You nervous yet? Cold feet?"

"Nope and nope. Calm and toasty. You?"

"Never been warmer," I admitted, shifting onto my side so I could see his face better. He looked happy, or at least happier. It had been a long process over the last couple of months, but this look of contentment was my new favorite on him. "You wanna come and give charm and charisma some love before you become a married man?"

"You wanna stop asking your future husband stupid questions and shift over already so I can grope my future wife?" He smirked.

Shuffling back in the bed, I flung the comforter back from my body with a quiet flourish. "Since when have you needed an invitation?"

"I don't." Drew moved around carefully, kicking off his sneakers and propping himself up on a pillow, opening his arm for me to lay on his chest.

He'd been outside. I could smell it on him when I buried my face into his chest. I had been checking the weather almost obsessively over the past few weeks, and I knew it was going to be sunny, hot and dry, just like every other day.

Sinking into him, I let my eyes slide closed and took in the moment. I liked to memorize the little things that I loved.

These were the things I wanted to tell our kid about when they asked how I fell in love with their dad, or what I loved about him most. I couldn't tell them about his strength and bravery, or how I adored that crazy martyr side of him that had taken on the world with his two bare hands to protect the ones he loved.

I also wanted to selfishly bask in the moments where it was just he and I. The two of us alone.

In another month, we were going to be able to find out if this bun in my oven was a girl or a boy, and I had a feeling that the whole world was going to change then. The baby still felt like a dream, but that would make it real.

"Before the madness of tomorrow starts, and I break down and allow my hormones to take over, I want to say thank you." I lifted my head and twisted to find his eyes.

"Thank you?"

I smiled up at him. "Yeah, thank you. Thank you for reminding me what it feels like to be happy. For pulling me out of my own personal Hell and loving me even when I was a pain in the ass."

Drew's jaw ticked as his eyes searched mine. "I loved you *because* you were a pain in the ass, Ayda. I love you now because you refuse to make things easy for me. If you'd have been softer, weaker even, I wouldn't know how lucky I am to have you. I wouldn't appreciate everything you brought to the table for me, too. So I guess the gratitude works both ways, right?"

I felt that familiar love rise inside of me with every word he said. I hoped my smile told him everything I was feeling because those damn hormones also made me a crazy emotional at times. I was dangerously close to being a blubbering fool again.

"I guess what I'm saying is I love you, and you've made me happier than I thought I could ever be. I didn't think about getting married or having kids much after Mom and Dad died. I didn't see much of a future at all. I wasn't living. Then along you came, and I've never felt so alive in my life. I don't think I could have given you up, even if you'd tried to make me."

He reached up with his free hand, brushing a thumb across the apple of my cheek. "I remember trying to make you give up this life a few times. Thank God you were born stubborn. But I could argue this with you all day, telling you I feel like I'm the one who should be thanking you while you tell me you're the one who should be thanking me. So, let's agree to disagree on who deserves who more. Let's be thankful we're here, doing this, waiting for tomorrow, and let me tell you that you're welcome, Ayda Hanagan. If I had to walk into a diner again and pick out any waitress in any part of the world, I'd walk right back into Rusty's and pick you all over again."

"Remind me to thank Tate one day, when he's not a hormonal jackass with an attitude." I sniffed trying to hide those emotions I'd tried so hard to suppress.

"Ayda?"

"Hmm?"

"You're trying not to cry right now, ain'tcha?"

Slapping his chest, I dropped my head and buried my face in his shoulder before the first tear fell, a muffled, "asshole," falling from my lips.

I couldn't imagine my life without Drew Tucker in it, and tomorrow I would be marrying him. Who knew that the man who'd stumbled onto my driveway, making threats and demands, would turn out to be my forever?

"Drew?"

"Yeah, darlin'."

"Can you do that thing you do to stop me from getting emotional?"

"I'm really not in the mood for doing puzzles right now, Ayda."

"So you're asking me to be clearer?" I asked his chest sweetly. My eyes on the hound inked into his skin.

"You're about to become a Tucker. Blunt and to the point is all we know. Consider this part of your training."

I raised my eyes to meet his as my hand skimmed his abs and worked under the waistband of his gray sweats to wrap my hand around his erection. "Fuck me. Please."

His eyes darkened, the intensity of them penetrating mine. I'd said everything I needed to say. "Yes, Ma'am," he whispered, moving quickly to pull me closer to him so he could press his lips against mine, a whisper of a groan echoing in his throat from the feel of my palm around his dick.

I sank into the kiss; heat flooding my body and riding my veins. These were the moments when he belonged to me, when I had all of him to myself, and truth be told, I enjoyed being greedy. Tomorrow we were to be married, and I planned on making the most of today.

CHAPTER FORTY-SEVEN
DREW

I kissed her goodbye somewhere around 5:00 p.m. that afternoon, with Autumn ushering her away from me, peeling us apart with threats of superstitions and a lifetime of bad luck if Ayda didn't get out of there quickly. Somewhere along the way, with the help of Sloane, Libby, and a few of the other women in The Hut, a bridal party had been formed to help things run smoothly.

All day, Ayda and I had seen our brothers walking around carrying logs, boxes of candles, flowers, before looking at me with a roll of their eyes to let me know they weren't all too happy with being ordered around by a bunch of testy women.

Once Autumn had done all she needed to do around the yard and The Hut, she'd packed Ayda into a car and driven her away from the night. I stood there on the porch, my hands tucked in my pockets, and I watched her disappear down the road.

That was the last time I'd ever spend quality time with Ayda Hanagan.

Tomorrow, she'd become Ayda Tucker, and the thought made me silently giddy.

I'd been staring at the road she'd disappeared down when Jedd, Slater, Kenny, and Deeks came charging out from The

Hut, their arms flying around my neck, hands roughing up my hair, and the cries of The Hounds of Babylon filling the air. I was fought, tackled, mocked, and teased until they managed to drag me back inside with a promise of whiskey all night long—enough that would make sure I slept the night away without waking up, pining for my woman.

Eric stood behind the bar, taking the position Harry once owned with a cloth thrown over his shoulder as he slid tumblers of liquor up and down the bar, laughing freely, without the shadows around his eyes I'd come to expect.

Rubin and Tate amused themselves among the enthusiastic young women, even though I believed Libby was still very much a part of Tate's life. He was entering that stage where the boy was dying, and the reckless man was coming to life, and as I glanced over to keep checking on him, I vowed to try steer him onto better paths once the wedding was over.

"Refill?" Eric asked, dragging my attention back to him.

"One more," I told him.

"Right." He laughed to himself. "Because these lot are going to let you sleep tonight."

"They'd better." I studied the happiness on my father's face as he went about his business. "It suits you, you know."

"What does?"

"Happiness."

Eric's face fell, his eyes finding mine.

"If that's what you are," I added. "Maybe I'm just seeing you differently than I ever did before, but I like seeing you without the cloud over your head. The secrets, the regret… they all seem to have faded away. You're not bad to be around when you're like this."

"Save your declarations and vows for tomorrow." He

smirked, but I could see the effect my words had had on him. The happiness shone a little more every time he realized our bond was growing tighter.

"Roger that." I tipped my glass toward him before taking a sip and looking back over at my men.

As far as nights before your wedding day go, it was tamer than I expected.

Maybe they realized how important this was for me now. Ayda wasn't just some chick riding through my life to satisfy a craving. She had become my life, and the build-up to this moment had been a rollercoaster of loving, losing, fighting, and trying to survive. Tomorrow marked the start of a new forever. The old one now dead and buried.

Tame or not, though, I still rolled into bed with a heavy thud, with Jedd laughing over me as he slapped my cheek and tucked me in for the night.

"Love you, brother," I slurred, enjoying the warm buzz that flowed through my body.

"Get some sleep, shithead."

I raised my middle finger, smiled dopily, and closed my eyes.

When I woke, it was morning, and the light poured through the open blinds. The haze of a new day meant I needed a second to catch up, and I threw my arm over my face, groaning as I rolled over and tried to open my eyes.

The minute I did, water was thrown on me, forcing me to gasp and sit bolt upright, my hands digging into the mattress as I breathed through the shock.

"Wakey, wakey, rise and shine. It's lose your freedom for the rest of your life time," Slater sang.

I flicked water from my eyes, shaking my hair as I looked

up at him.

"You bastard!"

"Really? The first words you're gonna say on the morning of your wedding are *You bastard*? Today is a sacred day, brother. Thou shalt not cuss or do anything little wifey wouldn't approve of."

"The fuck is wrong with you?"

"Not a damn thing." He grinned brightly.

"Screw you." I laughed, reaching for a pillow to throw at his head.

He dodged it, and ran over to me, rubbing his hand over the top of my wet hair. "Come on, Fucker. Get up. I have promises to keep and women to please. If you're not in that shower within the next five minutes, my ass is on the line."

"Anyone would think you were taking this best man shit seriously."

"Don't get me started. I'm still pissed about that."

"You really expected me to choose between my best friend and my VP?"

"Fuck, yeah, I did. VP is his job. Being your best friend has been voluntary, and I deserved the good karma that went along with that."

I reached for another pillow, tossing it at him as hard as I could and earning an exaggerated grunt for my efforts. "Fine. I'll share the role with Jedd. Blah, blah, whatever. Now get in the shower."

For the first time in my life, I did as I was told without argument, moving where Slater told me to, showering, trimming my beard down and spraying whatever shit he told me to spray over my body and on my neck.

When it came to getting dressed, I stood in front of the

clothes hanging off the curtain rail and smiled to myself.

"Stepping into the shoes of a new man, Drew," Slater said with excitement. "You ready?"

"I was made for this," I told him proudly, and then I reached up and pulled down my clothes, eventually shrugging into my crisp white shirt before I stepped into the smartest pair of black suit pants I'd ever owned.

Deeks and Eric had helped me pick them out after I'd told them both I didn't want to do the traditional MC wedding attire. I wanted this to be a once in a lifetime day for both of us—one where I'd look like me, only different. I wanted to knock her off her feet as much as I knew she was going to knock me off mine.

By the time I was dressed, standing in front of the long mirror, I palmed down the front of my shirt and shook out my legs to make my trousers fall right.

Slater was standing next to me, holding onto the black vest we'd had made with white embroidery on the back in the design of my club's patch. The Hounds and Reaper were with me… we were just being a bit fancy for the day. Slater held it out, and I pushed my arms through, shrugging it into place and pulling down the edges to make it fall as perfectly as it needed to.

"Smartest cut I ever did see," Slater admitted softly.

"Yeah." I cleared my throat and began to fasten the buttons up, stretching my neck out as I did.

It had been a hard decision, choosing not to wear my cut. A decision I didn't take lightly. It was as much a part of me as my legs and arms were, and even though there was a tiny bit of regret at not feeling the weight of it on my shoulders, the weight was exactly what I'd wanted to be free of for just one day.

That cut was covered in responsibility, death, and mistakes.

Those weren't welcome at the altar. I didn't want the ghosts of anyone looking at Ayda while I told her all the things I needed to tell her. I didn't want my mind to drift when the familiar smell of leather reminded me of a time I'd rather forget. My cut would go on later that night, once the ceremony was over, but for now, I needed this. I needed peace.

I wanted this for both of us.

"You think it's too much?" I asked, staring at my own reflection as I bounced on the balls of my feet.

"Not even a little bit, you handsome fucker."

I grinned and caught his eye, watching as he turned away and rubbed at his brow.

"Allergies, Slater?"

"Yeah," he croaked. "Give me a minute."

"Take all the time you need," I said, rolling the sleeves of my shirt up to my elbows before I reached over to grab the black bow tie on the side. "Well, maybe not all the time you need. Ayda will kick your ass if you make me late, and one of us needs to figure out what the fuck to do with this." I held out the bow tie and watched the fear shine from Slater's eyes.

"Shit. We need Eric, don't we?"

"I guess we do after all."

CHAPTER FORTY-EIGHT
AYDA

I watched the scenery of Texas and Babylon pass by the window of the car as the ladies with me chatted with excitement. I couldn't stop smiling, and my cheeks ached from it. Janette and Autumn had organized the whole morning. A cleverly designed RV bus had been converted into a mobile spa, including full hair, makeup, and even massages. I was now waxed, buffed, and coiffed into perfection.

The plan was to drive to The Hut, where Deeks would be waiting for us outside the gates. The car would take the ladies in, and they would proceed down the aisle. Deeks would be giving me away in his own unique way.

This was a day I'd dreamed about in several different ways since I'd been a little girl. But marrying Drew was a dream I'd never been smart enough to conjure until I'd known I couldn't survive without him. I couldn't seem to find it in myself to be nervous. Every time I thought about walking down that aisle, all I could think about was finally becoming his wife in front of our friends and family, and for it to be recognized legally by the great state of Texas.

"You ready?" Janette asked, leaning into me. She and Autumn were on either side of me, my rocks, as always. My two mother hens making sure every dream I'd ever had came true while making sure every part of the machine they'd put together ran smoothly.

"I am," I admitted, moving my bouquet to the other hand and gripping hers. "I think it's the only thing I've ever been this certain about."

Tears welled in her eyes as she assessed me.

"No. None of that. You'll just set me off," I pleaded. "You can make me cry as much as you want after Drew's seen the full effect."

"Oh, look," Sloane said quietly, her face practically pressed against the glass of the window. We all seemed to lean in at the same time as the limo slowed and pulled off onto the shoulder by the gates of The Hut.

There were flowers everywhere, and on either side of the gates sat logs in various heights, ranging tallest to shortest, blooming out from the gates to the street. Each log held two mason jars—one with flowers, and one with a candle flickering in the breeze. The open gates had beautiful wreaths made of waxy green leaves and romantic flowers.

"Wow."

This hadn't been something I'd arranged, and from the grin on Janette and Autumn's faces, they'd not only known about it, they'd arranged it. The two had struck up quite the friendship since the real planning for the wedding had begun.

"You like it?" Autumn asked as the car stopped completely on the shoulder, just before the gates.

Like was an understatement. The whole thing was breathtaking, as were the emotions rising inside of me. It had been like this for the last week. The closer the wedding had come, the more the hormones had tangled with the excitement, leaving me to become a blubbering mess no one was quite sure how to handle. I think I'd scarred Tate and Rubin for life.

"It's stunning." I finally choked out, doing my best to blink back the tears that were already rising.

"There are a few more surprises, but I promise, we stuck to your rules."

If the surprises were all like this one, I was more than happy to concede everything to them in the future. The entrance to the yard looked civilized and graceful in a way I'd never seen it. It was welcoming, warm, and everything I could have hoped for.

I was still gawking when I finally noticed Deeks leaning against his bike, just to the side of the gates. The chrome of his bike was bright in the sunlight, and the paint was polished to utter perfection. Deeks looked handsome and regal, wearing a suit with his cut in place of a jacket.

"Dapper."

"My God, the man cleans up good." Autumn hummed wistfully, all the love she had for him evident in her tone. "But he only does it rarely, and only for the people he loves the most."

"Y'all are determined to make me cry," I accused, picking up the small train of the dress in my free hand and sucking down oxygen like it was going out of style.

"Then we'd better get you down that aisle and to the man at the other end of it." Janette opened the door, her hand gently holding my forearm as I stepped out and into the warm summer air. "We love you, sweetheart."

"I love you, too."

I walked toward Deeks, who had pulled off his sunglasses and was now staring at me with wide, watery eyes. I swore I wasn't going to make it down that aisle without mascara down my cheeks. I knew this was all out of the love these people had for me, but I was barely holding my shit together as it was, and Deeks' reaction just made that lump in my throat grow as my smile returned in full force.

"How do I look?" I asked, spreading my arms and turning slowly. I lifted the bottom of the dress in my hands and twisted my foot at him, an ivory colored cowboy boot sitting there comfortably.

Deeks stepped forward as the limo started to pull into the yard. They were gone by the time Deeks stepped in front of me. Gripping my hands in his, he squeezed them tightly, his face lighting up with a smile I'd never seen there before. It was filled with love and pride, and an emotion I couldn't quite put my finger on.

"You're perfect, kid." Lifting one hand, he twisted a finger into one of the loose curls falling around my shoulders, and let it spring free with a wistful shake of his head. "That boy ain't gonna know what hit him."

"Take me to him?" I asked, my voice trembling with barely contained emotions.

"It would be my distinct honor."

Deeks turned to look at his shiny bike with a shit-eating grin I hadn't seen there in a while. "Think you could manage sidesaddle?"

"On your bike?"

When I raised an eyebrow at him, he shrugged. "We all have our traditions, Ayda, and you're about to experience one of the rare ones."

I waited as he swung his leg over the bike and pulled it upright, offering his hand to me and grinning when I accepted it with a playful roll of my eyes. With my bouquet in hand, I gathered up the train of my dress and raised it up as carefully as I could once I was sitting behind him. It wasn't as dignified as I'd have liked, but it felt right. Drew had warned me the guys had some things of their own planned, and I guessed this was one of them.

Deeks took off slowly, barely fast enough to make a breeze as he rolled toward the gates and into the yard.

The whole place was as transformed as the gates had been, with logs, flowers, mason jars, and candles filling the spaces surrounding us. Fairy lights and lanterns were strung all the way around the yard and crisscrossed overhead, leading toward where we'd agreed on placing our altar of metal and willow branches. This was where I knew my bridesmaids had just arrived and stepped into place and where Tate waited so he and Deeks could give me away together.

What I hadn't expected was the club guys there, sitting on their bikes, each man lined up on either side of the aisle, parked diagonally and facing Drew with their bright lights on. My jaw dropped as I studied each of them looking at me the way Deeks had just done, their smiles authentic and filled with love.

I almost dropped my dress as my emotions threatened to overwhelm me.

The club was as much of the family as every one of the guys, and this was a way of acknowledging that. This act was their way of respecting this day, and this marriage, and the tears welled in my eyes only long enough for me to blink them away again. I couldn't have anything hindering my view when Deeks got to the end of that Harley-lined aisle, and it was worth it all.

The moment Deeks turned that corner, I could only see what waited at the other end of it.

The man I'd been waiting to see all day.

Drew.

He looked amazing in his version of a tuxedo. His wide shoulders filled out the shirt that was rolled up to his elbows. A bow tie that was a bit wonky but totally him, sat around his neck, and a sexy as sin tailored vest hugged those abs of his.

He was all could see from that point on.

I took the hand that was offered to me and rose from the bike to my full height before letting the train of the dress go. I was barely aware of the girls slowly heading down the aisle before me. All of those little details that seemed so important to me in the planning suddenly fell away when Drew glanced around and saw me for the very first time.

Yes, I thought to myself as his eyes widened with hunger and awe. *I'm yours.*

CHAPTER FORTY-NINE
DREW

She was breathtaking—beyond anything I could have conjured in my mind, and I had to shuffle my stance, push my shoulders back, raise my chin and swallow the emotion in my throat as I held my hands together in front of me and waited.

Her blonde hair was a relaxed halo around her body—a body that carried my child and made me love her in ways I could never have imagined loving her.

The dress she wore hung in all the right places, showing me her strong, slender arms, her tanned skin, and just enough cleavage to make me contemplate ditching the wedding just so I could drag her back to her our room and ruin her.

Fucking perfect.

I had to swallow again, the world around me fading away until all I could see was the glow of lights from the bikes lining the aisle, and my woman. My savior. My soon-to-be-wife.

Whatever I'd done in life to deserve this moment, I would be forever grateful for it.

My slow rising smile soon turned into a grin of disbelief as she grew closer, her eyes locked on mine.

Get here to me, darlin'. Let's live this good life.

It was like she read my mind. Her smile was brighter than

the Texas summer sun and filled with happiness and love that was aimed directly at me.

The closer she got, the more I struggled to hold onto my emotions.

I wanted to run my hands through her hair, drag her to me and hold her there forever, in our forever—a forever no one could ever touch now.

It took a different kind of forever for her to reach me, and when she did, I sucked in a breath and held it in my chest as I watched Deeks and Tate take turns to kiss her cheeks and hide their need to cry like babies, too. When Ayda turned back to me, her eyes sparkled with unshed tears.

Stepping forward, I reached out to take her hands in mine, any cool I'd ever possessed gone as I broke the rules, pulled her to me, and pressed my lips to hers in a slow, sentimental kiss I needed to take for nobody else but myself.

The men around us cheered, but I couldn't hear a word a single one of them said.

Ayda relaxed into me, the hand not holding the flowers rising to run over my cheek as she returned the kiss with just as much enthusiasm. When she slowly pulled away, she kept her eyes closed, and her smile was bright.

Then she unleashed the sea of blue on me. "Hi," she whispered.

"Fuck, hi," I whispered right back, a wave of laughter rising from the crowd, no doubt at my toothy grin. "You look sensational. Out of this world."

A single tear escaped the corner of her eye. "You stole my line."

I held her hand in the air and took a step back, looking her up and down like I wanted to eat her… because I really fucking did. So many things ran through my mind. I wanted to ask her how she'd made it possible to look better than she did when she was riding my dick, but I was trying really hard to keep this moment semi-pure for her. A fairy tale. The dream she deserved. The start of a brand new chapter and adventure for both of us.

"I could fuck you right here, right now," I let slip. *Dammit.*

She let out a quiet laugh, her cheeks turning pink as her own hunger flared in her baby blues. "How about you marry me first. Maybe later, you'll get lucky."

Tate's groan of disgust only made my smile brighter as I stared at Ayda, giving her those bedroom eyes of mine she told me turned her legs to jelly.

"I'm already lucky," I told her, lowering her arm down and bringing her to my side to place a kiss on her forehead.

A rough cough forced out to grab our attention came from the officiant in front of us, and I looked up to find a familiar face smirking back at me as he stood there under an iron arch, which was covered in leafy twigs. His hands were clasped in front of him, and it was nice to see him wearing a suit that made him look more human than cowboy.

"Let me know when you're ready. It's not like I've nowhere else to be," Sutton mocked, his brow rising high.

"If you weren't the man about to marry us, you know where I'd tell you to go, don't you?"

"I have a feeling it would begin with F and end in—"

"That's right," I interrupted on a laugh, squeezing Ayda's hand in mine one last time and taking another look at her. The two of us had chosen Sutton to go through the ordeal of becoming ordained. He was the only man among our family committed and intelligent enough to pull it off without any swearing involved—although he almost came close.

"You ready?" I asked Ayda softly.

"I've been ready for a long time."

"God, me too, darlin'."

CHAPTER FIFTY
AYDA

I'd never felt more confident and clear-headed in my life. Having Drew next to me, holding my hand as Sutton began the ceremony was like a ship being put to anchor.

I felt good, happy, and so alive.

I heard the formal part of the ceremony as though it was a song playing in the background. Most of my focus seemed to be on the man holding my hand, smiling over at me with as much happiness and rightness as I felt in every pore of my body. As much as I tried to concentrate on the ceremony so I could hold it in my memories, I always found my attention drifting back to Drew. I could only imagine how dewy-eyed and love-struck I must have looked.

As Howard Sutton read through the usual formalities, I finally relented and let my eyes stay on Drew, my future finally rolling out in front of me in a happy image of laughter, love, and children. When he turned and met my eyes again, all I could do was stare back in wonder at the man.

"Ayda?" Sutton whispered quietly.

"Hmm?" I said, hearing a small chuckle from our friends.

"Your vows?"

My cheeks warmed again, and I closed my eyes for a

moment to center myself as I beat back the sudden surge of emotions that rushed forward. I couldn't remember why I'd insisted on going first now. Not until I met Drew's eyes again and let myself drown in them for a moment.

"Right," I said, letting out a long, steadying breath. "Drew, I think I loved you before I'd even met you. You were like this beautiful dream I forgot to have, a longing wish I'd forgotten to make. You were the perfect future I never saw coming. From the first time I met you, you've surprised the hell out of me, and you've kept me on my toes every day since." I stopped, my throat growing thick with emotion as tears blurred everything in my line of sight but him. "We've been through the worst of times, both alone and together, but we've also been through some of the best. No matter what was thrown at us, no matter what we endured, we did it together, and it only made the two of us stronger, both individually and as a couple. You know, from the moment you kissed me under the bleachers at Babylon High, I figured out two unshakable facts that have never once changed from that moment. I knew you would always be my shelter in the storm, and I knew I would belong to you for the rest of my life, whether you wanted me or not. Thank God you did," I added with a full, tearful smile. "You consumed me in every way possible. You make me feel safe, you make me feel loved, and when you look at me, sometimes I feel like we're the only two people on the planet. The more time we spend together, the more I know my life will never be a life worth living without you in it. I'm yours, Drew. I've always been yours, and I always will be. I'll weather every storm by your side. I'll be your can when you can't because you're my person, forever."

Drew's eyes were heavy with unshed tears, but he wore

them with pride, his smile fixed in place as he reached up and brushed his thumb under my eye and rested his palm against my cheek, holding me when he knew I needed him the most.

"Drew?" Sutton urged him to go.

Pushing his lips together, he rolled them back and forth, his nostrils flaring before he swallowed and unleashed his smile on me again.

"There's an intimacy in me that I never knew existed before you brought it out. The thought of speaking this way in front of my brothers would have sent me shrinking into a dark corner only twelve months ago. Now, here I am, ready and willing, *desperate* to let all the things I need to say to you fall free. That's what you do to me, Ayda. There was a version of me that existed before you, and that man was robotic, hard, miserable, and always seemed to be searching for some warmth. I could never find the warmth. The whole world seemed heavy and cold until you opened your mouth outside your home that night—the night you caught my attention. I haven't looked back since." He blew out a breath. "No other woman would have stood by me the way you have. No other woman would have forced me to believe in myself when all I wanted to do was fail, admit defeat, and give up on everything. You saw something in me before I saw it in myself. More importantly, you saw something in *us*, and you fought for us, baby. You fought for us and showed me what *true* strength is. This life you've accepted as your own hasn't been easy on you. At times, it's broken me to see the way you've been tested and forced to endure things you should never even have witnessed. But through all of that, I've looked on at you in awe because I've never seen another human being heal hearts the way you do. I've never witnessed anyone hold a group of men together the way you do. I've never wanted to be everything for someone the way I want to be everything for you. I'm stronger now. Life is brighter, and I'm a man I never knew I could be. So, my vow to you is that I'll be everything you need me to be and more. You'll never have to doubt my love. You'll never have to question my adoration. You'll never have to lay awake at night wondering if we're going to go the distance because I can promise you with every beat of my heart that you're it until the day I die. You're my girl. My wife. My old lady." He paused and released his slow smirk. "You're my darlin'."

For a moment, I couldn't breathe. He had stolen my breath away. I couldn't see him through the tears that slowly tracked down my cheeks, but I felt him everywhere. Felt his words coursing through me.

It seemed to take a moment for anything to happen. Even Sutton let off a subtle cough of his own before he continued. I listened to what was going on better now, but my eyes stayed on that magical color of Drew's, even when we exchanged our rings. Truthfully, I really wasn't sure that I wanted to see anything but him for the rest of my life.

If nothing else stayed with me from the whirlwind that was our wedding day, I knew his vows would be with me in my heart for eternity. Drew Tucker had effectively ruined me for anyone but him in this life and any other life that followed.

I could tell we were getting close to the end of the ceremony when the buzz started working through every one of our family and friends. It was like an electrical current that beat over the two of us and even pushed Sutton along, his words coming in a steady rhythm until he stopped altogether and smiled down at the two of us looking nothing short of satisfied.

"By the powers vested in me by the great state of Texas, I now pronounce y'all husband and wife," he said, rocking back on the heels of his boots for a moment before raising a hand as though to ask what we were waiting for. "You can kiss your old lady now, Drew."

And boy, did Drew kiss me…

CHAPTER FIFTY-ONE
DREW

*H*usband and wife.

Those three words set me on fire.

When I pulled away from our kiss, I opened my eyes to take her in.

"Happy forever, darlin'," I whispered.

"Forever," she whispered, her smile so big she'd made herself some dimples. "Doesn't sound long enough to me."

Before we could say anything else, Slater was slapping me on the back, and Tate was reaching out for Ayda, the two of us holding hands as we turned and laughed along with our friends.

Ayda's grip never loosened on my hand as she was passed between friends and family alike, unwilling to give up the physical connection between us for a second.

As we made our way down the aisle, the men reached out to congratulate us both, revving their bikes in celebration. I'd never felt such a natural high before. It was a buzz no amount of whiskey or drugs could ever provide. It was like winning the jackpot of life, and my prize was holding onto me with everything she had.

Before long, we'd reached the end of the aisle where Eric stood, tall and proud, an older version of me with his silver flecks running through his combed back hair, and his old cut on his shoulders. It was the smartest I'd ever seen him. The happiest, too.

"Congratulations," he said, stepping in to kiss Ayda on the cheek. "Welcome to the Tucker family. I have a feeling you're going to run this show better than either of us ever did."

"Couldn't be happier about being a part of the family," she practically sang at him, squeezing my hand as she bounced on her toes, full of energy.

Eric turned to me and held his hand out. "I'm proud of you, son," he said softly, and something about those words on that day made another part of that wall around my heart fall down. As much as I hated to do it, I broke from Ayda, stepping forward to my father and wrapping my arms around him to slap him on the back three times.

He'd done things for me when I thought I needed to hate him.

I knew he'd do them all again if he had to.

It took him a moment, but eventually, I felt the rise of his arms before he gripped me tightly and hugged me right back.

"Cheers, Dad," I said so only he could hear. "Wouldn't be the same without you here."

"Give it a rest already." He sniffed, clearing his throat and pushing me away.

My laughter was quiet as I stood back and reached for Ayda's hand again.

Eric pretended to look over his shoulder at something before he rubbed his forearm over his eye. *Those damn allergies*, I thought with a smile on my face.

Deeks slipped through the crowd with a black box in his hands, breaking the emotional tension running between Eric and me. Deeks looked proud as he held it in his arms so Ayda could open it. He watched eagerly with the rest of The Hounds around us as Ayda teared up all over again when she pulled out a small cut from the confines of it. She released my hand and held it up, staring at the patch on the back with TUCKER embroidered under it.

"Tradition," Moose grunted with a nod of his head. "Old ladies get cuts."

Ayda turned her glassy blue eyes on me and pulled the leather on over her dress with a smile.

"I like this tradition," she said, picking up my hand. "What do you think?"

"I think you're in danger of giving me a heart attack. Jesus, Ayda. Quit getting hotter."

Her smile grew coy as she studied my face, her tongue darting out and brushing over her bottom lip suggestively. Running her hands down the leather that hugged the subtle curve of her waist, she let out a satisfied sigh. "You gonna take me for a ride?"

"Yeah, but not the kind of ride you had in mind," I muttered, moving closer and grabbing her hips. "Is it time for bed yet?"

"That was exactly where my mind was," she teased.

"All right, you two, enough of that," Slater said, pushing through the crowd to come and peel us apart. I eyed him like I hated him, groaning as he looked at me like the smug bastard he was. "Sorry, pres, but rumor has it we have a little party to attend. I'm under strict orders from Autumn to keep your asses in *line*."

"Who died and made Autumn boss?" I scowled, half joking, half not.

"I believe Harry did," Autumn said, making her way toward us with a smile on her face. "And he left us all with very strict instructions of what you had to do to not mess this up and give your loving wife the wedding of her dreams."

"Pretty sure her dreams include me fucking her and calling her my wife over and over again, but whatever."

"Not a mental image I needed." Slater groaned.

I smirked, turning back to Ayda with raised brows. "Sorry, darlin'. What Harry wants Harry gets. I'll take you for a ride later."

The bikes behind us revved and began to move around us, and I took a moment to look around as everyone walked on by, making their way across the yard. The smile on my face was ridiculous—a smile I couldn't ever remember setting free before that very moment.

Every man and woman I adored was there, surrounding us with their love.

Deeks. Slater. Jedd. Kenny. Moose. Sutton. Tate. Rubin. Eric. Autumn. Everyone who mattered wore a look of pure happiness on their face because of us.

Because of my wife. The woman looking at me like she couldn't believe all this was real.

"Who knew loving you could feel this good?" I said, pulling her close for one final moment of intimacy before we were to be dragged away to the party.

"I can't stop smiling," she confessed quietly, ignoring the groans from our friends as she allowed herself to be pulled into my embrace. Wrapping her arms around my waist tightly she squeezed again. "I didn't know I could be this happy."

"I haven't shown you anything yet." I smiled and pressed my hand to her stomach.

CHAPTER FIFTY-TWO
AYDA

I was reluctant to let go of Drew, even as we were ushered into the huge barn we'd built where the training room had once stood. It was destined to become the training room again, but before they'd ordered the equipment, Janette and Autumn had commandeered the space for our wedding reception. One end of the building was opened up to the new lawn area where a bonfire, more lights, flowers, and mason jars were dotted between seating areas and several coolers were filled with drinks.

It looked amazing.

The lights continued inside the barn, the same weaving pattern working their way between the exposed beams, while lanterns hung cheerfully, casting romantic lighting over the tables. It was like they'd pulled every dream I'd had and made it into a realization. In the center of it all was a log-lined dance floor lit only by the mason jars with candles. It was perfect in every way.

Drew led me to the table that was very clearly set aside for the two of us. Behind it was a banner that had the reaper and hounds nestled in a bed of flowers, which matched the ones we'd used for the wedding. It was a way of making the club a part of our wedding. As I stared up at it in awe, I couldn't help thinking it would make an amazing tattoo one day.

After the baby was born, of course.

We'd barely taken our seats when Slater and Jedd came and stole Drew with a promise to return him soon. Most of the guys were congregated around a cooler of beer, anyway. This was our day, and I wanted him to enjoy every aspect of it as much as I did. So I gave him a long lingering kiss and issued a warning to Slater to behave, and then I watched him go, beaming a smile at him when he glanced over his shoulder.

My kid brother soon slid into the seat next to me. He sprawled out with his long legs and crossed them under the table, shooting a lazy smile in my direction. He'd been spending so much time with Rubin and the girls lately, and I hadn't seen much of him. He was making the most of the summer before football training started again.

"You know what this means, don't you?" he asked, rolling his head in my direction and grinning with all his boyish charm.

"With no context, call me clueless. How about you enlighten me?" I teased, ruffling his hair and chuckling when he swatted my hand away and twisted from my reach.

"I'm the last standing Hanagan. The only hope to carry on the family name."

"God help us all."

"Hey."

"It's okay. You're sixteen. There's hope for you yet." I studied his face. I wasn't sure if he was hiding hurt about that under his bravado because he was unreadable as we stared at one another. He'd grown up so much in the last year, and it was almost hard to find the punk kid hiding under the weight of new responsibility he'd taken on for himself.

"What?" he asked, his palm flattening his hair down.

"Does it bother you?"

"Does what bother me?"

"Being the last Hanagan."

Tate let off a huff of laughter and sat upright before turning to me. He took on a pose that was pure Drew, his elbows on his knees and hands linked together. Drew had become a mentor for him without really knowing it, and it was the small things like this that I loved to see.

"If you're asking me if it bothers me that you're married? No, A. You're happier than I've ever seen you. I mean you're glowing and shit, sis. I can be an asshole sometimes, but I'm not that much of a dick. You're right where you need to be."

"You're not answering the question."

"Not having the same last name doesn't mean you stop being my sister." He smiled, his dimples popping. "I know you love me. You know I love you. Now stop being a girly girl and getting all emotional. You're setting a bad example for my nephew."

"Nephew?" I asked, raising my eyebrows. "You know something I don't?"

"There's a pool going."

"Tate!"

"What?" he asked, too innocently. "Everyone's in on it."

"Sutton?"

"He's hoping you have a girl. Said it would make Drew crazy."

"Rusty?"

"Girl."

"Moose?"

"Girl and boy."

"What?" I asked, my voice taking on another octave.

Tate shrugged. "He said he talked to Eric. Twins run in the family."

I was on my feet before I realized I'd moved, and Tate, the little bastard that he was, sat in fits of giggles, his arm wrapped around his ribs as he snorted out a laugh. My eyes were already scanning the guests looking for Eric in the crowd.

"Ayda, I'm kidding. Most people are just having fun with it. We don't care as long as y'all are happy." He sobered a little, his laughter dying into a smile that took me back to his preteen years. The emotional little kid that wasn't afraid to wrap his arms around me and tell me that he loved me. Pushing to his feet, Tate wrapped his big arms around me; the new leather of my very own cut creaking as he squeezed me tight. "I love you, sis. I love that you're happy, and the only thing I would change about today is having Mom and Dad here. They'd be proud of you, you know."

"Tate..." I felt my throat tighten with emotion as I wrapped my arms around him. Just when I'd thought the tears were over for the day, here he was, bringing them back with a vengeance. Mom and Dad were here with me today in the form of a locket Janette had given me. It was my something new, and she'd had Tate find pictures of my parents to put in it. I fingered it as I pressed my cheek into his shoulder. Looking out over the crowd, I met a pair of concerned blue-green eyes, and all I could do was smile brightly as a tear rolled down my cheek.

"I love you, Ayda," Tate whispered into my hair. "But if I make you cry, Drew and Autumn will kick my ass, so stop already."

"I'm not crying."

"You're still a bad liar."

"Shut up."

"'Kay," he said with a chuckle and hugged me tighter.

CHAPTER FIFTY-THREE
DREW

"So, you gotta treat her right," Deeks said for the hundredth time, his finger pointing right at me as he leaned forward, resting his gut between his parted legs.

"I heard you, brother."

"You don't get second chances with angels like her, you understand?"

"More than you know," I said, slapping his shoulder firmly and gripping it tightly. "Thank you."

"For giving you a lecture?"

"For loving her almost as much as I do."

Deeks dropped his finger, his shoulders relaxing, and his familiar smile rising into place. "If I'd have been twenty years younger..."

"Don't make it weird." I laughed, and he laughed, too. That's all any of us had done: laughed. No dark cloud hung over Babylon that night. Our town was clear, the stars shining bright overhead, blessing our day with a new sky, a new air—a new road to ride upon.

Man, my heart had turned from stone to feathers, the lightness of it a joy, so full with the fluttering twirling around inside my chest.

I'd spent the night talking and laughing with friends who were more than friends. They were family, and where I once thought the responsibility was mine to carry them, it felt good to let them carry Ayda and me for a night.

Deeks was halfway through telling a shit joke when Slater and Jedd came up to me with a huge tumbler of whiskey, thrusting it in my face for the fifth time in the last hour.

"Come on, you pussy. Just one."

"Fuck off," I told them again, pushing the drink away carefully. "I've told you already. I don't want to drink tonight."

"Remind me why not…" Slater slurred, the effects of all his consumption enough to make him sway when he walked now.

Resting my forearm on the table, I looked up at him and pressed my free hand to my knee. "I always said you were too pretty to be intelligent, too."

"Is that why you're ugly as fuck, brain box?" He grinned.

"If I didn't love you so much, you'd be seeing stars right now, brother."

"Come on, Drew." Slater jabbed my shoulder with a weak fist. "Tell me, your best friend, and tell Jedd, your VP, why you won't have one teeny, tiny, lil drink with us after all we've been through."

"Because, shithead. This is a day I want to remember forever. Every detail. So much of my life has been a blur. I want tonight to be crystal clear. All of it."

"You've changed."

"God, I hope so."

Kenny and Moose joined us, Ben not far behind, and the rest of my brothers soon gathered around. The night was growing darker, and I'd yet to spend any reasonable amount of time with Ayda. Every time I looked her way, she was beaming, talking to someone with enthusiasm and an energy I wished I could bottle for my darkest of days. In this world of mine, where darkness had always been present, she had become the bright light I couldn't look away from.

I imagined a nice country boy—someone with a plot of land, a homely ranch, several horses, and a mom who could take Ayda under her wing and drag her into a loving family. Into a home where they ate together every Sunday and baked pies for each other just because their love was pure. I imagined someone loving her who wasn't me—a man without any stains on his heart or blood on his hands. When I looked at her, I knew with every part of my soul she deserved that man.

But none of that mattered.

Because when I looked at her, I also knew no one, no cowboy, no straight-laced, church-going momma's boy could ever love Ayda the way I did. They could never cry out to the universe for them to rain pain down on their lives every day, so long as they got to curl up in bed with her at night and fall asleep in her arms with her lips pressed against their head.

She could have done better.

She never would get better than me.

Together, we were perfect, a fantasy I never realized I'd had until I saw her laughing with her friends, wearing a wedding ring that marked her as mine for life.

"I hope I look at a woman like that one day," a voice sighed.

I turned to see Rubin standing beside me, happy and carefree, like a young kid his age should.

"You will," I told him. "Just go for the one who makes

you angry the first time you lay eyes on her, and know that that anger isn't because you hate her… it's because you know she's going to be the one to break down all your bullshit and expose you for who you really are. Then watch that hate slide right into love, brother."

Rubin smiled, reaching out to grab onto my shoulder. "Mind if I come to you for advice if that happens?"

"You'd better." I reached up and rested my hand on his, tapping it twice. He was a new feature in my heart—another thing for me to protect and provide for. I planned on upholding all the promises I'd set to him in recent months.

"Happy wedding day, bro." Rubin offered, his eyes sparkling with contentment.

"Thanks, kid."

Laughter erupted behind us, pulling our attention in that direction, and when I looked behind me, Autumn was charging forward, her eyebrow raised as she approached.

"Oh, hell," I muttered under my breath, but she was on me before I could ask any questions or try to protest, pulling me up by both hands, her strength surprising me.

"Up you get," she said through a heavy breath, standing me on my feet and brushing her hands down over the chest of my tailored vest to smarten me up.

"Autumn?"

"Come on now, Drew. You know more than anyone that the best part of a wedding is always the first dance with your lady. I do believe she's wearing the right boots for a bit of two-stepping. Go spin her around while we all watch on like fools."

When I looked up, Ayda was being led to a small dance floor by Sloane, the two of them giggling, and their eyes bright with enthusiasm.

With a small flourish, Sloane spun Ayda into the middle of the dance floor, leaving Ayda to slow to a stop in front of me. Pulling her dress up, she flashed a pair of white cowboy boots and tapped the toes together before glancing back up at me.

"You owe me a dance, husband," she called out above the buzz of conversation, silencing almost everyone between the two of us.

Husband.

Fuck, yes.

I turned to her fully, my legs shoulder-width apart as I reached up to unfasten my bowtie, my eyes on hers the whole time as she watched me. I unraveled it and left it hanging around my neck before I popped the top two buttons of my white shirt open, and then moved to open every button on my black tailored vest, pushing the edges back before I walked over to take her in my arms. With one hand around her waist, the other holding her hand tightly, I pulled her close, so our faces were only an inch apart.

"At your service, wife," I whispered.

"Say that again," she moaned quietly.

I dropped my mouth to her ear, my lips brushing against her lobe as I breathed warm air onto her skin. "Yours for life, wife."

She closed her eyes for a moment, her lips still smiling. When she opened them again, all I could see in those pools of blue was warmth, love, and raging hormones.

"I think I'm ready for that ride now," she said quietly, the last words fading as the music started.

Together, we danced a dance so natural, the two of us moving in perfect time as our song rang out around us—a song I'd chosen to tell her what I felt about her. *Tangled Up in You* by Staind led us around the dance floor, the lyrics I'd listened to a thousand times now there for everyone to hear and understand how I felt about the woman in my arms.

I couldn't take my eyes off her, couldn't get her close enough or tell her how much I loved her. Everything I felt was all-consuming, wrecking me, and reducing me to what I was as we danced together. I mouthed the lyrics to her as we moved around, and when it came to an end, I didn't stop dancing, needing to hold her this close for so much longer.

"You and me now, darlin'," I told her softly.

Pushing her fingers into my hair, Ayda pressed her body to mine. "Forever," she whispered.

Deeks and Autumn joined us on the dance floor, as did Kenny and Sloane, and an awkward-looking Tate, with Libby dragging him along. Once the space around us was crowded, I knew it was time.

We'd shared enough of our day with everyone else.

It was time to step into the night on our own.

With a small kiss to the forehead, I pulled away from Ayda and jerked my head in the direction of the exit. She didn't have to say a word. The blush of her cheeks and the excitement in her smile told me everything I needed to know. She couldn't wait for us to be alone either.

I led the way, pulling her along as I walked backward and she followed. We'd almost made it to the exit when I turned around and slammed straight into the chest of my father. He was there, as always, blocking the way, his arms behind his back and his legs parted like he was a doorman or some kind of security. Standing right beside him was Sutton, and that familiar smirk of his made me step back and raise a brow as I pulled Ayda into my side.

"What's going on?" I asked, eyeing them both.

Sutton shrugged, enjoying every second of whatever this was.

"Sorry, son. We can't let you leave yet," Eric said smoothly, pulling an envelope out from behind his back and holding it in front of me.

"Why not?"

"We're under orders ourselves," Sutton said, his southern drawl dragging the words out longer than they needed to be.

"There's someone important here who wanted to say something before the night was through," Eric added.

I stared into my father's eyes for far too long, taking the envelope from him with a slightly shaky hand before glancing at Ayda for reassurance. With reluctance, I peeled myself away from her and opened the envelope, pulling out a one-page letter with a script I recognized in an instant.

Looking up at Eric, I wanted to tell him I couldn't do this. I couldn't read the words in front of me, but my father looked like a father then, and his encouragement forced my chin down, for the words of my other father to drift into my heart.

> *Well, look at that.*
>
> *You're reading this damn letter, written by my beat-up old hands.*
>
> *I wouldn't blame you if you needed a minute.*
>
> *Would understand if you needed to put this aside and come back to it another day—a day less important than this. I don't want to make this about me.*
>
> *But you know I needed to be there in some way,*

right, son?

The kid I'd given grief to his whole life.

You think you'd get away with that on your wedding day? Did Ayda think she'd get away with that? Not a chance. I told you both before: I'll never die.

My body may have given up, but this soul of mine lives on in splattered ink and wrinkled paper.

So…

Looks like you both made it.

The white wedding, the tears of joy, and the promises of forever.

It's gone down that way, yeah? God, I hope so. As I sit here writing this with a lump in my throat, all I hope is that you got what you both deserved.

I've never seen two people look at each other the way you looked at each other. The minute she walked into The Hut, ready and willing to bend so you could break her, Drew, I knew she was the one.

Do you believe in magic? I did. All my life. I believed in magic, fate, and all that other bullshit most men scoff at when someone mentions it.

Seeing you two together was some kind of magic.

Oh, boy, oh, boy. Never lose that. I hope, even after I'm long gone, bored up in Heaven (because I'm too pure for Hell… and Hell is just a lie created to scare those of us who want to live fast and die young) that you two understand what you've got in each other.

You're gonna face hard times.

You'll face good times, too.

You'll have babies, argue, fight, want to run away, want to go back to the beginning, and you'll struggle. No one is immune to that. Not even you.

But none of that matters because even when at your weakest, the two of you are stronger than an army of beasts. An army of Hounds. A motorcycle club filled with old men and young dreams.

I'm not here today to make you cry.

I just couldn't let the pair of you get married without telling you some facts.

I'm proud of you.

I believe in you.

I love you.

Until we meet again, keep being the perfect version of you.

With more love than you can imagine a man like me could give,

Harry.

P.s. Eric is about to hand over a key.

You're gonna stamp your feet and tell him you can't accept it.

I'm gonna be up on this cloud, son, not giving a shit.

Take the key.

Go and see your new home.

Walk around in it. Spend time in it. Imagine a room for a baby someday.

And know I made that house yours long before

Ayda even came along.

You're so much more than you'll ever believe you can be, Drew.

The Hounds are your family.

You, though... You're allowed to be you, too.

Go and make a life for yourself. Live it every day.

Love you, pres.

I wish I could be there to tell you that to your face.

I could barely see Sutton and Eric when I looked up. My tears fell silent, but hard, the ache in my chest unbearable as I stared at them, speechless.

Eric held out a key. "Follow FM 709. Veer left about a quarter of a mile down. You'll see a turn in. Follow it up."

Taking the key from him with a shaky hand, I parted my lips to say something, but nothing came out, and all I could do was turn to Ayda to help me.

Tears fell freely down her cheeks as she looked between me, and the key in my hand with absolute wonder. Her chest stuttered as she drew in a breath. "We should go and see," she whispered. "For Harry."

I ran my forearm over my eyes, sniffing up hard and clearing my throat. "For Harry." I nodded.

Eric stepped forward, embracing me for the second time that day, his chin resting on my shoulder as he patted my back.

"So much love in one room for you," he whispered to me and me alone. "If you can't see what you're worth today, I don't know when you ever will. Be proud of yourself, Drew." And just as quickly as he embraced me, he uncurled his arms and slipped away.

"You need a police escort, or…?" Sutton smirked at me.

I huffed out a laugh, wiping my weeping eyes again like a fucking pussy, before I shook my head and pulled Ayda close. "We're good, man. Thank you."

Like a friend, he looked between the both of us, his smile pure. "Yeah. You're good."

When he drifted away, too, I looked at Ayda and started to walk us both into the fresh night air, and I sucked in a much-needed breath as I glanced up at the stars in the clear night sky.

"Fuck," I whispered.

Running her fingers under her eyes, Ayda let off a small tear-filled chuckle. "That's one way of putting it. What a day."

I rolled my head her way, reaching up to cup her neck as I blew out a heavy breath. "Tell me you're okay."

"Baby, I've never been better."

"Jesus Christ, Ayda, I've never felt this much before. I'm raw… open, vulnerable… fucking broken apart," I whispered, exposing all my truths. "And the weirdest part is that it feels like I'm finally living, you know? And that's all because of you."

"All those things you're feeling, that is life. That's living. It's what you've done for me."

I didn't wait. I moved and kissed her. I kissed her hard, my need to express everything I was feeling taking over as I curled myself around her and held her tight. My tongue slid over hers, the heat of our chemistry making me blind to the fact we were only a few feet away from so many people. I'd have taken her there and then if I could, but when a small shiver of delight ran over her body, making her shudder in my grip, I reluctantly pulled away, littering softer kisses over her face.

"Come ride with me, Mrs. Tucker."

"With pleasure."

We didn't have a threshold there and then, but that didn't stop me from scooping her up in my arms, enjoying the way she curled hers around my neck as I led her to my bike. With another kiss, I guided her down, and before long, the two of us were in a position we'd been in a hundred times before.

I guided my bike back, feeling the weight of love and responsibility at my back.

My wife.

My baby.

Arms wrapped around me and hearts pressed into my back.

With a squeeze of my hand around hers, I stared at the gates of the yard, and I sucked in a breath.

So much was changing, but these changes felt right. A forever without change means you're stuck in the same place for far too long. We were meant to travel down different paths, and Ayda was the one guiding me into unknown territory, showing me how life could be lived if I opened my eyes and heart enough to let the good stuff in.

The Ayda kind of stuff.

I closed my eyes for just a second, thinking of Harry, Pete, and my mom. With a single thanks to each of them, I stared in front of me, focused on what lay ahead instead of what rested behind, and I led us both out of the yard.

To a home we hadn't yet seen.

Down roads we'd yet to explore.

To a life waiting.

A life I knew would be more than I ever imagined it could

be.

EPILOGUE
AYDA

"*I fucking hate you, Drew Tucker*!" I screamed. The pain in my body was immense, and I had been verging on exhausted hours ago. I was a mess, my hair stuck to my sweaty forehead, legs spread for the room, and stretch marks cradling my exposed belly. Yet, there stood my husband with his top off, looking perfect for the entire world.

But, I could see how tense the muscles in his bare shoulders were as I squeezed his hand. He was enduring the torture I was inflicting on him as yet another contraction rolled over me, and I was beginning to wonder what I'd done to myself when it finally eased enough for me to breathe again.

"Maybe hate is a strong word," I mumbled as the nurse checked the machines.

Drew was scowling and trying to smile at the same time, but it came off as some weird kind of grimace, his eyes drifting to the hand I'd just tortured. "You could never hate me, Ayda." Leaning closer, he reached up to brush some damp strands of hair away from my face. "And you can do this. You're the toughest old lady I know."

"*Old*—" my words were cut off as the now familiar pressure started again. My skin felt too tight for my body, and my grip tightened around Drew's abused hand again. They'd told me to hold off on the pushing while they'd made sure everything was okay, but the pressure was making it impossible. For the millionth time, it felt like it was too much—like I couldn't do this. There was no way in hell I could push this baby out, not even when my body was demanding I do it.

"Ayda," the doctor said, rolling her stool closer, in between my parted legs. This whole baby thing was really hard on my personal space. "This is it now. We're ready. You can start pushing."

I released a long breath, my eyes meeting Drew's before I pulled in another. Digging my nails into the back of his hand, I finally started to push.

"Come on, baby," Drew hissed, his body working with mine, leaning closer as though he wanted to push for me. I would have let him, too. I felt like I was trying to shit out a watermelon. I curled forward as I pushed with everything I had. The pressure was so intense that I was convinced I was being ripped in two.

"You're crowning," the doctor offered in a way of an update, but I felt her reaction was delayed. I could feel the baby's head pushing, stretching, burning.

"I can't," I wailed, trying my best to remember how to breathe. My eyes found Drew's as my body took over and pushed with every ounce of strength I had. My fingers were buried so deep into the back of his hand, I couldn't seem to release my grip.

I was contradicting myself it seemed.

A scream started and stuck in my throat as the doctor moved around between my thighs and smiled up at me. Her mouth was moving but the words were drowned out by my body's sudden chanting of *push, push, push*.

"Stop pushing now, Ayda."

What the fuck?

"Can't."

"The baby's head is out, sweetheart, but we have to check that the cord isn't around the neck."

I felt my bottom lip tremble. My body demanded that I rid myself of this pain immediately. My head was almost fuzzy with the odd feeling of being held open.

"Holy shit," Drew whispered beside me, his attention drifting to where the doctor's hands were holding onto the baby we'd yet to meet.

I tried to lift my head to look, but I couldn't see over my stomach while I was fighting to catch my breath.

"You're doing so well, Ayda. Now we're going to have you give one last big push for us."

Sweat trickled down my forehead and slid into my eye, forcing me to brush it away with my free hand before pushing up on my elbows and curling around my belly. Gritting my teeth, I could hear the strangled cry tearing free from deep inside me as the pain soared to a point I wasn't sure was normal.

Then, I pushed.

Time slowed down as the stretching sensation left my body. The pain was receding, but my breaths wouldn't come as a nurse cut the cord and swaddled the baby before whisking her away. Drew and I looked after them, the time ticking painfully away until a high-pitched wail came from the other side of the room.

My skin broke out in goosebumps at the sound of our

baby, and tears clouded my eyes, that cry making my arms ache, and my heart soar in my chest. Knowing that the baby was healthy had me searching for Drew.

His mouth was parted, his eyes wide as he stared at me, unable to believe the baby was here.

"You did it," he finally whispered, wrapping a hand around my neck and dropping his forehead to mine. "Ayda, you did it. She's here. Our little girl is here."

I started crying. I couldn't help myself. I was so overcome with emotion that I just fell apart. I needed to hold my little girl, see her beautiful face—kiss all ten fingers and toes. Everything in me seemed to ache for it. But this moment with Drew, this moment called for something more. Pressing my palm to his face, I pressed my lips against his and smiled a tearful smile.

"Our little Harriet," I whispered sounding hoarse and weak.

Drew huffed out an emotional laugh, his eyes glazed as he stared at me in that way he always did recently… like he was in awe of me. "We're fucking parents," he said quietly. "We have a *daughter*."

I held those beautiful eyes with mine for as long as I could, making a hundred unspoken promises to him and Harriet for our future. My heart was pounding so hard that I found myself suddenly distracted by the new silence that descended over the room. When I glanced over, I saw a beautiful little face peering from a blanket being offered to me.

Our little girl.

It took everything to not burst into tears when I accepted Harriet from the nurse. I cradled the tiny bundle to my chest and tried to catch my breath as I looked down at the utter picture of perfection I was holding in my arms.

Harriet Linda Tucker was beautiful in every way.

She stared up at me curiously, little grunts coming from her as I stared right back. The connection felt instant, another small puzzle piece of my heart suddenly locking into place like it had always been there. I loosened the blanket enough to find her tiny hands and the tiny fingers on them and ran my lips over them reverently.

I couldn't stop stroking her fingers and running my thumb down her cheeks. This tiny little human being had just come from me. She was already the best parts of Drew and me, and the most loved human on the face of the planet.

I glanced up at Drew the moment I was able to drag my eyes from our little Harry and smiled.

"You want to hold your daughter?"

"More than anything in the world," he answered, with pure love shining from his eyes.

Slowly, and carefully, I placed our daughter into her father's arms and watched as he pulled her to him.

I loved Drew. I had since the day I'd met him, but the sight of him with our baby in his arms, her cheek pressed against the hound on his bare chest, and her tiny hand wrapped around his thumb did something to me that I would never, ever forget.

All of his power and strength wrapped around her delicate frame with such love and adoration, I could feel it myself. The sight of it warmed my heart and made tears flood my eyes as the future lit up like a sunny day. Drew's rough edges and darker days all melted away as he looked down on his daughter like she was the most magnificent thing he had ever seen. I knew the feeling. For me, Drew had never looked so good. Watching him rocking our baby back and forth in those powerful arms as he bounced in place, I knew this little girl would never know true fear. He wouldn't let her. I knew that her pain would always be eased by this man, who was already so in love with her, that he was lost to the world. I also knew that she would always be loved by Drew, by me, and the entire MC family she would grow up surrounded by.

Harriet Tucker was going to be the brightest spark in our lives.

She was perfection wrapped in a swaddling blanket and cradled by the most perfectly imperfect man I had ever met.

This right here was my world.

These two divine beings were my life.

And really, it was only just the beginning.

"She looks like a little angel," I said, propping my head up with my hand on my side of our enormous California king-sized bed, watching as Harriet kicked her arms and legs at the ceiling above her. It was so good to be home with the newest addition to our family. Harriet was wearing a ridiculously cute onesie with the Hounds logo that one of the girls had ordered for her in baby pink. Happy little gurgles emitted from her when her daddy ran a finger over her miniature-sized palm.

We were besotted. Even sleep deprivation hadn't stopped our complete adoration when it came to Harriet.

Every moment Drew spent holding her, rocking her in his arms and dropping little butterfly kisses all over her face, the more I fell in love with them both. The contrast of her delicate little body in his strong arms was indescribable. Watching him with her was one of my favorite pastimes now.

Glancing over at him on the bed, I smiled. Since we'd moved into this house that Harry had given us, Drew had been peaceful, happy, and content. Being here with Harriet seemed to take that all to a whole new level. Reaching over, I traced his brow with a finger, not really saying a word in explanation, just needing to touch him. I always needed that connection these days, whether it was with him, Harriet, or both of them. It was almost as though I was making sure they were both still real, and this was my life.

Drew glanced up, a soft smile in place. It was a part of him now. The smile I used to long to see more of had brightened up his face more than ever before, making him even sexier than I ever thought he could be.

"You okay?" he asked quietly.

"Better than okay," I admitted, smiling back at him. "Just have to keep reminding myself this is real life."

"Pretty special, ain't it?"

"You, sir, are looking at the luckiest woman alive."

"Damn right." He smirked. "I'm a catch."

I let off a small laugh and dropped my hand to where Harriet was gripping his thumb with a white fist, my finger gently stroking her knuckles.

"You also give good sperm. Just look at her. She's gorgeous."

Drew immediately propped himself up on his elbow, attempting to cover Harriet's tiny ears with his huge hands as he looked up at me. "Ayda! We don't talk about the S. P. E. R. M in front of my daughter. I don't want her to know what that is until she's at least a hundred and eight."

I playfully rolled my eyes and dropped my head lower, pressing my lips to her chubby little cheek. "She doesn't know what I'm saying. Do you, sugar?"

Harriet gurgled again, kicking out both of her legs as her eyes moved about the ceiling, occasionally darting to me when I gave her more kisses. I was addicted to the baby smell of her. It was so unique and clean.

"How many more do you think you would want?" I asked, suddenly curious. I'd been a mother less than a week, and I wasn't willing to give up these little moments yet. The thought of her growing up was almost soul-crushing. "Babies, I mean."

"Right now, I feel like I've got so much love inside of me, I could father a hundred tiny babies." His hand glided over her delicate little tummy. "Seeing you as a mom is, without a doubt, the sexiest thing in the world to me. I don't know how many I want or how many we'll have. All I know is that this isn't the last time. I already want to do this again with you, if that's what you want, too."

"I really, really do," I said gently. "Life's funny, isn't it? Two years ago, I wasn't even sure I wanted kids. Now…?" I glanced down at Harriet. "A week, and I can't imagine life without her." When I glanced up and found his eyes again, all I could see was love there. "And you… seeing you with her is possibly the most beautiful thing I've ever witnessed in my life, Drew. I feel so happy sometimes, I think I'm losing my mind. You, this house Harry gave us, Harriet… all I need now is a dog and a pony."

He looked at me for a moment, his eyes searching mine. "I used to think that what goes around comes back around, you know. I believed that, so in a way, I think I had my whole life mapped out in my head when I walked out of those prison doors. I'd come back to Babylon, cause more trouble, make a stand, and live my life chasing my own ass all over the place.

Now I'm starting to think it doesn't work that way. What goes around doesn't have to come back to you. Sometimes it just goes because it needs to go. It needs to get out of here so you can live a better life. Every day since we got married, I wake up next to you, and I feel that this is how life is meant to be. The last year with you has been the only year I've truly lived, and if you're losing your mind, I'm right there with you, Ayda. I may still be the president of The Hounds, but I'm more than that now. I'm a different version of Drew Tucker. I can't wait to get home to you and Harriet. I can't wait to go to bed... sober. Everything I once loved is insignificant, replaced by things I never knew I could crave." He reached over to trail a finger up and down my bicep. "So, if my girl wants a dog and a pony, I'll find a way to get her them, because I need you to feel full like I do." He smiled. "But you're picking up their sh..." He trailed off, glancing down at Harriet.

I started to laugh, unable to help myself.

This man, who had always dropped his expletives so freely, now watched every word he said in front of a week-old baby. It was possibly the most adorable thing I'd ever seen, but I didn't say that aloud. Instead, I scooped Harriet up and laid her face down on his chest before wriggling under his arm. When she'd been born, she'd almost looked like a little old lady, all wrinkles and frowns. Now she was coming into her own, and I loved seeing the parts of her that belonged to Drew. When they were laid together, Harriet on his chest like this, it was a double-Drew stare. She had the same shaped eyes as him, the same dark hair, and when she had gas, she looked like she had his signature smirk.

"Right now," I said gently, resting my head on his shoulder. "I just want to stay like this. Imprint it all into my memory."

Drew ran his hand down Harriet's back, his other arm wrapping around me as he kissed the top of her head and rested his mouth there. "Then let's stay like this a little while longer," he whispered.

I didn't fear the future anymore, and I didn't worry about the unknown. Life would always test us, but with Drew by my side, I knew I was ready to take it all on. I was ready to fight because I'd had a taste of happiness, and I wasn't ever going to let it go.

Drew was my forever, and maybe every forever that followed.

DREW

One Last Round

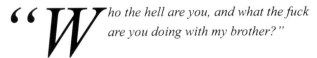

Those were the first words Ayda ever said to me.

"Where the hell do you think you're going? Hey, we're not finished here, dude."

"Yeah, we are, sweetheart."

"Do not walk away from me!"

"You have no idea who I am, do you?"

"That's Drew Tucker, Ayda. Shut the fuck up."

The memory made me smile every time I thought about it.

Her smart mouth mixed with my bad attitude had equaled one hell of a life.

"We have some fantastic humble pie, or apple if you'd prefer."

I remembered her face that day in the diner so clearly. She was tired, a little broken, and I was a fucked-up mess who'd decided I needed to feed off those who were suffering more than I was.

A petty man. A man I no longer recognized as I drove our Ford Explorer toward The Hut with Harriet strapped up in her car seat, the two of us heading to meet Ayda who had been instructed to take a girly day with Autumn and the others.

She'd left us that morning in our home away from The Hounds. It was a home I never expected to have. A private space among the trees with a wraparound porch and plenty of land for me to convert into play space for Harriet and any other kids we may be graced with. Ayda loved it, saying it reminded her of a more secluded version of her parents' home—a place she hadn't realized she'd missed as much as she had until Harry had gifted us with his generosity, even in death.

I'd kissed her goodbye that morning, assuring her that I'd be fine with our daughter. The two of us would miss her, sure, but she needed to remember who she was besides a mother and a wife. With her hair thrown up in a messy bun, a loose white tank, and a pair of light blue jeans, she'd walked out of that house looking sexier than ever. She was barely recognizable from the woman I'd first stumbled upon thanks to her brother. She seemed freer, like she was where she was always meant to be.

Now, I was taking Harriet to see her many uncles and grandpa—a group of big, burly men who turned to mush the moment she looked up at them with her sparkling blue-green eyes. Eric had taken a room at The Hut permanently, and Tate had insisted he stay with the men, knowing full well that Ayda and I would be living in both homes on and off whenever the mood struck us. My room, bathroom, and office were still ours and ours alone, and no one batted an eyelid when we'd carried a bunch of baby things in there to make it Harriet's as much as ours.

We may not have been a conventional family, but I dared anyone to tell us there was a family out there who loved harder than we loved.

I pulled into the yard, chuckling to myself when I saw Deeks and Eric tussling on the top step of the porch the minute they saw us, each desperate to get to Harriet first.

She was the princess of a king, and boy, was she going to use that to her advantage when she was old enough.

For now, though, at just five months old, she took it all in her stride, loving each and every man who let her grab hold of their beard so she could yank away at it as much as she wished.

"Me. No, it's my turn. Get out of here, you old fool," Eric said as he opened the back door, pushing Deeks out of the way with his ass, his face coming to life the minute he saw his granddaughter kicking away in her chair in front of him. "*Hello, baby girl*," he cooed, using the most ridiculous voice I'd heard a grown man use.

"Goddammit, Tucker, you—"

"Hey!" Eric cut him off, pulling Harriet out of her chair

and propping her up in his arms as he turned back to Deeks. "Remember what Ayda said. There'll be no bad language in front of the baby."

Deeks was practically bursting with anger by the time I'd gotten out of my car, walked around it, and slapped him on the back.

"Don't worry, Deeks. She needs her diaper changing soon. We both know Eric can't handle that S. H. I. T."

Deeks grumbled something that sounded like a cuss word before he shook it off and stepped closer to Harriet, his eyes alive as he lifted a finger to her tummy and greeted her with a tickle.

I watched them walking her toward The Hut, and I found myself turning around to the gates of the yard when a tourist bike flew down the road, the thunderous sound of the engine grabbing my attention.

A flash of Ayda walking through those gates all those times she came to clean our club's shit up to pay a debt to me she didn't really owe, and the defiance she wore every time she did it had my face falling. I'd treated her like shit because I feared what she could become, but, like she always did, Ayda had managed to break into my iron heart without me even realizing it, her quick one-liners and her beautiful eyes making me weak for her.

"You're quite the confusing creature, Ayda Hanagan."
"Me?"
"You."
"I'm pretty sure I'm the bleakest person around. I'm an open book."
"Is that really how you see yourself?"

I shook away the idea of her not knowing who she was and what she was capable of, the warmth of even those early memories making me smile in disbelief as I walked through the yard, up the steps of the porch, and I pushed open the door to The Hut.

Inside, Harriet was circled, with Eric holding her proudly while Slater, Jedd, Rubin, Kenny, Moose, Ben, Deeks, and yes, Howard Sutton, all cooed around her, their voices high pitched as they made her smile grow, each of them laughing when she laughed—happy because she was happy, too

Tate was soon walking out of the corridor, wearing nothing more than his gray sweats as he waltzed forward, a cocky, arrogant son of a bitch now. His body had grown even more, the muscles of his chest and shoulders expanding to make him appear manlier than he'd ever been. He may have been a moody teenager, but the minute he saw his niece, his face lit up, and he was in among the men, removing her from Eric's arms and claiming her in his own. I watched him as he bounced her up and down, asking her who her favorite uncle was, while Rubin chipped in with a witty comeback.

I'd never grow tired of seeing them this way.

Sutton caught me staring with a stupid grin on my face, and he stepped out from the circle, walking over to me in his uniform like the old cowboy he used to be.

"You'll never have to look too long and hard for a babysitter," he said, coming to a stop in front of me.

"I think the real problem will be keeping these lot away when we want some privacy."

"That too." He laughed, looking back at them all as the noise of Harriet's laughter grew before he turned back to me.

"So, I have some news for you that I thought you might wanna hear."

"Yeah?"

"Come on." He tilted his head toward the door and began to walk out onto the porch. I followed him, walking over to the railing and leaning against it, the same way Sutton had done.

The two of us looked over the yard as the Texas sun beat down on our land.

"Thought you should know that Walsh has messed up on the inside already."

I frowned, turning to study Sutton's face. He seemed lighter these days, too. More settled in his skin and less likely to start firing at random targets just to prove a point. "What do you mean?"

"Rumor has it that he tried to cut some deals. Bribed a few officers. Tried to play some gangs off against one another. Got caught in the middle of it all and—"

"Shit," I whistled, imagining the trouble he'd gotten into.

Sutton nodded slowly, glancing down at his hand on the rail as he twisted it around the wood and leaned back, rocking on his heels. "Turns out he's had another few years added to his sentence. He won't be out for a long time." When he turned to look at me, there was a small smile hiding under his tash. "The Navs that got sent down won't be around either. Especially not since they got caught smuggling drugs inside."

"Drugs?" I asked, my eyes widening. "You'd have thought they'd have learned their lesson with that shit already."

Sutton shrugged a shoulder. "They may have. That didn't stop me getting someone to plant that shit on them to make sure they weren't out any time soon."

I stared at him, my mouth falling open, and my eyes practically popping from their sockets. "Are you... are you serious?"

Turning back to the yard, Sutton raised his chin and sniffed the air, looking at the clear blue sky above. "You looked after me and my girls when I wasn't so nice to you. I decided I could do something to look after you and yours. We're even now."

I studied him, this new friend of mine, like a younger father figure who I wanted to go to when I was troubled. One who I trusted with my life and knew would always be in it for the rest of my days.

There were many things I could have said and argued, but instead, I simply slapped his back once, leaned over the railing, and said two words.

"Thank you."

"Don't mention it."

The Hut door slammed open, and out rushed Tate with Harriet in his arms, holding her to me with a look of disgust on his face.

"Dude, I think she needs her diaper changing."

With a roll of my eyes, I laughed and took her from him, shaking my head as he walked back inside, groaning like a chump.

"I'll go see if he's all right." Sutton chuckled, walking away and leaving me to stand on the porch with my baby girl in my arms.

Looking down at Harriet, I grinned widely, holding her close to my chest.

"Did you do that on purpose so Uncle Tate would stop bouncing you up and down, princess?"

Harriet looked up at me, her eyes bright and her mischievous smile making my heart melt as she lifted a finger and pointed it right at the end of my nose.

"You don't stink that bad." I laughed, pulling her close.

I was about to take her inside when I heard a car drive through the yard, the stones kicking up dust as the tires ran over them. The minute I saw Autumn driving, I knew who was about to charge toward us.

Ayda wasted no time, acting like she'd been away from us for weeks, not hours, as she jumped out of the front passenger seat, slammed the door closed and jogged over.

"Look at Mommy, Harry," I whispered in her ear. "Isn't she gorgeous?"

Harriet gurgled something that I told myself was *abso-fuckin-lutely, Daddy*, and I waited for Ayda to come closer so I could kiss her already.

"I don't want to hurt you anymore."
"Then don't ask me to leave."
"I won't. I can't."

Her smile grew as she got closer, the hair falling loose from the bouncing bun on top of her head.

I couldn't imagine a time where I'd ever have found a reason to ask her to leave when now all I ever needed her to do was stay. Her absence made me ache. Her smile was what I lived for. She'd been a little piece of Heaven in the palms of my hands, and I'd somehow held on tight through it all.

"How are my two favorite people?" Ayda asked breathlessly, swooping in to kiss Harriet's cheek before rising and pressing her lips firmly against mine. "I missed y'all."

"We're better now you're here." I grinned, pulling her into my other arm and holding her tight. I gestured to Harriet's diaper, bouncing her in my arm. "Little Tucker has a present for you."

Ayda laughed and swept Harriet away from me, swinging her into the air and sticking her face close to the diaper with an exaggerated gagging noise as she brought our daughter back to eye level with a bright smile. "You know, sugar, you still smell better than The Hut's toilets when I used to clean them. Don't let these men make you feel bad. Let's go and get you smelling good again."

Pressing her lips to mine again, Ayda grinned and headed toward the door.

"Be right back, and then our little princess will be reset and ready to torture the boys."

I watched her as she danced toward the door, her attention solely on entertaining her daughter. Everything I felt for her swelled in my chest to the point of it being painful. It turns out being happy can fucking hurt, but this would always be a pain I would welcome.

"I think, deep down, I always knew I'd get you to stand at the end of my bed, half naked."

"That's because you're Drew Tucker."

"Damn right, I am. I always get what I want one way or another. I just like to go the long way around sometimes."

"Ayda?"

She spun, the action making Harriet chuckle out loud and brightening Ayda's smile in turn. "Yeah, Drew?"

I smiled brightly at them both, finally feeling nothing

but permanent warmth in a world that had once felt bitter and ice-cold.

"I really love ya, darlin'. More than you'll ever know."

Her smile turned into a grin, before she whisked my daughter inside with a flourish, leaving me standing there, soaking up the warmth in my life with a satisfaction that made my chest and cheeks ache.

With one last glance at the Texan sun beating down around me, I turned and stared at the porch steps.

And I swear, for one single moment, I saw Pete and Harry sitting on top of them, both glaring at me with their arms resting over their knees and their eyes tight from smiling.

"It's only just begun, son," Harry whispered.

"See you at the end of a fucking good life, brother," said Pete.

No sooner had they arrived, I blinked, and they'd disappeared, leaving me to look up at the sky as two birds flew by.

A fucking good life, I smiled to myself.

Yeah.

I liked the sound of that.

The End

The Hounds of Babylon Motorcycle Club
Babylon, Texas.
Thanks for passing through.
Ride safe.

THE HOUNDS OF BABYLON MOTORCYCLE CLUB TEXAS

WITHOUT FOREVER
SUGGESTED PLAYLIST

Feral Roots - Rival Sons
The End - Pearl Jam
Gravedigger - MXMS
Tangled Up In You - Staind
Bloody City - Sam Tinnesz
Movement - Hozier
Front Porch - Joy Williams
Dark Nights - Dorothy
Vacant - Zola Jesus
Dig your Grave - Erick Serna & The Killing Floor
Battle Born - Five Finger Death Punch
45 - Shinedown
The Red - Chevelle
Put the Gun Down - Andy Black
Hunted - Little Hurricane
Cryin' Like a Bitch - Godsmack
Shoot Em Dead - Trouble Andrew
Do Your Worst - Rival Sons
Leadfoot - No Sinner
Never Take Me Alive - I WAS THE LION
Smoke Rising - Brown Bird
Gun in my Hand - Dorothy
Never Meant to Be - Welshly Arms
Ain't Our Time to Die - Dorothy
99 Problems - Hugo
I'll Follow You - Shinedown
Over and Over - Reignwolf
Prison - The Pretty Reckless
Legendary - Welshly Arms
House of the Rising Sun - Nomy
Future Days - Pearl Jam
Burn Down This Road - Josh Wolfe
For Whom The Bell Tolls - Metallica

Machines - Biffy Clyro
Born for This - Royal Deluxe
Waiting Game - Banks

If you're a member or L.J. Stock or Victoria L. James groups on facebook, or you have the ebook, there are links to the playlist on both spotify and youtube.

23103736R00251

Printed in Great Britain
by Amazon